HIGH SOCIETY
MURDER
IN DETROIT
Peacock-tail Mirror

M A R I E   H A R R I E T T E   K A Y

BALBOA.PRESS
A DIVISION OF HAY HOUSE

Balboa Press books may be ordered through booksellers or by contacting:

Balboa Press
A Division of Hay House
1663 Liberty Drive
Bloomington, IN 47403
www.balboapress.com
1 (877) 407-4847

Because of the dynamic nature of the Internet, any web addresses or links contained in this book may have changed since publication and may no longer be valid. The views expressed in this work are solely those of the author and do not necessarily reflect the views of the publisher, and the publisher hereby disclaims any responsibility for them.

The author of this book does not dispense medical advice or prescribe the use of any technique as a form of treatment for physical, emotional, or medical problems without the advice of a physician, either directly or indirectly. The intent of the author is only to offer information of a general nature to help you in your quest for emotional and spiritual well-being. In the event you use any of the information in this book for yourself, which is your constitutional right, the author and the publisher assume no responsibility for your actions.

Any people depicted in stock imagery provided by Getty Images are models, and such images are being used for illustrative purposes only.
Certain stock imagery © Getty Images.

Print information available on the last page.

ISBN: 978-1-9822-4172-8 (sc)
ISBN: 978-1-9822-4174-2 (hc)
ISBN: 978-1-9822-4173-5 (e)

Library of Congress Control Number: 2020903310

Balboa Press rev. date: 02/26/2020

DEDICATION

I dedicate this book to my mother, the late Eva Kay,
who with love of family and by example,
instilled in me honesty, compassion, and
the ability to see all issues fairly.

To my children Jane, Robert, Steven, and my son-in-law Tom,
who encouraged me to write.

To my mentor, teacher, and friend, the late June Black,
who awakened my natural intuitive ability.

My understanding of God is a universal consciousness, a powerful
loving energy that oversees and unites all people of all faiths, in
physical body and in spirit, in interconnected love.

An historical murder mystery which demonstrates the human frailty of misinterpreting information, and the psychological destructive effect of self guilt. It challenges the reader to decide who is to blame for each tragedy as it occurred.

The story starts in 1931 in Detroit Michigan during the Great Depression. Lillian Hansen, a wealthy socialite, flaunts her social position. After ten years of marriage, unable to accept she has given birth to a deaf child, she becomes emotionally unstable. Her husband, Edward Hansen, a wealthy, unassertive man, is dominated by his wife, Lillian. He presents his wife with a large, gold-framed mirror. This mirror witnesses the difficulties of life swing from love, cut-back to hate, then to tragedy. The mirror is the catalyst that brings the story to full culmination.

One person commits murder and disguises it as an accident. However, self guilt and fear of discovery cause a paranoid and self-destructive behavior. The killer dies by the eerily strange scenario that he/she invented to hide the murder.

HOW I CAME TO WRITE THIS STORY

Being a psychic medium, I was called to a home to examine an exquisite, but unusual antique mirror. The owner recently purchased it from an antique store and claimed to have seen a strange face in the glass. Though I saw no face, nor sensed anything unusual on that visit, I asked permission to remove a splinter of dry wood from the back of the mirror to examine it later.

That evening, I closed my eyes and took several slows, deep breaths. This began the process of slowing down my brain waves to enter a state of mediation. I held the splinter of wood in one hand to feel the vibrations, and a pen in the other. My hand began moving, penning the impressions as they came into my mind. This process is called psychometry-tuning into the vibrations of an object while automatic writing.

I sensed what the face looked like, and why it was in the mirror. I also received several names, and the era in which these tragedies occurred. Using my creative imagination, I expanded the story, building on the characters personalities and the role each played in the tragedies. Keeping with the crux of the story of why this spirit came to be imprisoned in the mirror, I revealed the innermost meaning; the human frailty of misinterpretation and the psychological effect of self guilt.

CHAPTER 1

Sarah entered her friend's living room and stopped abruptly, startled to see an old mirror standing against the wall. "Where did you get that?"

Jane's eyes twinkled with excitement. "It was in the window at the Salvation Army store. You know how I love antiques. I couldn't resist."

"I wonder where they got it?" Sarah murmured.

"I know it's just an old-fashioned mirror, but it fascinated me."

Sarah fixed her attention on the well-worn antique. *Could it be the same mirror?* she thought, as she made her way across the room.

"What's the matter? You look like you've seen a ghost."

Sarah lowered her voice to a whisper. "I know this mirror."

"You do?" Jane replied as she placed her hand on the wooden frame. "Isn't it beautiful?"

Sarah moved closer to the mirror, her mind deep in thought. *What act of fate brought it back to me now?*

"The glass looks dirty, like it's veiled in a haze. Spooky isn't it?" Jane chided with a wide grin. "I wonder what makes it shine."

"It smells like lemon oil," Sarah said, sniffing the air.

"Um-hum. Look. There's a small crack at the bottom."

Sarah nodded.

"Someone tried to clean it."

"I saw this mirror years ago. The frame was brushed with real gold then." Sarah pointed to the carved scrolls on the wooden frame. "See! There's only a trace of gold deep in the crevices."

"Yes. I see. It looks like someone scrubbed it. Must have been expensive. I often wonder what secrets these old antiques have seen."

"It wasn't new when I first saw it. It was already an antique." A somber look crossed Sarah's face. "It still gives me the creeps."

"How on earth can this old thing frighten you?"

A slight movement behind the glass caught Sarah's attention. She leaned closer. *Is something moving inside the mirror?* She stood mesmerized, watching a misty haze drifting behind the glass.

"What's the matter? You're as white as a sheet. Are you all right?"

Sarah gripped the chair to steady herself, and eased herself down.

Jane knelt down and grasped Sarah's hands. "You look like you've seen a ghost."

"I'm okay." Once again, Sarah studied the antique with intense curiosity. She brushed Jane's hand aside and retraced her steps to the mirror. This time, she approached more cautiously, as if she feared the well-worn relic. Her hand trembled as she slid her fingers across the wooden frame.

Jane flipped her blond hair with a quick toss of her head and made her way to her friend. "You've seen this before?"

"Yes," Sarah said as she fingered the scratches across the top. "Most of the gold is worn off, but I remember those dents." She pointed to the top of the frame. "There. Where it looks like the tail of a peacock."

"Oh, those dents. Hum. It does look like a peacock's tail. Those birds are known for showing off their fancy feathers, aren't they?" Jane giggled.

A somber look crossed Sarah's face. "I remember because . . . ." Sarah gazed aimlessly across the floor and shuttered. "It still gives me the chills."

"Why?"

"This is the same one that belonged to Mister Hansen."

Jane eyes sparkled, and her voice rose to a high pitch. "You mean Edward Hansen? The wealthy industrialist?" Jane grabbed the frame and tilted it forwards. "Let's see if there's a name on the back." As she moved her hand along the warped veneer, splinters of wood flecked off and fell on the carpet.

"Yes. Edward Hansen," Sarah murmured, unable to conceal the admiration as she spoke his name. She glanced up, hoping Jane hadn't detected the emotional tone in her voice.

Jane, too excited to notice, set the mirror against the wall. "He's such a celebrity."

Sarah stepped away from the mirror, toward the center of the room.

Jane gathered up the flecks of wood, inspecting them as if they had a secret to tell. "He's so handsome, and wealthy too. I've read about his affairs with other women. Such a rascal. I'll bet he led a colorful life." Jane stopped when she saw the serious expression on her friend's face. "What's the matter?"

"If only he had known what tragedy it would bring."

"Tragedy? What do you mean? Did you know them?"

Sarah nodded several times ever so slightly. "I understand this was a family heirloom. The maids said it belonged to his grandmother, then handed down to his mother, Priscilla. When Edward Hansen inherited it, he gave it to his wife as a birthday gift. Let's see. It must have been 1929, or 1930. That was long before I met them."

"You met them?" Jane's voice rose with excitement. "You never told me that."

"There's a lot of things I haven't told you."

"I've known you for over two years. You never mentioned his name before."

"I couldn't."

"Why?"

"It's something I couldn't talk about," Sarah replied as she backed away from the mirror.

"He's so famous." Jane giggled and covered her mouth with her hand. "Or, should I say infamous. How could you forget to tell me?"

"I had other things on my mind."

"I know we never lived close as neighbors, but you're my best friend."

"I couldn't confide in anyone. I had to keep my private life a secret."

"A secret? Can you tell me now? When did you meet those wealthy people?"

Sarah made her way across the living room, heading toward the kitchen. Her voice softened as she spoke. "I was just out of high school. That was over seventeen years ago. Yes. I knew him and his wife. She was a strange woman. Let's go in the kitchen and have a cup of tea. I'll tell you about them."

Jane started toward the doorway, but her attention was drawn back to the mirror. She lowered her voice to a whisper. "Do you see something moving?" She stopped, rubbed her eyes and took a closer look.

Misty gray shadows drifted behind the glass and the room turned uncannily cold.

Sarah stood at the kitchen doorway watching, and the hair on her arms stood on end, but she said nothing.

"What is that?" Jane turned to see if her friend was watching, and indeed she was. "Did you see that?"

Sarah turned ashen.

The eerie haze slithered behind the glass.

Still, Sarah would not answer.

"You see it too, don't you? Are those shadows moving?"

Sarah clasped her hand over her mouth, too shaken to speak.

The girls watched in horror until the mist began to fade.

The faint image of a face appeared through the shadowy background. The mouth drooped, taking on the appearance of agonizing torment. The image lasted only seconds, vanished, leaving a string of gray orbs drifting in the darkness.

Jane stood spellbound, watching the orbs tumbling in the hazy background. "Do you see those shadows?" Jane whispered. "They look like a string of pearls."

Sarah gripped the kitchen doorknob. "Pearls? Oh no!"

The beads faded, and fragmented image of a frightened face levitated beneath the glass. Within seconds, the eerie face was gone, leaving two dark stains resembling pleading eyes. Soon the black orbs faded, the icy chill disappeared, and the room became warm once again.

Sarah stood at the doorway mesmerized, then turned and hurried toward the kitchen.

Jane, seeing the horrified expression on Sarah's face, knew her friend had seen something. "It's probably just a flaw in the glass," she called out. When she entered the kitchen, she found Sarah sitting at the table, apparently deep in thought. Hesitating to interrupt her friend's somber mood, she filled the tea-kettle with water and set it on the stove. Still unnerved, she hesitated to mention what she had seen. She wasn't sure what it was. Or, if she had seen anything at all. It all happened so fast. Jane shrugged, casting aside her suspicions.

An eerie stillness permeated the kitchen until a shrill sound broke the silence.

Sarah's head jerked up, startled by the piercing whistle of the tea-kettle.

Jane filled two cups with hot water, dropped a tea bag in each, and set the cups on the table.

Could the warped wood on the back have caused those weird shadows? Sarah tried to push aside the image of the haunting black eyes, but they had burned in her memory like searing hot coals. She raised her cup, staring deep in the steaming tea, gathering her thoughts before she spoke. "I heard from the maids that the mirror was given to his wife on her birthday. That was long before I worked for them."

"You worked for them?" Jane replied, her voice piqued with curiosity. She slid her chair closer to the table. "Tell me about the celebrity who owned my mirror."

Sarah forced a weak smile. "I remember the day I met him. He was so pleasant."

"You really met him?"

"Yes. He hired me on the spot. They lived in a house off East Jefferson. It was huge, like a mansion." A slight smile slipped across Sarah's lips, as she reminisced. "We had a lot of happy times."

"You were in their house?"

"Um hum." Sarah's smile disappeared and her voice turned cold. "There were sad days too. I've always been fascinated by how that mirror affected the lady of the house." She thought about the real reason, that she felt the mirror had a mind of its own, and had struck back. She had seen the pendulum of life swing from love, cut-back to hate, then to tragedy. "If only he had known, he might have saved his family. But, he was so dominated by his wife that he didn't see the thin line between reality and insanity that his wife walked." Sarah lowered her voice and murmured. "But then, maybe he did. I often wondered why he didn't." Her voice trembled as she began her story. "It all began before I met them."

CHAPTER 2

November 1930 in Detroit Michigan. Most people were barely surviving the financial crisis of the stock market crash. In the poorer sections of town the bread lines had closed down for the night. Homeless people roamed the streets searching for a warm place to sleep. While across town, Lillian and Edward Hansen, owners of a tool and die business, were hosting a grand celebration.

Lillian gave little concern for the poor. She was interested in impressing her wealthy friends who did not lose their money in the stock market.

Shiny black Fords, Cadillacs, and Duesenbergs pulled around the curved driveway in front of a large four-story fashionable home. Lights shone through the beveled-glass windows, casting long amber shadows across the snow. A bitter wind swirled snowflakes around the brass lamp-posts, lighting the porch for the guests' arrival.

Although the Tool and Die company's stock dropped and money was tight, Lillian was determined to make the society page of the Detroit News. This celebration of her thirtieth birthday was meant to impress the prominent political leaders and wealthy socialites.

During prohibition, alcohol flowed freely for those who could afford it. Though it was against Edward's better judgment to deal with bootleggers, he again yielded to his wife's demands and sent a shifty, street-wise employee to purchase wine for the party.

Lillian was a new bride when Edward built this house for her. Reveling in the power of money for the first time, she decorated extravagantly, often overruling her mother-in-law's suggestions. She designed the foyer, and the curved staircase to be conspicuously visible when she made her grand entrance on special occasions. Now, after ten years of marriage, she was in the prime of her life, and ready to entertain prominent guest.

Lillian slipped out of her bedroom, leaned over the banister, and peered down at the foyer below.

The sound of laughter rose above the orchestra coming from the spacious parlor.

"It looks like the guests have arrived," she murmured, then returned to her bedroom. "Just one last look in the mirror before I go downstairs." Lillian checked each tiny detail of her gown, pursed her painted lips and swirled gracefully, pleased she still had her youthful figure.

It was last year, on her twenty-ninth birthday that her husband had given her this antique vanity and oval-shaped mirror. The wooden frame was carved with leaves intertwined within the curved scrolls. The frame was hand-rubbed with gold and carved across the top was a peacock-tail in full spread. Although she would have preferred a modern dressing table, she had accepted it, making sure her husband took notice of her indifference.

Lillian had spent the morning at the beauty parlor, and even though her hair was dyed a shade darken than she preferred, she was pleased with the wiglet of curls the hairdresser had set on top. She stood in front of the mirror admiring her reflection. The rounded neck of the purple, velvet gown was scooped seductively low, and the waist cinched tight. "Ugh. This is tighter than when

I purchased it last month. Oh well, it's still an elegant gown. Just a touch of pink rouge and I'll be ready to greet my guests."

Although Lillian had been feeling poorly the past several weeks, she arched her back, held her head high, and moved gracefully down the curved staircase. The boisterous voices singing Happy Birthday spread a smile on her face. She passed through the foyer greeting each guest with a smile. Lillian was quite adept at playing the part of an elegant socialite and did so with the adoring approval of her husband.

Edward, a handsome, well-built man, watched his wife making her way across the parlor. He was a quiet man, seldom raised his voice, and preferred to stay out of the limelight.

Maybe opposites attract, he thought as he admired her vivacious personality. He searched the room, studying the sullen faces of guests who had lost their zest for living since the stock market crash. *I'm glad I procrastinated and didn't invest all my money in stock. If I had, I couldn't have given Lillian all the beautiful things she deserves.*

A burst of laughter interrupted his thoughts.

He brushed a strand of blond hair off his forehead, reached out and drew his wife close to him. "For my lovely wife, who is as beautiful now, as she was when I married her nearly ten years ago." Edward reached in his pocket and withdrew a small, velvet box. He presented his wife with an exquisite ring, inset with an oval shaped diamond, surrounded by ten rubies.

"It's absolutely perfect." Lillian held out her hand while he slipped it on her finger. She studied the ring admiringly, then twirled playfully around him. "Come. Let's dance. They're playing our song."

"You are the peg of my heart," Edward sang as he swept her up in his arms. *Everything is so perfect,* he thought as he whirled her toward the center of the parlor.

Later that evening, a lavish dinner was served in the formal dining room, and vintage wines flowed freely.

During the evening, Lillian feigned a pretense of enjoying the party. But, as the evening drew to an end, her smile disappeared, and she felt tired and irritable.

Doctor Johnson, a personal friend and the family physician, took notice of Lillian's irritability during the evening. Aware of her temperamental mood swings, he made it a point to be the last to leave. He stood by the door stroking his gray beard. "You look tired my dear."

"I'm fine." Lillian passed off his concern with a forced smile. "Perhaps I've had a bit too much wine." She twisted the doorknob and eased the door open, hesitated, as if to speak. She wanted to apologize for her irritability, but felt too exhausted to explain. "Thank you for coming to my party," she said, opening the door wider.

A cold as a gust of wind sent snowflakes fluttering on the floor.

Doctor Johnson, seeing Lillian wasn't about to explain, patted her arm. "Come to my office next week if you're not feeling better."

"I'm just exhausted from the party. I'll be fine in a few days." Lillian again forced a smile as she bid him good evening.

After the guest had left, Edward approached his wife. "Your party was a success. Everyone had a good time."

Lillian glared at her husband. "This dress is killing me, and I feel awful. Your friends were getting rowdy and that damn maid didn't bring the canapés out on time."

"Everything was served on time, my love. Maybe the party was too much for you." Seeing how angry his wife was, he backed away. After ten years of marriage he had become accustomed to her mood swings and, rather than face her wrath, he would wait until her anger passed. It was not in his nature to argue, and being tired from the long evening, he hurried across the foyer and stepped behind the library door.

Lillian stomped back in the parlor to confront the serving crew.

Edward stood in the shadows and watched Lillian, her hands on her hips, scolding a maid. *Should I ask her what bothering her this evening? If I do, it's sure to start an argument. Oh well. It's late and I'm tired.* Edward crossed the foyer, finding it easier to procrastinate, than start an argument. "Perhaps tomorrow will be a better day," he mumbled as he trudged up the stairs.

The second week of December, the doctor made a house call at Edward's request.

"My wife hasn't been herself lately. She's exhausted and more irritable than usual. She complains about the food not tasting good, and she's raising hell with the maids. My nerves are on edge." Edward pointed toward the bedroom. "She's upstairs. See what you can do to help her."

Doctor Johnson, a slender, nattily dressed man in his mid fifties, nodded assuredly. His black suit and brocade vest added an air of authority to his already confident mannerism. "I'll give her a thorough examination. Don't worry. It's probably nothing serious." The doctor started up the stairs with his medical bag in hand, tapping his black-enamel cane on the wooden edge of each step. When he entered her bedroom, he saw his patient lying on the bed.

Lillian raised her head when she saw the door open.

"Well Lillian. What's the problem? I hear you've been under a strain lately." The doctor placed his black bag on the bed while studying the tense expression that scowled back at him.

"I'm so damn miserable. It's hard to explain. Everything annoys me more than usual. I'm nervous and aggravated, and I don't know why."

"Let's find out what's wrong. " After a brief examination, the doctor placed the medical supplies back in his bag and tightened the leather strap. "I've known you for nearly ten years and I've been waiting for this day." He leaned forward, and a smile crossed his face. "Have you ever thought about having children?"

Lillian's forehead furrowed in disbelief. "Children? You mean I'm pregnant? How can that be? Not after all these years?"

"What's wrong? You don't look pleased."

"No. It can't be."

"You're probably upset because of the morning sickness. You'll be all right soon." Surprised by Lillian's lack of enthusiasm, he patted her on the shoulder. "The nausea won't last much longer. Well, this is quite a way to welcome 1931."

"How could I have let this happen?" Caught off-guard by her own miscalculation, she stared aimlessly across the room. "Never mind. You don't understand," Lillian mumbled under her breath.

Edward, hearing the doctor's cane tapping on the oak stairs, rushed to the foyer. "Is she all right?"

The doctor pulled his wool coat off the brass coat-rack and smiled. "It's not serious. Just as I suspected. Your wife is pregnant."

"Pregnant?" Edward shouted, his voice rising in blissful surprise. "But I thought we couldn't have children."

"What ever gave you that idea? Lillian's in good physical health. There's no reason why you can't have more after this one," he jested with a mischievous wink.

"A baby? But . . ., ah . . ., I mean. We just assumed after all these years. Are you sure?" Edward helped the doctor with his coat and hustled him out the front door. Bubbling with excitement, he dashed up the steps and burst into the bedroom. "We're going to have a baby. Lillian, I love you." He swept her up in his arm. Tears moistened his cheeks as he cradled his wife tenderly.

Lillian, still dazed with the unexpected news, felt her husband's arms around her, but her listless body didn't respond to his embrace.

Several months later, Doctor Johnson chanced to meet Edward on the street. He grabbed the sleeve of Edward's coat, and escorted him into a drugstore, out of the cold. "I've been meaning to talk to you. How is your wife?"

"Fine. Fine" Edward removed his homburg, gave it a quick snap against his knee, knocking a mist of rain off the rim. "She saw you a couple weeks ago. Everything is okay."

The smile disappeared from the doctor's face. "That's what I want to talk to you about." He removed his glasses, and to avoid eye contact, begin inspecting the lenses. "I'm concerned about your wife." He pulled a white handkerchief from his pocket, wiping it across the lens with a slow, deliberate motion. "I want you to keep an eye on her. She's not very enthusiastic about this pregnancy." He paused and his voice turned serious. "Just watch her closely."

Edward, taken off guard by the blunt comment, stared in disbelief. "What do you mean her attitude? I haven't noticed anything unusual. She spends a lot of time in her bedroom. But, isn't it customary for a woman to hide from the public when she's pregnant?"

Doctor Johnson adjusted his glasses on the bridge of his nose. "Your wife is more troubled than she lets on. Why is she so upset about having this baby?"

"My wife is a private person. She hasn't complained to me, but she does seem more depressed."

"You better talk to her. I'm concerned she may take something."

"Take something?" Edward responded as he nervously twisted the rim of his homburg through his fingers. "Do you think she would do something?" Edward stared down at the sidewalk, unable to reply.

"Just watch her carefully"

Edward, unwilling to accept the life-threatening criticism, hurried out the door and headed down the street. A gust of cold wind sent a chill through his body. The message was thrust upon him like a sword, piercing the blissful event, stabbing at his happiness. He heard the doctor's footsteps following close behind. He walked faster, hoping to escape the reality of the moment.

Later that evening, Edward decided to mention his concerns to his wife. Knowing her quick temper, he chose his words carefully. "Doctor Johnson says you're upset about this pregnancy. Is that true, my dear?"

Lillian glared at her husband, but seeing the worried look on his face, she stopped crocheting and forced a smile. "He's just overly cautious." She clenched her jaw, gripped a strand of yarn, and jabbed the brass crochet-hook through the weave.

"The doctor seemed troubled." Edward was about to question her further, but was interrupted by Lillian's sharp reply.

"Oh, shut up! Haven't I got enough problems?" Lillian slung the half-done afghan on the floor exposing her swollen belly. "Look at my figure. I'll never be slim again."

"You're only few months along. You look good honey." Edward started toward his wife, but the high pitch of her voice made him turn away.

"I can't go out looking like this. I'll be stuck in this house with a damn child hanging on me."

Edward hadn't noticed his wife's thick waist, nor the dark circles under her eyes. He had accepted her solitude as normal.

He didn't understand her inability to cope with the pregnancy, and, not knowing what to do, he slid his hands deep in his pant pockets. "Perhaps she will feel better," he muttered as he walked out of the room.

As the months passed, Lillian became moody and reclusive. Gazing in the mirror, the face that reflected back was not the sophisticated woman she intended to be. She laid her hand on her swollen stomach, disgusted by the stretched seams of her nightgown. She turned and glared at the walk-in closet full of expensive dresses. "It's been months since I've worn a nice dress. Will I ever fit in them again?"

The afternoon sun burst from behind the clouds, sending a glaring light reflecting on the glass.

Lillian squinted and shielded her eyes from the blazing light. When she again looked at the mirror, the golden scrolls on the frame appeared to be whirling. She clutched her forehead as she watched the scrolls twisting and whirling, taking on the appearance of grotesque mouths, jeering and laughing at her.

"Why are you mocking me?" Lillian felt a pressure building in her head. The room seemed to fade in and out of the darkness. In an uncontrollable urge, she ran in the hall and stood trembling at the top of the staircase. Tears blurred her vision. She gripped the railing, edging her way closer to the stairs. *Something is telling me to go down in one flying leap. Th*e stairs faded in and out of the darkness. Spastic lights flashed before her eyes. The *ceiling is caving in on me. Is someone calling my name?*

"Misses Hansen. Misses Hansen," a distant voice called out.

Lillian hovered at the edge of the staircase, staring at the black void below. Voices inside screamed. *Let go. End this!* In a moment of conscious logic, she gripped the banister and hung on. A sharp pain raced across her forehead. The hallway seemed to be whirling, pushing her forward. Her knees gave way, and she felt herself falling. She felt an excruciating pain as her head smashed against the wooden steps. She heard someone sobbing.

Darkness, and a deadening silence engulfed Lillian as she lay unconscious at the foot of the stairs.

Edward, having been summoned, returned home within minutes of the doctor's arrival.

The housekeeper, Hilda, was leaning against the bedroom door, her apron covering her mouth, smothering her sobs.

Lillian, seeing her husband standing at the foot of the bed, turned away.

"You're a lucky girl. You didn't lose the baby," the doctor said.

Even though Lillian heard the words, they sounded muffled, distant, and returned his comment with a blank stare.

"The baby's heart beat is strong. Everything seems fine." Doctor Johnson glanced across the room. "Your wife is all right. The baby is okay too." He turned toward Hilda. "I want her off her feet until the baby is born."

Hilda, still holding her apron over her mouth, nodded in reply.

The doctor turned to Edward. "I gave her something to make her sleep. Why don't you go downstairs? I'll be down shortly." Even though the doctor saw Lillian's irritability increasing, this accident caught him off-guard. He waited until Edward left the bedroom, then motioned for Hilda.

Hilda followed the doctor into the hall wringing her hands in her apron.

"How did she fall?" he asked, hoping to get a clearer picture of the accident. "Did she call for help?"

"Ya. She was screaming something. I come to the foyer and saw her at the top of the stairs." Hilda sniffed and wiped her finger across her nose. "I was scared, so I called up to her. I say

Missus Hansen, I'm coming. But she just stood there. I don't think she heard me. I was up one step when she started swaying, like dis." Hilda's buxom body rocked, and she lowered her voice apologetically. "I was trying to help, but I couldn't get up there fast enough."

"It's all right," he said, patting the housekeeper on the arm. Hilda's explanation shed no light on the accident. He started down the stairs, stopped midway, glanced up at the bedroom, shaking his head to cast off his suspicions. He knew Lillian was troubled, but didn't think she would hurt the unborn baby.

Edward reluctantly summoned his mother to take charge while his wife was confined to bed. *Lillian's going to need my mother's help. After all, it's only until the baby is born.* He didn't look forward to her visit. She could be quite domineering, constantly badgering him to be more aggressive.

Priscilla Hansen, a stern, stoic woman, agreed to take charge until the baby was born. She was a teenager when she arrived in the United States in 1885, along with the influx of immigrants from Germany. After living in Detroit for three years, she had the good fortune to marry the wealthy industrialist, Henry Hansen, who was quite a bit older than she. Even though she had been raised on a humble farm with meager necessities, she quickly adapted to the sophisticated life style of the wealthy. After a tumultuous twenty-five-year marriage to a meandering husband, Priscilla was widowed and inherited, along with her son, the Hansen Tool and Die business. She ran the company until her son took over, and though it irritated her daughter-in-law, she maintained an office, overruling many of Edward's business decisions.

Priscilla had been living at her son's home for several days when she noticed her daughter-in-law's depression worsening. She approached Lillian. "You seem so worried. Why don't you talk to your doctor?"

"I'm not talking about my feelings," Lillian retaliated.

"But you seem so depressed."

"You don't know how I feel." Lillian turned away, refusing to confide her true feelings.

Later that evening, Priscilla took her son aside and insisted he seek medical attention for his wife. Several days later, after hearing Lillian had again refused medical help, Priscilla took matters into her own hands, and made an appointment with the family physician.

"Doctor, I'm concerned about my daughter-in-law. Lillian and I have always had our differences, but now she resents, not just me, but everyone."

"I know she's having a tough time."

"She's so unreasonable. It's causing problems among the household staff."

The doctor nodded, but didn't reply. As a professional, it was his duty to keep his patients private life in confidence. So, he didn't inform Priscilla he had already warned Edward about Lillian's increasing depression.

"What will happen when this baby arrives?" Priscilla twisted a lace handkerchief between her fingers, searching for the right words. "Will she be able to take care of the baby?"

"I'm sorry. My hands are tied. The patient has to ask for help," he said, shaking his head in regret. "What do you want me to do?"

"She's getting worse. My son can't…, ah, he won't insist she see a specialist."

"If something happens, I'll intervene. I understand your frustration, but it's all I can offer at this time."

"I'm concerned Lillian will make me leave after the baby is born."

"Let's hope not. She's going to need help."

Priscilla left the office disappointed. She knew it would be difficult, but was determined to remain at her son's home as long as possible. Her grandchild needed protection from Lillian's temper tantrums, and she intended to keep peace in the family.

Behind closed doors, the young maid, Ester, whispered her suspicions to the housekeeper. "The missus been getting real mean lately. Whenever I change her bed sheets, she complains about everything." Beads of sweat glistened on Ester's forehead as the hot iron pressed against the dampened cloth, sending a cloud of steam into her face. "Yesterday, I heard her screaming at the mister. She say it's all his fault."

Hilda, grateful for the position of head-housekeeper, would not reply. She filled a bowl with hot, chicken soup. "Take this up to the missus," she said as she handed the serving tray to Ester. "Don't you worry. Things will be different now that the mister's mama is here."

Ester picked up the tray and sauntered up the stairs. She paused near the half-open door, about to present the lunch, when she heard Lillian's voice.

"You mock me! You laugh at my repulsive body."

Ester, hearing the footsteps pacing the floor, hesitated to enter the room. She waited until the sound stopped, then peeked through the half-open door.

Lillian was leaning close to the mirror. Her hair hung loose, straightened and matted from the humid summer heat. "Just a week or two, then you won't mock me." She turned when she noticed Ester reflection in the mirror. "Why are you spying on me?" she screamed, waving her hands in the air. "Get out of here!"

Ester, hesitating to speak, pushed the door open with her foot, holding the tray as a peace offering.

"Put it down! Get out of here!" Lillian flopped on the bed, smothering her face in a satin pillow, already dampened from perspiration.

Ester set the tray on the bedside table and dashed out of the bedroom. She returned to the kitchen, covered her mouth with her hand and whispered. "I know the misses is supposed to be in bed all the time. She ain't fooling nobody. She's up to no good."

"Just you never mind. Get on with your work," Hilda grumbled.

Ester spread a white, linen tablecloth across the ironing board and returned to her ironing.

Hilda slopped a wet cloth across the kitchen table, wiped the loose crumbs to the edge and dropped them into her hands. "I wonder vhen all this is going to end."

CHAPTER 3

As the time for the birth neared, Edward paced the foyer. He glanced up, and heard Hilda calling from the balcony.

"It's time to call the doctor."

After phoning the hospital, Edward stood at the front door waiting impatiently. When he saw the doctor and his nurse coming up the front sidewalk, he held the door open, urging them to hurry.

Doctor Johnson entered the foyer, shook the rain-drops off his umbrella and set it aside. Laying a firm hand on Edward's shoulder, he said. "Relax. This isn't the first time I've delivered a baby."

It wasn't common practice to have a nurse assist the birth. Most patients preferred their own midwife or relatives. However, Lillian was adamant that a nurse assist the birth, and not her mother-in-law.

After checking his patient, the doctor returned downstairs to the breakfast room. "It will be a few hours before the baby is born. I'll stay here until it's time."

The evening seemed to drag by. It was eleven-thirty when Hilda's voice echoed down the stairs. "It's time."

The doctor started up the stairs, stopped midway when he saw Priscilla following close behind. "You're not needed," he said. Seeing the determined look on Priscilla's face, he knew this grandmother would not be dismissed so easily. "Lillian won't like this," he grumbled under his breath as he hurried toward the bedroom.

It was well past the midnight when the wailing of the newborn broke the silence.

Edward rushed to the staircase. His heart beat wildly. He waited in silence, looking up at the balcony.

The bedroom door opened slowly.

Hilda shuffled into the hall wiping her hands across her blood-stained apron. She leaned over the banister and called. "Come on up."

Edward entered the dimly lit room, and the silence disturbed him. The smell of talcum powder barely smothered the repugnant odor of warm blood. He glanced around to catch someone's attention.

No one turned to face Edward.

Detecting a sense of urgency, he thought it strange that his mother didn't turn around and greet him with a reassuring smile. The doctor didn't turn around either, but continued washing his hands in a bucket of cold water that Ester had placed on the night table.

Hilda broke the silence, motioning toward the bassinet. "Come. See your baby girl."

Edward bent over the bassinet and the baby's misshapen face left him weak in the knees. His expectation had been anything, but this.

The baby's tiny nose flattened against her malformed face and her forehead marred with purple bruises from medical instruments.

"She is much smaller than I expected. Is she supposed to look like that?" Edward scanned the room, searching for consolation.

Priscilla turned to observe her son's reaction to the newborn, but remained silent.

The doctor's weary shoulders sloped forward as he slid off his white gown. He nodded, gesturing for Edward to follow him into the hall. "I'm concerned. Your wife had a hard delivery. I was afraid that we might lose her." Seeing the terrified look on Edward's face, he changed the tone of his voice and spoke with authority. "She's out of danger now. I gave Lillian something to make her sleep. Let' go down. Hilda and the nurse can finish up here."

After the men left, Priscilla took one last look at the tiny infant. "These imperfections often correct themselves," she muttered to herself. After tucking a blanket around her granddaughter, she headed down to the breakfast room.

Hilda gathered the bloody linens and stuffed them into a wicker basket. Thoughts of Lillian's falling down the stairs came to mind. "It all comes back, one way or the other." Being a religious woman, Hilda feared God's vengeance. Yet, she knew He would be merciful. "That baby's gonna be born just the way she wants to be."

The nurse turned toward Hilda. "What are you talking about?"

"Nothing," Hilda muttered with a wave of her hand. She tucked the corners of her apron into her waistband to hide the crimson stains. After taking a last peek at the sleeping infant, she started down the hall. "She just doesn't look right," she muttered, shaking her head in pity. Hilda hurried to the breakfast room, curious to hear about the newborn.

An early morning breeze floated through the back screen door, and the room took on a somber silence.

Edward shifted nervously in a chair, listening to it creak as he leaned forward. "My daughter isn't what I expected. Do all babies look like that when they're born?"

"No. Not always," the doctor replied. "Some features are not fully developed when they're first born." Hesitant to express his

23

own thoughts, he nodded a 'thank you' as he accepted a glass of ice tea from Priscilla. It wasn't the baby's facial features that bothered him, it was something else. He sipped his iced tea while mulling over the facts, separating the uncertainties in his own mind.

Hilda, having remained quiet in the background, spoke. "Did you tell the what I found on the baby's hand?" Hilda smiled, pleased that she had noticed what the others had overlooked.

"Found what?" Edward interrupted.

Hilda, noticing the doctor seemed reluctant to answer, spoke with confidence. "The lines on the baby's hands just don't look right. They're not long enough."

"Lines on her hands? Isn't that what palm readers do? That's nonsense. What's that got to do with my baby?"

Priscilla interrupted. "I've heard of this before, but I've never seen it." She held her hand out, palm open. "See this center line. This is the simian line. Sometimes it's called the headline. This length of this line shows the mental ability."

Edward felt his stomach tightening into a knot. "Mental ability? Are you saying my daughter is mentally retarded?"

"No. No," the doctor interrupted. He too, had seen this under-developed line on a palm before, and found it often was an accurate indicator of a problem. Because the medical profession frowned on palm reading, most physicians didn't speak of palmistry. However, since the Hansen's were personal friends, he felt he could express himself more freely. "The line is not that short."

"What the hell are you talking about," Edward asked.

The doctor's hand shot up, halting the discussion. "I'm not sure, but there's a slight possibility your daughter's intellect will develop slowly."

Edward slumped back in his chair, unprepared to deal with the bad news.

"Your baby will be okay," Hilda said in an assuring voice. She picked up the basket of linens and headed toward the laundry room.

Ester took the basket and dumped the linens into a large, metal tub of cold water. She leaned close to Hilda and whispered. "Is that baby okay? She sure don't look right."

"Sure is a strange-looking baby," Hilda mumbled as she plunged the linens down with a wood bleaching-stick, pushing them into the cold water.

Ester covered her mouth with her hand and whispered. "That baby's gonna get back at the misses."

"Eh, huh. The Lord moves in strange ways."

"I gotta feeling that baby ain't gonna pay no mind to the misses."

"We'll see," Hilda replied.

CHAPTER 4

By the time Bridget was six months old, her face improved slightly, although not to Lillian's satisfaction. Each day the baby's voice grew stronger, and her screaming louder.

Priscilla, concerned about her granddaughter's constant crying, spoke to her daughter-in-law. "When are you taking the baby for an examination? We should find out why she cries so much."

"That child has a bad temper. It's just her way of getting attention," Lillian retaliated.

Priscilla, concerned about her granddaughter, waited until the family gathered at the dinner table, and again approached the subject. "Perhaps Bridget should see a doctor," Priscilla said, directing her attention toward her son.

Lillian's head shot up, and she glared at Priscilla. "That child is just ill-tempered. She doesn't seem to be in pain. She's just rebellious."

Priscilla shot a quick look at her son. "Don't you think a doctor should see Bridget?"

Edward glanced up from his dinner. "Yes, we should." Noticing the scowl on his wife's face, he turned toward his mother, and with a defeated shrug replied. "Maybe she'll outgrow her crying."

Priscilla frowned, frustrated by her son's passive attitude. After dinner she whispered to Edward. "Meet me in the library."

Edward reluctantly followed his mother across the foyer.

"You must find out why Bridget cries so loud, and so often."

"I know," Edward muttered as he reached for the light-switch. He felt his mother's hand edging him further into the library. "I can't go against Lillian. It's her child too."

"It's your child too," Priscilla snapped, guiding him into the room.

Edward bowed his head in regret. "You know how Lillian gets when I confront her."

"I know how unpleasant she can be," Priscilla retaliated in a whisper. "Why do you always give in to her demands?"

Edward wrenched his grip from his mother and hurried out of the room.

As the months passed, Lillian's temper tantrums increased. The maids gossiped behind closed doors, all agreeing Lillian intended to drive her mother-in-law away.

Priscilla, determined to stay, avoided Lillian. She was especially careful not to intrude upon Lillian's parental authority. To keep Bridget from crying, she attended the baby whenever possible. Worried about the baby's health, she decided to take matters into her own hand. She waited until Lillian would leave for the day, then took the baby to Doctor Johnson's office.

"Something is wrong with Bridget," Priscilla explained. "She cries constantly. It's not normal for a baby to cry so loud."

"Why didn't you come sooner?"

Priscilla sat down and lifted Bridget up, onto her lap. "I told my son about the baby's crying."

"What did he say?"

"He seemed concerned. But as usual, Lillian overruled him."

"I understand," the doctor replied with a slight smile and a nod of his head. "Let's see what's bothering this little one."

After a lengthy testing, the doctor returned to the waiting room. He handed the baby to Priscilla and smiled reassuringly. "Bridget has no serious medical problem. However, she has a severe loss of hearing. She can only hear high-pitched sounds."

Priscilla suspected something was wrong, but this diagnosis took her by surprise. "Why does she scream so loud? Is she in pain?"

"No. No. Physically, she is healthy. My guess is she's mimicking sound. I think she's trying to hear her own voice."

Priscilla was relieved that Bridget's cries were not of pain, but of curiosity. "Is there anything we can do? An operation or something?"

"I'll do some research." Doctor Johnson raised his eyebrows and a stern look crossed his face. "When are you going to tell Lillian?"

"I'll talk to my son. He can tell her."

"Wasn't Lillian worried about the baby's crying?"

"No. She doesn't seem to care at all. My daughter-in-law refuses to discuss Bridget's crying with me. She's very cunning and hides her frustration from Edward. I hear her complaining to the maids, but not to me. She rarely talks to me at all."

Later that evening, Priscilla cornered her son in the upstairs hall. "Edward," she said, clutching his shoulder and nudging him into her bedroom. "I took Bridget to the doctor. I guess I should have asked for permission, but someone had to find out."

Edward felt his knees grow weak. "Bridget's not sick, is she? What did the doctor say?"

"Bridget has a hearing problem. But she's not ill, or in pain."

Warm perspiration dampened his brow at the thought of facing his wife. "I'll tell Lillian," he muttered under his breath. He knew Lillian's wrath would be inescapable. He had intended to tell his wife that day, but his timid mannerism once again led to procrastination.

Several days later, Edward waited until it was time to leave for work. He paused at the back door, twisting the rim of his homburg between his fingers. "Lillian. My mother took Bridget to a doctor," he said, his voice trailing to a whisper.

"What?" Lillian shouted, slamming her coffee cup down on the table. "What business does she have taking *my* child to a doctor? She had no right. Your mother went behind my back."

"Bridget can't hear very well," he replied, quickening his pace toward the back door.

"She what!" Lillian shrieked as she headed toward her husband. "Just a minute! What else did you discuss?"

"Just Bridget, my love," Edward gripped the doorknob and eased the door open.

"That woman's overstepped her bounds this time," Lillian shrieked. "Tell your mother I'll take care of my own child."

Edward felt his stomach tighten, and a nauseating taste filled his mouth. He closed the door behind him. "It's not my fault," he muttered as he headed toward the garage. "Lillian should have taken Bridget to the doctor herself. Then, my mother wouldn't have intervened."

Over the next three years, Lillian appealed to many specialists. The medical examinations always ended with the same diagnosis– eventual total loss of hearing. After each medical visit, Lillian became moody and despondent. Many days she refused to see or care for her daughter. On those days she would complain of a headache and remain in her bedroom.

Because society encouraged concealing the handicapped behind closed doors, Lillian insisted Bridget be confined to the house.

Priscilla, troubled by the unreasonable command, managed a cordial relationship with her daughter-in-law. She heard the neighbor's insensitive remarks about the deaf and understood why Lillian had become so defensive. Priscilla obeyed Lillian's instructions and kept Bridget hidden behind closed doors. Not because she was ashamed, nor because society expected her to do so, but because she knew of Lillian's inability to cope with Bridget's deafness.

As Bridget grew, her loud screeches sent the maids scurrying to her attention. When she didn't get her way, she sprawled on the floor kicking and screaming. Her inability to understand resulted in temper tantrums and her screams became louder, and more frequent.

Lillian took every precaution to keep her daughter's deafness from prying eyes. She demanded the windows say shut so the neighbors couldn't hear Bridget screaming. Each day she had the maids arrange indoor activities to keep Bridget entertained. However, on this weekend, Lillian was so preoccupied with trying on new dresses that she forgot it was Saturday.

Edward paused at the back screen-door and breathed in the fresh spring air. "Come on Bridget," he said, mouthing each word with visual expression. He opened the door wide, coaxing her with hand gestures to come outside.

Bridget shook her head, refusing to budge. She remembered the last time she ran in the yard, and how it hurt when her mother smacked her hard across the back.

Edward continued mouthing unheard words, waving his hand in friendly gestures.

After a while, encouraged by her father's pleasant smile, Bridget dashed out the door screaming with joy.

Lillian, hearing the loud screams, threw her new dress on the floor, and pulled the lace curtain aside. She shrieked with disgust when she saw Bridget tearing roses off the latticework of the gazebo. "That child is an animal." Lillian dashed down the stairs and stood on the back porch with her hands planted firmly on her hips. "Get that damn child in here," she demanded in a low, but stern voice. "Right now!"

Edward held his hand over his face, shielding his eyes from the sun. "She's okay," he shouted, mindful of the angry tone of his wife's voice. "I'll watch her."

Lillian stomped down the brick path toward the back of the yard.

When Bridget saw her mother, she dashed across the yard toward her father's open arms.

"Get her in here. Now!"

"She wants to play, my love. Let her be." Turning his back on his wife, he took Bridget by the hand and lead her toward the swing that hung on the old, oak tree.

Lillian clenched her teeth and lowered her voice. "Shut that damn child up. The neighbors will hear her."

"What? I don't give a damn about the neighbors."

"Well, I do! That child doesn't need to go outside. She has plenty of toys in the house." Lillian clenched her teeth and muttered in a low voice. "She is not allowed outside! Ever!"

Edward glanced up, startled in disbelief. "Do you mean she's never been outside before? That child needs the sunshine." A gasp of surprise tightened his throat when he realized how little he knew about his daughter's daily routine. "Must I stay home from work to see that Bridget gets proper care? From now on, my daughter is to play in the yard. Do you hear me?" Edward had no stomach for arguing. And, responding in such an assertive manner surprised him. He took Bridget's hand, turned his back on his wife, and headed toward the back of the yard.

Lillian, infuriated by her husband's aggressive attitude, hurried toward the house "He'll embarrass us if he keeps this up." Lillian stomped into the kitchen. "Hilda. Where is Ester? Tell her to go outside. Keep that dam child quiet."

"Yes ma'am," Hilda nodded, turned and hurried to the laundry room.

"Go outside. Keep that damn child from screaming." Lillian shook her finger. "Don't you dare discuss my business with the neighbor's maids."

Ester, reluctant to speak, nodded.

"What do you girls gossip about while you're hanging up the wash? I'll bet they talk about Bridget up and down the boulevard, don't they?"

"I never talk about your daughter," Hilda replied.

Lillian scowled at Ester, waiting for a reply.

Ester, still shy at eighteen, looked down at the floor, shaking her head in denial. "I ain't heard no talk bout her."

"Well, just keep it that way."

"You want me out there now?"

"Yes! Now! Keep that brat from screaming."

Hilda nudged her head toward the door, urging Ester to leave. "Misses Hansen, the neighbors don't care about the noise."

Lillian pulled the curtain aside. "I see the neighbors came out in their yard. They heard Bridget screaming." Lillian was glad it was customary, or at least understood, that her friends not discuss Bridget's handicap. She was grateful most people skirted around the truth to avoid embarrassment. Still gripping the curtain, she noticed Ester talking to Edward. She could tell by his hostile glance toward the house he was angry.

After Ester finished speaking with Edward, she headed toward the side-fence. Even though she saw Lillian looking out the window, she knew Mister Hansen would protect her. Ester leaned her elbows on the fence to chat with the neighbor's maid. After a while, she sauntered across the yard and entered the kitchen. "The mister say it's okay to come inside He's gonna play with Bridget."

"What were you and the neighbor maids talking about?"

"Oh, let's see. The cleaning lady talked about Bridget. But I ain't gonna talk about her."

"What did she say?"

Ester hesitated, stared up at the ceiling, trying to remember the exact words. "She say apples don't fall far from the tree. I don't know what she means, so I come in the house."

"Is that what you maids do? Spread gossip over the back fence?" Lillian's voice quivered, finding it difficult to control her anger.

Ester backed away, wide-eyed and innocently bewildered. "What I do?" she whimpered.

"Apples!" Lillian placed her hands over her ears, cringing at the screeching in the backyard. She slammed the window shut and dashed up the stairs, sobbing uncontrollably.

Hilda shook her finger at Ester. "You dummy. Why you tell her that?"

"What I do?" Ester replied as she strolled to the laundry room.

As the weeks passed, Bridget grew more curious. Barely able to hear a sound, she screamed to feel the vibrations of her own voice. This strange feeling in her throat amused her, and she started to shriek louder. It didn't take long before she realized her screams would bring the maids scurrying to help her. When her screaming didn't get the results she wanted, she retaliated with temper tantrums. Because she didn't understand her silent world, her voice became louder, and her demands more unreasonable.

Lillian only saw her child growing worse. She didn't understand Bridget's tantrums were a result of her own behavior–a mirror image of her own hostility. If Lillian had taken the time to understand, she might have seen the damage she was causing. But, Lillian blamed the student, not realizing that she was the instructor. So the vicious circle began.

Bridget became the aggressor.

CHAPTER 5

In 1936, in the state of Michigan, it was customary to hide deaf children behind closed doors. The public had little interest in educating the deaf. Although Priscilla repeatedly asked her son to hire a sign-language tutor, he always found an excuse to procrastinate.

The past five years of guarding Bridget from Lillian's temper tantrums had taken its toll. Priscilla kept her failing health a secret from the family. Now she decided to take action; acceptable or not, sign-language was the only way her granddaughter could live a more normal life.

Meeting her son in the upstairs hall, she shoved a paper in his hand. "Here's the name of the sign-language teacher. I know your wife will be upset, but you must consider Bridget's future."

Edward scanned the paper. "What if Bridget can't understand? You know she has a quick temper. She'll just stamp her feet and scream."

"It's Bridge's inability to understand that makes her quick-tempered. She's nearing school age. It's time she learned to communicate."

Edward cast his eyes down. "You know how Lillian feels about sign language."

"Edward. No more excuses." Priscilla set her hands on her hip in disgust. "Promise you'll phone this woman."

Hearing the harsh tone of his mother voice, Edward nodded in agreement and slipped it in his wallet. Though he wasn't sure what he would do, he must offer his mother a ray of hope. "I'll do what I can." He turned away and hurried down the stairs.

March winds blew heavy, gray clouds overhead, and rain poured down with a vengeance. Priscilla woke to the sound of the wind battering branches against the window. She lay in bed as visions of her dream flashed across her mind. She remembered the black box looming overhead, growing larger, and larger, engulfing her in its darkness. *They're premonitions of death,* she thought.

Priscilla bolted upright, startled by a loud thud.

A black crow landed outside the window, darkening the room.

Its piercing squawk sent a chill through her body. She slid down and pulled the blankets up to her chin, waiting for it to fly away.

The crow sat on the ledge determined to show its ominous presence. After a while it flew away and perched on a leafless branch.

"Oh no. Not so soon," Priscilla whimpered, conscious of its prophetic warning. She snuggled under the blankets and closed her eyes. Memories of her childhood in Germany flooded her mind.

Priscilla was only a child when she first saw the black harbingers of death circling over her farm house. She remembered the small farm where she was raised, and the death of her overworked parents. The villagers had tried to scare away the black messengers, but only scattered them into the woods nearby. Later that day they returned and circled the sky for hours, screaming their fateful prophecy. The next evening they returned and perched in the trees near the farm. Though it was long ago, Priscilla still remembers the uncanny silence that engulfed the farmland as the crows waited for their premonition to be fulfilled. That was the day the villagers buried her mother.

Priscilla wiped the tears from her cheeks. It was not for herself that she cried, but for Bridget. "Hilda! I need you," she called out in a feeble voice.

Hilda shuffled up the stairs. When she opened the door, she jumped back, startled to see a huge crow looking through the window. "Goot en himmel!" she shouted, whipping her apron in the air with a snapping sound.

The monstrous intruder flapped its huge wings against the glass, battering out its grim omen. Still, it refused to move. Its beady eyes peered through the rain-spattered glass as if searching out its victim.

After pulling the winter drapes closed, Hilda turned on the bedside lamp. "There. That's better. Don't pay attention to those black devils."

Priscilla patted the bed, motioning for Hilda to sit beside her. "It's near my time."

"Now don't talk like that." Hilda sat on the bed and held Priscilla's hand. "You're going to be okay."

"Listen to me. This is important," Priscilla said, her voice barely a whisper. "When I go, I want you to watch Bridget."

"I've got no business up here. Ester's the upstairs maid. Besides, I've got my job in the kitchen."

"You and Ester must take charge of Bridget whenever you can. Now go. Tell my son I need him. Don't tell Lillian that I'm ill."

Hilda, smelling the foul odor of death, scurried down the stairs, toward the cheerful sound of music in the parlor.

Edward was pounding hard on the piano keys.

Bridget's hands were pressed flat on the sounding board, feeling the vibrations through the mahogany frame as she bounced to the beat of the rhythm. She stopped when she felt the vibrations of heavy footsteps entering the parlor. Bridget yanked her father's sleeve and pointed to the door.

Hilda stood teary-eyed in the doorway. "Your mama is real sick."

Edward's face turned ashen when he saw the serious expression on Hilda's face. "Oh my God!" Brushing Bridget's hand off his jacket, he dashed toward the stairs. "Tell Lillian to call the doctor."

"I'll call him, but she doesn't want Miss Lillian to know. You best hurry," Hilda said as she scooped Bridget up in her arms.

Edward dashed up the stairs and paused to catch his breath before opening the door.

Priscilla was laying motionless, her hands lay limp across her chest. A weak smile of relief spread across her face when she saw her son.

Easing himself down on the edge of the bed, he grasped his mother's hands. "You'll be all right. We've called the doctor."

"There's no time. Promise you'll hire that woman. The one that teaches sign-language."

Edward, hearing his mother gasping for air, gripped her hand tighter.

Priscilla stared up at the ceiling. "Look. There's your father. He's come to take me with him."

The air grew uncannily cold, yet a peaceful feeling of unconditional love encompassed the room.

Though Edward saw nothing, he felt the ethereal feeling of love embrace him.

Priscilla turned toward the corner of the bedroom. "Do you see that beautiful gold cloud?" Again she gasped and her voice became barely audible. "Mama and daddy are here. They want to take me home."

Beads of sweat poured down Edward's forehead as he watched his mother laboring to breathe.

Priscilla closed her eyes. A faint smile swept across her face as if greeting an unseen visitor. A rasping sound released from her throat. Her smile froze in a final goodbye.

Edward slipped off the bed and buried his head in his hands.

Later that evening Bridget rushed into grandma's bedroom, but was surprised to find someone had stripped the linens off the bed. Puzzled by the unfamiliar routine she stomped her feet and screamed as loud as she could.

Ester, hearing the loud screams, ran from the kitchen to help Bridget. She tried to calm the child, but it was to no avail.

Bridget continued screaming, running from room to room, searching for her grandmother. She bolted into the parlor and yanked at her father's sleeve.

Edward, unable to explain, wrapped his arms around Bridget and held her tight.

Bridget, sensing the grief, pulled his face toward her and wiped the tears from his face.

"I wish I knew how to explain. Grandma's gone sweetie."

Bridget laid her head on her father's chest. It was the first time she saw her father cry, and though she didn't understand, she felt his sorrow. The following days, she would peek in her grandmother's bedroom, but the empty room brought no comfort. Though she was angry and confused, she remembered her father's tears and no longer objected with temper tantrums.

Over the next several months Lillian showed little interest in consoling her grieving husband. With her mother-in-law gone, she took control of the household with a firm hand. She was thrilled to learn that Edward had inherited the tool and die business. And, that both she and Bridget had inherited numerous shares of stock.

By the time spring arrived Bridget was past school age. Edward tried to persuade his wife to enroll Bridget in a private educational facility, but it was to no avail. Whether it was pride, or fear of public ridicule, Lillian refused to allow Bridget to attend a public school, much less a school for the deaf.

Edward dared not press the issue, fearing Lillian would retaliate and take her anger out on Bridget. In his attempt to educate his daughter, he began spending more time with Bridget, and less time with Lillian.

Lillian took this as a personal insult, believing her husband was intentionally neglecting her. In her attempt to get his attention, she purchased a collection of high fashion clothing, and raised her skirts shorter than fashion allowed. Mid-calf was acceptable, but to show the knee was outrageous.

"Why are you dressing like that? People are talking."

"What's wrong with the way I dress? Your secretary dresses like a streetwalker, and you never complain about that. I'll do as I damn well please."

"Miss Chalmers is a good secretary," Edward replied, attempting to answer with an assertive voice.

"She's a cheap, gutsy woman. Fire her!"

"I can't. I promised my mother." Edward lowered his voice. "I depend upon my secretary."

"Can't you think for yourself? Your mother is still running the show. That secretary irritates me! That's why your mother wanted that hussy to work for you."

It was against Edwards nature to be disagreeable, and he found it difficult to stand his ground. "I will not argue with you. Miss Chalmers stays," Edward replied firmly. To avoid further argument, he turned and walked away.

Each day that passed, Lillian grew increasingly irritated by her husband's lack of attention. To alleviate her feeling of rejection, she wore high-fashion clothes to cover her insecurity and heavy makeup to mask her sorrow. The social facade of being wealthy temporarily eased her loneliness.

CHAPTER 6

Hilda stood on the back porch enjoy the morning sun when she noticed movement in the back of the yard. "Hum. Must be the new gardener."

A robust young man was approaching with a bushel-basket straddled on his hip, and a rake slung over his shoulder. "Good morning. My name is Patrick," he said, shifting the bushel onto the ground.

Hilda wiped her hands across her apron and leaned over the railing. "How's the garden coming along?"

"Just fine ma'am. It'll be a pleasure to see it in full bloom. The man of the house ordered me to hang the little girl's swing near the house," Patrick said, pointing to a large tree near the patio. Spotting pieces of hemp rope on the ground, he picked them up and tossed them into the bushel. "When the lady of the house saw me hanging it, she made me cut it down. I put it on that oak tree, way back of the yard by the burning barrel. Ya know, like she said, so it's out of sight."

"That's fine Patrick. The misses joined the garden club. She wants the yard to look especially nice today."

"Yes ma'am. I'll make it real pretty."

"The missus is mighty fussy about things around here. So pay attention to what she says."

"Yes ma'am," he said, pushing a lock of red hair from his freckled face. "I am a hard worker. That's why she hired me."

"Come in the kitchen when you're done. The missus bought you a nifty, black chauffeur's outfit. You can wear it today when you open the car doors for the ladies."

"But ma'am. I'm a gardener. Ah, I don't know much about tending ladies."

"You'll do just fine. Best you get back to your work."

Patrick tipped his well-worn cap and nodded. "Yes, ma'am." His face reddened at the thought of wearing such a pretentious uniform. He waited until Hilda left the porch, then muttered under his breath. "Tis a bloody nuisance. But, I guess I have to wear that monkey-suit and scrawny cap." He hoisted the bushel onto his shoulders and headed toward the burning barrel.

Hilda returned to the breakfast room just as Lillian was giving her final instructions.

"Oh, there you are," Lillian called out as she tightened the belt on her silk bathrobe. "My friends will be here later this evening." She handed Hilda two gray, J.L. Hudson boxes. "I bought these fancy uniforms and fancy aprons. I want you and Ester to wear them tonight."

"But Misses Hansen. I'm wearing a clean skirt. And besides, I'm not serving, Ester is. I'm gonna be in the kitchen with Bridget."

"Do as I say. Wear those cute outfits today."

Hilda lifted a small white apron out of the box. "That ain't no bigger than a doily. It's not gonna keep me clean."

"Just wear it. And don't forget! Keep Bridget away from my friends."

Ester took the box from Hilda, and her head dropped submissively. "Thank you, ma'am." Though she was excited to see her new outfit, she waited until Lillian left the room before opening the box.

Lillian returned to her bedroom and gazed in the mirror. Pleased with the social status she had attained, she was determined to make this afternoon a success. She slipped on a snug-fitting, rose-colored crepe dress; straightened the seams of her silk stockings and twirled in front of the mirror. She was glad women were wearing more makeup. Her cheeks needed the rouge, and the powder covered the dark circles under her eyes. As she leaned close to inspect her makeup, her elbow bumped against the vanity, shaking the heavy mirror.

"Someone could get hurt if that ever fell," she mumbled as she steadied the vanity.

The door chimes echoed through the foyer.

Lillian headed toward the stairs, prepared to greet her guests.

As the day proceeded, Ester strutted proudly in her new uniform, keeping a keen eye on Lillian, lest she makes a mistake. She didn't want to be reprimanded in front of these elegantly dressed ladies.

Madeline Warren, an amply built woman in her mid-fifties, brought the meeting to order. Her dark hair hung in a cascade of waves, and soft curls partly covered each diamond earring. She began the lecture with great emphasis on the unique hybrid rose which she sponsored with a generous donation. "It will be named The Madeline." Holding the rose in her diamond studded fingers, she rattled on and on about the uniqueness of its brilliant color.

The room grew uncomfortably silent.

The ladies turned their attention toward a small figure standing passively in the doorway.

A rush of fear swept over Lillian. Her facial muscles twitched, and her stomach tighten. *My God! What's Bridget doing here?*

Bridget stood in the doorway and stared at the women. She had never been out of her bedroom when company was present and was surprised to see so many faces. Encouraged by the ladies friendly smiles, she started toward the piano.

Madeline Warren, as head of the club, felt it was her duty to speak. "Who is this fancy-dressed little girl? Won't you come in and say hello to the ladies?"

Lillian, too frightened to speak, nodded to Ester, shifting her eyes toward the kitchen.

Ester's brow furrowed into an inquisitive frown.

Lillian felt a flush of heat rush on her face. *What should I do? Do they expect me to introduce my daughter?*

Ester's raised her eyebrow, and understanding Lillian's fear, she replied with a slight nod.

Lillian glared at Ester, again nudging her head. *Why doesn't she do something?*

Ester had to act fast before Bridget started screaming. She nodded, ever so slightly, and eased the silver serving-tray onto the table. Slowly, steadily, she made a casual move toward Bridget who was moving toward the center of the parlor.

Again, Madeline spoke, raising her hand in a friendly gesture. "Come in. Say hello to the ladies."

Bridget watched the woman's brightly painted lips moving, but only understood the friendly gestures. The woman's smile reminded her of her father when he played the piano. Bridget dashed across the room and grabbed Madeline's dress, pulling her toward the piano.

Madeline, startled by the child's brazen behavior, lost her balance and stumbled forward. To keep from falling, she reached for the piano. A horrified expression crossed her face when she heard her dress splitting. She grabbed the piano, braced herself upright with one hand, and knocked Bridget aside with the other hand.

Bridget landed on the floor with a startled look on her face. Determined to have her way, she ran to the piano and began banging on the keys.

Lillian felt her heart was beating wildly. She dashed across the room, grabbed Bridget by the arm and yanked her away from the piano.

Bridget grunted and screamed in protest. When she couldn't free herself from her mother's grip, she dug her heels in the carpet, and with a shrill screech, struck her mother with all her might.

Madeline shrieked in horror. "What is that child doing?" Realizing she had attracted attention, she backed up toward the couch, hoping the ladies didn't notice the split seam of her dress. When she was safely seated, she leaned back against the couch to hide the gaping hole.

The loud screaming brought Hilda huffing and puffing up the basement stairs. She stopped in the parlor doorway long enough to catch her breath. After a quick survey, she snatched Bridget and hoisted the child up, onto her hip.

A hushed silence encompassed the parlor.

Hilda carried the screaming child out of the parlor.

The women turned to Lillian, expecting an explanation to a child's deplorable behavior.

Lillian felt her throat tightening as if someone was twisting a vice around her neck. She gazed around the room, too embarrassed to speak. *I have to say something, but what?*

The room grew sullen and quiet.

Time seemed to stand still. Several minutes passed before Lillian spoke. "I'm sorry if this startled you. My daughter is deaf. She didn't understand," Lillian said, concealing the quiver in her voice. It had taken only a few minutes, and the secret she hid for the past five years had been exposed.

Ester stepped back, eager to leave the parlor.

Lillian clenched her lips in anger. *Everyone hides their secrets behind closed doors,* she thought, *but for me, it's all over.* Her precious dignity had been shattered in one agonizing scene.

The grim-faced German lady was the first to speak. "Well, my dear. You didn't tell us you had a deaf child," she said in an accusatory tone of voice.

Whose fault was that? But the memory of falling down the stairs came to mind, and Lillian felt guilty. Feeling lightheaded, she grabbed the chair and braced herself upright. Her legs felt rubbery as if they would give way at any moment and send her crashing to the floor. The room seemed to change to a misty gray, and the guest's faces faded into shadowy images.

Ester, realizing Lillian was about to faint, edged her way across the room, ready to catch her if she fell.

Lillian stood motionless. Withing minutes the shadowy faces became clear once again. Somehow, she had fought off the fainting spell. "Yes, my little Bridget lost her hearing. I mean, she was born deaf. We love her though. She's such a pleasure. Her deafness hasn't bothered me." Lillian paused, forcing a weak smile. "Perhaps we should continue."

A low whisper spread across the room and soon gained momentum. The women begin chattering as if nothing interrupted the meeting.

Madeline leaned her back on the couch, covering the bulging skin protruding through the seam of her sleeve.

Lillian held her composure for the next hour, even though it seemed like an eternity. After adjourning the meeting, she positioned herself at the door cordially thanking each lady for attending. When the last guests left, Lillian leaned her back against the door, closed her eyes and breathed a sigh of relief.

The ticking of the grandfather clock echoed sharply against the marble floor of the foyer.

The sound of rattling dishes in the dining room drew Lillian's attention. She opened her eyes and saw Ester balancing a tray of cups and saucers.

The sun caught the edge of the silver tea-set, reflecting a blinding streak of light into the foyer.

Lillian squinted and turned from the glaring light; away from the shame she had tried to hide. She felt a pressure against the back of her eyes, and a deafening whirling sound inside her head. Unable to control the hatred building inside her, her mind exploded in anger. "I'll kill that brat," she screamed as she dashed up the stairs.

That evening, Lillian informed her husband of Bridget's uncontrollable actions. "That child made a horrible scene in front of my garden club. She embarrassed me."

"Bridget doesn't understand when she's doing. She's just a child."

"You're always defending her. She made my lady friend tear her sleeve. It was an expensive dress."

"If that was Madeline, her dress was probably too tight, anyway. That's why it tore."

Lillian covered her mouth with a dinner napkin. "What am I going to do? Everyone knows I have a deaf child."

Edward glared at his wife. "You can't even say the word *daughter*, can you? It's this child, or that child."

Bridget let out a loud scream and pointed to the dish of steaming, hot rolls.

"Does she have to scream so loud?" Lillian cried, covering her ears.

When Bridget didn't get a roll, she crawled up on the table and grabbed one.

"Look at her deplorable table manner. That damn child knows she's driving me crazy, but she does it anyway."

"You're just too touchy. She can't hear, so she doesn't understand what's right or wrong." Edward slammed the dinner napkin on the table. "I don't want to discuss Bridget's behavior anymore."

"She made a fool of me today," Lillian bellowed as she bolted out of the dining room.

Edward raised his hands in disgust. "I can't please that woman no matter what I do." Having no stomach for arguing, and rather than listening to her complaints, he spent the night in the spare bedroom.

CHAPTER 7

The house was uncannily quiet and an unusual chill permeated the kitchen. Hilda tried to ward off the strange feeling, but the sense of danger wouldn't go away. Shoving the curtain aside, she leaned closer to the window.

Patrick was in the backyard poking at the trash barrel with a wood-charred stick and Bridget was swinging through clouds of gray smoke.

Even though they were quite a distance from the house, Hilda heard Bridget screeching with joy. Yet, the feeling of an unidentified threat drew her to watch more carefully.

Patrick dropped his rake, scooped up a handful of leaves and tossed them in the burning barrel. He poked the hot cinders, sending flecks of ash drifting in the air.

Sooty black smoke billowed from the cast-iron trash barrel.

Hilda needed time to get rid of this eerie sense of danger. She slipped in the foyer and glanced up at the balcony.

Lillian's bedroom door remained closed and the hall quiet, and empty.

An icy breeze brushed against Hilda, making the hair on her arms stand up in rebellion.

The grandfather clock struck the brass chimes, sending out four mellow tones.

Hilda looked suspiciously over her shoulder. Grandma Priscilla came to mind. *Watch Bridget.* The words came as thoughts in her head, like a message from beyond the grave. She hurried to the kitchen window and again eased the curtain aside.

Bridget was still swinging through gray clouds of smoke. The hemp rope made a groaning sound as it rubbed against the huge branch of the oak tree. Patrick had moved from the burning barrel and was now raking leaves along the edge of the fence.

A sense of uneasiness gnawed at the pit of Hilda's stomach. It was too quiet, and it worried her.

The clinking of Ester's metal pail broke the silence.

Ester strolled in the kitchen and plunked a bucket on the sink. "Why ya looking out the window?"

"Shh. Is she the misses in her bedroom?"

"Yeah. She axed me when I be done washing the upstairs windows. I told her I was done. I'm gonna change the water. She axed me what I'm gonna do now."

"What did you tell her?"

Ester dumped a bucket of dirty water in the sink and turned on the faucet. "I told the missus I was fixing to wash the front windows."

"And, what did she say?"

"She say that's okay and went in her bedroom."

Hilda wiped her sweaty hands across her apron. "Did she seem mad, or anything?"

Ester gave her wet rag a firm twist and tossed it in the pail. "No. She seems fine. Why? What you so fired up about, anyway?"

Hilda glanced at the wall clock. "It's twenty minutes after four. The mister will be home in forty minutes." Retracing her steps back to the window, she again pulled the curtain aside. "I just don't know," Hilda muttered under her breath. Movement at the side of the yard caught her attention, and she leaned closer to the window.

"What you looking at?" Ester asked.

"At the misses. She's standing by the side of the fence. She just handed the gardener a sheet of paper."

"In the yard? I just saw her upstairs," Ester replied, pushing the curtain aside. "Let me see."

"Shush. Be still," Hilda whispered. "I didn't hear her come down either. I wonder what she's doing out there?" Hilda tilted her ear toward the window, straining to hear the voices. But they were too far away to be audible.

Patrick slipped the piece of paper in his pocket, set his rake against the fence, hopped on his bicycle and sped out of sight. Lillian headed toward the house and disappeared from view.

Hilda checked the time once again. It was four thirty. Pressing her finger against her lips, Hilda motioned for Ester to be quiet.

The grandfather clock chimed the half hour.

Hilda moved quietly toward the kitchen doorway to listen.

The sound of the French doors in the dining room closed softly. Faint footsteps crossed the foyer, and someone tiptoeing up the stairs.

Hilda lifted her apron and mopped the perspiration from her forehead. "Did you hear a window opening upstairs?"

"Huh? You want me to go upstairs and check?"

"No." Hilda slipped quietly into the foyer and tilted her head toward balcony.

"What you listening for?" Ester asked, as she followed Hilda.

"Hush. Let's get back in the kitchen," Hilda whispered, nudging Ester out of the foyer.

The sound of the back-door slamming broke the silence. Bridget dashed through the kitchen and up the stairs.

The muffled sound of a bedroom door closing made Hilda move quickly. "Ester! Never mind the washing the windows. Get upstairs fast. Help Bridget change her clothes for dinner. Run!"

Ester, sensing the urgency in Hilda's voice, wasn't about to argue. She bolted up the stairs. Several minutes later she strutted casually in the kitchen. "Miss Lillian say I should wash the front windows. She's gonna dress her own child."

Hilda's face turned pale. The sense of danger weighed heavy on her mind. "Why is she gonna dress Bridget today? She rarely dresses that child."

Again, the icy chill of an unseen presence passed through the room.

"Burr. Did you feel that? That cold went right through my body."

Ester's head jolted up. "Yeah. That cold air is following us for sure."

Hilda decided she must change her daily routine. Do something different without risking a reprimand. "Ester!" Hilda whispered. "Grab the trash basket under the sink. Go outside and burn it. While you're out there, keep your eyes on all the upstairs windows. Watch them all the time. Ya hear me?"

"But Patrick done burned the garbage this morning," Ester whined, trying in her usual manner to get out of work.

"I said git," Hilda scolded, swishing her skirt in the air, shooing Ester toward the back door.

Ester picked up the half-full paper-basket and sauntered across the grass. "That woman's gone loco. She's always hollering for me to hurry. Now she wants me to take my time. Well, I'll just take my time."

Ester strolled slowly across the yard to the burning barrel and dumped the trash into the smoldering ashes. Striking a long wooden match against the sooty barrel's edge, she lit the paper.

She glanced up as the curtain in Bridget's window fell slowly back in place.

Hilda grabbed the pail from the sink, filled it with cold water, and hurried to the foyer. Crouching on her knees, she slopped water over the shiny floor, and swished a wet cloth over the marble. From time to time she stopped mopping and listened.

She heard the creaking sound of a bedroom door opening.

Hilda glanced up just as a stream of sunlight filtered through Bridget's half-open door.

The light spread across the hall and disappeared as the door closed ever so quietly.

The mellow chimes of the clock sounded the quarter-hour.

Hilda sloshed the rag across the floor and started singing loud enough to be heard upstairs. "He's got the little tiny baby in his hands. He's got the whole world in his hands." Hilda stopped singing. It was too quiet. The silence overhead made her feel uneasy.

The clock ticked rhythmically, echoing against the marble floor of the foyer.

The sound of Edward's car pulling into the garage behind the house broke the silence.

Bridget, feeling the vibrations of her father's car, dashed down the stairs. She ran into the yard and greeted her father with open arms.

Hilda gave the wet rag a firm twist and wiped up the last puddle of water from the floor. "Thank the Lord." Sensing someone was watching her, she glanced up.

Lillian was peeking though a crack of Bridget's half-open door.

The grandfather clock chimed a victorious five o'clock. The sound of happy voices filled the house once again.

Hilda rushed to the kitchen and yelled out the back door. "Ester! Quit fooling around out there. We gotta get dinner on the table. The mister is home."

CHAPTER 8

Bridget shoved the curtain aside and peeked out the parlor window. When she saw her mother's car heading down the street, she dashed up the stairs and into her mother's bedroom.

Hilda noticed the child's fascination with Lillian's bedroom. Today curiosity got the best of her. She decided to investigate. Hilda crept up the stairs, opened the door to Lillian's bedroom and peeked in.

Bridget was sitting at the vanity with her chin resting in her hands. She appeared mesmerized by her own reflection.

Hilda eased the door open a little wider.

Bridget, startled by the movement reflecting in the mirror, jumped off the vanity bench and cowered on the floor. She remembered when her mother caught her sitting in front of the mirror, and had struck her so hard on the back that it sent her flying across the room.

Seeing the startled look on the child's face, Hilda opened the door wider. "Bridget! What are you doing here? Child, I wish you could hear me. You know your mama smacked you last time she caught you here." Hilda took Bridget's hand, helped her up and gently pulled her toward the door.

Bridget yanked her arm away, grabbed hold of the vanity and jutted her chin out stubbornly.

"All right!" Hilda replied, knowing how defiant Bridget could be. Rather than start a commotion, she let go of Bridget's hand. "You can stay awhile, but you better get out of here before your mama comes home."

Bridget pursed her lips, glared stubbornly and refused to move.

"I always get in trouble vhen you don't mind your mama."

Bridget grunted and gripped the vanity tighter.

"No point in scolding. You'll just sneak back upstairs, anyway." Hilda shrugged, turned and trudged down the stairs to the laundry room.

Ester was sitting with her feet propped up on a chair, reading a magazine. Piles of soiled clothes lay sorted on the floor, ready for the washing machine.

"Bridget's upstairs in her mama's bedroom."

"Uh, hum." Ester mumbled, her eyes never leaving the page.

"You better listen for the missus car. Ester! Do you hear me?"

"Eh, huh. I hear you."

"When you hear the misses' car, you best get that child out of the bedroom. Miss Lillian will throw a fit if she finds Bridget in her room again."

Ester lowered the magazine. "Yes ma'am. Don't I always git up there before she comes home?"

Bridget leaned her elbows on the vanity and stared into the gold-framed mirror. These secret visits with the mirror had become her sanctuary, a place to live in a world of fantasy. Bridget's first encounter with the mirror occurred when she was four years old. After months of gazing into the mirror, Bridget found companionship in her own reflection. One day, after staring at her reflection, she noticed colorful movement shimmering behind the glass. Fascinated by the brilliant colors, she began returning to the mirror more often. Each visit became longer, and the images became clearer. Bridget's imagination separated her from a silent world, into a fascinating new existence.

In Bridget's make-believe world, the mirror revealed rainbows spreading out like a magical path, coaxing her to enter. The glistening colors swirled in circles, drawing her deeper, and deeper, into an imagery garden. In her imagination, she entered a meadow where birds chirped a song of welcome. Bridget had never heard birds before, and the melodious sound held her mesmerized for hours.

By the time Bridget was five years old, her imagination had conjured up playmates in the mirror. She would sit in a beautiful meadow and listen to children singing. She had never heard human voices before and, even though she didn't understand language, she understood the meaning of the song.

Lately, when visiting her garden, Grandma Priscilla would be waiting for her in a field of purple heather. Granny looked younger, and more beautiful than she remembered her to be. The mystical visits lasted longer, and each time it became more difficult to leave. Bridget believed her fantasies were real, and no one had told her differently.

Today, her imagination guided her through the shimmering rainbow into a magical garden. She pranced gracefully along a pathway, sniffing the fragrant flowers as if each one had blossomed just for her. Bridget, so engrossed in her make-believe world, didn't feel the vibration of her mother's car.

Ester, hearing a car make its final stop in front of the house, dashed up the stairs.

When Bridget felt the heavy vibration of approaching footsteps, she snapped back to reality. Her eyes grew wild. She waited in fear for the footsteps to reach the bedroom.

Ester burst in, scooped the frightened child up, and carried her out of the bedroom.

Once safely in her room, a smug grin slipped across Bridget's face. Mama didn't catch her. She tilted her head when she felt the vibration of someone stamping up the stairs

Lillian flung the door open and peered in with an angry expression on her face.

Bridget watched her mother's painted lips blaring out soundless words.

Ester started to cry and ran out of the bedroom.

Did mama know I was in her room? Would she hit me again? Bridget watched her mother's mouth spewing words she neither heard, nor understood. She cringed at the sharp vibration of the bedroom door slamming shut. After waiting awhile, Bridget peeked out the door.

The hall was empty.

Bridget, being curious, crept down the hall and peeked in her mother's bedroom.

Lillian was lying on the bed with a washcloth covering her eyes.

Ester, noticing Bridget at the door, laid her finger on her lips. Moving silently across the room, she scooped Bridget up and carried her down the hall.

Bridget was furious. She tried to scream, but Ester's hand was covering her mouth. She kicked and flung her hands. But it was no use. She couldn't get away.

Ester dragged Bridget down the stairs and into the maid's kitchen.

Hilda, hearing the screeching, reached out with open arms and lifted Bridget onto her lap. "My poor baby," Hilda cooed, comforting the bewildered child.

Bridget nestled her face in Hilda's bosom, tears streaming down her cheeks. She watched Ester's mouth moving. Judging by the serious expression on their faces, she wondered what had happened to her mother.

"The misses got those headaches again. She's getting a lot of them lately, ain't she?" Ester leaned close to Hilda and whispered. "Why doesn't she see a doctor?"

Hilda pointed to the stove. "Put the tea-kettle on. I'll brew some sassafras and peppermint tea. That usually helps."

"Maybe he should take her to a doctor." Ester filled the porcelain tea-kettle with water. "I swear. Maybe he don't care how she feels."

Hilda slipped her finger over her lips. "Shush. It's none of our business."

"Maybe she's just loony in the head," quipped Ester, screwing her face comically while scratching her head.

"Hush up. You better watch out. Someday he's going to catch you bad-mouthing his wife." Hilda had been employed by the Hansen's for many years, and although she wondered about Lillian's instability, she had never expressed an opinion. The Hansen's had been exceedingly generous when her family needed financial help, and because of that, she vowed to protect their privacy.

The shrill screeching of the kettle penetrated the kitchen.

After filling the teapot with hot water, Ester covered her mouth with her hand and whispered, "Maybe he knows a doctor can't help her none."

"Don't talk like that," Hilda reprimanded sternly as she lifted Bridget off her lap. She returned to the sink, sprinkled a pinch of herbs on white mesh, twisted it into a pouch, and tied it shut with a grocery-string. "We don't know what's wrong," she said, dropping the pouch in a teapot of hot water. "Maybe that uppity Missus Warren mentioned Bridget being deaf. You know how touchy the misses gets when those ladies say mean things."

Ester reached for the tray. "Sure. That's when she gets those bad headaches."

"I'll take that," Hilda said as she reached for the tray. "Hand me that bottle of oil-of-cloves. Maybe she has a toothache. Watch Bridget while I'm upstairs."

"If she's got a toothache, maybe she should get them pulled out."

"Mind your own business" Hilda scolded. She picked up the tray and trudged up the stairs. After catching her breath, she pushed the door open with her foot and tiptoed in the bedroom.

Lillian gave a faint smile of relief when she saw Hilda entering the room.

"Do you have a headache again?" Hilda asked, lifting the washcloth off Lillian's face. She laid the back of her hand on her forehead. "Hum. You don't have a fever."

Lillian closed her eyes, clenched her jaw and gripped the bed sheets with a tight-fist. "My head hurts,"

Hilda noticed an aspirin bottle on the bedside table. "How many of these did you take?"

Lillian held up four fingers.

"That's too many for a small woman. I made some sassafras tea. Drink it while it's hot. It'll help ease the pain."

Lillian slipped the wet compress off her forehead and with trembling hands, drank the tea.

"This washcloth is warm. I'll rinse it with cold water," Hilda said as she left the room. After rinsing the cloth in cold water, she returned and laid it on Lillian's forehead. "Try to sleep. I'll check on you later."

By the time Edward arrived home from work, Lillian had recovered from her headache. Determined to play upon his sympathy, Lillian wiped the makeup off her face and made her way slowly into the parlor. "Edward. I've been in bed with a headache again."

Edward ignored his wife's complaints and nodded nonchalantly. "I'll call Bridget in for dinner," he said as he hurried toward the French doors in dining room.

Lillian followed her husband, and in a demanding voice, said. "That child is eating in the maid's kitchen this evening. I thought it would give us a chance to talk. You know how noisy she is."

"Talk about what?" A frown of discontentment crossed his face when he saw only two place setting on the table. Although he wanted to object, he considered Lillian's pale complexion and remained silent.

"About the dentist," Lillian insisted.

Edward flopped down at the head of the table. "Don't start that again. You want your teeth fixed so you'll look like your fancy friends."

"No. My head really hurts."

Edward frowned impatiently. "You saw the dentist last month. He said your teeth are okay," he replied, hoping a denial would end the conversation.

Tears filled Lillian's eyes. "Why don't you believe me? I had a headache."

Edward slammed his napkin on the table. His wife had played this sickly game too many times. "I don't want to hear about the dentist again," he growled, shoving his chair away from the table. "I'm eating in the maid's kitchen tonight." He turned away so his wife couldn't see the smile of relief. He preferred to hear Bridget screams rather than his wife's whining complaints.

Lillian, taken off-guard by her husband's unexpected rebellion, stammered to explain. "All I want is a little sympathy," she called out as she watched her husband scurry to the kitchen.

Hilda entered the room carrying a serving tray. "Misses Hansen? Do you want me to serve now?"

"Take it back. I'm not hungry." Lillian, fuming with anger, sat alone listening to the muffled sound of voices coming from the kitchen. The sound of laughter taunted her. She clenched her jaw, wondering if they were plotting against her.

The sun disappeared behind the oak tree leaving the dining room gloomy and dark.

"Alone again," Lillian whimpered. A sudden burst of laughter from the kitchen startled her. She slid her chair away from the table and blew out the candles. "Just one drink," she muttered as she poured a double shot of whiskey in a glass.

CHAPTER 9

———◆———

Edward had trouble sleeping, wondering about wife. *Perhaps Lillian really had a headache.* He laid his hand on Lillian's back to assure her of his love.

Her taunt body lay beside him, responding with cold hostility.

His wife's frigid rejection felt like a stab in his heart. He knew their daughter's behavior was unacceptable at times, and he wished he could make life easier for her, but there didn't seem to be an easy answer. Thoughts of his mother's dying wish came to mind. A promise he had intentionally set aside rather than face his wife's unreasonable objections.

Tomorrow I'll *hire someone to take over for Lillian. Someone who will teach Bridget.* Edward lay for a long time mulling over how to tell his wife. *Should I ask permission to hire the woman? Perhaps I should insist.*

*N*o matter how he approached the subject, he was sure Lillian would object. She would lecture him on the degrading stigma that sign language would bring to their family. Though he knew it could cause trouble, he decided to fulfill his mother's request. *If a teacher can help Bridget, then it must be done.*

Edward tossed and turned for hours before finally falling asleep. In the dark entanglement of a dream, he saw his mother drifting toward him, her hands grasping at gray webs as she made her way through the darkness. In the distance he could hear her voice.

"Remember your promise. Your promise."

He felt himself moving in slow motion, reaching for her hands, but recoiled when his hands became tangled in a sticky mass of gray webs. Terrified, he struggled through the maze of spider-like webs.

The scene grew darker. Nightmarish. The gray webs begin quivering and trembling until they lay shriveled in the darkness.

Drifting in the darkness, he found himself surrounded by turbulent gray clouds. He tried to scream, but no sound came from his mouth.

In the distance a shadowy image began rising from a bottomless abyss. Lillian appeared from the haze, drifting toward him encased in a churning black cloud. Her gauze-like, black cape fluttered in the darkness. She burst upon him like a monstrous storm. A fierce wind sent her skirt snapping in the air, billowing out like wings of a vicious vulture. Lillian stood defiantly between him and his mother. Obstructing his view. Smothering his mother's cries of a forgotten promise.

Edward reached for his mother's hands, but churning gray clouds blanketed him, obscured his view.

The dream moved into pitch-black darkness.

Edward felt himself moving in slow motion, drawn into a helpless state of confusion.

The scene changed. Somehow, he had moved past his wife and was looking down at party below. Piles of jewelry, gold coins, and glittering gems lay in a quagmire beneath him. Blurred images of Lillian's friends stirred in the darkness.

He watched the despicable scene until he felt himself being drawn downward. Though he struggled to rise above the amoral setting, he landed in a gaudy cluster of jewels.

Shadowy images of Lillian's pretentious friends moved in the darkness.

Desperate to get away, he crawled over the tarnished jewels that lay snarled beneath him. With hands outstretched, he forced his way through the shadowy figures, crawling through sticky muck. Panic set in when he felt something pulling at his feet. He looked down.

Lillian stood with her arms outstretched, blocking his way.

He felt paralyzed, stuck between his wife's gaudy possessions, and his mother's promise.

Eward awakened the next morning with the dream of his mother's promise still in his mind. To avoid discussing the matter with Lillian, he slipped quietly out of bed. *Today, I'll see about hiring the tutor.*

When Edward arrived, he felt relieved to see the office running smoothly. He stopped, as was his morning custom, at his secretary's desk. "Quiet today," Edward said as he took the daily mail off his secretary's desk.

"Yes Sir," Betty replied, smiling seductively.

Betty Chalmers had been his private secretary for many years. Betty, a plump, abundantly endowed woman, was in her late forties. Her bleached blond hair and pencil-thin eyebrows complimented her sensual, throaty voice. Though she had an eye for Edward, she always failed at tempting him.

"Here are the invoices, but I expect there's more."

"Just hand them to me," Edward interrupted. He didn't mean to speak quite so sharply, but hiring a tutor today had him on edge.

Betty's smile disappeared. She stacked the invoices, tapped them firmly on the desk to even out the edges, and handed them to Edward.

"Get me a list of teachers wages." he asked casually, hoping to add a note of disinterest to his request.

"Yes sir. What kind of teachers? Do you want grade school or college teachers?" Betty jotted the information on her steno pad.

"Just grade school," Edward replied brusquely, hoping to discourage further conversation. "Get me a phone number for this woman." He scribbled a name on a sheet of paper and handed it to her. "I need this now," he added, before scurrying to his office.

Edward, uneasy about the impending phone call, leaned back in his chair to mull over the consequences of hiring a tutor. A gentle rap on the door startled him, and he bolted upright. "Yes. Come in."

Betty smiled flirtatiously as she moved sensually across the room. "Is this sufficient?" Betty cooed, bending close enough for her breast to touch his shoulder.

Edward swiveled his chair back at the sensation of warm breath on his neck. The titillating scent of perfume wafted from her cleavage. A faint smile surfaced as he breathed in the perfume, amused that another woman might be interested in him.

"This is fine. Did you get the phone number?"

"No sir. I checked the phone book and spoke with the operator. The lady's name isn't listed anywhere. Apparently, she doesn't have a telephone."

"Why didn't I think of that?" Edward mumbled under his breath.

"What?"

Edward signaled Betty away with a casual wave of his hand. "Nothing. Never mind." *The woman's probably deaf. Naturally she wouldn't have a phone.*

"Anything else?"

"No. No," Edward replied absentmindedly.

Betty, seeing her boss had other matters on his mind, hurried out of the office.

Edward leaned back to mull over the situation. Normally, he would have an employee seek out a teacher but this was something he had to do himself. His mind wavered with indecision. *Will Lillian refuse to have a tutor in our home. People are bound to find out.* He drew in a deep breath and heaved a sigh of regret. It *seems everything I do is printed in the Detroit Newspaper. I'm damned if I do, and damned if I don't. Oh hell. Not everyone feels the same way about sign language as my wife does.*

It was nearly noon when Edward began his search for the tutor, driving past rundown storefronts and ramshackle houses. After traveling several miles, he turned onto a narrow side-street. He slowed his car and scanned the porches for an address. Following the numbers, he pulled in front of a weather-worn, frame house.

The afternoon air had turned muggy and warm. The blazing sun sent heat-waves rippling off the metal hood of his shiny black Chrysler.

As he pulled up to the curb, a blast of hot air rushed through the open window. *How will I speak to this woman? How much should I tell her?* He wiped his sweaty hands across his pants, and made his way across the dry, weed infested lawn toward the sidewalk. He walked carefully between the cracks, a habit he carried from childhood.

The rickety steps creaked as he stepped onto a small porch. He stood in front of sun-blistered door, pondering what to say. Taking a deep breath to bolster his courage, he knocked gently on the door. While he waited, he scraped his fingernails on the scars of hinge marks where a screen door once hung. Digging his nails into the blistered paint, he watched the flecks fall to the ground.

His mind drifted to the chips of paint as if to escape his purpose for a moment.

No one answered the door.

He waited, listening. *Perhaps, if I stamp my feet, that will attract the teacher's attention.* He rapped again, his time much louder, and stamped his foot several times just to be sure. "There, she should hear that," he muttered to himself. He stepped back, wondering if he had overdone it with his foot stomping.

The door opened slowly. A young, attractive lady stuck her head out and smiled. "Yes?"

Edward, intent upon being heard, bellowed loudly. "I would like to talk to the woman who tutors deaf children."

The lady opened the door wider. "Yes. I'm she. My name is Sarah Woodward. Won't you come in?"

"Yes, of course," he shouted as he followed her into a small parlor.

"It's not necessary for you to speak so loudly. I hear quite normally," she said in a soft voice.

Edward's face reddened, embarrassed at his mistake. "Oh, I'm sorry. I just assumed you were deaf."

"No. My brother is deaf. That's why I learned sign language." Sarah led him across the room to a well-worn couch. "How can I help you?"

Edward scanned the scantly furnished living room as he made his way to the couch. *She seems rather shy,* he thought as he edged his way past the girl. The pleasant scent of ivory soap wafted from her auburn hair. As he sat down on the couch, the fresh odor of Fels-Naptha soap drifted from the frayed, cotton slipcover.

The small room was dimly lit and the shades partly drawn. The carpet was clean, but threadbare. Worn paths of hemp backing showed though, exposing a path to another doorway.

Sarah seated herself across the room, and smoothed her skirt down, discreetly covering her legs. "You need a teacher?"

A calm feeling of relief swept over Edward. He wasn't nervous about hiring this teacher as he thought he might be. In fact, he felt rather comfortable. The compassionate look in the girl's blue eyes caught his attention, drawing him away from his intended purpose. His eyes followed the delicate features of her milk-white skin and blushing cheekbones. He didn't mean to stare, but was fascinated by the soft folds of her thin, well-worn blouse, clinging to her youthful body.

Sarah shifted into a more comfortable position.

Edward glanced up, embarrassed when he noticed her again adjusting her skirt. It was apparent she was waiting for him to explain his visit.

"Can you manage a child who is completely deaf? My daughter understands very little," he said leaning forward with interest.

Sarah smiled and nodded. "Yes."

"My daughter needs someone near her at all times." He stopped speaking abruptly, wondering if he had said too much already. *I better not mention Bridget's belligerence or temper tantrums. She'll soon find out soon enough.* "My wife is frustrated because Bridget refuses to cooperate."

"Yes. I understand your daughter's handicap. I know exactly what she's going through."

"We can't make her understand anything."

'Have you ever read the book on the life of Helen Keller? She was quite a handful until she understood what was going on."

"I never thought about that. So that's why she gets angry so easily?"

"Yes. How old is she?"

"She's nearly six. Sometimes we can't communicate with her at all." Though he didn't mean to reveal quite so much, he found it easy to express himself, saying more than he intended.

Sarah leaned forward to give him her full attention. "I understand."

Edward's eyes followed the folds of her well-sworn cotton blouse. The cloth seemed almost silken, nestling in the curves of her soft breasts. Once again, his eyes moved to the skirt draped seductively over her knees.

Sarah shifted upright in her chair, intentionally interrupting his curious stare. "That's because you don't understand how your daughter feels, or what she's thinking. How would you feel if you couldn't speak? She doesn't know how to verbalize her frustration."

"She has quite a temper when she's upset."

"If she's constantly confused, that would make her temperamental. Well, you understand what I mean."

"I'm sure you're right, but...." Edward stopped, hesitating in mid-sentence. *Perhaps it's best not to volunteer too much information.*

"Don't worry. I'm sure when your daughter learns to sign, much of her frustration will disappear."

After discussing the work arrangements, and since Sarah had no transportation, it was decided she would live at his house. Edward quoted a weekly wage which included free room and board.

Sarah nodded in agreement. She hadn't expected such a generous salary and was eager to start the job. First, she must get her mother's approval. Sarah excused herself and headed toward the kitchen.

Edward rose as she left the room. *I've kept my mother's promise,* he thought as he flopped down in the couch. *It's finally done.* When he heard footsteps returning, he again stood up acknowledging the young lady's presence.

"I can start any time," Sarah announced with a smile.

"Good. Next week. Monday will be fine." Edward wrote his address on his business card and handed it to her.

By the time Edward left Sarah's house, the afternoon air had grown stifling hot. He opened the car door and stood for a minute, waiting for the heat to escape. A waft of hot air flew in his face reminding him of the heat he would face when he got home. His mind shifted from his wife's rage, to the young girl. *I'm glad I hired her.* Again, he wondered about wife's reaction. *Will it be worth the trouble it might cause?*

As he drove home, he thought about the pretty girl and the dilapidated old house. *A gentle girl. Or is she a woman? She seems so out of place with her innocent beauty concealed beneath her loose-fitting clothing.* Edward never had reason to stray, and yet, there was a sensual emotion stirring within him. An excitement he had never expected.

Being a Libra, it was his nature to weight each decision over, and over, again. *Will Lillian be pleased? Will she allow this woman to take charge?* His conflicting mind wouldn't let him rest. *After all, Bridget is getting out of hand, and Hilda is getting older.* He vacillated, weighing society's prejudiced opinion of the deaf, against the benefit of educating his daughter.

I feel more confident since I met the teacher. Again, indecision struck like a swinging pendulum. *Why am I so indecisive?* The weight of his decision fell heavy. He recalled his wife's high-pitched voice screaming, forbidding a school teacher in their house. Edward shook the thoughts from his mind. "I've got to go against society, and my wife. Damn it. I've made this commitment, and I'm going to keep it." He delayed entering the house, and stood in the shade of an oak tree, catching the afternoon breeze. Still uneasy for hiring a teacher against his wife's approval, he wondered. *How will I tell Lillian?*

The leaves overhead rustled with a slight breeze that cooled him temporarily.

His mind hammered at his decision. *Have I done the right thing? Will it set off Lillian's tantrums?*

Later that evening he remained silent, reluctant to tell his wife about the teacher. *Perhaps tomorrow would be better.* When tomorrow came, it seemed no different than the day before. Again, he remained silent.

CHAPTER 10

Several days later Edward stopped at the jewelry store and paced the familiar showcases. A single string of pearls caught his eye. "I'll take those," he said pointing through the glass enclosure.

"Ah, a marvelous choice. A special occasion Mister Hansen?" The jeweler slid a silver box out of the showcase, removed the pearls and draped them gracefully over the palm of his hand.

"No special occasion. I'll take them," Edward said, sliding his fingers over the milky-white beads. "Ah, those are perfect."

"Quite a story behind those pearls," the jeweler responded, eager to elaborate on his expertise. Albert Adams was a lean, willowy man with olive skin and curly black hair slicked back with a film of oil.

Edward nodded, eagerly accepting his invitation. Actually, it was his way of delaying his trip home, if only for a few minutes.

"Yes. An interesting story. Each pearl starts as a grain of sand." Albert held the beads in the hollow of his palm. "If a single grain of sand sneaks into the shell, it can't get out."

"The oyster clams shut, huh?"

"Yep. It can't push the intruder out; so it covers the grain with a milky film. This takes time. Sometime years. In the meantime, that speck of sand grows, and grows, until it becomes a beautiful pearl."

"The oyster can't get rid of its intruder? It just has to live with it?"

Albert braced his elbows on the showcase and leaned forward. "Eh, huh. It has to live with its tears," he said with a toothy grin. "That's what they call a pearl. A teardrop. Tears caused by an unwanted guest."

"Can the clam force the sand out?"

"I don't think so. Maybe, but it would be rare. Nothing short of death, I suppose. Only if the oyster dares to open its shell. Then, it becomes vulnerable." The jeweler draped the pearls through his fingers and spread his palm wide. "You see! It's defenseless. And, that my dear fellow, is the kiss of death." Touching his fingers to his lips with a soft kiss, he laid the necklace back in the box. And, with a quick snap, slammed it shut. "It has to keep the intruder or sacrifice itself."

"That was very interesting. I'm sure my wife will be pleased with the necklace."

When Edward arrived home, Bridget was waiting in the backyard. *This is the light of my life,* he thought, picking up his daughter and cuddling her in his arms.

Bridget thin legs dangled, nearly touching the ground as he carried her through the door. A swell of pride surged through him. *She is the reason I return home each evening.*

Hilda opened the back door. "You're home early today,"

Edward nodded, grinning as he transported his frisky passenger through the breakfast room and into the parlor. "I have a special surprise for my little girl." He set Bridget down and flopped in his favorite chair. "Fix me a double scotch and water."

Hilda nodded and made a quick turn toward the liquor cabinet. "Hum. Wonder why he's having a drink so early in the day?" After filling the glass to the rim, she returned and handed it to him. "What's the good new?" she asked, smiling with expectation.

"Is Lillian home?"

"No sir. She's downtown shopping. I suppose she'll be coming home soon."

Edward took a large gulp of liquor. "Prepare the spare bedroom for a guest. I've hired a tutor for Bridget."

"A teacher? Oh my!" Hilda blurted in surprise. "What about your wife's clothes in the dresser? Should I empty the drawers?"

"Yes, of course. The woman needs to put her clothes some place."

"You want all your wife's stuff out of the drawers?" Hilda raised her voice rose to a high pitch, drawing attention to the seriousness of his request. "The missus is mighty fussy about moving things without her permission."

"I know. I know," he assured her with a nonchalant wave of the hand. After finishing the drink, he held up the empty glass up. "Fill it up again. I don't give a damn where you toss those frilly things."

A frown crossed Hilda's brow and her voice turned stoic. "Where should I put your wife's clothes?"

Edward waved his hand as if pushing the problem away. "Do whatever you think. Why are you asking me? I don't know where she would want them."

Hilda, taken aback by Edward's brusque reply, headed to the liquor cabinet. "Hum. I guess he didn't tell the missus about the teacher. He looks nervous. I better make this a strong one. He might need it." Hilda tilted the bottle upright and poured a generous double shot. She returned to the parlor, handed him the glass. "Anything else I can do?"

"No. No," Edward replied, waving Hilda away. He sipped the drink as he mulled over his defense. *Oh, how I dread confronting Lillian. Mostly, I detest her stinging, unreasonable comments. He* took a large gulp to bolster his courage. *The hell with society! The hell with Lillian! I need some peace around here. I've got to help my baby.*

Lillian arrived an hour later carrying an arm full of packages. "Sweetheart! I didn't know you were coming home this early today," she said, setting several shopping bags on the overstuffed chair. "Do you like my hairdo?" she cooed, moving gracefully like a child displaying a treasure. "It's the new page-boy look." She twirled around several times, allowing her hair to flow with the movement of her body.

Edward glanced up, smiled halfheartedly and gave a disinterested nod of approval.

Lillian, craving a compliment, continued whirling gracefully in front of him. Seeing she couldn't attract his attention, she slid a bright red dress out of a box and held it against her body. She moved sensually toward him, enticing him with provocative movements.

A loud screeching interrupted Lillian's seduction.

Bridget ran in the parlor, and when she saw the boxes, she started tearing at the ribbons.

"Stop her. Look what she's doing," Lillian screamed.

Bridget grinned at her mother, tucked a box under her arm and ran screaming with joy. When she was out of her mother's reach, she tore the box open, ripped out the tissue papers and tossed them high in the air.

"You brat! Get back here." Lillian grabbed Bridget's arm. "That's mine. Give it to me."

"Let her alone," Edward shouted.

Bridget twisted and squirmed until she was free. Spotting the dress, she grinned mischievously and snatched it out of her mother's hands.

"Stop her!" Lillian shouted as she grabbed the dress and held it firmly.

Bridget tightened her grip and yanked with all her might.

"She's tearing it," Lillian shrieked. When she realized Bridget wasn't about to let go, she struck her hard on the arm.

Edward's hands shot up as a protective halt. "Don't touch her!" he bellowed in a voice loud enough to be heard throughout the house

Lillian stepped back, startled by her husband's loud outburst. He had never challenged her with such boisterous hostility before, and it took her by surprise. "Make her give it back," she whined.

Edward opened his arms and Bridget ran to him, dragging the red dress across the floor. "She's just a child. Put your packages away. I'll get it your dress from her," he grumbled as he cradled his grinning daughter in his arms.

Lillian clenched her thin lip. "That brat. She always gets her way." Lillian kicked a box out of her way and dashed out of the parlor.

Bridget dropped the dress and slipped away from her father's grip. Now that her mother was gone, she began kicking the boxes.

Edward placed his hands over his ears blotting out He stared at the tissue paper scattered over the floor, feeling defeated and frustrated. "It's too late to give Lillian the necklace today."

Bridget stopped screaming when she saw Hilda in the doorway.

Hilda studied the untidy mess. "Who tore all that paper?" she said, shaking her finger at Bridget.

"Can you get that away from her?" Edward grumbled, pointing toward the dress.

Hilda pulled a cookie out of her pocket, coaxing Bridget toward the kitchen. "Come on, sweetheart. Ester will play with you."

Bridget dropped the dress and followed Hilda into the kitchen. A few minutes later, Hilda returned and paused in the doorway. With her usual stoic posture, she tightened her apron strings and examined the untidy floor. "What happened here?" she asked, shaking her head in dismay.

Edward rested his head between his hands. "How can I tell my wife about the tutor now? She'll be furious when she finds out. I guess, I should have asked her first."

"Um hum," Hilda mumbled. She picked up the tissue papers, crunched them into a wad and shoved them in her apron pocket.

"How can I convince Lillian that I hired the teacher just for her?" Edward whined.

"I don't know," Hilda mumbled as she folded each dress and placed them in the boxes. "You best take these to the missus. Tell her Bridget didn't mean any harm. You can sweet talk her. Tell her everything is gonna be okay."

"Bridget tore that red dress."

"That's okay. I'll sew it real quick."

Edward picked up the packages and reluctantly trudged up the stairs. When he reached the top step, he heard Lillian sobbing. He eased the door open and peeked in.

Lillian jerked her head up, and she glared angrily.

Edward forced a weak smile as he tiptoed into the bedroom. "Everything is here, my love. Bridget didn't understand."

"Where's my new dress?" Lillian whimpered.

"Hilda is sewing it."

Lillian made no attempt to suppress her hostility and began pounding her fist on the bed. "That child is an animal," she cried, muffling her voice in the pillow.

Edward sat on the edge of the bed and patted Lillian gently on the shoulder.

Lillian stopped crying when she felt her husband warm body. She rolled over, gripped his shoulder, and looked deep in his eyes. "Edward. I feel so alone. I cry, but the loneliness won't go away."

Edward understood what it was to feel depressed. He had never told his wife that he too, felt lonely. Even before Bridget was born, he felt an emptiness that he didn't understand. Now, with his own loneliness locked deep inside, he could only offer hollow reassuring words. He wrapped his arms around Lillian. "I know Bridget upsets you my love. There's nothing I can do."

Lillian placed her hand on his chest, pressing him away. "Have you ever been so lonely that you're tired? You don't see me anymore." Lillian buried her face in the pillow. "You only see Bridget."

Edward lay down next to Lillian's trembling body. Though he felt helpless, he was reluctant to speak. *What did I do to make her feel lonely?* He wondered. Then, he remembered the pearl necklace. *I wanted to put a smile on her face, but now it's too late.* He set the box on the bedside table, slipped his arms around his wife and held her close.

They lay for a long time wrapped in each other's arms. The orange sun dipped behind the trees, casting an eerie, red glow across the room, changing the white satin bedspread to an angry shade of pink.

The next morning Edward took great care not to disturb Lillian. He hoped the smell of freshly brewing coffee wouldn't wake her. After he finished dressing, he remembered the necklace. He tiptoed to the bedside table, scribbled several words on a paper and tucked it under the silver ribbon. Not ready to face her this morning, he slipped quietly out of the bedroom.

Hilda held a steaming cup out to Edward. "Here's your coffee," she said with a comforting smile.

Edward waved the cup aside. "I haven't got time this morning," he muttered as he hurried toward the back door. He hesitated, turned to Hilda and spoke in a sobering voice. "Keep Bridget away from my wife today. At least until she feels better." Edward felt confident that Hilda would find the right words to pacify his wife. *Hilda always knows what to do. She had the simplest, nicest, easiest answers to my problems.* Edward didn't consider her as just another employee, he relied on her as a friend.

Lillian yawned awake and the glitter of a ribbon caught her attention. She slipped the note from beneath the bow. 'Because I love you,' was scribbled across the note. She lifted the strand of pearls out of the satin-lined box. "Perhaps he does love me best," she murmured as she lifted the pearls to her neck.

CHAPTER 11

The morning of the tutor's arrival had finally come. Edward dawdled through breakfast until it was time to leave for work. "I hired a live-in tutor for Bridget," Edward said, trying to sound firm, but nonchalant. "She'll be here this morning."

Lillian slammed her coffee cup down and jumped up. "You what? When did this happen?" Lillian jutted her jaw out stubbornly, waiting for an answer.

"I hired her several days ago," he muttered, turning his back on his wife and hurried across the kitchen toward the back door.

Lillian rushed ahead of her husband and stood with her hands on her hips, blocking his way. "A live-in! You expect a teacher to live here?"

Edward circled around his wife and grasped the doorknob. "I did it for you, my love."

"What kind of teacher?"

"The woman teaches sign language."

"No! Not sign language," Lillian bellowed. "You know how I feel about that. Cancel this tutor, whoever she is."

"You're overreacting my love. No one cares."

"I won't have that woman in this house," Lillian shouted, shaking her finger in protest. "What will the neighbors say?"

Edward shrugged submissively. "I've already hired her my love. If it doesn't work out, we'll ask her to leave." Edward skirted around his wife and hurried out the back door.

Lillian glared at Hilda. "Did you know about this?"

"Well, he did mention something about it." Hilda held her hand up to head off further conversation. "It's not my place to speak."

"It's too late to stop her now," Lillian mumbled under her breath. "She's already on her way."

Hilda pushed the curtain aside and looked out the window. "Hum. Looks like the sun's up already. Suppose it's gonna be a hot one today?"

Sarah, eager to start her new job, had packed two bags. In a brown leather suitcase, she folded several Navy blue skirts and white cotton blouses. Along the side, she tucked toiletries in the pocketed edge. In the needlepoint bag, she jammed as many books as it could hold. She had never worked away from home and the excitement of living elsewhere made the job more appealing. She kissed her mother and brother goodbye and set out for the streetcar boarding station.

The August sun blasted down as Sarah made her way to the boarding station. The streetcar station was several blocks away and the heat of the scorched pavement penetrated her well-worn shoes. She found it necessary to stop several times, stand on the grass to cool her burning feet. At the end of the fourth block, her hands began to hurt. Setting the luggage down, she switched the heavy bag to the other hand, and started out again. Shorty after she arrived at the boarding station, the loud brassy bell sounded the streetcar's approach.

The wheels of the big yellow trolley made a scraping sound as it rode the metal railway tracks, then stopping with a loud screeching sound. Two narrow doors creaked open.

Sarah stepped up the step and made her way to the back of the car. Exhausted from the sweltering heat, she dropped the luggage and plopped down on a brown leather seat.

The car rumbled along, leaving the poorer section of town. It wasn't long before the conductor shouted, "Vernier. Next stop."

Sarah reached to the top of the window and pulled a grimy, cotton cord to signal her departure. When he trolley jerked to a sudden stop, she picked up her bags and stepped down into the affluent suburb of Detroit.

A waft of fresh air swept off Lake St. Clair. The breeze was cooler, the streets cleaner, and the homes more opulent.

It was well past noon when Sarah arrived at the Hansen's residence. She dropped her luggage at the end of the long brick sidewalk and stood admiring the grandeur of the three-story house, the spacious grounds, and the neatly trimmed shrubbery.

Again, she picked up the heavy bags and made her way up the wide steps, onto the over-sized porch. She stood or several minutes admiring the brightly polished brass lamps hanging overhead. Feeling intimidated by her opulent surroundings, she rapped lightly on the huge oak door.

I wonder if there's a servant's entrance, she thought. She cupped her hand over her eyes and peered through a beveled-glass window. The shades were drawn, so she couldn't see if anyone was home. Hot and tired, she stepped into the shade of the porch, lifted her long auburn hair to dry the perspiration from her neck.

Several minutes later a kindly face peeked through the half-open door. "Is you the teacher?"

Sarah nodded and stepped forward.

"I'm Ester," the girl said, beckoning with a tilt of her head. "Come on in."

Sarah stepped inside a spacious foyer and set her luggage on the marble floor. She gazed across the foyer at the wide oak staircase that led up to an open balcony, and at the crystal chandelier hanging high overhead. Even though the foyer was elegantly decorated, it felt cold and uninviting. So unexpectedly different from the small, cozy home where she had been raised.

The afternoon sun shone through the open door, lighting the crystals teardrops dangling from the chandelier, sending shafts of pink and orchid dancing on the vaulted ceiling.

It's so immaculately clean and sterile, Sarah thought as she stood humbly uncomfortable and feeling out of place.

Ester pushed the heavy door closed and the delicate shafts of rainbow colors disappeared from the ceiling.

Sarah shivered. The foyer dimmed and turned cool without the brilliant sunlight.

"The misses wants the door closed so it don't fade the carpet." Ester studied the two pieces of luggage, picked up the smaller bag and heading up the stairs. "Follow me."

Sarah grasped the larger suitcase, stepped gingerly around an oriental carpet, and followed Ester up the stairs. She stopped midway and glanced down at the bronze statue of Apollo that sat on a small Chippendale table at the foot of the stairs. *It all so immaculate and tasteful. Perfect, yet empty.*

Ester reached the hall and dropped the needlepoint bag down with a thud. "You sure got a powerful bunch of clothes in that little bag." She strolled toward an open door, leaving the small bag standing in the hallway.

Sarah picked up both bags and followed Ester into a large, sunlit bedroom. "I don't have clothes in that bag," she said, pointing to the needlepoint bag. "It's full of books." She glanced down at her loose-fitting blouse, wrinkled and limp from the humid summer air. "You can see I'm not a fashion plate," she said with a humorous giggle.

Ester never judged a person by their appearance. Either she liked them, or she didn't. At first, she noticed the newcomer's friendly smile, paying little attention to her well-worn clothes. Only now, did Ester take a second look. Sarah's Navy blue skirt was faded as if it had seen too many washings. Her white blouse, though clean and starched, appeared flimsy and well-worn. Ester didn't care what Sarah was wearing. This new girl was like a breath of fresh air, and her friendly smile filled the room with a pleasant energy.

"Is this where I'm to sleep?"

"The mister say you take this room, cause it's near Bridget. You kin put your clothes here," Ester said, pointing to an empty closet.

"It's a beautiful room." Sarah eased the suitcase open, careful not to scuff the plush carpet.

"Use this dresser for your other stuff. And, don't set nothing on top. The misses is mighty fussy if we scratch her furniture. The missus is going to a big dinner party tonight, so you might have to wait awhile, but I spec she be by when she done dressing." Ester twisted her fingers nervously through her apron, shifted her eyes suspiciously toward the door and whispered. "I just want to tell you about Miss Lillian."

"Is Lillian the lady of the house?"

Ester was about to answer, but stopped when she heard footsteps in the foyer below. She grabbed the doorknob and set the door ajar. "You kin unpack. Somebody gonna show you around pretty soon," she said, then scurried down the hall.

The bedroom walls were papered with delicate white flowers, spread across a pink background. Starched, white curtains crisscrossed a large window overlooking the back yard of the vast estate.

The accommodations were more than Sarah expected, and felt overwhelmed by such perfection. After hanging her clothes in the closet, she placed several undergarments in the top drawer. In the drawer below, she laid a blue sweater her mother had crocheted several years earlier. She hadn't noticed how worn it looked before. But now, in the midst of such newness, the frayed edges seemed even more ragged. She shrugged her shoulder and closed the drawer.

"I can't worry about how it looks. It's all I have, anyway." Sarah turned when she heard a child's laughter outside. She went to the window, drew the curtain aside, and looked down.

The spacious, manicured yard was in full bloom with colorful flowers. A frail little girl with straight, mousy brown hair, scampered after a butterfly.

So this is my student, Sarah thought. *She looks small for six years old.* She held the curtain aside while she studied the child's movements.

The girl seemed oblivious to the neighbor's housemaids peeking over the fence. Nor, did she pay attention to the black maid passing nearby, toting a paper-basket of rubbish.

Of course, thought Sarah. *The child has no way to communicate, so she ignores what she can't understand.* Sarah's attention was drawn by movement at the back of the yard. The figure was too far away to see clearly through clouds of smoke, so she leaned closer to the window.

A handsome, young man was standing by a burning barrel. His curly red hair tumbled over his forehead. His plaid shirt-sleeves were rolled up, exposing tan, muscular arms. He was poking the fire with a charred wooden stick, sending sparks flying in the air.

"Ah, who could this be?" Sarah murmured with a whimsical note of interest. She knelt down and rested her elbows on the windowsill. A glimmer of hope enticed her to take a second look the handsome man.

Hours passed. Still, no one came.

Sarah's eyelids drooped, drowsy from boredom.

The late afternoon sun cast long shadows across the carpet, and the room grew dimmer.

Sarah peeked out the door to see if anyone was coming.

The hall was empty and quiet.

She returned to the window, sat on the floor and looked across the spacious yard. The young man and child were no longer in sight. Still, she waited. A sudden rapping sent Sarah's heart thumping. She jumped up just as the door opened.

An elegantly dressed lady entered, and the fragrance of her perfume permeated the room. The woman's long, silk dress rustled as she moved across the carpet. Her dark hair was smoothed in a fashionable soft wave and her red lipstick had been meticulously applied. The sun caught the prisms of the lady's diamond necklace, casting a glitter of blue and orchid reflections on the wall.

"I'm Lillian Hansen, my dear," Lillian said, extending her hand limply.

Sarah gave a shy handshake. "I'm Sarah Woodward." Feeling awkward and overwhelmed by the sophisticated woman, she stepped back.

"I'm sure we'll get along just fine. My daughter is six, and very difficult at times. I understand you'll be able to teach her," Lillian said, feigning a firmness to her voice.

"Yes. Oh, yes. I'm sure I can teach her."

Lillian interrupted. "I don't mean, just teach her, my dear. I mean reach her. We want her to cooperate with us."

Sarah smiled. "Oh yes, Misses Hansen. I'll teach her to understand everything you want."

Lillian folded her arms across her chest, eying the new girl from head to toe. "You may take your clothes up to the maid's quarters. Use the back stairs to the attic. Starting tomorrow, you and Bridget will take your meals in the maid's kitchen. I'll expect you to teach Bridget proper table manners. You do know proper table manners, don't you, my dear?"

Sarah nodded, but didn't reply. Underneath she bristled at the sarcastic innuendo. *Just because I wasn't raised in a splendid house, doesn't mean I don't know proper etiquette.*

"You will also teach her to dress herself, and to obey commands," Lillian continued, intentionally projecting a cold, unemotional tone to her voice.

Obey commands? thought Sarah, again nodding in agreement to the woman whose softness and beauty was vanishing with each word.

"You can go home on the weekends."

Sarah glanced up in surprise. "Oh. I thought, ah."

"You thought what?" Lillian interrupted. "What did my husband tell you? Seven days?"

"No. I mean. I thought," Sarah backed away, deciding not to explain. She had assumed the generous salary included weekends, which she was willing to work.

"You have a home to go to, don't you?"

"Yes. I live with …."

"How old are you?"

"Nearly twenty."

"You're too young to have finished college. Where did you go for your training?"

"I never went to school for sign language. I taught myself."

Again Lillian interrupted. "Are you married? Where do you live?"

"No. I'm not married. I live with my mother and brother. We live quite a distance from here."

"Good. You have a home to go to. We'll only need you on weekdays. My husband will be home on the weekends with that child." Lillian studied the girl haughty. "I'll have Ester show you to the attic."

Sarah nodded. *Hum. It looks like I'm going to have a tough time pleasing Misses Hansen.*

Lillian sauntered down the hall with a smirk of satisfaction. Even though she had masked her face in heavy makeup and wore expensive jewelry, she felt a twinge of insecurity. There was something about this shabbily dressed girl that made her feel uneasy. Hearing Ester's voice, she called down to the foyer. "Ester! Come up here."

Ester glanced up the staircase. "Huh?" She dropped a cleaning rag in a bucket of water and shuffled up the stairs.

Lillian waited with her hands set firmly on her hips. "Take that girl up to the attic."

Ester hesitated, wide-eyed and innocently naïve, before she spoke. "But Miss Lillian. The attic's too hot for a white gal."

"Do as I say. Go!"

Later that evening, Lillian, intent upon showing her disapproval, approached her husband. "The tutor seems satisfactory. I moved her up to the maid's quarter."

Edward's head shot up, taken off guard by his wife's stern comment. "The attic?" Though he was angry and upset, he dared not confront his wife about the sleeping arrangement. He was sure she had sent Sarah to the attic just to overrule his authority.

Lillian huffed with disgust. "We can't have a stranger sleeping in our bedrooms. What will people say? I've decided to make the best of the situation. That woman sleeps in the attic."

Edward didn't answer. He was upset because Lillian was just like his mother, with her stuffy, social pride. He wished he could be more aggressive and confident like his father, but was raised to respect his mother's social position, and his strict heritage held him socially bound.

CHAPTER 12

Bridget, uncertain of the new member of the family, kept her distance. Day after day, she watched the tutor waving her hands and making exaggerated facial expressions. At first, she found the finger-gestures puzzling, but amusing. Entertained by the comical expressions, she followed the tutor's every move; learning, not by listening, but by watching. With repetition, the connection between the face and hand movement began to make sense.

By the time the autumn leaves turned golden brown, Bridget had learned to communicate. Instead of striking out; her small fingers spelled out questions. Simple matters others took for granted; such as books, summer storms, and winter cold. Most of all, she wanted to know why her mother was so angry.

As the days passed, Lillian tolerated the tutor until the day she noticed her husband set aside his evening newspaper and pick up a sign-language book. "Why are you pointing your fingers like that?" she grumbled while watching his hands moving in clumsy gestures. "You look stupid. What will the neighbors say if I use my hands to speak?"

Edward set the book in his lap and gave his wife a look of disapproval. "It's time you learn to communicate with your daughter."

Lillian gritted her teeth and backhanded a stack of books, sending them flying off the coffee-table. "You're making a fool of yourself. Think about our social status."

Edward turned his attention to the book, poising his fingers awkwardly to convey a message of disapproval.

As the weeks passed, Lillian watched with bittersweet anticipation. Although satisfied with Bridget's progress, she refused to take part in sign-language.

Edward, encouraged by his daughter's progress, approached his wife. "Sarah should be teaching Bridget social skills, like table manners. It's time Sarah joins us in the dining room as a family," Edward said, emphasizing the word 'family.'

"That woman is *not* part of our family."

"Come now, my love. It's time Bridget learns table manners. If we watch Sarah, we can all learn."

Lillian scowled, lashing back in her defense. "I will not have an employee dining with us."

It wasn't Edward's nature to argue. He really wasn't very good at it, anyway. Rather than challenge his wife today, he devised a plan that would give him an excuse to eat in the kitchen. Several days later, he waited until dinner time, and again approached his wife. "I want Bridget and Sara to dine with us this evening," he said, keeping his voice firm and unwavering.

"Absolutely not!"

"If our daughter can't eat in the dining room with us, then I'll eat in the kitchen with her."

"You're a damn fool. Go ahead. Eat with the servants."

Edward grabbed his dish and bellowed. "Hilda. I'm having my dinner with Bridget tonight." He stomped out of the room with a smile of satisfaction. *Isn't this what I wanted, anyway?*

From that day on Lillian dined alone, listening to laughter coming from behind the closed kitchen door. Worse than the laughter, was the silence. She was sure they were gossiping about her, and her suspicions were increasing her paranoia.

The warm weather had come to an end. The evenings were growing cooler and the days shorter.

Lillian opened a window and a cool breeze drifted in, bringing with it the sound of laughter. A scowl crossed her face, and she slammed the window down, blocking out the noise. "Look at that damn kid! She's in the back yard screaming again. She's embarrassing us!"

"It's okay, my love. Let them be." Edward shook his head in disgust and returned to his newspaper.

Lillian's voice rose to a higher pitch. "The neighbors can see them. Come here and see! They're using their hands in public. Edward! Do you hear me?"

Edward slipped his watch out of his vest pocket and checked the time. "They'll be in soon. Let them be."

Lillian's face turned red and her voice grew demanding. "Make them stop."

"I'm not going to argue with you. Can't you let them alone?" Edward rose and started to leave the parlor, but stopped in his tracks when his wife started screaming.

"Don't you dare walk away from me! Where are you going?" Lillian followed her husband into the dining room. "The neighbors are gossiping. Fire that tutor before we're the laughingstock in town."

Edward ignored Lillian's comment. He edged his way past his wife and stood by the French doors overlooking the yard. A smile slipped across his face as he watched Sarah gently coaching his daughter.

"What are you looking at?"

Edward snapped back to attention. "People don't care what Bridget is doing."

"If you don't do something, I will," Lillian demanded, pointing her finger accusingly. "Make them stop that."

Edward quickened his pace and stepped out, onto the patio. He raised his hands and signed, informing Bridget it was time for dinner.

Lillian, seeing her husband relaying the message, opened the sliding door and rushed to the porch. "What are you doing? Now you're using your hands in public?" Angry and humiliated, she rushed through the dining room and up the stairs. She slammed the bedroom door to shut out the embarrassing noise. *How could he do that in public? He did that on purpose.*

Later that day the housekeeper, Hilda, spoke with Edward. "The misses won't be coming to dinner. She said you made a fool of her talking with your hands."

Edward, impatient with his wife's refusal to accept signing, replied in disgust. "What does she want? More attention from me? Does she want me to feel guilty? Well, I won't." He rose and started toward the foyer. "I'll go upstairs and talk to her."

"I wouldn't go up there. The misses is real upset. She threw a vase against the wall. You know that pretty one your mama gave."

"My mother's vase?"

"Yes sir. I went upstairs when I heard her crying. She screamed and chased me away."

Edward gripped the door-jamb to steady himself. "How could she do that? She knows how much I treasured that keepsake," he said, holding back an emotional sob in his throat. "Have the maids clean it later." Edward, tired and frustrated, turned and headed toward the sound of laughter coming from the kitchen.

Several weeks later, Bridget was in the backyard by the burning barrel, swinging high in the air. Sarah and the gardener were standing quite close, talking.

Lillian peeked from behind the curtain at the yard below. She felt a twinge of insecurity as she studied the contrast between the two girls. Sarah was a natural beauty with ivory skin and rosy cheeks, but Bridget was the opposite, with a homely flat-face and straight, mousy brown hair. She smoldered with anger as she watched the handsome gardener moving closer. "I'm paying that kid to work, and there he is, flirting."

A coy smile slipped across Sarah's face. It was apparent that she was enjoying his attention. She picked a frost-nipped rose from the fence, reached out mockingly as if to give it to him. With a coy smile she pursed her lips, and tucked the rose deep in her blouse.

Patrick eyed the red rose protruding from her cleavage. He looked at Sarah, laughed flirtatious and reached out as if to take it from her.

"She's teasing him with that rose. How dare he pluck the bloom from such a young girl."

Sarah noticed the curtain in the upstairs window fall back in place. Her smile disappeared, interrupting her moment of seduction. "Someone is watching us."

Patrick's face turned sullen. He returned to the burning barrel and began poking at the ashes.

Lillian stepped away from the window, envious of the attention Sarah was receiving from the gardener. She tried to remember when her husband looked at her with the same passion, but it had been a long time ago, and she couldn't recall if he ever looked at her adoringly. She wondered, *could Edward be attracted to Sarah? Could he be captivated by the tutor's charm?*

Autumn arrived leaving a mist of frost across the yard. A cool breeze rustled through trees, blowing crisp brown leaves to the ground.

Sarah raised the window, and feeling a nip in the morning air, she opened the dresser drawer and pulled out a bulky, blue sweater. As she slipped her arm into a sleeve, large holes appeared and strands of yarn fell onto the carpet.

"What on earth happened?" Sarah pulled the sweater off and laid it on the bed. "It looks like it's been cut." A feeling of uncertainty gripped the pit of her stomach. She picked at the shredded fibers, her mind accusing the person she thought responsible. *Lillian has been acting strange lately. I dare not accuse anyone, least of all her.* She shook the sweater, letting the threads fall on the carpet. There wasn't time to fret about it. Bridget is waiting for her morning walk. Sarah stitched the loose threads and patted the fibers flat. Though it was barely acceptable, she slipped it on and hurried to the maid's kitchen.

Hilda was standing at the sink when Sarah entered and didn't turn around while she spoke. "Sarah, I gotta tell you this. Now don't get mad. The misses doesn't want her little girl outside."

Sarah glanced up in surprise. "Why?" she replied while buttoning Bridget's coat up to the fur collar. "Mister Hansen said it was all right." While she spoke, her fingers informed Bridget of the news.

"I don't know. The misses doesn't want you strutting down the street like a peacock." Hilda rinsed the last dish, wiped her hands across her apron and turned. "Goot en himmel. What happened to your sweater?"

Sarah patted the fibers across her stomach, flattening a bulging knot. "I found it in the drawer like this." Sarah's fingers moved in a graceful flow of motion, propelling out each word.

"For shame. Looks like somebody been playing games."

"Oh no! Not Bridget," Sarah said, shaking her head. "She doesn't know what happened. Make no mention of it. I don't want anyone to know what happened."

Bridget interrupted the conversation by yanking on Sarah's sweater, gesturing with her fingers.

"What's she saying?" Hilda asked.

"She doesn't understand why she can't take a walk. Frankly, I don't either," Sarah answered, her fingers still conveying the message.

Hilda lowered her voice to a whisper. "The misses is a proud woman. Now mind you, I'm not saying there's anything wrong with that. I'm just saying sometimes she gets her pride up a mite too high. She doesn't want her little girl making monkey shines in public."

"Monkey shines! Is that what she calls signing?" Sarah stammered, refusing to relay the message to Bridget.

"Now, I'm just telling you what she said. Don't get all riled up."

Bridget again yanked at Sarah's sleeve.

Sarah ignored the request and nudged Bridget out to the yard.

Patrick stopped raking when he saw them approaching. "What took you so long today?"

Sarah returned his question with a weak smile. "Had to sew my sweater. See. It's full of holes," Sarah said, poking her finger into a snarled knot.

"What happened? Didn't someone like your sweater?" he asked, glancing accusingly at Bridget.

"Oh no, not her," Sarah whispered. "Someone doesn't want me taking Bridget out on the main street."

Patrick wrapped his arm around Sarah's waist, drawing her closer to him, and slid his other hand across her breast. "Sweater feels good," he teased with a mischievous grin.

"Stop that," Sarah scolded, pushing him away with a coy grin.

A slight movement in the upstairs window caught Patrick's attention. "Someone's watching us again," he mumbled under his breath. He backed away, positioned the rake firmly ahead of him and began pulling the leaves toward him.

A strong wind kicked up, pitching the dry leaves against the fence. Sarah folded her arms across her chest, pressing her sweater against her body to ward off the cold. Her fingers brushed against the frayed edges, and she trembled with mistrust. She glanced up.

The lace curtains in an upstairs window dropped slowly back in place.

"Why is Lillian always watching me," Sarah muttered under her breath.

That evening, Bridget pouted through dinner, upset because she didn't go on her daily walk. She waited until her parents left the dining room, then peeked in the parlor. Satisfied her mother was occupied reading the evening newspaper, she tiptoed up the stairs and entered her parents' bedroom.

The large bedroom was dimly lit by a Tiffany lamp sitting on an elegant bedside table. Purple fringes dangled from the lampshade, casting eerie shadows across the room.

Bridget headed straight for the vanity, and gazed in the mirror, just as she had done many times before. Within minutes her reflection drew her into a world of make-believe. In Bridget's mind, she entered a place of certainty that was not available in the real world because of her deafness.

A fragrant scent of sachet drifted from beneath the silk pillows on Lillian's bed.

Bridget breathed in the fragrance, believing it came from her garden. Drawn by the scent, her thoughts guided her along a glistening pathway, into a make-believe garden. It had been months since she visited her friends and was eager to tell them of her tutor.

"There are new words," Bridget signed with confident gestures. She told them of her teacher, and of the new things she had learned. Engrossed in her fantasy, she didn't feel the sharp vibration of her mother's high-heels coming up the steps.

An icy chill swept over Bridget's body. Darkness shrouded the garden and a gray mist swept over the rainbow path. The delicate flowers recoiled, folded their petals inward and shriveled on the ground. The children, frightened by the oncoming darkness, ran to the end of the meadow and disappeared in a swirling tunnel of light.

Bridget, sensing a threatening presence, turned and looked out through the glass.

A vaporous gray image of a woman appeared. A gust of wind blew the woman's cape, billowing it out like monstrous black wings. Spiny claw-like fingernails reached in through the frame.

Bridget, still suspended in her imaginary garden, tried to hide in the heather. She crouched down but, the wind had flattened the foliage to the ground. There was nowhere to go, except out of the mirror, into the claws of the sinister figure. She closed her eyes. A sharp pain raced across her shoulders, sending her tumbling off the vanity bench. When she opened her eyes, her mother was standing over her with hatred burning in her eyes.

"Mah-ma. Mah-ma." Bridget huddled on the floor watching her mother's mouth moving, bellowing out unheard words.

"I am not your ma. I'm your mother. Do you hear? Your mother."

Bridget covered her head with her hands.

"You're not my child," Lillian shouted, again striking Bridget across the back. "You're a devil from Hell. Why have you ruined my life?"

Edward, hearing his wife shrieking, dashed up the stairs and into the bedroom. Seeing his daughter sprawled on the floor, he scooped her up, soothing her with words she couldn't hear, yet understood. He glared at his wife. "Control your temper! You're the one who's ruining everyone's life."

Bridget peeked from the safety of her father's arms. Her garden had disappeared. Only the reflection of her mother's black dress appeared, blocking her from the mystical garden.

Edward, angry and frustrated, carried Bridget down to the kitchen. "Hilda! Move Sarah's clothes to the spare bedroom. Today! Someone has to protect my baby."

Lillian entered the kitchen just as Edward was shouting his orders. "Don't you dare. What will the neighbors think? What will the newspapers print when they learn we have a common teacher living in our home?"

"That damn newspaper isn't running my life. Sarah is not sleeping in the attic!"

Within the hour, Sarah's clothes were moved into the upstairs bedroom. This new arrangement made Sarah feel confident that this job could be a long-term position.

Several weeks later, Sarah noticed Bridget once again sitting at her mother's vanity. The child appeared mesmerized, staring in the mirror. Sarah stepped aside to watch.

The sudden vibration of a door slamming downstairs jolted Bridget to her senses.

Sarah, seeing the fear on the child's face, moved quickly. She opened her arms wide, hoisted Bridget on her hip and carried her into her bedroom. When she was safely in the bedroom, she cradled the trembling child. "It's all right," Sarah signed. "Why do you go in your mother's room? You know she doesn't want you there."

Bridget, clung to Sarah, waiting for the vibration of footsteps to stop. When she realized no one was coming, she raised her hands and signed. "I go to my happy place in the mirror. I have friends there, and grandma is there too."

"You mean like make-believe?"

"No. A real place. Real people."

"Have you ever seen these people before?"

"They live in my mama's mirror." Bridget didn't understand the difference between her reflection, and her imagination. No one had taught her that through the sense of touch we perceive what is real. What we cannot touch, may be a reflection or our imagination. Unable to make that distinction, Bridget believed her imaginary friends were real. If she had learned that touch was real and sight partially real, she might not have wandered so deeply into such a fantasy. But, because she had years of silence and unanswered question, her imagination had become her sanctuary.

Sarah understood how visual contact was a deaf child's way of communicating, so she coaxed Bridget to explain.

"I go to my garden when I'm upset." Bridget's hands spelled out the story of her mystical garden. "There are children to play with."

"Who are they?"

"They are like Ester's little sisters."

"Haven't you ever played with other children?"

"Only when Ester's sisters came in the yard one day. I liked them. We played until mama came home. She took a switch and chased them out. I thought it was something bad."

Sarah was amazed that this child had such a vivid imagination. *So this is her place to daydream.* "But, why the mirror? Can't you see your friends anywhere else?"

"I never had friends. When I was young, no one ever talked to me."

"When you look in the mirror, your face is only a reflection."

Bridget's head moved from side to side in denial. "When I was little, I looked in the mirror for a friend. At first my own face was my friend but, after a while I found my magical place."

"Your mother doesn't want you there."

"I feel better when I visit my friends. They understand my feelings. They listen to me. When I'm in my garden, flowers talk to me. Why is that Sarah?"

"Flowers can't speak. What you're seeing isn't real."

Bridget's lower lip pouted outward. "Grandma is real."

"Your grandmother is gone to heaven, and she won't come back."

"No. No. Grandma only went away for a little while." Bridget reached for the photograph of her grandmother on the bedside table, holding it close to her. She remembered how granny protected her from her mother.

Sarah wrapped her arms around Bridget, comforting her. She realized how desperate the child must have been to have created such an imaginary place. "Does your father know about your visits to the mirror?"

"No. Only Hilda and Ester. They protect me from my mother. I didn't know how to sign words, so I couldn't tell them."

"How many times has your mother caught you at the mirror?"

Bridget pulled the blankets up to her neck and shivered. "Mama hit me many times. Sometimes she shook me until my neck hurts."

"What about your grandma? Didn't she stop your mother?"

"Granny saw me cry, but never knew why. I didn't know how to tell her."

Outside, the wind howled as the evening settled in. Bridget started to relax and nestled in a fluffy pillow. The two huddled in bed, signing in silence until their heads nodded in sleep.

CHAPTER 13

Sarah lived at the Hansen's home for three months and was pleased with Bridget's progress, especially with the new sleeping arrangements. Now it was time to retrieve her winter clothing. After packing her summer clothes, she made her way to the front door.

Edward was waiting in the foyer. "The radio forecast a winter storm. It's too cold to travel tonight." Edward stepped closer and lowered his voice. "Let me drive you."

"Thank you. I really appreciate it."

Edward slipped on a heavy winter coat and tilted his homburg smartly to one side. "I've parked in front." He picked up Sarah's suitcase and eased the door open. "I didn't want you transferring from one streetcar to another. It looks like it's going to be quite a storm."

"Will your wife mind? You usually listen to the radio about this time, don't you?"

"I don't think Lillian paid any attention to me or the news."

Sarah followed his long strides down the snow-covered sidewalk and slid into the front seat. "Thank you. It's thoughtful of you to care."

"I'm glad there's something I can do for you, after all you've done for Bridget."

As they drove along the sun was setting behind rows of barren trees and gray clouds darkened the sky. The falling snow veiled the road in a maze of white.

Edward glanced at Sarah out of the corner of his eye. He turned away, feeling self-conscious when she faced him.

Sarah broke the awkward silence. "Why is your wife angry at Bridget?"

Edward shrugged. "I don't know."

"I asked her why her mother hit her."

"What did she say?"

"Bidget tells me she's not allowed in your bedroom."

"Why does she go there?"

"To see the mirror. She talks about an imaginary garden in the mirror." Sarah turned away and blushed, embarrassed when he returned her look.

"A garden? What's that about?"

"Just a child's imagination."

"I know my wife is difficult. I hope she's not too hard on you," Edward replied, making a point to keep his eyes on the road.

"I mind my own business." Sarah turned away and gazed out the window. *He's such a handsome man. I wonder why he lets his wife control him.*

"A penny for your thoughts," Edward chided, again breaking the embarrassing silence.

Sarah offered a weak smile, but didn't answer. The memory of him stirring in the bedroom next to her room brought a warm blush to her cheeks. *He doesn't know I'm wide awake when his wife is screaming at him in the middle of the night. Nor, does he know I listen to hear his footsteps pass by my room.* Although he was older, and certainly unavailable, she imagined him as her lover, but in the daylight reality set in, and she scoffed at her desires as foolish and impossible.

The blustery wind kicked up, coating the street with a sheet of ice. Headlights of oncoming traffic sent fragmented prisms flashing across the window-glass. Snowflakes melted against the window, dripping down like weeping teardrops.

Edward eased the car to a stop.

Sarah felt her heart beating faster. She wished they could stay and talk, but dared not ask. Reaching for the door-handle, she paused when she felt his hand touching hers.

"I'll open it for you," he murmured, pressing his arm against her body, preventing her from leaving.

Sarah closed her eyes, mesmerized by his warm breath on her neck. Languishing in the moment, she breathed in the scent of aftershave wafting from beneath his starched collar.

Edward had also fantasized about this moment. Especially the nights he spent alone in the guest room.

If only he knew how I feel, thought Sarah. The rhythmic rise and fall of his breath was now on her cheek. She leaned back, giving in to the passionate moment, eager to feel his lips pressing on hers.

Edward drew her closer, kissing her lightly at first. Feeling confident she had not stopped him, he slid his hand under her sweater, caressing her warm breast. Though he knew the consequence of this affair could cost him, he couldn't resist.

Sarah felt his body pressing against her leg, closer than she intended. She placed her hand against his chest, creating a distance between them. "Edward. I can't."

He moved away and looked at Sarah as he had never seen her before. His face reddened with embarrassment, yet, he couldn't resist, even if he tried. "You're beautiful," he whispered, sensing something must be said.

Their eyes met, holding the passion of the moment.

Again, Sarah reached for the door-handle. This time she didn't stop him when he pulled her closer. She melted in his arms, returning his kiss with passionate lips.

The next two days Edward lived in anticipation of Sarah's return. When he was alone, he relived the memory of her tender kiss. He could think of nothing else. A passionate new emotion stirred within him. He began looking at his wife differently. Now, Lillian appeared bitter and uncaring. He tried to remember why he was attracted to her, but the past seemed blurred. Tonight his life had taken on a new meaning. This was more than a physical attraction, it was a sensual closeness he had never experienced before.

Sunday morning Edward made it a point to say out of Lillian's way until it was time to leave. He set the door ajar before he spoke. "I have to stop by the office this morning. I'll pick Sarah up on my way home."

Lillian's head snapped up, and a startled expression crossed her face. Before she could answer, she heard the front door slam shut.

Edward had previously informed Sarah he would pick her up before noon. As he stood on the porch in the chilling wind, indecision struck a chord, and he worried that she would doubt his sincerity. Taking a deep breath, he rapped softly.

Sarah opened the door and cast her eyes down, afraid to betray her true feelings. *How can I ever look at him again without recalling his passionate kiss? Was this something he had taken lightly?* She heard of married men who strayed and wondered. *Am I just another conquest?* Feeling awkward standing in the cold, she gripped the luggage and stepped out, into the blowing wind.

Edward reached for the suitcase, making sure his fingers touched hers. He paused, as if to hold this precious moment, to assure her he still cared.

The warmth of his hand sent a flush of passion rushing through her body.

After driving only a few blocks, he parked at the curb, leaving the motor idling to warm the car. He leaned close while dialing the radio to sentimental music. "I've never done this before," he whispered, drawing her closer. "I didn't expect this to happen."

Sarah returned his embrace, hoping this was not just a passing fancy.

Edward was aware of the predicament he had placed himself in. Still, he lingered in her embrace, casting aside his guilt.

The afternoon passed quickly. Edward glanced at his pocket-watch. "We better go. It's past three o'clock," he murmured, reluctant to leave her embrace.

"What will you tell your wife?"

"I told her I was going to the office for a while, and would pick you up later. Please don't misunderstand. I had to talk to you."

"Wasn't she upset? She knows you don't work on Sunday."

"I left the before she asked any questions."

"We better hurry. She's going to be mad at you, anyway."

Edward nodded, started the motor and headed down the snow-covered street.

"Did you talk to your wife? Did she say why she hit Bridget?"

"No. I didn't ask. Lillian might not tell me, anyway. I've been sleeping in the guest room. I guess you knew that, didn't you?"

"Yes, I know," she murmured, remembering the times she heard him pacing the hall in the still of the night. She thought about those nights, how she wanted to comfort him, to confess her love, but they were impossible dreams. When she first came to work as a tutor, she had been impressed with his public statue and his wealth. As the days and months passed, she saw him in a different light. It was his gentleness and the concern he had for his daughter that caught her attention.

Edward interrupted her thoughts. "It seems Lillian is having more tantrums lately. I don't know how to protect my daughter."

Sarah nodded. "I've noticed how quickly she gets annoyed with Bridget."

"My wife flies off the handle for no reason at all," Edward grumbled as he pulled to the curb.

Bridget feeling the vibrations of the approaching car, squealed with delight. She greeted her father with a hug and signed a welcome to Sarah.

Lillian, hearing Bridget's scream, hurried to the balcony and stood in the shadows overlooking the foyer. When she saw the smile on Edward's face and the attention he was giving to Sarah, she fumed with anger. Gritting her teeth with envy, she tiptoed back to her bedroom.

As the days passed, Edward took every opportunity to meet Sarah behind closed doors; innocently at first, but the desire was growing. His life with Lillian now became a double-edged sword, cutting back with intense resentment. Deep in the core of his being, he felt that he had been living alone, drowning in an ocean of darkness. He wasn't aware he was starved of affection, but after seeing the joy Sarah brought to the household, he realized how empty his marriage had become. Sleeping alone gave him time to analyze his feeling. It was not just a physical separation from Lillian that made him lonely; it was his wife's coldness and unemotional response.

Though mindful of the consequence, he decided to separate himself from his wife. Casting aside his conscience, he contrived petty criticisms to anger Lillian. It was not in his nature to be devious, but he was determined to be closer to Sarah.

Several days later, after one of Edward's stinging remarks, Lillian could no longer control her temper. She ripped his suits off the hangers and threw them in the hall. With a loud slam, she locked him out of their bedroom.

Edward's plan worked. This gave him an excuse to move the rest of his clothes to the spare bedroom.

Behind closed doors, Lillian panicked and her headaches worsened. Edward had always catered to her every whim. Now that he was pulling away, she realized how much she needed him. After analyzing his trivial excuses, Lillian came to the conclusion; his heavy workload at the office coincided with Sarah's trips home on the weekends. Fearing she would appear jealous, she refused to confront her husband. Lillian stood in front of the mirror fingering the pearls that lay heavy around her neck, unable to let go of the resentment burning inside her. She must find a way to make Edward return to her bedroom.

CHAPTER 14

Lillian looked over the railing and listened while searching the foyer.

The house was quiet, except for the clinking sound of dishes coming from the maid's kitchen.

Lillian's spirits soared with anticipation when she heard Sarah had left for the Christmas holidays. "Alone with my husband for a whole week," she murmured, as she headed toward the aroma of freshly baked pies. "Mm. It smells good. Hilda, where's Edward?"

Hilda hesitated to answer and continued washing the dishes.

Lillian, too excited to wait for an answer, hurried to the dining room.

The crystal chandelier lit the room. A burst of afternoon sun hit the prisms, casting orchid beam across the walls. A large table was set with gold-rimmed china, placed side-by-side, just as she had instructed. Two slender white candles, set in crystal candlestick holders, and a bottle of champagne lay chilling in a silver ice-bucket.

After finding the room empty, Lillian returned to the kitchen. "Hilda! Where's Edward?"

Hilda, hesitant to face Lillian, continued bustling about the sink. She gave a towel a quick snap in the air and placed it over the steaming hot pies. "He took Sarah to her mother's house," she mumbled under her breath.

"What! When did they leave?"

Hilda released a soft sigh. "Oh my. Some time ago."

"Why didn't Patrick take her?" Lillian's voice grew louder, more demanding. "I told him to drive Sarah home on the weekends." Turning on her heels, she stomped out of the room. "Damn. Sarah outfoxed me. She ruined my plans for the evening." Lillian grasped her breast, feeling as if the world was slipping out from under her, leaving her drifting in a sea of uncertainty.

Returning to the parlor, Lillian switched off the lamps, so she could see outside more easily. Evening was setting in and a howling wind whipped icy crystals against the glass. Lillian paced the floor, from window to window, until it was too dark to see the road. *Perhaps he's delayed by the storm,* she thought, preferring to deny her suspicions, rather than face the truth.

Hilda choose to keep out of sight that evening. "Ester, you better get going. The storm is getting worse by the minute. Ya?"

Ester matched the last pair of cotton stockings, rolled them together and placed them in a wicker basket. She cocked her head to one side, listening. Cupping her hand over the side of her mouth, she whispered. "Is the missus still slipping around the parlor like a polecat on the prowl?"

Hilda flipped her apron in the air with a quick snap and lowered her voice. "Roust! You should be glad you're going home for the holidays."

Ester packed a hearty portion of leftover food in a brown paper bag, crunched the top down with a firm twist. "Well, it's her own fault," Ester whispered. "I figure she chased him away with her peculiar ways." Ester moved closer, again placing her hand over her mouth. "You speck he's messing around wit Sarah?"

"For shame! That's none of your business." Hilda handed Ester the over-sized wool coat hanging on a hook by the door. "You best get going."

Ester rolled her eyes up to the ceiling and grinned. "Ah. Come on Hilda. Ya know them two been carrying on fer quite a spell."

"Why you talk like that? Those folks been good to you."

"Ya know what I'm talking about. Ya see how Sarah looks at him when he struts in the parlor. And, how he leaves his good suit on when he comes home. He ain't never done that before."

"You shouldn't be talking like that. Look at the table scraps they let you take to your family."

Ester slipped on her coat and tied a bulky wool scarf around her neck. "The missus don't know about the left-overs," Ester replied as she tucked the grocery bag under her arm. "It's okay, cause the mister say I kin take the left-overs."

"He's a generous man."

"I like Sarah too. She's been teaching me to read," Ester replied, her eyes beaming with pride.

"You can do sign-language?"

"A little. Sarah's been teaching me to read and write, just like you. I kin read magazines now. What you think about that?"

"You best not say bad things about them two."

"I ain't blaming Sarah. Miss Lillian is strange. Ya know, wacko."

"Roust! Git on before the weather gets any worst," Hilda opened the door and ushered Ester onto the snow-covered porch.

By eight o'clock a howling wind whirled veils of snow across the ground.

Lillian stood by the drafty window. Watching. Waiting. With each approaching headlight, Lillian gripped the frosty ledge until her fingers turned bluish from the cold. The hours seemed to drag by slowly. Mounds of snow piled high on the window ledges, making it difficult to see across the lawn.

After a while, the headlights on the road ceased, except for an occasional car that braved the winter storm. She waited, pacing from window to window., each moment expecting Edward's car to pull into the driveway.

However, the evening took on a different meaning for Edward and Sarah. They rendezvoused at a quaint inn on the outskirts of town, where, in the past, they had spent many evenings nestled in each other's arms. For them, time passed as quickly as the flicker of a firefly. In the passion of the moment, they didn't realize how many hours had passed. Only now, as they entered the main dining room, did they notice the countryside blanketed in freshly fallen snow.

The main dining room was lit by crimson lanterns centered on each table. Soft music flowed from a mahogany piano hidden in the shadows of a dark corner. A gray-haired gentleman, barely visible, spread his ebony fingers over the ivory keys, sending a romantic melody meant for lovers. The man cast his dark eyes down and never glanced across the room.

Edward guided Sarah to a table, next to a large picture-window where they could watch the falling snow while they dined.

Sarah lifted her glass. "To the end of a beautiful day."

Edward touched his glass to hers, ever so lightly, creating a mellow chime that reaffirmed their secret love. "I wish it could last forever," he whispered.

The faint tinkle of wine glasses chimed across the room.

Sarah nodded, half smiling.

"I don't know how much longer we can keep this a secret. It's getting harder to get out of the house without starting an argument."

"I know. I can feel your wife's resentment toward me."

Edward swirled his wine glass, biding time before he spoke. A sullen expression crossed his face. He released an uneasy cough and his voice cracked. "I spoke with my lawyer last week."

"You did?"

"If I divorce Lillian, I could lose custody of Bridget."

Sarah stared down at her glass avoiding eye contact. "You're a powerful man. You can do something."

"Yes, I know. My attorney claims there are ways." Edward lowered his voice apologetically. "How can I live with my conscious? I'm the one committing adultery. I broke the marital contract."

"But Bridget is afraid of her mother. Won't that make a difference to a judge?"

"The law is on my wife's side. I'm guilty, and she will hire powerful attorneys to prove it. I can't take the chance of leaving my baby alone with Lillian. You understand, don't you my dear?"

Sarah hesitated to question Lillian's sanity for fear of sounding vindictive. "We can't let Bridget get hurt again."

Edward nodded in agreement and raised his empty glass to attract the waiter's attention. He knew their secret affair had jeopardized his chance of getting legal custody of his daughter. "Even if I file, Lillian has the right to refuse a divorce. It's the law. She'll make my life a living hell."

Sarah waited until the waiter filled the glasses and left before she spoke. "You've got to do something."

Edward leaned across the table and whispered. "What if the newspapers find out? They will expose my infidelity. My reputation ruined. I have employees who count on me." He griped Sarah's hand, holding it tight. "It's not only the business, I just can't leave Bridget alone with Lillian."

"I understand. Our first concern must be for Bridget's safety." Sarah reluctantly accepted this relationship as an occasional rendezvous. It was the most she could expect under the circumstances.

"There's no solution except time. We have to wait for my daughter to grow up. When she's out of danger, I'll do what is best for her." The mutual concern for Bridget had sealed their alliance and bonded their love to secrecy.

That evening, Hilda tossed and turned, listening to the creaking floor overhead. The rhythmic patter caused an ache in her heart. Because Hilda arrived before the maid's quarters were built in the attic, Lillian had assigned her to a room at the back of the house, directly below the master suite. Hilda remembered the first day she came to work at the Hansen's estate, how proud she was to be the head-housekeeper. Through the years, they treated her with respect, and she came to regard her employers as friends.

It was well past three o'clock in the morning when Edward's Chrysler coasted silently into the garage behind the house.

The pacing stopped.

The faint creaking sound of the back door opening broke the silence.

Hilda lifted her head off the pillow to listen. She could tell by the muffled footsteps that Edward had slipped off his shoes and was tiptoeing up the stairs. Tilting her ear, she faintly heard footsteps heading toward the guest room at the end of the hall. She listened.

A door slowly closed with a muffled click.

Again, the rhythmic creaking coursed through the ceiling.

Hilda climbed in bed and pulled the comforter up to her chin. She wondered if Lillian would remain silent tomorrow, or would she challenge her husband's suspected infidelity?

The house became uncannily quiet, except for the rhythmic pacing overhead.

Lillian woke the next morning to the sound of wind striking branches against the window. The constant click..., click..., click..., reminded her of her youth, when her nimble fingers moved swiftly across a noisy keyboard. Memories of yesterday passed across her mind. She was twenty years old when she started working for the Hansen Tool and Die Company. Lillian closed her eyes, replaying the days gone by.

It was 1920, and the new owner, Priscilla Hansen, had arrived to take charge. It had been weeks since her husband's death, and the office wondered if her son, Edward, would take over his father's position.

Indeed, that is exactly what she had in mind when she marched in the office appropriately dressed in a black dress, black cotton stockings, and black lace-up oxfords. Her son trailed meekly behind.

Edward had just turned twenty-five. He was tall and quite slender, almost to the point of being too thin. A pleasant-looking man with sensual blue eyes like his father. His wispy blond hair was parted in the middle, clipped clean behind his ears exposing a pale, gawking neck.

That was the first time Lillian saw young Edward. She remembered how timid and overly courteous he was. He appeared awkward that day and used his smile as a way of excusing himself. Even though he masked his shyness with a stern face, his weak chin betrayed his uncertainty.

Lillian remembered slowing her typing as Edward passed close to her desk. She fluttered her eye-lashes and smiled, welcoming him behind his mother's back.

Edward took notice and responded with a secret half-smile.

From that day on Lillian made an effort to attract his attention. She began by imitating Priscilla Hansen's every move. She lowered her skirt to a fashionable ankle length and mimicked her quick, demanding voice. After several months, it had accomplished its goal. Edward reached out, finding comfort in her familiar mannerisms.

Lillian rolled over, buried her face in the pillow to block out the light. The past continued to flood her mind.

She recalled the week before the wedding. Her future mother-in-law had made arrangements for the bridal shower and the wedding reception to be held at the Detroit Yacht Club. Without consulting Lillian, a wardrobe of expensive clothes had been shipped to her home. Even the wedding gown wasn't what Lillian would have chosen. Feeling intimidated and overwhelmed, she gave in to Priscilla's wishes. An entirely new way of life was opening up for her. Lillian was too excited to realize she was being guided like a pawn on a chessboard. Being prepared to dress and behave like a socialite. Groomed to be a Hansen.

The front-door chimes echoed up the stairs.

Lillian set her memories aside and slid the satin sheets off her body. *Where is the gentle man I used to know? Why did he change?* She hurried to the breakfast room expecting an explanation of Edward's late hours. Or, at least, an excuse. A reconciliation of some type. Disappointment swept across her face when she realized he had left for work early that morning. Feeling betrayed, and ashamed to face the serving staff, she turned away, unsure of how to handle this situation.

On Monday morning, as planned, Edward picked up Sarah from her weekend visit.

Bridget, feeling the vibrations of her father's car, ran to greet him. She leaped in her father's arms, greeting him with kisses. She stretched her hands out and signed to Sarah. "Bur-Dee haw-pee," Bridget screeched, attempting to perfect each awkward word.

"My Birdie. My Birdie." Sarah sang as she swept Bridget up in her arms.

Lillian, hearing voices in the foyer, rushed to the top of the stairs and leaned over the balcony. It angered her when she saw Bridget signing, obviously excited at Sarah's return. She stepped back in the shadows when she saw Sarah wearing a new coat. *She can't afford that on her own salary.*

Edward wrapped his arms around Bridget and Sara, hugging them tightly.

Lillian, infuriated by the closeness of their embrace, tiptoed back to her bedroom. She stood in front of the mirror, staring at her reflection. "I'm glad I don't look like Bridget." She fingered the pearls, and today they lay like a heavy burden on her neck. After dusting her face with powder and patting a dab of dry rouge on her cheeks, she applied bright red lipstick on her pursed lips.

"There! That's better. I'm not like Bridget at all." She brushed her hair down in a soft wave and pinned a small wiglet of curls on top of her head. After gathering her confidence, she arched her back and casually made her way into the foyer.

"Welcome home, Sarah," Lillian said, while examining the coat more closely. "Did you enjoy your holiday?"

Sarah smiled, nodding her reply.

"Is that a cashmere coat?" Lillian feigned a smile, but her stoic voice betrayed her indifference.

CHAPTER 15

Spring arrived with a steady downpour, and a strange chill settled throughout the house. The house took on an unnatural quiet, and an eerie breeze drifted from room to room.

Though Hilda was troubled by the icy chill, she had set it aside, until the day the frosty breeze brushed against her face. The hair on the back of her neck stood up, sending her scurrying to the maid's kitchen. "Do you feel that cold?" she whispered to Ester who was preparing the evening meal.

"Um-hum. When you came in the kitchen, it got real cold." Ester' eyes widened, and she stepped away from Hilda. "What ya suppose it is?" she replied, shifting her eyes, searching for a disembodied spirit.

"It's a ghost," Hilda mumbled under her breath. "Maybe it's Grandma Hansen watching all the strange things going on. She's probably turning over in her grave."

Again, a gust of icy air blasted Hilda in the face.

"Goot en himmel! That's what it is!"

"You say what?" Ester grabbed her coat, slung it over her shoulder, snatched a brown grocery bag off the table and dashed out the back door.

Hilda clutched the bib of her apron and took a deep breath. She, like her mother, had the ability of intuition, sensing things that others could not, and she used this as her conscience. She wondered if a spirit had touched her face. As the thought passed her mind, another waft of air touched her cheek. This time the feeling was threatening, like a foreboding message of danger. Not wanting to be alone, she rushed to the parlor.

Edward jerked his head up when he saw Hilda standing in the doorway. "Good God! You look like you've seen a ghost."

Hilda peeked back, over her shoulder and scanned the doorway. "Yes, sir." she whispered as she moved cautiously into the room. "Something strange is going on."

Edward set his newspaper on his lap, giving the housekeeper his full attention. "Strange? What's the matter?"

"I feel like I'm being followed." Hilda cupped her hand to the side of her face and lowered her voice. "I think there's a spirit roaming this house."

A humorous smirk slipped across his face. "For heaven's sake. Don't tell me you believe in such nonsense?"

"Ah, huh. There's something strange sneaking around my kitchen. It scared Ester. She run out the house like a scared jackrabbit."

Edward grinned at the amusing scenario. "That's just a breeze. It' s been unusually cool this April."

"I know it's cold outside. But," she stopped and took several steps into the parlor. "I got a funny feeling your mama is trying to tell me something."

"That's ridiculous. She's been gone for years." The remembrance of his mother's passing still weighed heavy on his heart, and thinking of her as a ghost angered him. His smile disappeared and his voice turned stoic. "I don't believe in spirits."

"I know it sounds strange. But, I believe souls live forever, and spirits never die." Hilda glanced over her shoulder toward the kitchen. "Sometimes they come back to haunt us."

"Oh. Come on," Edward said, tossing his head back with a snicker. "Once you're gone, you're gone. That spirit business is just foolishness."

"Maybe not. I got a feeling I'm being watched."

"You mustn't worry about such things," Edward replied with a wave of his hand. "Maybe a nice glass of wine will settle your nerves. Why don't you retire early this evening?"

"Well, perhaps I've been a bit hasty. Maybe a drink would do me some good." A quick nod of her head and a smile sent Hilda ambling off to the wine cabinet.

"Ghost. What next?"

"Who are you talking to," Lillian asked as she entered the room.

"Nothing important. Hilda's going to bed early this evening."

"This room is cold." Lillian shivered and rubbed the sides of her arms. "Are there any windows open?" Lillian shoved the curtain aside, searching for a draft. "I'm chilled to the bone."

"The windows are closed tight." A frown crossed Edward's forehead as he watched his wife examining the windows. *Hum. Just a coincidence,* he thought, recalling Hilda's message.

"Did you have the bedroom window fixed yet?"

"The handyman couldn't fix it today. He set a wood board on the ledge to prop the window open. He'll fix the window when the weather warms up."

"A stick of wood? An ugly 2 x 4? You call that fixing it?"

"It's just temporary."

Lillian huffed her disgust and pushed the curtain aside. "Look. The frost nipped the buds of my bushes. This will be the first year my Nipponese vases won't be filled with lilacs."

Edward raised his eyes to the ceiling and waved his hand the air. "Hilda tells me the cold is a ghost. A spirit of some sort."

"Nonsense! This is a big house. We can expect a draft now and then." Lillian pushed the curtains together. "I'm going to bed. It's too damn cold in here," she grumbled as she headed toward the stairs.

"Good night, Edward said, then returned to his newspaper. He had been reading only a short time when his attention was drawn to the doorway. He wasn't sure why, but his curiosity lasted only a second or two. *Is there a person standing there?* He sniffed the air. The familiar fragrance of his mother's perfume drifted by, but it was gone as quickly as it came. *Just imagination.* He closed his eyes. Thoughts of his mother invaded his mind. He could almost hear her voice.

"Watch Bridget. Watch Bridget."

I will, he thought to himself. A cool breeze brushed against his face and his eyes popped open. "Ah, you're letting those spooky stories get to you," he murmured, feeling foolish for being caught up in such tomfoolery.

The peculiar coolness traveled throughout the house touching each member of the household. Even with the heat of summer, the strange chill did not disappear. Months passed. The days grew cooler with the onset of fall. Still, the eerie breeze drifted silently from room to room.

Though Lillian spoke no more of the icy chill, the negative feeling left her feeling despondent and moody. There were times she displayed fits of anger and separated herself from the family by staying in her bedroom. Days later, her mood would change, and she would continue her daily routine as if nothing had happened.

Although Edward was concerned about Lillian's depression, it was his nature to procrastinate. *She's done this before,* he thought. *Is it just her way to get attention?* After nearly twenty years of marriage, he had learned to keep his distance until her moodiness passed. Also, he wasn't ready to admit his affair with Sarah might have caused his wife's depression. So, to justified his guilt, he showered his wife with extravagant gifts and elegant jewelry.

Lillian used the jewelry as false hope, a facade to cover her failing marriage. She had been moody all week and tonight she locked herself in her bedroom.

That night Edward tossed and turned, replaying his wife's unpredictable behavior. When the house became quiet, he eased the door open and peered down the hall. *Is there a light coming from beneath Lillian's door?*

A shaft of moonlight streamed through his partly open door, barely lighting the hall. He looked down the hall.

Lillian's bedroom remained dark.

Edward slipped out of the room and stood quietly in the darkness. There was no sound. He tiptoed to the staircase and leaned over the banister, listening. *Could Lillian be downstairs?*

The house remained unusually quiet.

He made his way down the hallway and tapped lightly on the door. "Sarah," he whispered.

Sarah, wakened by the sound of Edward's voice, jumped out of bed and eased the door open. A wave of passion swept over her. She opened the door wider.

Edward slipped in the bedroom and pressed the door closed behind him. In the glow of moonlight, he could see the soft curves of Sarah's thighs, and the passion rose within him. "Hush," he said, putting his finger over his mouth.

"Edward. It's four o'clock in the morning."

Drawn to the fragrant scent of her body, he reached out and wrapped his arms around her.

Sarah slid her hands under his pajama top, pulling him close. The sensual odor of sleep made her draw him closer, smothering her face in his chest.

"I need you," he whispered as he pressed her closer, edging her toward the bed.

Sarah hesitated momentarily, reflecting on the guilt of her indiscretion, but the warmth of his body had weakened her resistance, and she backed toward the bed.

Edward knew the risk he was taking, but the desire that burned within couldn't be smothered, the risk of being caught made this liaison more sensual.

"What if Lillian wakes up?"

The sound of his wife's name made him step back in the shadows. "I worry about her," he whispered. "She hasn't snapped out of this yet. These spells don't usually last this long."

"Maybe you should take her to a doctor."

"I've tried, but she accused me of butting in her business. I think it's best if I wait awhile."

"Is this our fault? I feel guilty when she looks at me." Sarah was glad they were standing in the dark. She didn't want him to see the guilt on her face. "Did we make her ill?"

"Lillian's always been temperamental. We had nothing to do with that," Edward retaliated softly.

"She's been acting strange for weeks. Is there something wrong with her?"

"My wife's had depression for years."

"It's not just her moodiness. She can't control her temper. Do I anger her? Am I to blame?"

"She's always had a bad temper. Don't blame yourself. If anyone is to blame, it's me."

"Why? What did you do?"

"It's what I didn't do. I never spoke up. I always backed down when her temper exploded."

Sarah felt his hands sliding up her thighs, lifting her nightgown. "What if Bridget comes in?" she murmured, sliding willingly onto the bed. Sarah gave her love freely, justifying her infidelity with excuses that were once against her own moral code.

CHAPTER 16

———◆———

"It's time we hire another tutor," Lillian said, determined to get rid of Sarah. "Bridget should learn something new."

"Why? Sarah's doing fine. Leave good enough alone. At least we can take her out in public now."

"You think she can behave in public? Well, we'll see."

The following day Lillian called Ester into the parlor. "Get Bridget dressed. I'm taking her out for the day."

"Yes-um. Where she going Miss Lillian?"

"Never mind. Don't forget her boots. It's snowing"

Ester scurried up the stairs, and into Bridget's bedroom.

After waiting a half hour, Lillian stomped up the stairs and pushed Bridget's door open. "What's keeping you?" she urged with limited hand movement.

Bridget turned her back and continued setting books in the bookcase. Any change in routine was upsetting and wearing a fancy dress early in the day left her feeling suspicious. She dawdled, hoping to escape the unexplained situation.

"Damn it! Hurry up. What on earth makes you so dumb?" Lillian yelled and shoved Bridget toward the door.

Bridget, fearful of the unknown, dug her heels in, determined to stay in her bedroom. Though she wanted to sign a question, she folded her hands across her chest, fearful of getting her hands slapped.

"Enough is enough!" Lillian bellowed, impatient with her daughter's procrastination. She grabbed Bridget's arm and dragged the screaming child down the stairs with Ester following behind.

The household staff, hearing the commotion, rushed to the foyer.

"Help that child with her coat. The red velvet one. At least she'll look respectable."

"Yes-um," Ester replied as she hurried to the closet.

"Let me do that," Hilda said, shoving Ester aside. She patted Bridget on the head and smiled assuringly, while buttoning the fur collar around her neck.

Bridget turned toward Hilda and secretly signed, begging for an explanation.

"Miss Lillian. Let me tell her where she's going."

"I'm not making monkey-shines in public. She'll find out soon enough."

"Ma'am. The child's upset."

"We'll do just fine." Lillian grabbed Bridget's hand and dragged the crying child to the car. With a hefty push, she shoved Bridget in the back seat and sped away.

Bridget pressed her face on the window, tears streaming down her cheeks. Am I being punished? Where am I going? She saw Hilda sending a reassuring gesture, but that did not sooth Bridget's fears.

As the car sped along, a winter storm blew snowflakes across the highway. Glaring headlights reflected on the glass blinding the road ahead.

Each time a car whizzed past, Bridget gripped the door handle tighter. The vibration of the fast moving traffic upset her equilibrium.

The car approached the downtown area. Tall buildings loomed like snow-covered towers.

A faint rumbling vibration resonated through the back seat. The abrasive vibration grew stronger, and stronger, until the car began to shake. Bridget, being sensitive to vibrations, gripped the door-handle tighter as the strange trembling resonated through her body.

The vibration grew stronger, more intense.

Bridget crouched down in the back seat.

A long, yellow streetcar clattered past. Metal wheels scraping against the steel railroad tracks transmitted an eerie quivering sensation.

Bridget slid deeper into the seat.

The strange trembling became fainter, and fainter, until it disappeared.

Bridget sat up and again pressed her face against the window.

Huge buildings cast long shadows on the pavement. Clusters of people hurried across the walkway through blowing snow.

Lillian pulled into a busy parking lot. She yanked Bridget out of the car and guided her through ankle-deep snow toward a large building.

Bridget had never been downtown before, and the swarms of people terrified her. She clung to her mother's hand, too frightened to let go.

Near the entranceway of the building, a group of people stood around a red kettle hanging on a tripod.

Lillian grimaced at the piercing sound of the brass bell clanging in the distance. She gritted her teeth, clutched Bridget's hand, and led Bridget toward the main entrance.

Bridget didn't hear the clinking of coins being dropped in the big kettle, or the people singing in the corner, and the pounding vibrations of the brass tuba made her grip her mother's hand tighter. The constant movement of people and flashing lights affected Bridget's equilibrium. Feeling dizzy, she stopped to catch her breath.

Lillian, oblivious to her daughter's anxiety, shoved her daughter toward the entrance.

When Bridget saw the huge glass doors spinning around, and around, and the people disappearing inside, she dug her heels in the snow. She refused to go forward, afraid of being devoured by the horrible doors that were swallowing people.

"Get in there. It can't hurt you." Lillian yelled as she yanked Bridget's hand.

Bridget, resisting in fear of her life, squatted on the sidewalk. She didn't hear the laughter as people passed by, ridiculing her with pointed finger. Nor, the stern remarks from a somber gentleman.

"Why do you allow that girl to throw a tantrum?" he grumbled.

Lillian, realizing it would be impossible to go through the revolving doors, scooped Bridget under her arm and carried her in, through the side door. "Why are you making such a fuss?" She plunked Bridget down in front of a glittering Christmas tree.

Bridget, fascinated by the Christmas wonderland, forgot her fear and calmed down.

The Christmas tree glowed with colorful blinking lights. Tiny winged fairies twirled on top of pedestals covered with fluffy white cotton. Small elves in green suits tapped their hammers on glittery cotton.

Bridget had never imagined such beauty. It was like the story books were coming alive.

"Now that you've calmed down, we can go upstairs to see Santa," Lillian said, as she grabbed Bridget's hand.

Bridget pulled back. I stay here, she signed.

Lillian clasped Bridget's hands together, silencing her before anyone would notice. "That's enough of that," she muttered under her breath, then shoved Bridget toward the escalator.

When Bridget saw the moving stairs, she let out a scream that echoed through the store. Panic-stricken with fear, she tried to free herself from her mother's grip. In her limited understanding, she believed her mother was putting her in harm's way, and the moving stairs would carry her into the unknown. Her only escape was within her own silence. She flopped down on the floor and covered her eyes with her hands.

Lillian was frantic. She grabbed Bridget, tucked her under her arm, and carried the child past the crowd of snickering faces. After a while, she set Bridget down in front of two highly polished brass gates.

Bridget opened her eyes and scanned the room. She wondered why the people were standing in front of the gates, and what are the red blinking lights on the wall? The lack of movement calmed her momentarily.

The tall metal gates slammed open.

Bridget felt the vibration of the gates opening, and it frightened her.

"Going up."

Bridget felt herself being jostled by the crowd, forced into a small room.

"Step to the back of the car, please." The door slammed shut.

Bridget, smothered by bulky, wool coats and poked by ladies' handbags, wondered why the people were standing still? A sudden jolt and an upward surge made her stomach feel peculiar. Because of her deafness, she again lost her equilibrium and stumbled forward. To keep from falling, she grabbed a lady's purse, sending the contents flying across the floor.

"I'm sorry," Lillian said, yanking Bridget's arm, prodding her to stand.

From Bridget's sitting position, she could see the woman's mouth spewing an unheard reprimand. In her effort to stand up, she clawed at the woman's silk stocking until they lay in folds around the woman's ankles. Bridget could tell by the expression on her mother's face she had done something wrong.

The elevator stopped with a sudden jerk. Two metal gates slid open.

Lillian grabbed Bridget's arm and dragged her out of the elevator. Halfway across the room, she stopped and cupped her hands on her temples.

Bridget, seeing the sickly look on her mother's face, signed to the people, pleading for help.

A crowd bustled past, ignoring the child's pleas.

Lillian, feeling light-headed, could not go further. The room grew dim. People faded into vague, blurry images. She crumbled to the floor.

Busy shoppers swarmed around the fallen customer.

Bridget tried squirming her way back to her mother, but was pushed aside. Not knowing where to go, she edged her way along a row of glass showcases until she found a dark space under a counter. To escape the trampling feet rushing past her, she crawled under the counter and covered her eyes. The silent darkness calmed her. She didn't know how long she had been asleep until a gentle nudge on her arm wakened her.

Edward peered under the counter with a wide smile.

A grateful smile slipped from Bridget's lips. She wrapped her arms around her father's neck and smothered him with kisses.

Edward turned to his wife who had overcome her fainting spell. "Come on. We're going home." He carried his daughter past the glittering Christmas trees, past the angels twirling on sparkling pedestals, and past the tiny green elves.

Lillian followed behind, barely keeping up with Edward's long, stride. Once outside, she pulled her fox-fur collar up, covering her face from the bitter wind. "Put that damn child down. She can walk," Lillian shouted, her voice muffled by her collar.

Edward ignored his wife and continued walking several paces ahead.

"She's too big to be carried like a baby. Look at those long legs dangling. Put her down. Now!" Lillian yanked her husband's arm, loosening his grip.

Edward glared at his wife as he eased Bridget to the pavement. Even though he wanted to defend his daughter, he held his tongue rather than make a fuss in public. He gripped Bridget' hand and led her toward the icy parking lot.

Bridget, spotting her father's Chrysler, dashed into the street. She didn't hear her father's scream, nor the shrill sound of squealing tires as a huge automobile swerved sideways. Glaring headlights rushed toward her like a sidewinder. Sharp pain raced through Bridget's body, and she was hurled to the pavement.

Bridget woke several hours later with her mother and father hovering over her bed.

Hilda, Sara, and the maids stood in the doorway.

Bridget turned away, angry at her father for letting her get hurt. She tried to move her hand. Panic showed in her eyes when she saw her arm covered in a stiff white bandage. She wanted to sign to Sarah, but her fingers were tightly bound in the bandage.

Sarah, seeing Bridget's hand rise, stepped forward to sign an explanation.

Lillian's head jerked up, sending a damning glare of resentment.

"I wanted to explain about the cast on her arm. She doesn't understand." Sarah stepped back in the doorway when she saw the scowl on Lillian's face.

Bridget remembered her mother pulling her arm until it hurt and wondered why she did this? What is this thing on my arm?

Is it to keep me from signing? Bridget's limited understanding led her to believe she was being punished; bound to silence by a stiff bandage.

Later that evening, Lillian tried to defend her actions. "I wanted her to see Santa. This is all your fault. I tried to prove I'm a good mother, and this what I get for trying."

"It's always about you. Bridget is the one who got hurt, not you." Edward, finding his wife's actions inexcusable, buried his face in the evening newspaper.

"It's all her fault. That child was horrible. She screamed every where I took her." Lillian, seeing the disgusted look on Edward's face, changed her tone of voice. "I don't understand that child," she whimpered. "Why does she cry when I do something nice for her?"

"What did you do?" Edward sputtered, slamming the newspaper down on his lap.

"That child wouldn't get on the escalator, and she made a fuss in the elevator. She even pulled some fat lady's stocking down."

Edward picked up his newspaper, shielding his grin. "Good for her," he snickered, picturing the woman's awkward position.

"Edward! That's not funny. I was so embarrassed I could have died."

"So you nearly killed my child."

"How can you say such a thing! I would never hurt my baby." Lillian again, softened her voice. "I love Bridget as much as you do. I tried to be patient, but she's impossible to handle."

Edward frowned in disgust.

"Do you hear me? Your daughter screamed so loud everyone could hear her. She embarrassed me. People were staring at me. That's why I became ill in the store."

"That's all I hear is me, me, me." Edward flipped the newspaper page with a quick snap and resumed reading.

"She hid from me. This would never have happened if that child did what I told her to do."

Edward's patience had reached its limit. "What she was told! How could you tell her anything? You refuse to speak so she can understand. No Lillian. It's your fault. Don't tell me you were ill because of her. It's you! You cause your own problems."

Lillian blotted the tears with her lace handkerchief. "Why doesn't anyone believe me? I was trying to be a good mother. Why do you always take her side?"

Edward slouched down in his chair. His wife's words turned into an irritating hum. Drumming at him. Building like a time bomb. He put his hands to his head and covered his eyes. *When will this end? When will I find peace for Bridget and me? I wish I could make her stop.* But, he didn't have the courage to speak up, and Lillian's voice droned on, and on.

Several days later Bridget explained to Sarah. Though she found it difficult with the heavy cast on her arm, she signed. "Moving stairs scared me Whirling glass doors swallowed people. It scared me. People pushed me away, so I hid."

"They didn't understand sign language," Sarah signed.

Images of trampling women flashed across Bridget's mind. "Christmas is horrible. Flashing lights make me dizzy. Why does my arm have a heavy bandage? Will I ever sign again?"

"The cast must stay on a while longer. Your hand will soon heal."

Edward was passing down the hall when he heard Sarah's voice. He opened the bedroom door and peeked in. "Is everything okay now?"

Sarah smiled, and closed her robe over her flannel nightgown.

Edward grinned and winked. "Does she understand now?" He opened the door a little wider, and was about to enter the room, when he heard footsteps coming up the stairs. He eased the door closed and hurried to the spare bedroom.

CHAPTER 17

On the 7th of December 1941, the radio blared the earth-shattering news; Japan bombed Pearl Harbor. The word spread like wildfire, consuming everyone's thoughts and conversations. The following day President Franklin D. Roosevelt declared war on Japan. Posters were pasted on billboards and telephone poles with a picture of Uncle Sam pointing his finger. The captions read; Uncle Sam want you! It encouraged young men to enlist in the Army. All Americans were advised to turn their lights off at night so the enemy couldn't see where to drop bombs. People were warned to watch their words, lest they reveal a service man's whereabouts.

The shocking news drew Lillian back to the parlor to listen to the radio broadcast. Once again, feeling a sense of purpose, she joined her family in moral support of their country.

Patrick threw down his snow shovel, packed a burlap bag and slung it his shoulders. He hurried to the parlor and proudly announced."Ma'am, I'm enlisting in the Navy."

"What about the yard work? And my garden?" Lillian demanded.

"Sorry ma'am. Tis my patriotic duty."

"When are you leaving?"

"Today."

Lillian's eyes lit up as a devious thought crossed her mind. "On your way out tell Sarah to come to the parlor."

"Yes ma'am. I'll see you after the war is over." Patrick tipped his hat and marched out of the room.

Minutes later Sarah entered the parlor. "You want to see me?"

"Patrick joined the Navy. You'll have to take over his chores."

"Yes ma'am. I can shovel the snow and still tutor your daughter."

"Never mind tutoring. Someone needs to run my errands."

"I can do that too."

"Shh. My husband's coming in the back door. Leave the room. Hurry," Lillian whispered, waving her hand, shooing Sarah out of the room.

Edward entered the parlor with a broad smile on his face. He draped his black wool over-coat across the couch and turned to his wife. "What a day. The government accepted my bid to build tanks. This will expand my business. I'll have to build more factories."

"My business? Don't you mean our business?"

"Yes. Yes. Of course. Our business."

"By the way, did you know Patrick joined the Navy?"

"He did? That's okay. I'll hire a handyman to take over this winter. We'll worry about your garden in the spring."

"I've taken care of that. Sarah's taking over Patrick's chores." Lillian folded her arms across her chest, waiting for husband's reaction.

Edward, annoyed at his wife's inconsiderate decision, raised his voice. "You expect Sarah to do a man's work? Have you forgotten about our daughter's education?"

"Sarah can do both," Lillian responded with a smirk to irritate her husband. "Teaching that kid can't be too difficult."

"You're not being fair. I'll hire a man to take over Patrick's chores."

"Ha! All the men are in the service."

"There are plenty seniors who would like the job."

Lillian scowled and her voice turned stoic. "Don't bother. Sarah's willing to do the yard work."

Edward's voice rose to a higher pitch. "Sarah can't do two jobs."

Lillian flung her book on the floor and pointed her finger at her husband. "I'm in charge of this damn house. Don't you dare interfere with my decision."

Startled by his wife's spiteful attitude, Edward backed away. Still determined to keep Sarah as a full-time tutor, he went behind Lillian's back and hired a handyman.

When Lillian met the handyman, she was furious. In the past she had always had her way and took this as a personal insult. Feeling stripped of her power, she was determined to get rid of Sarah.

The strain of the war affected everyone. Bridget's world turned upside down. Her father was seldom home to play the piano. The radio no longer vibrated with happy, foot-stomping music. And, it was especially upsetting when she placed her fingers against the side of the radio and felt the thumping vibration of a marching band.

"Who is this man called Uncle Sam?" Bridget signed. She had always been encouraged to speak, but now everyone was asked to be silent. "Why can't we talk? Why must we turn off the lights at night?"

Sarah explained what she could without frightening Bridget. The silent world of the deaf is confusing enough, and Sarah didn't want to add to the child's anxiety.

Bridget was left alone most of the time. She seldom saw her parents and didn't notice the lack of communication between them. Her world remained the same-silent

The excitement of the war vitalized Lillian health. To fill the void in her life, she began sponsoring patriotic charities. She used the limelight as an excuse to dress dramatically and to display her newly acquired jewelry, temporarily easing the stress of her failing marriage. Yet, she was determined to get Sarah out of the house. She waited until Edward was at work to approach Sarah.

"Why don't you do your patriotic duty? Get a job at a factory?"

"I have to tutor Bridget. She still needs help with reading."

"You can make good money," Lillian chirped with a spark of enthusiasm. "The factories are hiring women to work on the assembly line."

Sarah nodded with interest. "Well, it would make me more independent."

"The government is running buses right to the factories."

"But your daughter still needs my help."

Lillian, seeing she was losing ground, made the job more appealing. "What if you worked at the factory every day and tutored Bridget on the weekends? Would that please you?"

Sarah eyes widened, surprised at Lillian's generous offer. "It's okay if I work only weekends?"

"Yes, of course," Lillian replied quickly. "Then, it's agreed? You'll tutor Bridget part-time, on Saturdays and Sundays." Lillian left the room satisfied that she could keep her eye on Sarah, especially on the weekends.

Later that evening, Sarah waited behind the library door. "Psst," she whispered, motioning to Edward as he passed through the foyer.

Edward hurried toward the whisper and peered in the dark library. "Are you okay? Why are you standing in the dark?"

"I wanted to tell you before your wife did. I'm going to apply for a job. The factories are hiring women to work on the assembly line."

"What?" Edward's whispered, easing the library door closed. "You have a job here."

"Bridget is getting older. She won't need my help in the future."

"She's not ready to communicate with people yet."

"Since I've been running errands for your wife and doing chores too, there hasn't been a lot of time to teach Bridget."

"When did you decide on factory work?"

"Your wife said it's my chance to get a steady income."

"Lillian told you to get a job?"

"Not exactly. She suggested it." Sarah's head dropped submissively. "Your wife doesn't want me here, anyway."

"What is Lillian thinking? I'll take care of this," Edward grumbled as he marched toward the parlor.

Lillian, expecting an argument, was prepared. When Edward entered the parlor, Lillian was quick to call out. "What's the matter with you? You look so damn grumpy."

"Did you tell Sarah to get a job? Our daughter still needs tutoring."

Lillian jumped up and hurled her book on the floor. "It's done. Sarah agreed to move back with her mother. She's getting a factory job."

"Move back home? Oh no! She's staying right here." Edward's voice grew louder, more demanding. "Bridget needs a companion. Someone to help her deal with everyday problems."

Lillian clenched her teeth and set her hands on her hips. "It's too late. Sarah agreed to move. That's final."

"We'll see about that." Edward stormed out of the parlor angry and frustrated, determined to persuade Sarah to stay. He entered the kitchen and approached Sarah. "Please stay. My baby needs a live-in tutor."

"I'm being forced out. Can't you see that?"

Hilda and Ester glanced at each other, then turned their back to the conversation.

"Would it help if I hired *you* at my factory as a part-time employee? That way you can learn an office skill and still tutor Bridget. Lillian doesn't have to know where you're working."

Sarah's head bobbed up and down, thrilled at the prospect of working in an office and still have a secure job of tutoring. She turned to Hilda. "Please don't say anything to Misses Hansen."

Hilda nodded. "If that's what he wants, then it's okay with me."

Edward had been so engrossed in pleading with Sarah that he didn't realize the maids were in the kitchen. He turned to Hilda. "Of course, I want to keep this a secret. We're doing this for Bridget."

Several days later, Sarah approached Lillian. "I started a new job. I've been working three days a week. Is it okay if I tutor Bridget on the days I'm not working?"

"Well that's a start. You can do better. I'll help you find a full-time job."

Lillian, determined to get rid of Sarah for good, waited until everyone left for work, and slipped in Sarah's bedroom and rummaged through the dresser drawers. "There must be something I can use against her." She opened the top drawer and picked up a manila envelope. "Ah, what is this? Pay check receipts." She thumbed though the receipts and gasped. "That tramp isn't working at a factory. She's at our main office." Everything was becoming quite clear. Sarah had been at the office with her husband every day, alone.

Lillian waited at the kitchen door, ready to attack her husband when he arrived home. "You hired that tramp. Sarah's working at your office? Why is she getting two payroll check?"

Edward, still gripping the doorknob, stepped back in surprise. "What?"

"You heard me. What's going on?"

"Hush. The staff can hear you. Who told you about her salary?"

"None of your damn business. That girl isn't worth it."

"Sarah's working twice as hard." Edward closed the door and hurried through the kitchen to escape his wife's accusations.

"And another thing," Lillian shouted, trailing behind. "You went behind my back. You bought that tramp a car. You had no right to do that without my permission."

Edward stopped in his tracks, turned and lowered his voice. "Who told you I bought the car?"

"Well, she couldn't afford to buy it herself."

"Sarah needs transportation." Edward, stunned by his wife's bitterness, kept his voice stern while defending his actions. "Sarah needed a car to drive here every day. She still needs to teach Bridget."

"What good did it do?" Lillian chided. "That dumb child still can't talk."

His wife's attitude left him saddened and disgusted. "Can't you be more understanding? Maybe Bridget can't speak clearly, but she can communicate with us now."

"She talks like she's got a mouth full of marbles. A lot of good that sign language did!" Lillian, seeing her husband's face flush with anger, backed up and hurried out of the room.

Lillian spent the next several nights consumed with envy. She fingered the pearls hanging heavy on her neck, and like the grain of sand inside the clamshell, she couldn't get rid of the intruder. She pictured her husband and Sarah having a secret rendezvous at the office. Yet, she would not openly accuse him of adultery.

The need for war supplies increased, demanding longer hours at the office. Edward found himself in charge of an expanding enterprise beyond his wildest dreams. Overwhelmed with government contracts, he assigned his closest friend and attorney, Robert Michaels, to take charge of several renovated factories.

Lillian filled her evenings by attending public charities. With the much-needed attention she was receiving, she was easily persuaded to donate large amounts of money to the service-men's clubs. The Detroit News applauded her as the patriotic citizen of the year. After months of whirl-wind public charities, and swallowing aspirins to ease her headaches, the fast pace finally took its toll on her health.

Edward noticing his wife's pale complexion and irritability, confronted her. "You're wearing yourself to a frazzle. It's time you slowed down."

"I'm fine. You're not the only one who's important. We can afford to contribute money."

"It's not the money. I'm concerned about you."

"You're just jealous because I'm influential. My name is mentioned in the newspapers too."

"Those public appearances are killing you. You're tired all the time. You're neglecting Bridget."

Lillian, refused to slow down. Caught up in the limelight excitement, she continued entertaining until hospitalized with exhaustion. During her hospital stay, she demanded Edward visit her daily in spite of his busy schedule. This was her chance to demand his attention, and because he was in the public eye, he would have to comply.

Edward made his daily obligation day after day without complaint. "How are you today?" he asked as he entered the hospital room.

"I still feel exhausted. It takes time to get well."

"That's good. You need the rest."

Lillian leaned back and started to relax when she noticed a faint smile on her husband's face. Edward looked more robust and happier than usual. It didn't take long before she realized Sarah had been alone in her house with him. Lillian bolted up in bed. "I've changed my mind. I'm coming home today."

"Won't you stay a couple more days? You still don't look well."

"No! I want Sarah to quit working at your office. I'm too sick to watch that child. You know I can't speak that kid's language."

"I've hired a nanny for Bridget and another maid to help out. Sarah wants to work. Business is booming. We need the office help."

"I'll bet you do!" Lillian snarled. "Fire the maid and nanny. Sarah can do the work. We're paying her far too much, anyway."

"Please stay until you feel better."

"No! I'm going home today."

Edward huffed in disgust. "All right, if you insist. I'll hire a nurse for you, but I need Sarah at the office. She can tutor Bridget after work."

Lillian was released from the hospital that very day. Upon her arrival home, she exaggerated her illness, demanding unreasonable attention from the household staff, and especially from her husband. Still not well enough to resume her public appearances, and with the time on her hands, paranoia again took over. Lillian drew lewd conclusions of her husband's affair that was far from the truth. Lillian paced the bedroom each night consumed with envy. Still, she wouldn't accuse him of adultery, nor would she threaten him with divorce.

CHAPTER 18

———— •◆• ————

Bridget stood by the window watching the wind blowing crisp, brown leaves across the lawn. The vibration of a door slamming drew her attention. She ran to the window and saw Sarah and Ester walking toward the car with shopping bags in hand.

It was grocery day, and they would be gone for hours.

She tiptoed across the foyer and peeked in the parlor. When she was sure her mother was busy crocheting, she made her way up the stairs. Easing the door open, she crept into the room and sat down in front of the mirror. It had been a long time since she visited her magical garden. Bridget's imagination drew her into the fantasy world. In her mind's eye, she entered a field of colorful flowers. Deeper, and deeper, she drifted into the world of make-believe. Bridget had been in her garden a short time when a heavy, oppressive feeling swept across her shoulders.

The meadow took on a sobering darkness. Huge gray clouds, roiling and swirling in the distance, moved closer, siphoning the colors from the flowers.

A threatening sense of danger snapped Bridget back to reality. Once her imagination was outside the mirror, she saw a black silhouette reflected in the mirror.

Glaring, red eyes stared down at her. A wooden board loomed in the air.

Too frightened to run, Bridget lay her head on the vanity and covered her eyes.

The board crashed down, striking Bridget across the back, knocking her off the vanity bench.

Bridget clutched the back of her neck, looked up at the image and mouthed the words. "Mama?"

The ghoulish figure sent a message of fear with its eyes.

Confused and frightened, Bridget crawled toward the vanity-to the safety of her garden.

The menacing figure had moved and was now standing between her and the mirror. Again, a huge hand hovered in the air. Or was it a board? The hand crashed down, striking Bridget across the back.

A sharp pain pierced Bridget's neck, sending her reeling to the floor.

"Why Mama?" Bridget felt herself, as if in slow motion, lowering her head to the floor. She closed her eyes and a numbness spread through her body. She felt herself floating above the room, and a tranquil feeling surrounded her. Bridget opened her eyes and looked down at her mother standing over a lifeless body. Though she knew it was her dead body, she felt no anger about what had happened

A brilliant light radiated from within the glass mirror. Grandma Priscilla appeared beckoning with open arms.

Bridget drifted toward the light. Once inside the mirror, her magical garden became brilliant-alive with brilliant flowers. She took her grandmother's hand, drifting peacefully on a rainbow. As she floated in the light, the reality of His truth consumed her being. She connected to the universal knowledge. Became one with the God consciousness. Bridget understood she wasn't one person, but a part of all people; of all life forms; a part of the trees, the flowers, the clouds, and everything that emitted energy in God's light.

Bridget and her Grandmother disappeared into the light.

Lillian stood over the lifeless body for several minutes, too stunned to feel emotion. In a brief instant of clarity, the death scene became lucid, like a sobering decay.

What have I done? Got to get help. No, I can't. Someone will think I did this. I've got to be quiet. Got to wait.

Still in a state of shock, Lillian picked up the wooden board. *Got to hide the board.* She scanned the room *Where? Under the bed.* She tiptoed across the room and shoved the heavy board beneath the bed. Slivers of wood jabbed her fingertips as she pulled her hand away from the sinful object.

Got rid of the board. Now what do I do? Lillian moved as if in a nightmare, toward the lifeless body. *Can't let anyone know. Got to hide her.* She grabbed the vanity and tipped it forward, sending it crashing down to cover her guilt.

She waited. Listened.

The house remained quiet.

Who is home? She stretched her neck toward the door. *Can't hear anyone.* Still in a state of denial, she tiptoed down the hall, leaned over the banister and stared down the staircase.

The house remained eerily still. A faint voice on the radio announced the bombing in London.

When Lillian was sure no one was in the foyer, she crept down the staircase. Pausing at the bottom step, she tightened her grip on the handrail and listened. *Could someone point an accusing finger at me?*

A faint voice on the radio broke the silence. "Citizens! Remember to darken your windows at night so the enemy can't strike."

Lillian stood in the foyer listening. *Where's Hilda? Did she hear the vanity fall?* When she was sure no one was in the house, she tiptoed into the parlor.

The late afternoon sun disappeared behind the clouds, leaving the parlor dim and dreary. The room took on a depressing atmosphere.

Lillian flopped down on the sofa. Feeling faint, she gasped for air and heaved a dry cough. Time seemed to stand still. She waited in dead silence.

No sound came from the kitchen. Only the sound of the radio pouring out a warning. "Loose lips. Sink ships."

Lillian's thoughts drifted upstairs. *What should I do?* She picked up a brass crochet-hook, stabbed at the yarn and drew up a loop through the weave. Her hand trembled as she jabbed the thread, pulling it into a tight knot. Her insides screamed for this nightmare to end. Yet, she remained silent.

Why isn't someone coming? Why isn't Sarah back?

She wanted to run up the stairs and help her daughter, but could not move. *I must sit here until someone comes.* Lillian cocked her head.

A faint noise drifted from the kitchen.

Is someone coming?

The sound became clearer. Shuffling footsteps coming from the cellar broke the silence.

Hilda's coming to help. Hurry, Lillian screamed within her mind. She listened.

Slippers flapping on the steps grew louder. Clinking of glass jars being set on the porcelain sink. Hilda's voice softly chanting. "He's got the little tiny baby in his hands. He's got the whole world in his hands."

Lillian gripped the yarn, again jabbing at the afghan. She pulled the yarn so tight that she couldn't move the hook through the twisted fiber.

Hilda! Help my baby, Lillian's insides screamed. Again, her thoughts twisted, unable to accept reality. *How could someone do this to my child?* Her denial brought a surreal calmness. She brushed her hand across her hair and smoothed the wrinkles from her dress. *It's important I look presentable.* Calmly, with no feeling of remorse, she spread the half-finished afghan across her lap, took a deep breath and waited.

Several minutes passed.

The silence smothered her, making it difficult to breathe. After a while her thoughts cleared. Panic stricken, she felt as if the entire world was crashing down around her.

Be still, she thought. She tilted her head and listened.

The familiar sound of a door slamming echoed through the house.

They're back. Hurry Sarah! Hurry, her mind cried out. Yet, she could not move.

The sound of Sarah's voice in the kitchen. Footsteps passing through the dinning room, heading toward the foyer. Someone briskly climbing the stairs.

Lillian clutched her blouse, twisting it against her chest.

More sounds. Doors opening and closing.

She held her breath.

Sarah's scream pierced the silence. "Bridget! Oh, my God! Hilda! Help!"

Lillian waited until she heard Hilda's heavy footsteps stomping past the parlor. Then, she too, rushed toward the stairs. She paused at the bottom step and looked up.

The stairs appeared high, steep and unsteady. The hall overhead faded in and out of the darkness.

Lillian took another deep breath, then started up the stairs. When she reached the bedroom, Sarah was struggling to lift the mirror off Bridget's body.

Ester rushed in the bedroom, paused at the door and surveyed the situation. With a sudden burst of strength, she gripped the mirror and flung it off Bridget's body.

Lillian fell down on her knees and cradled the lifeless body-rocking and wailing uncontrollably.

Sarah, stunned with disbelief, lifted Bridget's wrist. At the touch of the cold, lifeless hand, the color drained from Sarah's face. "She's gone," Sarah whispered.

Upon receiving the news of Bridget's death, Edward rushed home. He dashed up the stairs and stood in the doorway. He shook his head, finding it difficult to accept what he was seeing.

Two medical attendants hovered over Bridget's body. Doctor Johnson was speaking to a man in a white jacket. Hilda, Sarah, and Ester stood in the corner weeping. Lillian glanced at her husband, searching his eyes, then turned away and flopped down on the bed.

"How did this happen," Edward wailed.

"I'm sorry you had to see this," the doctor said as he spread a white sheet over Bridget's face. He waved toward two men in white jackets. "You can take the body now."

The men lifted the small lifeless body onto a gurney and pushed it out of the bedroom.

Lillian rose from the bed, her eyes fixed on the floor as she followed the men down the hall.

"How could this have happened?" the doctor mumbled under his breath.

Edward, stunned by the tragedy, leaned against the doorway staring aimlessly across the room.

Lillian returned to the bedroom, her eyes cast down, refusing to look at her husband's face.

"Why don't you all go downstairs," the doctor said, shooing the family away with a sweep of his hand.

Sarah took Hilda's hand and led her down the stairs. Ester followed behind. Edward nodded and followed his wife down to the kitchen.

The doctor stayed behind and scanned the room, searching for clues.

The bedroom was clean. Nothing seemed out of place. The windows were closed. Curtains neatly in place. The bedspread slightly wrinkled. There were no signs of a disturbance. The mirror and vanity had been placed against the wall.

He gripped the mirror and shook it. The vanity stood steady, and the mirror remained attached to its wooden post.

After the doctor finished analyzing the scene, he joined the family in the breakfast room. "Call your household staff. I want to talk to them," he said to Lillian.

Lillian gestured with a weak smile and left the room. She entered the maid's kitchen, braced her hand on the door-jamb to steady herself, and leaned in the doorway. "Everyone in the breakfast room. The doctor wants to talk to you."

The doctor waited until Lillian and the staff returned before he spoke. "Did anyone hear Bridget fall? Did she cry out?"

Hilda gripped her apron, twisting it through her fingers. "No sir. I was in the cellar getting canned food for supper."

"That child is always climbing on things," Lillian interrupted.

Edward grabbed the table to steady himself and flopped down in a chair. "Wasn't anyone here? Didn't anyone see her fall?"

"No sir. Sarah and Ester were at the grocery store," Hilda explained.

"Perhaps something frightened Bridget," Sarah said in a low voice. "Maybe she bumped the vanity, and it fell."

"She must have stumbled and knocked the vanity down," Lillian added, dabbing her eyes with a lace handkerchief.

Doctor Johnson made it a point to look at Lillian when he spoke. "May I suggest you sleep in another bedroom tonight?"

Lillian glared at the doctor, arched her back and clenched her jaw. "I'll decide where I will sleep."

"You can take the guest room," Edward offered, his voice meek and sympathetic.

"And, where will you sleep? On the couch?" Lillian snarled as she stormed out of the room.

"There's nothing else I can do here tonight. I gave your wife a sedative. She's still quite edgy." Doctor Johnson headed toward the foyer. "Phone me if your wife needs help."

Edward nodded. "Thank you, doctor. I'll watch her."

The doctor left the house with unanswered questions racing through his mind. He found it difficult to believe a small child could have the strength to topple the vanity, and that the mirror was heavy enough to strike with such deadly force. The accident shed a veil of doubt in his mind. Although the doctor had suspicions, he signed the death certificate an accidental death. The Hansen's were influential and highly respected in the community, and he dared not raise a hint of suspicion.

CHAPTER 19

—◆•◆•◆—

Lillian pointed to the parlor window. "Hang the purple drapes over that window. Put the casket there too," she said to the funeral director.

Edward stood in a corner of the room and listened to his wife giving directions. *Her voice sounds cold and detached from emotion,* he thought. *Perhaps it's the tranquilizers.* He waited until the man left then approached his wife. "I don't think you should sleep in your bedroom. You can spend the night with me in the guest room," he said.

"I can do what? What do you mean, I can? Don't you dare pity me."

Edward, overcome with grief, had given little thought to his words, or what they might imply. He didn't mean the invitation to sound pompous or arrogant. He was at a loss for words. Secretly, he was relieved Lillian refused to spend the night with him. "I'm sorry. I didn't mean to . . . ."

"I'll sleep where I damn well please," Lillian snarled.

Edward glanced at Sarah standing in the foyer. Her face was hidden in the shadows, and the only thing he could see were the soft folds of her blue dress. He raised his hand to attract her attention and called softly across the room. "You'll stay on for a while, won't you?"

Lillian turned with a jerk, sending a damning look of disapproval.

Sarah stepped out of the shadows and nodded. "Just until the burial. Then, I'm going home." Seeing the hateful look on Lillian's face, she stepped back to give the grieving couple their privacy.

Lillian's head dropped and her eyelids started closing. She wanted to reprimand her husband, but the tranquilizers were taking effect. Feeling too disorientated to protest, she headed toward the foyer. As she approached the stairs, she gave Sarah a look of disgust then stomped up the stairs.

"Meet me in the dining room later," Edward said to Sarah. He waited until his wife retired for the evening before turning off the parlor lights. After his eyes adjusted to the dark, he groped his way across the room.

A beam of moonlight shone through the French doors, barely lighting the dining room. A shadowy figure stood by the window.

Feeling his way in the darkness, he headed toward the image. "Please don't leave," he whispered.

Sarah stretched her arms toward Edward. "I'm not needed here anymore."

"Don't let me lose you too," Edward slid his hands around Sarah's waist, drawing her close.

"I'm leaving right after the funeral." The sound of Hilda's footsteps crossing the breakfast room, made Sarah step back in the shadows.

Edward waited until the sound receded toward the kitchen. He grasped Sarah's hands and again drew her close. He wanted to beg her to stay, but knew it would be impossible.

Sarah nestled her mouth against his ear. "My happiness is gone, just as yours is."

"What will you do? Where will you go?"

"I'll find employment somewhere."

"You can work in my office." The pitch of his voice rose. "Say you will. I want you in my life forever."

"Yes. Oh, yes." Sarah heaved a sigh of relief. "Give me a few days then I'll apply."

"You don't need to apply. I'll make the arrangements." The sound of Hilda's footsteps returning to the kitchen made Edward step back in the shadows.

"I'll see you in the morning," Sarah whispered.

Edward stood in the darkness watching Sarah's shadow moving across the room. After she left, he felt hollow, almost empty. He shoved his hands in his pocket and made his way upstairs to the guest bedroom.

Three days later the velvet drapes were removed from the window and the black wreath taken off the front door. Even though the floral arrangements had been left at the burial site, the sickly odor of flowers still lingered in the parlor.

The next morning, Sarah packed her luggage, set them in the foyer and made her way to the kitchen. "I'm leaving," she said to Hilda.

Hilda wrapped her arms around Sarah. "We're all going to miss you."

"I hoped to talk to Edward before I left. Is he here?"

"No. He went to work early this morning."

"I'm surprised he's returning to work so soon. Perhaps it's best. Maybe it will keep his mind off losing Bridget."

Ester stood in the corner and lowered her head submissively. "I'll miss you too," she whispered

The next morning, Lillian woke with a throbbing headache. The tranquilizers had left her groggy and despondent. She placed her arm over her face, blocking out the morning sunlight. She was tired of the war; of noisy factories and smoke stacks that spew black soot in the air. Most of all, she was tired of competing for her husband's affection. Voices in the foyer drew her attention. She lifted her head off the pillow and listened.

Sarah and Ester were at the front door whispering their goodbyes.

Bittersweet memories came to mind. Lillian remembered how it used to be before Sarah came; when Bridget had terrible tantrums and her screams sent the household in a frenzy. How hectic it was in those days. Even though her daughter had learned to communicate, Lillian still regarded Sarah as an intruder.

The front door closed softly.

My husband will come back to me now, she thought. *After all, wasn't it Sarah who stole him from me? Wasn't it Sarah who stole my child's love? Lillian* heaved a sigh of relief. *Now, I'll be alone with Edward. Alone, like it used to be. Reality* edged its way back, and left her feeling uncertain. *I wonder if he will return to our bedroom?*

As the weeks passed, Lillian spent most of the time in her bedroom. Tranquilizers dulled her senses, allowing most days to pass without remorse or guilt. However, even with the sedation, there were times when she looked in the mirror and imagined it crashing to the floor. On those nights, she would wake from a horrible nightmare, crying for someone to rescue Bridget.

Tonight Edward woke to Lillian's loud scream. He dashed down the hall and barged into the bedroom. "You've got to move to a different room. It's not healthy to sleep here."

"No. This is my room."

"We'll sell the house."

"No! This is my home. I designed it. I'm staying here."

"The neighborhood is changing. There are race riots in Detroit. We can buy a larger place in the suburbs where we'll be safe."

Though Edward tried, he couldn't convince Lillian to move out of the bedroom, or sell the house.

Weeks passed and the war escalated. Edward accepted another government contract to manufacture war supplies. To suppress his loneliness, he worked longer hours at the office, creating a barrier between Lillian and himself. At the end of the fourth week, he found it unbearable to return home to the somber silence. He began spending the weekends with Sarah at an elegant resort in the suburbs.

"I can't live with my wife anymore," Edward said. "It's too depressing."

Sarah wrapped her arms around him and replied softly, "I understand. Without the sound of Bridget's laughter, I would feel lonely, too."

"And without you, the place feels empty."

"I'm sorry. I wish I could help. What are you going to do?"

"I'll file for a divorce as soon as Lillian feels better. Then, we'll get married."

"How can we make plans? Your wife is still having night terrors."

"That's because she's still sleeping in that damn bedroom. I asked her to sleep in the guest room."

"What did she say?"

She almost agreed until I mentioned sleeping in the room you once had. Oh boy. She went crazy. Ranting and raving like a maniac." Edward's shoulders drooped, and his head fell forward in disgust. "I need to get away from her."

"It's too soon. Don't make any hasty decisions."

"I know you're right. We have to wait until Lillian is more stable."

By the middle of July, Hilda became concerned about Lillian's strange behavior. "It's time to take the mirror out of your wife's bedroom."

"Why? Does she cry when she sees it?" Edward asked.

"No. That's not the problem. You're never home. You don't know what's going on. The missus hardly comes downstairs anymore. She just stares in the mirror and acts peculiar."

"What do you mean peculiar?"

"Sometimes, it sounds like she's talking to Bridget. I'm worried about the missus."

"I'll take care of it," Edward mumbled under his breath. A twinge of guilt crossed his mind when he saw the startled look on Hilda's face. He didn't mean to sound so blunt, but the words just slipped out. "I'm sorry, but I'm fed up with Lillian's refusal to help herself." Edward softened his voice. "I'll talk to her again about moving."

The following morning, Edward again approached his wife. "You've got to move out of that room. It's making you sick."

Lillian's eyes narrowed to a squint, and she sent him a damning glance. "I'll do as I please."

"We'll see about that," Edward grumbled as he grabbed his keys and stormed out of the house.

Edward hurried to his office and made arrangements with a local moving company. Because the mirror was a family heirloom, he decided to store it in the attic. The following morning he returned leading four burly men into the foyer.

Hilda, hearing noises in the foyer, hurried to the front door. "What's going on? Who are those men?"

"Where's my wife?" Edward whispered.

Hilda replied in a low voice. "She's in the breakfast room."

"Keep her there until I get that damn mirror out of her bedroom."

Hilda's head bobbed up and down. "Yes, sir." Though she felt guilty about the deception, she turned and scurried back to the kitchen.

"Go up those stairs and wait for me," he said to the movers, pointing to the staircase. "And for God's sake be quiet."

The men nodded and plodded lightly up the steps.

Edward guided the men into Lillian's bedroom. "Grab that vanity. Follow me," he said with a wave of his hand.

"Do you want me to unbolt the mirror from the vanity first?" the young man asked.

"Okay," Edward whispered. "But hurry."

The young man pulled a screwdriver from his pocket and the older man held the frame steady. Together they loosened the bolts. Within minutes, they detached the mirror from the vanity.

"Up there," Edward said, pointing to a door at the end of the hall.

The men followed Edward up the narrow stairway, into the dimly lit attic. "Put it over there," he said, pointing toward a dark corner.

"Do you want us to bolt it together again?" the man asked.

"No. Just lean it against the wall." Edward flipped a white sheet in the air, letting it float across the wooden frame. "Be quiet," he said as he hurried the men toward the stairs. "Close the door quietly on your way out."

The older man smiled curiously and waved his hand toward the other men. "Let's go."

After the men left, Edward locked the attic door and placed the key over the frame. Just as he started down the hall, he heard a sound in the foyer. He leaned over the balcony and saw Lillian slip behind the library door.

Weeks later, Lillian appeared to have recovered from her reclusive behavior. Whether it was the new medication or the removal of the mirror, she resumed her charity work.

Edward was finding it difficult to come home to an empty house each evening. Without his daughter, the house seemed depressing. He felt guilty about his adulterous affair and uncomfortable facing his wife. Needing a place to escape, he secretly purchased a magnificent house in the northern suburbs of Detroit.

"This is for you," he said, handing Sarah the deed. "It's safe from the racial turmoil in the inner city."

"We can spend our weekends together. I'll call it our love cottage," Sarah cooed.

Edward hoped the peaceful setting would bring back the passionate moments they had once shared, but the rendezvous seemed strained. Though he didn't speak of his loss, the circumstances of his daughter's death cast a shroud of depression over him.

After several months passed, Edward attributed his amorous restraint to the overwhelming business demands. Yet, he knew it was the loss of his daughter that had curbed his passion. He began to visit Sarah less often. Even though their physical relationship had lessened, he still held a place in his heart for her.

CHAPTER 20

Lillian began to fit the pieces together. Her husband's lack of communication, working overtime, and his time away from home, made it imperative she find out where he went on weeks ends. Her hand trembled as she dialed the phone. "Hello. Is this the detective agency?"

"Yep. Pete Rizzo detective agency. How can I help you?" a gruff voice answered.

"I want a woman followed. Her name is Sarah Woodward. Find out where this home wrecker lives and, what she's doing."

"Okay! Do you have any current addresses? Tell me what you know."

"I have her mother's address. You can start there."

"How quick do you want the information. Real quick will cost extra."

"I'm not concerned about the price. Find out what she's up to. Where she goes."

"I'm on it as soon as I receive a check for five hundred dollars."

"Start now. I'll have the cash delivered today."

The following day Detective Rizzo phoned Lillian. "I finished my investigation. Miss Woodward is working at the Hansen Tool and Die building. She must be a big shot. Nice swanky office."

Lillian gasped to catch her breath "What? At his office? What else did you learn?"

"She's living in a real nice apartment in Harper Woods. Respectable affluent neighborhood."

"Well, I'm not surprised."

"Do you want me to dig deeper?"

"Yes! Find out where she goes on weekends?"

By the time Edward arrived home that evening, Lillian had worked herself into a frenzy. She waited in the kitchen and attacked him at the door. "That home-wrecker is working in your office? Did you think I wouldn't find out?"

Edward's eyes widened and his heart pounded in his chest. "What the hell is the matter?"

"I see what's going on."

"Nothing is going on," Edward replied, shaking his head in denial.

"Either stop seeing that woman or I'll file for a divorce."

Edward stepped back, taken off guard by Lillian's threat. He grabbed his chest and took a deep breath. After giving his wife's threat a second thought, a calmness swept over him. "Go ahead. File. If that's what you want."

Lillian stumbled backwards, shocked by his unexpected response. "You can't do this," she cried as she bolted from the room.

That night Lillian paced the floor, hell-bent on making him pay for his adultery. The following morning she made an appointment with an attorney, Harry Shilling. She had used him for personal matters in the past and had been satisfied with his legal expertise.

Lillian barged in Shilling's office. "I want a divorce!"

Harry Shilling, a short, gray-haired man, leaped from behind his desk. "Misses Hansen! What are you saying?" Shilling feigned a feeble smile and led her to a chair. "What's this all about?"

"You know what it's about. Everyone knows."

Shilling lowered his voice reassuringly. "Now Misses Hansen. I've known you for many years. Perhaps you're overreacting."

"No. I'm not." Lillian slammed her fist on the desk. "I know he's seeing that tramp."

"You don't know that for sure, do you?" Shilling edged his way behind his desk, putting distance between them.

"No. I can't prove it." Lillian collapsed in a chair. "A wife knows these things."

Shilling straightened a stack of papers on his desk, avoiding eye contact as he spoke. "Now, lets take this slow. We have to talk about this."

"Edward hasn't slept with me in years. Ever since that damn girl came to work for us. She's just a teacher," Lillian said with a disgruntled scowl. "A young, stupid girl. She teaches sign language. Isn't that pathetic?"

Shilling forced a condescending grin, but gave no credence to her accusations. "I understood your daughter was learning . . ., ah, I mean. I heard you were feeling better after this woman took over."

Lillian's forehead creased to a frown. There it was again. That same senseless grin. She was never sure if he was smiling, or smirking. She was especially annoyed at the way he artfully dodged issues that were not in his best interest. "I didn't need anyone to help me. I was quite well until that hussy came to our house. That woman caused my illness."

"Let's not rush into this."

"Don't you see! Edward is pushing me into this. I think he wants a divorce."

Harry Shilling listened to Lillian's side of the story, knowing more than he dared disclose. "Let's wait until I research this more closely. If there's any truth to what you're saying, we'll take a serious look at the matter." Schilling leaned forward and lowered his voice. "You have a great deal to lose if you file."

Lillian stood up and clutched the back of the chair to steady herself. "I want a divorce," she demanded firmly.

"Please, let me give you some advice. There's so much money involved. It's in your best interest to remain his wife. He gives you everything you want, doesn't he?"

Lillian thought about his question and nodded reluctantly. The reassuring tone of his voice calmed her momentarily. "He's never refused me anything."

"Let's forget about this for the time being."

Lillian nodded in agreement until Shilling's peculiar smirk brought her back to her senses. "No! Either he stops seeing her, or I want him out of my house."

"You can't chase a man out of his own home. What if he fights you? Do you know how many attorneys he has on his staff? Do you realize how powerful he is? You could lose everything."

"Don't you dare threaten me! I want him to stop seeing that woman."

"Let's not rush into anything." Shilling began a long, tedious lecture, careful not to side with her, nor her husband. "If we can't get this matter resolved, I'll intercede on your behalf."

After Lillian left his office, Shilling mulled over the consequences. He was in a serious dilemma, and his first concern was to maintain a good relationship with the Hansen Corporation. He called his co-worker into his office. "Gordon! Better get over here. We need to talk."

Gordon Goldstein, a tall, gray-haired gentleman entered the room, lowered his spectacles and raised his bushy eyebrows. "What's going on?"

"Lillian Hansen was in my office today. She found out her husband and that young girl are running around. I think I talked her out of a divorce."

"A divorce?" Goldstein bellowed as he hurried across the office. "What the hell brought this on?" Goldstein stared hard at his friend waiting for an answer. He slid his hands deep in his pockets and started fingering several coins nervously. "Are you going to defend her?"

Shilling slid his chair back and headed toward the bookcase. "No. I'm not sure what do to."

"You could make a lot of money, if you do."

"It's not worth losing my relationship with the Hansen Corporation."

"Whew. What a pickle."

"She was serious. Mad as hell." Shilling scanned the shelves, pulled out several law books and slammed them on the desk. "We have to nip this in the bud."

Goldstein stopped jingling the coins and braced his hands on Shilling's desk. "You don't want *me* to help you, do you?" A serious expression crossed his face. "Are you ready to match your wits against his staff? They can be brutal."

"I know! I've thought of that," Shilling grumbled.

Goldstein stepped back as if to remove himself from the responsibility. "You can't let that woman file for divorce. Maybe you should tell him what's going on."

"Tell him? I can't do that," he grumbled as he thumbed through the pages. "I should have stopped her, but this whole mess took me by surprise."

"You should have scared the crap out of her. That's what you should have done."

"I'm not about to attack his wife. He's got a streak of . . ., ah, I guess compassion is the word. He might not like it if we're too hard on her."

"We? What do you mean, we?" Goldstein shrieked.

"I need help. We can't let her take control of his assets. There's too damn much money involved here," Shilling said as he continued thumbing through the pages.

"What are you looking for?"

"There must be a legal opinion or a precedence case we can use. We have to stop her from taking legal action."

"How many shares of stock are in her name?"

"I researched that already. Too damn much. That woman could split the corporation. She was a bitch today. Vindictive as hell."

"You better talk to him. Convince him his wife isn't thinking straight," Goldstein mumbled as he edged his way across the office.

"She asked me to be her personal counselor." Shilling slammed the book closed. "I should have convinced her that his attorneys will tear her apart. They'll make her look incompetent."

"You can't let her file," Goldstein called out, his hand gripping the doorknob, ready to bolt.

"You're damn right, I can't. I'm caught in the middle. If I represent her, I have to battle Hansen's attorneys. If I refuse to represent her, I'm deep shit too."

"You're in trouble," Goldstein muttered under his breath as he closed the door behind him.

Later that morning, after much hesitancy, Shilling requested a private meeting with Edward. Although he knew it was illegal, and he was violating the client-attorney privilege, he relayed Lillian's request. "Your wife wants a divorce."

Edward glanced up and his eyes widened. "What! She does?"

"She knows about the other woman."

"What does she know?"

"She's ready to charge you with adultery. If your wife files, she could put a hold on your executive decisions." Shilling's voice rose, exaggerating the possible consequences. "That could mean financial losses." Feeling weak in the knees, he lowered his voice. "Is it okay if I sit down?"

Edward nodded.

Shilling continued. "A scandal like this could send your stock crashing."

A hollow feeling coursed through the pit of Edward's stomach. "She really wants a divorce?" A slight smile crossed his lips and a sense of calm swept over him. The thought of losing Lillian seemed unimportant, almost a relief.

"This is serious!" Shilling grumbled. "Fault divorce is the law. You're at fault. You have to cool it with that girl."

Edward stared down at his desk, shook his head and murmured, "I don't think I can."

"What?" Shilling bolted out of his seat. "Has she got something on you? Is she pregnant?"

Edward's jaw dropped, taken off guard by the derogatory accusation. "No! She doesn't have anything on me. I won't give her up. And that's, that!" Edward, stunned by the attorney's comment, leaned back in his chair, unable to find the proper words to defend Sarah.

"Now, Mister Hansen. I know she's a beautiful woman. I mean, she's real nice and all. But, let's be rational. At least slow down. Be more discreet. A public trial would expose you and the girl. We don't want to embarrass your girlfriend, do we?"

Even with the threat of divorce, Edward felt an inner calm. "I'll talk to Lillian."

"No! You better not!" Shilling interrupted. "You can't tell your wife I confided in you. Why don't you make her feel more important? Maybe she'll forget about the divorce. Take this seriously."

"All right, I'll give Lillian more attention. But I won't stop seeing Sarah."

"I'll convince your wife to wait. That'll give you time to get your books in order. Anything else I can do?"

"Don't mention this to the other attorneys. I'll take care of it." After Shilling left, Edward mulled over the consequence of a divorce. He picked up the phone and called, Robert, his close friend and personal attorney. "I have a problem. Come to my office. Bring several staff attorneys with you."

Several hours later, after a long discussion, each attorney reaffirmed that during the divorce, Lillian could interfere. Edward could lose part control of his executive position.

"You're a public figure," Robert said. "Your relationship with Sarah would be spread across the newspapers. She'll be named your paramour."

"I don't want Sarah involved."

"She is involved."

Edward nervously fingered the papers on his desk, but said nothing.

"You've got a real explosive situation here," Robert advised. "Try to keep your meetings with this woman under cover. The courts must comply with Fault Divorce. It's the law."

"I can't give up Sarah," Edward mumbled. *How can I explain this isn't Sarah's fault? She was young and innocent when all this started.* Yet, he knew being naïve was not an excuse in the court of law.

Robert continued. "If the newspapers get a hold of this, it could mean trouble. Not just for you, but for Sarah. I'm concerned they'll print this as a sleazy sexual affair."

"How do I file for divorce and still protect Sarah from a scandal?"

"File! A divorce will affect your stock."

"Why are you considering financial issues? Why aren't you protecting Sarah? Keep her name out of the newspapers."

Robert's voice turned somber. "My advice is to stop seeing her."

"I can't," Edward replied as he gazed aimlessly across his desk.

Robert raised his eyebrows and glanced at the other attorneys, but refrained from pursuing the issue any further. "You have no choice if you want to protect Sarah."

"You mean if my wife files for divorce? But, if Lillian thinks my affair ended, she won't have a reason to file."

"If your wife finds out you're protecting Sarah, she could force your hand. You might have to offer a larger settlement. That means handing over more control. More stock. Is it worth it to keep Sarah's name out of the news?"

"I understand what you're saying," Edward whined. "I need those controlling shares of stock."

Robert pointed his finger at Edward. "Financially, you stand to lose a lot."

"I don't want Sarah involved in this mess."

"It would be wise to end relationship. That way, Sarah won't be named your paramour."

Edward rocked back in his chair. "How am I going to tell her?" he murmured under his breath.

"On second thought, it might be wise to keep quiet. Don't tell Sarah anything. If this ever goes to trial, Sarah can only say that *you* ended the relationship."

"Just avoid Sarah?"

"Stay away from her. Convince your wife the affair ended. Do it! Any way you can."

The following morning after a restless night, Edward arrived early at the office. He stopped by his secretary, Betty Chalmers' desk. "Refuse Sarah's phone calls. Use my busy schedule as an excuse."

Betty glanced up, startled at the request. "What! Just for today?"

"No! Refuse all calls," Edward grouched as he picked up the morning mail. He kept his eyes on the envelopes, avoiding his secretary's curious stare.

"Oh, okay." Betty, hearing the emotional sound of Edward's voice, dared not pursue the issue.

The following week, Sarah was puzzled by her unanswered phone calls. When Edward failed to show up at the cottage, she wondered if she had done anything wrong. Late one Friday afternoon, she waited until the staff had left the building, determined to hear an explanation. When his office door opened, she grabbed Edward's arm, preventing him from leaving.

"What have I done? Why haven't you returned my phone calls?"

Edward yanked his arm away and hurried into his office. He turned his back so Sarah wouldn't see the anguish he was feeling. "It's over. I can't keep up this charade. I can't do it anymore." *How can I explain I'm doing this to protect her?* He turned to Sarah, his voice cold and somber. "I'm not the person you think I am."

Sarah's voice quivered as she spoke. "You're not divorcing Lillian, are you? You never intended to, did you?"

"That's not it. I can't divorce her. If I do, she could be granted the controlling shares of stock." Edward held his hands up defensively. "It's a complex situation. It's a mess, Sarah."

Tears welled up in Sarah's eyes.

Edward wanted to hold her. To tell her he still loved her, but he cast his eyes down and spoke softly. "It's over."

"This all comes down to money, doesn't it?" Sarah replied, holding back the tears.

Edward stared at the floor and did not answer.

"If it's over, transfer me to a different building. I can't continue working here, in your office."

Edward nodded, and an empty feeling washed over him. Though it was the hardest thing he had ever done, he managed to get the words out. "It will be on your desk in the morning."

On Monday morning, Sarah began her new job as office manager at a building across town. The office was impressively elaborate, private, and closed off from the rest of the staff. She felt uncomfortable because the employees knew of her relationship with Edward. Sarah didn't defend her reputation, nor tell them the affair had ended. She never thought of herself as a mistress. Never meant to fall in love. It was just something that grew out of admiration. Though pleased with the new arrangements, she thought it had been a payoff; a way to appease her for ending their affair.

After several weeks, with no contact from Edward, she removed her clothes and personal items from the country home.

Edward opened the morning mail. "Sarah transferred the title to the county house back in my name," he said to Robert.

"Good. That shows you have no connection on paper with her. We don't want a paper trail. Keep your distance from her."

As time passed, Edward, feeling guilty for his unexplained departure, stayed informed of Sarah's needs and repeatedly increased her salary. He intended she remain financially secure and wasn't about to explain his actions to his staff.

CHAPTER 21

To take his mind off his daughter's death, Edward began spending longer hours at the office. After months of overwork, the stress finally caught up with him. He needed to get away from the house, away from the rooms where his daughter once played, and his wife's abrasive attitude. One spring morning, Edward took a long drive to northern Michigan. Winding roads cut across hilly fields, leading to the high cliffs overlooking the crystal clear water of Lake Michigan.

Traverse City had become the tourist's spot for vacationers. The cherry trees were in full bloom and the tourist roamed the local stores.

He registered at the Park Place Hotel, and after consuming more drinks than usual, he returned to his room. The quiet evening was passing much too slowly, so he decided to visit a local tavern.

"New in town?" the bartender asked, quick to notice the expensive suit and a gold chain dangling from the watch-pocket.

"Just for the weekend. Scotch and water on the rocks."

"Yes sir. My name is Joe. One scotch. Coming up."

"Too damn much pressure down-state," Edward mumbled as he tilted the glass to his lips.

"Yeah. This war is getting on everyone's nerves."

"War hell! How about a wife that's worse than the war? Fill it up again," he said shoving his glass across the bar.

Joe filled the glass to the brim, leaned his elbows on the bar, giving Edward his full attention. "Oh, marital problems?"

"My wife is . . ., oh never mind. I just had to get away."

"Yeah. Wives will drive ya crazy. Ya must have a lot on your mind."

After the second drink, Edward loosening his inhibitions, and the words came unrestrained. "My daughter died. Now there's talk of divorce."

"Oh, I'm sorry. How did your daughter die?"

Edward gazed aimlessly around the room. "Don't know. One day she's here, and the next day she's gone."

"Was she sick?"

"No. Did you ever hear of a mirror falling on a person and killing them?"

"Wow. It must have been a big one," Joe replied as he held the bottle in front of Edward. "Fill it up again?"

"The mirror isn't that big. That's what bothers me. It isn't heavy enough to kill a person."

"Oh. And you think your wife. Ah, I mean. How the hell did it happen?"

"My wife claims she didn't hear it fall."

"She didn't hear it?"

"That's what she said."

Joe leaned closer. "And you think she heard it, huh?"

"What?" Edward gasped, taken back by the accusation. The thought of his wife's guilt never entered his mind. "No! No," he blurted out, defending the inappropriate accusation.

The bartender, seeing he startled Edward, backed away. "I mean, you must have a big house. My apartment is small. I hear everything that's going on."

"I was so upset, I don't remember what happened that day." Edward lowered his voice. "Maybe, deep down, I blame her. She was home." Edward softened his voice. "It's hard to believe she didn't hear a thing."

"Now you're afraid your wife will divorce you, huh?"

"Not sure. I think she wants to keep control of the money."

The bartender raised his eyebrows at the mention of money. "Say, our annual cherry festival dance is next week. Why don't you come back and join us?" Joe turned his back and winked at the red-haired waitress.

Within seconds, a saucy woman was leaning her voluptuous breasts over the bar. "Hi," she said with a wide smile as she wiggled in front of him. "My name's Marilyn. I'll be your waitress. Can I get you anything else?" she murmured in a sexy voice.

"Thinking of staying for dinner. What's on the menu?"

Marilyn smiled and moved her tongue sensually over her upper lip. "Whatever you want," she cooed in a breathy voice. "I get off at eleven."

Later that evening, Edward wined and dined the waitress. After a few more drinks, and losing all his inhibitions, he invited her to his suite. It didn't take long before he fell willingly to her seduction.

The following week, Edward returned upstate and sought out the same waitress.

Marilyn, seeing Edward entering the bar, greeted him with a big smile and set a glass on the bar. "Last week you said you're getting a divorce. Are you?" she cooed as she poured out a generous shot of scotch.

"My wife is just threatening, that's all," Edward replied.

"Maybe she still loves you."

Edward took a large gulp and placed the glass firmly on the bar. "She'll never give me my freedom."

Marilyn placed her hand on Edward's and squeezed gently. "Why don't *you* divorce her?"

Edward jerked his hand away and shoved the glass across the bar. "I can't. She's deeply invested in the family business." After consuming several more drinks, he felt relaxed enough to ramble on, and on. "I can't get a divorce unless I prove my wife is at fault."

"Well, then find her at fault. A little lie never hurts anyone," Marilyn interrupted.

"My wife has done nothing wrong. I have. The law says someone has to be charged with fault, and she may refuse to charge *me*. Strange law, huh?"

"Well, what if she finds out about me, she might divorce you," Marilyn snapped.

"Lillian will never give up her life-style."

"Poor baby. How can I help you? Just tell me," Marilyn murmured as she leaned closer.

Edward, feeling her hot breath on his face, backed away. "I've had too much to drink. I'm just blabbering about something that can't be. She'll never divorce me. I'll never have children as long as I'm married to her."

"You don't have any children?" Marilyn squeaked, her voice reaching a high pitch.

"I've wondered about this. Maybe she never wanted children."

"Why? Did she have an abortion?"

Edward's head shot up, and he stared curiously at Marilyn. "What! No. She convinced me we couldn't have kids, so I accepted it." Edward's voice trailed off to a whisper. "I don't know."

"Some women don't care about kids. Now me. I love kids, and I'm still young."

"Forget it. There's someone else. I'm not that drunk," Edward grumbled as he tossed several large bills on the bar and headed for the door.

Edward's weekend escapades became a habit. He began bar hopping, acquiring a reputation as a hard drinker and a free spender. Within weeks the alcohol took over and repressed his moral ethics. Edward smothered his sorrow with booze and wild nights, allowing the pendulum of restraint to swing out of control.

Soon, another waitress caught wind of Edward's marital problems and began escorting him to nightclubs.

On these unrestrained rendezvous, Edward found a temporary escape from the loss of Bridget, and of Sarah, but, in the sobering mornings his Bohemian lifestyle weighed heavy on his conscience. He felt repentant and regretted his immoral actions.

After many weekends alone, Lillian was more convinced Edward was meeting Sarah. Without consulting her attorney, she again employed the Rizzo Detective Agency.

It didn't take long for the detectives to acquire the needed information. Pete arrived at Lillian's home carrying a bulging briefcase. "There's no evidence that your husband was with Sarah Woodward. Are you sure you want to see this?" Pete hesitated, waiting for her reply.

"Show me what you have."

"Okay," he replied, placing a sealed manila envelope on the table.

Lillian grabbed the envelope, ripped it open and withdrew several photographs. "Oh, my God" she shrieked when she saw photographs of Edward with other women.

"Yep! Looks like he's been pretty busy."

"Where were these taken? I don't recognize the area."

"Traverse City."

"How many of these do you have?" Lillian asked as she sifted through a stack of pictures.

"I wasn't the only one with a camera. The local news reporters were hanging around most of the evenings. Did you check the morning paper yet?"

"No," Lillian replied as she grabbed the newspaper.

On the second page of the Detroit News was a large photo of Edward leaving a bar with a young, attractive woman hanging on his arm. Written in bold print under the photo, Wealthy executive, Edward Hansen, seen with blond bombshell.

"He can't do this to me," Lillian cried, crumbling the paper into a wad. "No wonder he's so damn tired on Mondays. When can you get more evidence?"

"What? Local, or Traverse City?"

"Both," Lillian snarled.

Later that afternoon, Lillian waited until her husband entered the house. She met him at the door and waved the newspaper in front of his face. "If you don't stop running around, I'll file for divorce," Lillian shouted, her voice quivering with frustration.

Edward stumbled back, startled by the sudden attack. Though he detested arguments, he knew he had to make a firm stand. After regaining his composure, and still hung over from the weekend, he bellowed. "Go ahead. File. Now you have proof."

"You're deliberately embarrassing me." Lillian hurled the newspaper to the floor. Feeling a dizzy spell coming on, she gripped her forehead, and grabbed the back of a chair to steady herself. "Can't you see what you're doing to me?"

June 6, 1944, United States celebrated D-Day, signaling World War II would soon be over. The military applauded Edward Hansen as the patriotic citizen of the year. The public escapades of the flamboyant, but naughty, Edward Hansen, became a diversion for the readers. Steamy articles fascinated the public, temporarily taking their minds off the tragedy of war, and they forgave him his indiscretions.

Pete Rizzo went to Lillian's house and delivered the second part of his investigation. "This is a deed to a house in the suburbs," he said as he set the documents on the table.

"I didn't know he had another house," Lillian blustered.

"He bought it some time ago. Looks like he paid high dollar. This was deeded to Sarah Woodward."

Lillian scowled as she dragged the paper toward her. "This is Sarah's house?"

"Not now," Pete replied sliding another document across the table. "Look here. It was deeded back to your husband several months ago."

"What's this all about," Lillian's hand trembled as she studied the paper closely.

"I don't know. That's inside stuff between the two of them." Pete placed another document on the table. "Your husband has an apartment at the Book Cadillac Building in Detroit. Executive suite. Top floor."

"That ass. Nothing but the best for him. Was he in Detroit this weekend?"

"My investigators never saw him in the city." Pete slid several large photographs out of an envelope. "Your husband was up north. Here he is with a blond woman. And, here he's leaving a bar with a brunette." One by one, Pete laid out photographs of Edward with different women hanging on his arm.

What's happened to him? Lillian thought. Is he *intentionally provoking me to file for divorce?* Lillian, devastated and angry, returned to Shilling's office the next morning.

"Edward refuses to stop running around." She slammed the photographs on his desk. "I found out where he spends his time."

Lillian spread the newspaper across his desk. "Look at this. These aren't just rumors. I can't hide his affairs anymore. His face is plastered all over the second page. What am I supposed to do?"

Shilling, not willing to take on the Hansen's staff of attorneys, spent the next several hours skillfully persuading Lillian that it was in her best interest to remain married. As soon as she left his office, he made an appointment to see Edward Hansen.

"I'm in a tough spot. Legally, I shouldn't be here, but your wife brought me these articles," he said, spreading the daily news across Edward's desk. "The press exposed your affairs."

Edward dragged the paper toward him. Already aware of the articles, and preferring to show little interest, he shoved them back to Shilling. "Ah, huh. What did she want?"

"A divorce!" Shilling backed away from the desk and his voice quivered. "I talked her out of it. What do you want me to do? I can't hold her off forever."

"I'll take care of this," Edward replied, concealing his astonishment with a frown. "Thanks for coming in."

Later that afternoon, after discussing the matter with his personal attorney, Edward agreed to give the appearance of reconciling with his wife. To mislead the public, the newspapers were informed he would be enlarging his home. Though secretly, the west wing was to be his own private residency. He designed the building to jut out, so he could look across the lawn and keep an eye on the main house.

Lillian, frustrated with the constant noise of the builders, stomped into the parlor. "Why are you adding onto our house? It's big enough."

Edward tossed his newspaper across the chair and retreated to the piano. His fingers danced over the keys, softly at first, then pent-up, drowning out his wife's whining voice.

"Go ahead. Play the piano. But you can't drown out the noisy workers."

Edward turned a deaf ear to his wife and thumped harder on the keys to release his frustration.

"That's what you always do! Hide in your music. Why can't you play softer?"

"I play what I feel."

"Is this how you feel? Angry?" Unable to get an answer, Lillian stormed out of the parlor.

The builders worked long hours to finish the job before winter set in. As soon as the addition was complete, Edward hired movers to transfer his personal possessions into the west wing.

Lillian ran to the foyer when she heard a commotion at the front door. "Why are movers here?"

"I'm moving my office supplies and personal files."

"How? There's no connecting door."

"I didn't want an adjoining door. This is strictly my place."

"You're a crazy man," Lillian screamed. "This is not an addition. It's another damn building."

Edward ignored his wife's complaints and directed two burly men toward the library. "Take that mahogany desk."

The men hoisted the heavy desk on a dolly and toted it out the front door.

Lillian, frustrated and angry, waited for the men to return. She spread her arms, blocking their way to the library. "Don't you dare take my furniture."

The men stopped and frowned at Edward, waiting for an order.

"They're only taking my personal items," Edward pleaded, as he led them to the library. "Take those file cabinets."

Lillian stood with her hands on her hip. "You'll be sorry you're doing this. I'm not through with you yet."

The first few days in the west wing, Edward enjoyed the quiet, nestled in the familiar groove of his favorite chair. As days passed, he began to feel lonely and bored. To pass the evenings, he would often attend the local movie theater to view the recent military action. Tonight the tragedy of World War II was interjected with newsreels of his adulterous affairs. The screen showed old clips of him attending elaborate parties and noisy fund-raisers. Edward slid down in his seat, hoping no one had noticed him.

It's all a facade, he thought. *I'm not the flamboyant man they think I am. All this is just an act. I had to protect Sarah.* Edward left the theater with his head down, to avoid being recognized as he dashed across the parking lot.

By the time he returned home, the servants had retreated to their quarters for the evening, and the house took on a chilling stillness.

He made his way across the room and turned on several lamps. Feeling more comfortable now that the room was brighter, he flopped down in his chair and closed his eyes. Sarah came to mind, and he envisioned her radiate smile and sparkling blue eyes. That brought back memories of their passionate love behind closed doors. A faint smile spread across his lips as he thought about his daughter squealing with joy. "My baby was doing so well. She was so eager to learn sign," he murmured under his breath.

A cool gust of air touched his face and a comforting sensation moved through his body. As he swept his hand across his cheek to brush away the cold, his mother came to mind. "I'm glad she's not here to see what a mess I've made of my life."

Edward thought about the embarrassing news reels he'd seen earlier this evening. This brought to mind his own sexual encounters. The shallow women with painted faces. The meaningless relationships that left him neither proud, nor satisfied. He rose from his chair and stood by the window.

Across the yard, a single light shone through the window of the main-house. A brisk wind kicked up, tossing the crisp brown leaves dancing across the frost-nipped lawn.

Lillian will have the parlor decorated for Christmas. A gust of wind blew against the windowpane, and he shivered, not with the cold, but with loneliness. *I don't know if I can make it alone. The quiet seems to smother me. I can't handle the solitude anymore. Maybe if I move back, I won't be so lonely.*

Edward turned his back on the inviting lights outside his window. His conflicting mind argued his options. *Lillian will probably welcome me back, but, how do I tell her that I'll never sleep in the same room where my daughter died?*

After weeks of sleepless nights, Edward moved back into the main-house. His first meeting with his wife seemed strained, yet he listened to her frivolous chatter. As the days passed, Edward didn't find the peace he expected. He regarded Lillian's presence as an intrusion, rather than a diversion. *It's better than being alone,* he thought.

Lillian's high-pitched voice rattled on, spouting meaningless trivia. "Did you hear me Edward? Are you listening to what I said?" Lillian rambled on, unwilling to hear the discontent in her husband's somber replies.

Edward blocked out his wife's idle chatter. His mind wandered, recalling pleasant memories of yesterday, only to be brought back by the raspy sound of his wife's voice. He felt the tension building, ready to explode like a time bomb. He wished he had the nerve to file for divorce, but the mention of splitting his corporation curbed his appetite for freedom.

Edward had been living in the main-house for several weeks when he decided to visit Bridget's bedroom. He peeked in the dimly lit room. A small teddy bear lay on the dusty floor. In the corner sat a small wicker rocking-chair. On the seat lay several clothespin dolls. He moved across the room, nudged the rocking horse just to hear the familiar creaking sound against the wooden floor.

As he sat on the bed, a waft of dust floated up, catching him in the throat. *If only I had the courage to start the divorce proceedings.*

He desperately wanted to change, but fear of making a mistake haunted him. Indecision flooded his mind, and he couldn't turn off his fear. He knew what his mother had said about him was true. *I'm still the same indecisive person, I've always been. All the money that poured into my hands was an act of fate.* Edward felt the cruelty of war had brought him prosperity in spite of his own shortcomings. *Even though the newspapers articles named me the 'flamboyant man about town,' they only saw a facade of who I am.* "How easily we fool the public," he muttered.

With this memory of triumph, a sobering reality ensued. He rose from Bridget's bed and gazed around the room. *It's hard to believe she's gone.* As the thought crossed his mind, the room grew uncannily cool and his body shivered, reacting to the eerie presence. He looked suspiciously across the room. "Bah. I don't believe in ghost." He stood at the door and gave the room one last look. The gloomy emptiness depressed him, and he eased the door closed, shutting out yesterday's memories.

As he stepped in the hall, a shaft of moonlight streaked through the half-open door where Sarah once slept. He paused, reminiscing about the nights he caressed her body, and how guilty they both felt for their own misconduct. He turned his back on the streak of light. "It's empty. It'll always be empty." He headed down the stairs toward the parlor. He needed someone to talk to, but he knew the same emptiness would be waiting for him downstairs.

CHAPTER 22

Edward raised the window to let out the stale odor of winter. A waft of spring air drifted in, and with it thoughts of a new beginning. *Perhaps I'll phone Sarah. I haven't seen her in a long time.* The sound of his wife's high heels passing through the foyer interrupted his spark of enthusiasm. He flopped down in his chair, out of reach of the telephone.

Lillian entered the room rubbing her hands across her arms. "It's chilly in here. No wonder it's cold." She headed straight for the window and slammed it shut.

"Why don't you leave it open? The air is refreshing." Seeing the determined look on his wife's face, he huffed a disgruntled grunt, knowing the window was staying closed. His eyes fell on the telephone, and he wondered, *will Sarah still be interested?*

Lillian sat down on the couch and spread an afghan across her lap. Once nestled under the blanket, she began chattering idle trivia of the day.

Edward pretended to listen while the thought of renewing his affair stirred his imagination. He closed his eyes and reminisced about the passionate evenings they once spent together. Time had not diminished his love. Sarah still touched his heart.

An urgent tapping of the Morse code blasted from the radio.

Edward's eyes popped open, and he bolted upright. He reached for the radio and dialed the sound up louder.

President Truman's speech blared from the speakers. "Victory in Europe is imminent." His voice continued strong and reassuring as he broadcast to the American people. "An end of the war is in sight."

Lillian yanked the afghan off her lap, jumped up and shrieked with joy. "That's wonderful. Aren't you proud our factories were so prosperous? Look at all the money we made."

"Hush," Edward replied, tilting his ear toward the radio. His thoughts wavered like the Libra he was, and indecision swung like a razor-sharp sword. *Certainly, an end to the war would be good for the American people.* Beads of sweat formed on his forehead as he calculated his losses. *Factories will be abandoned. Government contracts will be canceled.* He always believed fate had burdened him with these responsibilities. Now, he took this as a sign that fate would finally release him.

Maybe I won't have to lead such a hectic life, he thought. *I might even find peace.* Edward's thoughts were interrupted by Lillian's grating voice. He slouched down in his chair and stared aimless at the floor. *How long must I remain in this marriage of indifference?*

The next morning, he arrived at his office, eager to share the news with his secretary. "Did you hear the president? The war is nearly over."

"Yes. I heard the speech."

"Hold all my calls," Edward said as he scooped up the incoming mail.

Betty nodded with a smile. She was still a spinster, but not of her own choosing. Since fate had dealt her the old-maid card, she found her own niche in life. She took it upon herself to guard Edward's privacy like an empress protecting her dynasty.

He hurried to his office, tossed the envelopes on the desk and sat down. It wasn't the end of the war that had him excited. It was the possibility of renewing his friendship with Sarah.

It's been two years since I've spoken to Sarah. I wonder what she'll say. The sound of typewriters in the outer office drew his attention. He could hear Betty's brash voice giving orders, and it brought back memories of Prudence Crowley, his father's secretary.

I was just a young boy when my mother brought me to my father's office. I remember when the clerks wore mid-calf black skirts and starched white blouses. My mother convinced my father that the staff obey the dress code. I remember my father's secretary, Prudence. *She was a beautiful woman with red hair piled high on her head. It was the early 1900s and I heard my father tell Prudence that she looked like the Gibson Girl.* "Funny how these things come to mind," he muttered under his breath.

That brought to mind the day Prudence bobbed her beautiful red hair. *I remember my mother screaming, demanding he fire Miss Crowley. But, my father just grinned mischievously.* "Now my love," he cooed. "I'll take care of this matter." *My father never disciplined his secretary about her outrageous hairstyle, and she remained in his employ. I always thought my mother was angry about the hairstyle. But, as I grew up, I watched my dad's secretary more closely. Now I see why my mother was upset. It was because Miss Crowley's blouse was always unbuttoned daringly low.*

Edward leaned back in his chair and closed his eyes. *I remember visiting dad's office when I was about four years old, barely able to see the desktop. I saw my father's hand on Prudence Crowley's shoulder. He was leaning close and whispering in her ear.* "Prude," *he said, in a low voice and a wink of the eye. Come to think of it, my father never called her Prude when my mother was in the office. It was always Miss Crowley. I can still hear my father's voice like it was yesterday. It had a teasing sound to it in those days.*

Edward smiled within. *Could it be true my father was the rascal, he was rumored to be? Is that why my mother visited the office so often?*

A surge of warmth flushed over him as he uncovered the truth hidden in his childhood memory. He thought about the time he saw Miss Crowley, years after her retirement. Time had tamed the brazen coquette, turning her flaming red hair to silvery gray, and creasing her once sensual mouth with wrinkles. *No wonder my mother objected to me marrying an office clerk. Is this why she suppressed my confidence? Was it because of my father's indiscretion?*

Is that why I hired Betty? Have I followed in his father's footsteps? Have I hired the same kind of brash, outspoken girl? Edward opened his eyes and raised his eyebrows as the thought crossed his mind. *Did I hire Betty just to upset my mother?*

Sounds in the outer office interrupted his daydream. "Just like my dad," he chuckled, comparing himself to his father for the first time. He picked up the phone, eager to begin his new adventure.

"Number please," the operator asked.

Edward recited the number he had memorized, but dared not use in years. He coughed, clearing the raspy sound from his throat, then waited.

"Purchasing department. Miss Woodward speaking. May I help you?"

Edward, hearing Sarah's pleasant voice, spoke softly. "Sarah? I've got to talk to you."

"What?" Sarah stammered, upon recognizing his voice.

"This is Edward. I need to see you." He waited for an answer, but could tell by the silence he had taken her by surprise.

The phone took on a deadening silence.

"It's good to hear from you," Sarah replied in a business-like manner, intentionally omitting his name. "How are you?"

"Fine. Fine." Edward changed the tone of his voice and pleaded softly. "Please. I must see you."

"I'm not sure we should. A lot has happened since we last spoke."

"I need to talk to you. I really do." He waited for an answer.

Again, the phone went silent.

"Maybe we could have dinner?"

Sarah hesitated before she spoke. "It's been such a long time. Why are you calling me now?"

"Just to talk. It's important. Can you meet me for dinner?"

Hearing the sincerity in his voice, Sarah relented. "All right. Nothing else. Just dinner."

"Yes. That's all. I'll pick you up tonight at seven."

"No! Meet me at Antonio's restaurant. You remember the place, don't you?"

"Yes. Yes," Edward replied, pressing the phone closer to his ear.

A faint click ended the conversation. The phone went dead.

Edward slumped back in his chair. It wasn't what he expected. He hoped Sarah would be pleased, perhaps even eager. *Is she angry at me? After all, there were all those other women. Maybe I should explain I was protecting her reputation. He* wavered, doubting his own judgment. *No. She won't believe me, anyway.*

Edward arrived at the restaurant shortly before seven. As he made his way through the parking lot, gusts of wind lashed at his face. He grabbed his homburg, holding it firmly against his head as he made his way toward the flashing neon signs. When he reached the front of the building, he peeked through the window.

A fine mist of rain covered the window, obscuring his view.

He brushed his hand across the glass, wiping away the moist film. *I wonder if Sarah arrived yet?* Unable to see through the glass, he pushed the door open.

197

The familiar tinkle of a brass bell hanging over the door announced his arrival.

Mama Rosa raised her eyebrows and gestured with a nod to Antonio. "Look who's here! Our favorite customer." She tightened the apron around her protruding belly and made her way across the room.

The sound of Italian music played from a neon-lit jukebox, and rows of wooden booths lined the walls. The savory aroma of parmesan cheese and garlic wafted from the wood-latticed window that separated the kitchen from the dining area.

Edward scanned the patrons for a familiar face, but no one turned to acknowledge his arrival. He motioned to Antonio, then headed toward a booth where he had secretly met Sarah many times in the past.

Antonio hovered over him with a big grin.

"Whiskey and water," he said, as he slid across the wooden bench.

"It's been years since you come here. Now you're a big, celebrity."

Edward acknowledged the greeting with a nod. "Another person will be joining me. On second thought, make it a double."

Antonio nodded, "You bet! A double it is."

Edward gazed across the room at the gray tile floor and the common wooden tables covered in red and white checkered oilcloth. This was certainly a step down from the elegant dining to which he had become accustomed. He kept his eye on the door as he sipped his drink. *Will she still have the same innocence in her eyes? Will she still care?*

The brass bell over the door tinkled, announcing a customer's arrival.

Sarah searched the back of the room. When she saw Edward, she couldn't hold back the unexpected smile. She had intended this meeting to be a casual encounter, but found it difficult to suppress the cordial smile.

Edward stood up while Sarah made her way toward him. As she approached, he reached out and took her hand. He felt Sarah's hand tense, then try to pull away. Though he sensed Sarah's hesitation, he held her hand firmly. The warmth of her touch still excited him. He looked in deep in her eyes, but the passion he felt toward her wasn't present in her eyes.

Sarah turned her back while she removed her wet raincoat.

He slid into the wooden bench while looking deep in her eyes. He knew he had wronged her, and understood why she wasn't enthusiastic about their meeting.

Antonio stopped at the booth, wiped his hands on his apron and grinned broadly. "Would the lady like a drink?"

Sarah nodded. "Yes. A glass of red wine, please."

Edward waited until the waiter left, then spoke. "It's been nearly two years. I've missed you terribly."

"You've been quite busy," Sarah replied coldly.

"Those women meant nothing to me!" Edward blurted defensively.

"I wasn't referring to your love life. Your business kept you busy."

Antonio returned and set a glass of wine in front of Sarah. "What can I bring you tonight?" he asked with a grin of approval.

After they placed their orders, and the waiter left, Edward took hold of Sarah's hand and spoke softly. "I need you Sarah."

Sarah snatched her hand away and picked up her glass.

"I can't live with Lillian anymore. I'm like an empty shell without you."

"It's too late for us."

"Please, don't say that. I've tried to make a go of it, but I can't. Living with Lillian smothers me."

Sarah waited until the waiter placed two plates on the table and left before she spoke. "Our lives have changed too much," she said as she set her left-hand flat on the table.

The sparkle of a diamond ring caught Edward attention. He gasped. "You're engaged?"

Sarah nodded, clasped her hands together, covering the small diamond that barely glistened.

"When did all this happen?" He felt like he had been hit in the stomach, and slumped back against the wooden bench.

"Several weeks ago. This shouldn't matter to you, one way or another."

Edward leaned forward and touched Sarah's hand tenderly. "It does matter." Even though she had not responded to his touch, he spoke from his heart. "There's never been a day I haven't thought of you. You're never out of my mind."

"I'm sorry. I didn't know," Sarah murmured, again pulling her hand away.

Edward hesitated, looking for words to justify his actions. He knew it would be difficult, but he had to try. "Those women meant nothing to me. I did it to protect you. To take the heat off you."

"It doesn't matter anymore," Sarah answered halfheartedly.

"I was trying to save my company." Changing the tone of his voice, he whispered. "I've always needed you."

"It's too late."

"Can't we try again?"

"No. My wedding is set for the seventh of May. I'm not mad at you, Edward. I thought you were just striking back."

"Not at you, Sarah. Never at you."

"Striking back at Lillian."

A frown furrowed his forehead. "At my wife? I don't understand."

Sarah leaned closer and whispered, "Because of Bridget's death."

Edward's body stiffened. He had always suspected something was amiss about his daughter's death, but to hear it from someone else took him off guard. "Do you think Lillian had something to do with Bridget's death?"

Sarah cast her eyes down, avoiding his curious stare. "I don't know. There's no point in discussing it now. You can't prove anything after all these years."

"Prove what? Do you think Lillian didn't tell the truth?"

Sarah spoke firmly, choosing her words carefully. "Didn't you wonder why the accident happened on the day Ester and I were shopping?"

"I never thought about that. I wasn't thinking straight."

"Your wife was there. I can't believe she didn't hear a thing. Not even a sound."

"You mean, she deliberately let my baby die?"

"She must have heard the mirror fall. She had to hear it."

"Why didn't you mention this years ago?"

"I'm not sure of anything, only my own feelings. You've seen your wife's temper go out of control. I wondered why you didn't." Sarah stopped in mid sentence, and her words turned cold and accusatory. "Why didn't you question her?"

"I was too upset." Edward slumped back hard against the wooden bench. "Now I understand why Lillian's constant chattering gets on my nerves. Something has been eating at me, but I never understood why."

"It's been seven years. Leave it alone."

Edward clenched his fist. "I've got to find out what happened that day."

Sarah covered his clenched fist with her hand. "What are you going to do?"

Edward didn't answer. He didn't know.

"Don't do anything foolish."

"Deep down, I've always wondered if she was covering up something. Maybe that's why I didn't care if my adultery upset her."

"Maybe you thought she was guilty. That's why you didn't care."

Edward stared curiously at Sarah. "Guilty! What do you mean?"

"I wondered why your wife tolerated your adultery. She could have struck back, but she didn't. Was it because *she* felt guilty?"

Edward nodded. The word 'guilty' ran like a buzz-saw through his brain. "Yes. Lillian was far too tolerant of my infidelity. Maybe she does feel guilty. That's why she never filed for a divorce."

"It's too late to do anything now," Sarah said, reaching for her coat.

Edward slid out of the booth and helped Sarah slip into her coat. "When can I see you again?"

"There's nothing more to say. I'm getting married in a few weeks. It's too late for us," she replied, then turned abruptly and headed toward the door.

That night Edward lay awake mulling over the day Bridget died. *Where was Lillian? Why didn't she hear the mirror fall? Was the radio on loud?* His mind probed every detail of the day of the funeral. *Lillian appeared numb or shocked that day. Was it the medication? When she stood by the casket, she seemed cold and unemotional.* Although Edward examined the facts, his own insecurity made him deny all probabilities. The morning sun was beginning to rise when Edward finally dropped off to asleep.

The following week Edward phoned Sarah. "After our last conversation, it was hard to face Lillian, so I moved out, into the west wing."

"Oh my God! What did Lillian do? She must be furious."

"She ranted and raved that the newspapers would find out. I tried to calm her, but she started on me again about not having an adjoining door to the west wing."

"There's no entry between the two houses?"

"Only from the outside. I built it to look like an addition."

"Why did you do that? You actually have two separate houses."

"My stock would drop if the public thought we were separated. I wanted the newspapers to print that we are still living together. Oh, why am I explaining this. It has nothing to do with us."

"There is no us," Sarah responded coldly.

Edward's voice turned serious. "Please, I need to see you."

"How can I help?"

"I need to clear things up in my mind."

"Okay. Just to talk. This will be the last time I'll see you. I'm getting married in a couple weeks."

"Will you meet me tonight at seven? I'm at the Book Cadillac Hotel. Please."

"Um," Sarah murmured.

The telephone clicked to dead silence.

Edward arrived at his suite early that evening. The sun was beginning to set when he heard a timid rapping. He opened the door and a wide smile swept across his face. Sarah's beauty still took his breath away. "I'm glad you came," he said as he guided her into a spacious room.

A large crystal chandelier dangled over an elegant, teak wood table. Gold-rimmed china and crystal goblets staged an amazing spectacle of elegance on a large table. Two sterling silver warming plates were placed on a white, Irish-linen tablecloth. Hot steam drifted from the covered plates.

Sarah handed Edward her jacket and moved across the room. "I see the table is set for dinner."

"I hope it's okay. The staff brought it in earlier. I gave them the evening off. No one knows you're here."

"I didn't intend to stay long. Only for a drink or two."

"Let's eat while it's still hot." Edward slid his hand on Sarah's back, unable to resist touching her as he led her to the table. "We can have a drink later, if that's okay?"

Sarah lay a linen table napkin upon her lap. "I was nervous about coming here tonight. You know. With my wedding being so close."

"Who is this man you're marrying?" he asked studying the ring on Sarah's finger. "Have you known him long?"

"Not long. A couple months. He's a nice man."

"A nice man? That's a strange answer."

Sarah offered a slight shrug of her shoulders. "What do you want me to say? That I'm madly in love. We're still getting to know each other."

"Are you sure you know what you are doing?"

"Why are you asking me these questions? I'm tired of being alone. I want a home, a husband, and a family."

Edward leaned across the table, staring deep in Sarah's eyes. *She's not turning away. Is she pleading to be with me?* Taking the compassionate look on her face as encouragement, he uttered softly. "If only there was a way."

"There's no way for us," Sarah replied, pushing her chair away from the table. "I can't be with you. You made that very clear."

Edward's body recoiled at the sharp tone in her voice. He rose from the table and stretched out his hand. "Come. Let's sit in the other room."

Sarah hesitated, nodded with a smile and took his hand.

"Can I get you a drink?" Edward said as he led her across the room.

Sarah nodded. "A glass of wine."

"I mixed martinis already. Which do you prefer?"

"A martini is okay."

Edward made his way across room. When he returned, he was balancing two glasses on a silver tray. "I think you'll like the way I fixed these."

Sarah accepted the drink and made her way across the room toward a large window. "It's so beautiful," she cooed, looking down at the buildings below. "The traffic headlights look like sparkling diamonds."

Edward stood across the room gazing at Sarah's slender body silhouetted against the pale moonlight. His love for Sarah was like a leaping flame, and he knew the embers could spark unsound judgment. He made it a point to change the subject. "I've talked to my attorneys about Bridget's death. Asked if they thought my wife was involved."

"And?" she answered coldly.

"My attorney didn't seem shocked." Edward longed to take Sarah in his arms, but her stoic voice made him step back. "How can I accuse my wife? We don't know what she heard. My attorneys made some valid points."

"You don't want to face this, do you?"

"My attorneys warned me to back off. Any allegations would bring inquiries. I can't jeopardize my position as head of the corporation." Edward, needing a moment to gather his thoughts, took Sarah's empty glass and left the room. When he returned, he handed her a glass filled to the brim. "My attorney asked if I thought Lillian was mentally incompetent."

"You saw her hide in her bedroom every time her temper exploded. That's not normal."

Edward paced the floor, his head meekly bent. "She did that for years. That's why it didn't seem unusual."

"What else did the attorneys say?"

"They said any accusation would open up a can of worms. I can't say Lillian's crazy, even if I think she is."

"You know something is wrong. What if she's not crazy?"

"That's exactly why I can't start anything. I might say the wrong thing and suggest Lillian is unstable. She could file charges against me for slander or defamation of character."

Sarah stepped away from the window and moved toward the couch. "You've never really confronted your wife, have you?"

"No. Not really. I talked to my attorneys about filing for a divorce."

"What did they say to that?"

"They discouraged me. I can't prove *she's* done anything wrong."

"You can get a divorce in Las Vegas."

"That would cause a bigger scandal. She'll make sure the court questions my affairs. That means you'd be investigated. She could drag your name through the courts."

"Well, your past performance certainly didn't help," Sarah replied sarcastically.

Feeling the sting of her remark, his voice turned stern and somber. "I'm sorry. I didn't mean to hurt you."

"Why? All those women?"

Edward stared aimlessly down at the floor. "I just lost it. When I lost Bridget, and you, I wanted to run . . ., and run . . ., and run."

"Didn't you realize what you were doing?"

Edward moved across the room. "No. I drank to forget. I haven't slept with Lillian in years."

"You're going to continue living apart? She's still next door. You're still alone."

Edward's voice rose defensively. "A divorce would devastate my corporation. There are thousands of employees to consider. Lillian could be awarded the lion's share of stock. That would give her too much executive control."

"I understand. It's all very involved,"

"My mother put a lot of stock in Lillian's name years ago. There's no way out. I'd move out completely, but she's so unpredictable. She might spread my past, our affair, across the newspapers."

"But, I haven't seen you in years." Sarah murmured as she flopped down on the couch.

"If there is a divorce, it's sure be tried by the newspapers, not the courts."

"Let it go, Edward. Forget about it."

"I have no choice." Edward replied as he headed for the couch. Feeling a need to be closer, he sat down and moved the pillow that lay between them.

"I understand. It not just a simple divorce. You have to consider how your wife's might retaliate."

Edward set his glass on the end-table, slumped back and closed his eyes. He felt Sarah squeezing his hand, and he felt comforted.

"I'm sorry. I shouldn't have criticized your judgment. You've got to think about the scandal it could cause."

The fragrant scent of Sarah's warm body close to him weakened his resistance. He opened his eyes. It was too late to stop the embers of love that burned within him. They were already out of control. He grasped Sarah's hand and pulled her to him.

Sarah, responding to his touch, laid her head on his chest.

Edward wrapped his arms around her, drawing her closer. "I never stopped loving you," he whispered. He could feel her body surrendering, melting into his arms.

CHAPTER 23

On the day of Sarah's wedding, Edward found himself repeatedly glancing at the clock. He opened the desk drawer and took out a silver-rimmed wedding card. He had intentionally selected a card with a simple verse, one that didn't reveal his true feelings. If he could, he would have told Sarah how her love had touched his heart. That she had become a part of him, like his soul-mate.

Robert peeked in the office door. "Are you busy?"

Edward dropped the card and covered it with his hand. "Come in. I wish I could stop Sarah from making a big mistake."

"Why?" Robert asked as he strolled into the office.

"I had Paul Logan investigated."

"Is that who Sarah is going to marry?"

"He's working on the loading dock. He's a troublemaker."

"Logan? Yeah, I heard about him. Several men filed complaints about his quick temper."

"Look at this investigator's report." Edward slid a copy of the report to the edge of his desk and read from his paper. "Paul Logan charges include petty larceny, aggravated assault, and jailed for drunken and disorderly conduct."

"You better warn Sarah before it's too late." Robert scanned his copy, nodding in agreement.

"How can I tell her about her future husband after all I've done?"

"This poor girl is heading for trouble. You should tell her something."

After Robert left the office, Edward wrote a check in Sarah's maiden name as a wedding gift. He wondered if the groom would misinterpret the gift, or if it would cause trouble between the newlyweds. "Too bad about the groom's feelings," he mumbled as he placed the check in the card, and sealed the envelope before he could change his mind. His thoughts swayed to their last meeting, and he hoped Sarah wouldn't misinterpret the gift.

Sarah married Paul Logan the first week of May 1945. A feeling of uncertainty swept over her as Paul slipped the ring on her finger. *Am I doing the right thing? It's been a whirlwind courtship, and I still don't know him very well.*

After a brief weekend honeymoon, they returned to Sarah's apartment. After going through the morning mail, Sarah searched through the stack of wedding cards until she recognized Edward's handwriting. She made sure her husband was still in the bedroom before pulling the card out of the envelope. *I wonder if Edward wrote a note? Maybe a secret message? Perhaps a plea, or regret?* There was none. Upon opening the card, she gasped, overwhelmed by the numbers written on a check. *How can I explain this amount of money? Paul might be angry, or refuse to keep it?* The memory of their last meeting came to mind, and she flushed with embarrassment. *Is this a payoff? Is this why Edward wrote it in my maiden name?* Before she had time to think over the matter, she heard her husband coming into the kitchen.

"What's that?" Paul snarled. "Is that a check?"

Sarah nodded and held it out toward Paul. "Yes. I'll put it in the bank."

"Where did you get this?" Paul grumbled as he snatched it out of her hands.

"Mister Hansen sent us a wedding gift. I wasn't sure if we should keep it. It's such a large amount."

Paul's eyes widened as he scanned the figures, and his grin changed to a scowl. "Why is it in your maiden name? Endorse it. I'll cash it for you."

"No. I'll put it in the bank."

"What's the matter? Don't you trust me? Why did he send so much money? Was there a note attached?"

The suspicious look on Paul's face made Sarah feel uneasy. "No. Just this card. We can keep the money, can't we? After all, this amount of money means nothing to him. We can use it for a down payment on a house."

Paul raised his eyebrow. "Is that a bankbook on the table?"

"It's my checkbook."

Paul grabbed the book and flipped through the pages. "You saved all this money?"

"Yes. It's my savings account."

Paul scanned the front cover. "Now that we're married you can make this a joint account."

Sarah nodded.

"Be sure you put that money in our account," he muttered, as he tossed the bankbook across the table. "We can use some for a down payment, but not all of it. I need money for other things."

"But Paul, we're both working. We can combine our income."

"Make sure you add my name on the saving account."

Several weeks later Sarah met with a real estate agent. Each time she presented Paul with a house listing, he objected to the price and turned it down. After many rejections, Sarah settled for a handy-man special; a fixer-upper in a suburb, north of Detroit.

On the day she finalized the purchase, she found Paul had drawn out half of the money from their savings. Sarah decided not to mention it that day. She would wait until they signed the purchase agreement and confront him later.

After moving into their home, Sarah approached her husband. "What happened to our savings? Where did the money go?"

"I paid bills," Paul responded.

"No, you didn't. I paid all the utility bills from my weekly paycheck."

Paul grabbed a shirt off the back of a kitchen chair. "Damn it! Stop nagging,"

"Don't wear that. It's dirty. It smells like stale beer and cigarettes."

Paul turned his back and slipped on the shirt.

"I'm asking you again. What happened to the money in my account?"

"My account. Don't you mean our account." Paul slammed his fist on the table. "It's gone. Don't tell me what I can spend," he bellowed as he headed toward the door.

"Why don't you stay home. We can save money if you help me make improvements on the house."

"If you want the walls painted, paint them yourself."

"Aren't you going to stay and help me?"

"What am I, your damn servant? I'm going out. I'll be back when you quit nagging."

Sarah soon realized her new husband had a quick temper and an argumentative nature. And, that the responsibility of repairing the house was completely on her shoulders. Each evening, after a full day of work at the office, Sarah made repairs, restoring the house to a more livable condition. Many days she asked Paul to help, but each time he found an excuse to storm out of the house for the evening.

Two months later, Sarah approached her husband beaming with pride. "Paul. I went to the doctor today. We're having a baby," Sarah said, hardly able to contain her enthusiasm.

"You're what? Ya can't be!"

"Aren't you happy?" Sarah replied, surprised by his hostile response.

"How the hell did you get pregnant? When did this happen?"

"I don't know. I'm not very far along."

Paul stared at the floor, searching his mind. "That son of a bitch," he mumbled under his breath. He headed toward the door, then stopped and stared curiously at his wife. "Pregnant, huh?" He suppressed a faint grin. "Don't think you're gonna quit work. We need the money."

"It's company policy. I have to quit when they find out I'm pregnant."

"Talk to your old boyfriend. He'll let you work a while longer."

"You promised you wouldn't bring up my affair with Edward. I told you it ended years ago."

"Yeah. You said it ended. I'm not so sure."

By the end of the third month, Sarah's could no longer hide her pregnancy. Reluctantly, she dialed Edward's private telephone.

"Hello, Edward," she said, her voice subdued and somber. "I have a favor to ask."

"How are you Sarah?" Edward's voice rose optimistically. "I haven't heard from you in a long time." He waited for an answer, but the silence made him press the phone closer to his ear.

"Fine," Sarah replied, forcing a lighthearted tone to her voice. "I want to thank you for letting me stay on after I got married."

"I know most companies don't hire married women. I don't feel it's fair. In fact, I think it's counterproductive."

Sarah's voice turned apologetic. "Would it be all right if I work a while longer? I'm having a baby and will need the money."

The phone went silent.

Sarah waited for an answer, but could tell by the silence, she had caught him off guard. "I'm having a problem paying the bills. I was hoping I could work a couple more months."

Edward coughed and cleared his throat. The word 'baby' had knocked the wind out of him, and he felt as if someone had kicked him in the stomach. "Your job? Yes. Of course." He took a deep breath and lowered his voice." I didn't know you were expecting."

"We need extra money for hospital bills. I know it's office policy, but I need the job."

Still reeling from the news, he softened his voice. "It's okay. Stay as long as you want."

A timid, soft voice whispered, "Thank you."

A faint clicking sound and the telephone went dead.

""Why am I so surprised? It was inevitable," he mumbled under his breath. Edward set the telephone down in the cradle gently. He swiveled his chair to the window and gazed at the gray clouds gathering in the distance. He hadn't noticed them before, but now he felt their heaviness.

The mounting thunderheads shrouded the afternoon sun, dimming the office.

"If I had married Sarah, that would have been my baby. Now there will never be another chance. Never."

CHAPTER 24

Robert entered Edward's office waving the morning newspaper. "Did you see this? The German are backing down. The war is finally coming to an end."

"Yes. That means no more army vehicles." Edward reached for the newspaper and shook his head. "No new contracts."

"You're always worrying," Robert replied as he tossed the newspaper on the desk.

"We'll take a hit financially when the contracts dry up."

"Is this really about your losses? Or, are you upset about Sarah's marriage?"

Edward glanced up and smiled meekly. "Is it that obvious?"

"Relax. Do something to occupy your time. The soldiers will be coming home soon. They'll need a place to live."

A spark of enthusiasm lit Edward's eyes. "Build houses?"

"I've done a lot of research on prefab housing. It's the quickest and cheapest way to construct a building."

"Prefabs huh?" Edward's voice rose with the prospect of starting a new business. "We'll have to renovate our factories."

"Then, lets do it."

"Funny how fate intercedes. Instead of our factories closing, we could start building houses for the soldiers." Edward took a deep breath and relaxed, grateful for the close relationship he had with his long time friend. Especially grateful for the times he procrastinated unwisely, and his friend took over and encouraged him to step forward.

"When the men return, a baby boom is sure to follow."

"We'll need more than one construction site," Edward replied, leaning forward with a spark of enthusiasm. "Several of our factories are still under contract with the government."

"The tank plants stay open until we hear from the authorities. There's a chance we might have some contracts renewed."

"I agree." Edward's voice grew stronger, more optimistic. "We'll construct new buildings. We need big yards to store electrical wires, roofing shingles, and a lot of lumber."

"The demand for housing is going to explode." Robert reached in his briefcase and withdrew a yellow legal pad. "We'll have to hire contractors, salesmen, and office clerks. I'll find out what permits are required. As soon as I know more, you can call your meeting."

"Sounds good. Go with it." A timid rapping on the office door drew Edward's attention. "Yes. What is it?"

Betty eased the door open and peeked in. "Your accountant is here."

"Send him in," Edward replied with a wave of his hand.

Alan, a thin, nervous man, hurried to Edward's desk. "I thought you should see these invoices," he mumbled, setting a stack of papers on the desk.

"What are they?"

"Copies of receipts your wife submitted."

"She's redecorating. Just pay them."

An inquisitive frown wrinkled Alan's forehead, and he stepped closer to the desk. "Don't you want to see these?"

"I can't be bothered with petty matters. Pay them. Decorating is my wife's way of releasing her frustration."

Robert, seeing the anxiety on the Alan's face, snatched the invoices off the desk. After scanning the pages, he turned toward the accountant. "Thank you, Alan. We'll take a look at these."

Alan nodded and offered a weak smile. "Your wife is doing extensive repairs. A lot more than you realize," he replied meekly, then scurried out of the office.

"Better take a look at these." Robert shoved the invoices across the desk. "You've been living in the west wing and don't know what's going on. This remodeling is quite extensive."

Edward dragged the stack of papers toward him and flipped through the pages. "These bills are outrageous," he grumbled while tracing his finger down the page. "Walls torn down. Re-plaster new walls. New carpets. Wallpaper. What the hell for?"

"Look at the upstairs renovations," Robert said, keeping his eyes fixed on his friend.

Edward flipped the page and scanned the document. "What has she done?" Edward crunched the paper in his fist. "She got rid of Bridget's furniture?"

"Take it easy. Calm down."

"That stupid woman. She trashed everything in Bridget's bedroom. Edward slammed his chair away from the desk started toward to the door.

"Where are you going?"

"To find out what the hell Lillian's doing."

"You must have seen the trucks parked in front."

"No. I always park in the garage. I never use the front entrance," Edward grumbled as he dashed out of the office.

Edward drove to main house, maneuvering his way through trucks and dumpsters parked on the lawn. When he opened the front door, he was bombarded with the deafening sound of hammering and the smell of wet paint. Rushing through the foyer, he nearly tripped on a paint-splattered tarpaulin. After regaining his balance, he made his way up the staircase and down the hall.

The door to Bridget's bedroom was open.

He tightened his grip on the door-frame to steady himself.

The room had been stripped bare. All the furniture, carpets, and curtains had been removed, and wood shavings littered the plywood sub-floor.

A soft sob slipped from his lips. "That damn woman threw everything away. She even ripped up the beautiful oak floor." Edward hurried down the hall, leaned over the banister and bellowed. "My God woman! What have you done?"

The sound of hammering ceased, and the men climbed down their ladders and stared up at the balcony. The house grew silent.

Lillian ran to the foyer and stood with her hands on her hips, glaring up at her husband. "Will you shut up? They can hear you down here."

Though it wasn't his nature to be assertive, Edward couldn't hold back the rage. His voice quivered as he shouted down the stairs. "Are you crazy? What did you do with Bridget's furniture?"

Lillian stomped up the stairs and stood in the hall with her arms folded across her chest. She glared at her husband, and with clenched jaw she lowered her voice. "I'm redecorating. I want that junk out of here!"

The word 'junk' made Edward stumbled back, stunned by his wife's cold demeanor. Even though his daughter passed away five years ago, he still found it difficult to let go. "How can you be so callous? You never loved our daughter, did you?"

"We can't hold on to memories forever," Lillian replied, deliberately keeping her voice dry and unemotional.

"How you can be such a bitch? I can't stand you anymore." Edward shoved Lillian aside and hurried down the stairs.

A heavy-set painter, seeing Edward stomping down the staircase, grabbed his ladder and dragged it out of the way.

Edward stood at the bottom of the stairs and looked up at his wife. "I'll never come in this house again," he bellowed, then slammed the front door behind him.

The Christmas season arrived with a howling wind, piling the snow in mounds across the lawn. Sarah, late in her pregnancy, sat at the kitchen table looking through a stack of unpaid bills.

Paul, still in his pajamas, wandered into the kitchen. "What's the matter with you? You look so damn grumpy."

"Why didn't you pay the utility bills?"

"Couldn't," he responded, shrugging nonchalantly. "My car broke down again."

Sarah hurried to the window and pushed the curtain aside. "Where is your car? Is it being fixed?"

Paul picked a cigarette butt out of the ashtray, lit it and inhaled deeply. "I've been too busy," he muttered, discharging a swirl of smoke from his nostrils.

Sarah let out a weak cough, waved her hand, pushing the foul fumes away. "How are you getting to work tonight?"

"It's all your fault. You shouldn't have sold your car."

"We needed money to pay the bills." Sarah grabbed a chair and flopped down. "Your car was in good shape until your last drunk-driving accident."

"Yeah. Well, it's not running now." Paul stomped to the window and peeked out. "Look at the damn snow. I'm not going out in that?"

"You've got to work tonight."

Paul threw his hands up in the air and shouted. "I don't have a job. I was laid off weeks ago."

"Laid off?" After a moment of thought, a frown of suspicion creased her forehead. "Weeks ago? Where do you go every night?"

Paul turned his back and headed toward the stove. "Where's my coffee?"

Sarah shoved the stack of bills across the table. "How are we going to pay these?"

Paul took a deep drag on his cigarette, then twisted the stub in the ashtray. "Stop bitching. I'll pay them."

Weeks passed and the utility bills had not been paid. Paul avoided discussing the matter, and would start an argument, using it as an excuse to leave each evening.

Concerned about Paul's late night jaunts, Sarah again approached the subject. "Now that your car is fixed, you've got to find a job. There's plenty of work in Detroit. They're hiring at the auto plants."

"Christmas just passed. No one's hiring now."

"Yes, they are. It's still early in the day." Sarah tightened the wool sweater around her stomach as a waft of cold air found it way though the crack in a weather-worn window.

"I'm not a damn factory worker. I want a good job." Paul stared hard in Sarah's eyes. "Call your old boyfriend. He can get me a good paying job. Not on the loading docks. One with prestige."

"I can't ask him for another favor. He's done so much for us already."

"You bet he has," Paul muttered under his breath. "What's the matter? Afraid of asking that prissy-ass man for a favor? Afraid of being turned down?"

"Please, don't ask me to do this."

Paul grabbed a heavy wool jacket off the back of a chair. "That man owes me," he grumbled, then slammed the door behind him.

Sarah ran to the front door and shouted. "Where are you going?"

"I don't mean a flunky job," he yelled, then plodded down the snow-covered sidewalk. The old car sputtered a few protests then rumbled down the street.

Sarah slammed the door as a painful contraction brought her to her knees. She crouched on the floor waiting for the pain to subside. Tears streamed down her cheeks. Though she dreaded making the phone call, she reluctantly dialed the phone.

"Number please?" the operator's pleasant voice chirped.

After reciting Edward's private number, she waited until she heard his voice. "Hello. This is Sarah. I feel terrible calling you, but I need a favor."

Hearing the quiver in Sarah's voice, Edward pressed the phone to his ear. "Are you all right? Do you need help?"

"My husband doesn't have a job. I don't know what to do?"

"He's not working in the warehouse? When did he quit?"

"He mentioned he was laid off."

"When? I didn't know that."

"He won't talk about it." Sarah lowered her voice. "He's upset and irritable. Could you hire him again?"

"Why didn't you call me sooner? Tell him to go to the Mount Elliott plant. I'll do the rest. Just get him there."

"I'm so embarrassed. The baby is due soon and . . ., ah."

Hearing the discomfort in her voice, Edward spoke softly. "Can I help? Do you need money?"

"No," she interrupted. "We can manage. I'll send Paul to the factory tomorrow. I can't thank you enough. You're always there when I need you." Sarah ended the conversation quickly for fear of breaking down and confessing how badly her marriage had turned out.

Sarah delivered a baby shortly after the New Year. The following day a courier arrived at the hospital and handed Sarah a sealed envelope. She ripped it open and pulled out a greeting card, congratulating her on the birth of her daughter. Inserted in between the card was a check with a note attached. "For the new arrival's college education. Respectfully, Edward Hansen." Again, the check was in Sarah's name. She heaved a sigh of relief when she saw the generous amount. Unsure of what Paul would do, she wanted to hide the card and tell him later, but it was too late.

Paul walked in the room. "What ya got there?"

A flush of embarrassment swept over Sarah's face. "A check for Heidi's education."

"Who gave it to you?"

"It's from Mister Hansen." Sarah replied, finding it difficult to face her husband.

Paul grabbed the check out of her hand. A slight grin appeared, then changed to a frown. "When did he give you this? Was he here?"

"No. It came by courier."

"Why is it made out to your name? Sign it! I'll put it in the bank."

"Paul please," Sarah pleaded, reaching for the check. "I'll pay the hospital bill."

Paul snickered, held the check up and dangled it out of Sarah's reach. "I said sign it." He slammed it on the table, keeping his hand pressed flat on the check. "You stay right here and rest sweetheart. I can do this."

"Please. Paul!"

"Sign it. I can't stay here all day. I have other things to do." Paul hovered over Sarah until she had endorsed the check. "Oh yeah. I'll see the kid tomorrow. Gotta get going." Paul grabbed the check, stuffed it in his pocket and dashed out of the room.

Sarah held her hand up, signaling him to stop. "Paul, stop. Remember. I'll need a ride home tomorrow."

The following day Sarah waited in the hospital room for several hours., but, as she expected, Paul did not show up. Frustrated and upset, Sarah telephoned her mother. "Would you call a taxi and pick me up at the hospital?"

When they arrived home, the house was in disarray. Newspapers lay scattered beside Paul's favorite chair, dirty dishes piled in the sink, and unpaid bills lay on the kitchen table.

It was past four o'clock in the morning when Paul stumbled in the front door.

Sarah lay still, listening to Paul stumble through the living room. When he entered the bedroom, she smelled the foul odor of liquor reeking from his clothing. She closed her eyes and pretended to be asleep, knowing in his drunken state, he was sure to start an argument.

The next morning Sarah confronted her husband. "I found these bills," she said, waving the over-due statements in the air. "You didn't pay the utilities again."

"I was at the factory every night." Paul staggered to the stove and poured hot coffee in a mug. It was apparent the alcohol had not yet worn off. He teetered unsteadily and flopped down at the table. "Relax. I paid the last ones, didn't I?"

"Where's the checkbook? I'll pay these bills."

"Quit nagging," Paul mumbled, then took a large gulp.

"You're still drunk. How can you work tonight?"

Paul ignored the question and staggered to the bedroom. Still unsteady, he braced his back against the dresser and removed his smelly clothes. He slipped on a pair of well-worn bluejeans and a wrinkled shirt. Leaning on the dresser, he stared in the mirror and rubbed the stubble of his whiskers. "Ah, what the hell. I don't have time to shave this morning." Paul grabbed a heavy wool coat and sneaked out the front door.

Sarah, hearing the click of the door, rushed to the window just as his car was pulling away from the house. "I wonder where he put the checkbook," she said as she made her way to the bedroom. After searching the dresser drawers without success, she opened the bottom drawer of his bureau. Hidden in the back, between a pile of summer shirts, was a stack green tickets bound together with a rubber band.

Her hand trembled as she loosened the stubs and read aloud. "Betting slips! Horse races. Forty dollars. Fifty dollars. Oh, my God! He bet his whole weeks pay!" Sarah felt her heart pounding as she hurried to the closet. After searching the pockets of several jackets, she pulled out the bankbook. A warm flush crossed her face as she scanned the last page. "He didn't deposit the check. Not a penny of it!"

Sarah waited until her husband returned home later that afternoon. "I found these," she said, slamming a stack of tickets on the table. "What are they? Betting stubs? Is this where our money is going?"

"Where did you get those? Did you go through my clothes?" He dashed to the bedroom and yanked the bottom drawer open. "Where's the rest of those tickets?" he shouted from the bedroom. When he returned to the kitchen, he had a terrified look on his face. "Where are they? They could be worth a lot of money."

"This is all I found. Take them, but you won't get your hands on my money again."

"What money? You don't have any." Paul stuffed the tickets in his pocket and waited for an answer.

"I'll get a job. You'll never get my paycheck again."

"What," he sputtered, surprised that his meek wife had finally stood up to him. Paul stepped back, unsure of how to stop her. "So it's your money, is it?"

"I wrote checks for the utility bills this morning. There's no money left in the checking account."

"You used all the money?" He rushed to the front window, eased the curtain aside and searched the main street suspiciously. When he was sure the road was empty, he grabbed his jacket and headed toward the front door.

"Where are you going? It's too early to go to work."

Paul glanced at his wristwatch and eased the door open. "I gotta get going. I'll be back when you stop whining."

CHAPTER 25

Within months, Paul's sporadic work attendance was brought to Edward's attention. Concerned with Sarah's well being, he again retained a private investigator. After learning of Paul's adulterous affairs and relationship with well-known gamblers, Edward summoned him to his office.

Paul strutted into the office with a cocky grin on his unshaven face. Stopping in front of Edward's desk, he shoved his thumbs deep in the pockets of his dirty bluejeans. "Ya want to see me?"

"Sit down. You've been missing a lot of work lately. Any particular reason?"

"Nope," Paul quipped, standing defiantly. It was obvious he wasn't about to be intimidated.

Edward frowned, repulsed by the odor of stale beer reeking from Paul's clothing. "I see your hospital bills aren't paid," he said, waving several documents in the air.

Paul stepped closer to the desk and glanced at the papers. "Did my wife give you those bills?"

"No! I had a detective investigate. You do some heavy gambling, don't you?" Edward pushed several dirty betting-stubs across his desk.

"Where did you git those?"

"You threw them away at the racetrack. My investigators picked them up."

"You're pretty sneaky, huh?" Paul grumbled, staring at the green stubs spread across the desk.

"According to this, you're spending more than you earn. Where do you get that kind of cash?" Edward leaned back in his chair, waiting for an answer.

"That's my business."

"It looks like you're dealing with big-time gamblers. Do you realize your gambling is out of control?"

"So what," he taunted, tilting his head back and jutting his chin out stubbornly.

"You're pretty cocky for someone who's talking to his boss."

"So fire me!" Paul replied with a smirking grin.

Edward huffed a sigh of disgust. "You amaze me. Don't you care about your wife and baby?"

"Let me tell ya something." Paul swaggered closer and looked Edward straight in the eyes. "Maybe that's *not* my baby. But, I'll bet ten to one, it's yours."

"What do you mean?" Edward sputtered, still not fully grasping the accusation. He furrowed his brow as the true meaning assaulted his conscious. "What are you saying?"

"Figure it out, pal. Where were you in March, just before I married Sarah?"

Beads of sweat settled on Edward's brow as the accusation became evident. He shoved his chair back, then bolted forward. "You son of a bitch! How can you say that? Get out of here."

Paul jumped back, raising his hands defensively in front of his face. With clenched fist, he planted his feet ready for a fight. "Hey! Wait, a minute. I got something to say." When he saw Edward backing off, a snide grin crossed his face. "I'm sterile. That's how I know."

The shock of Paul's paternity sent Edward staggering backwards.

"Yeah. That's right, pal. Hey! What if I tell your wife about our little secret?"

Edward backed up, momentarily stunned, and flopped down in his chair. "You're lying," he muttered, dazed by the accusations. "You're making this up."

"No, I'm not. Don't worry. Sarah doesn't know. I never told her."

"Sterile? You can't have kids?"

"That's not my baby," Paul taunted, stepping closer to the desk. "Hey! I'm kinda short on cash. How about a loan? Say a couple a thousand?"

"Not your baby?" Edward mumbled under his breath.

"Yep. It's true. I got proof." Paul reached in his pocket and pulled out a crumbled piece of paper. "Right from the doctor's office. One hundred percent sterile," he chided, tossing the medical document on the desk. "Take a look, pal."

Edward's hand trembled as he unfolded the paper. After examining the report, he stared curiously at Paul. "You're sterile?"

"Yeah! Can you lend me some money?" Paul pulled a toothpick out of his pocket and poked at his teeth with a twisted grin. "I can keep quiet for a couple grand."

"Get out," Edward demanded, his voice firm, but uncertain.

"I want my paper back," Paul said, reaching for the document.

Edward kept his eyes down as he shoved the medical report in a drawer.

Paul gripped the edge of the desk, leaned over and sneered. "That's okay. I got more copies."

Edward pointed to the door. "Get out."

"I only need a couple grand." Paul sauntered toward the door, turned and shouted. "Hey! Don't tell Sarah, or I'll tell the newspapers. I'll be back tomorrow. Only a few grand," he shouted before slamming the door behind him.

Edward sat for several minutes, the accusation racing through his brain. After the shock had worn off, he picked up the phone. "Betty! Tell Robert to come to my office, immediately."

Several minutes later, Robert entered the office. "What's the matter?" he asked, seeing the serious expression on Edward's face.

"This is confidential," Edward replied in a meek whisper.

"You look terrible. What the hell happened?"

"Strictly confidential. Close the door."

"Sure," Robert replied as he made his way across the room.

Edward shoved the medical report across the desk. "Look at this."

"What's this all about?" Robert sat down and scanned the wrinkled piece of paper.

"That's Sarah's husband." Edward's voice trembled as he spoke in barely a whisper. "I could be the father of Sarah's baby."

Robert leap out of his seat. "What! For Christ's sake," he bellowed, his broad frame hovering over the desk. "Did Sarah accuse you?"

"No," Edward responded quickly. "She doesn't know about this."

"What the hell are you talking about? Sarah doesn't know?"

"She doesn't know her husband is sterile. Paul Logan was just in my office. He accused me of fathering the baby."

Robert studied the report, and a frown furrowed his brow. "The son-of-a-bitch is sterile?"

"I don't know. He could be lying."

"I'll find out if this is true?" Robert grumbled, tapping his finger firmly on the paper. "Does anyone else know about this?"

"Just Paul Logan, I think." Edward's face turned pale as he reflected on the consequences. "What if the newspapers get wind of this?"

Robert paced the floor, searching his mind for answers. When he stopped, he stared curiously at Edward. "Were you with Sarah? Damn it Edward, are you the father or not?"

"It was more than a year ago," Edward mumbled, casting his eyes down. "I was with her before she got married."

"You what! Then, he could be telling the truth."

"For Christ's sake. I don't know for sure."

"Well, you damn well better think about it. What did that Logan guy want?"

"A couple thousand dollars to keep quiet."

"That's blackmail."

"I've got to pay, or he'll go the newspapers."

Robert again scanned the medical document. "Sterile, huh. If your wife finds out, this could affect her health."

"What?"

Robert's voice turned sullen. "How is your wife? She didn't look well the last time she was in the office."

"I didn't notice. Probably aging like the rest of us."

"Let's see the investigator's report again," Robert said, reaching for the folder.

"Paul threatened to tell my wife." He drew a handkerchief out of his pocket and wiped the perspiration from his forehead. "I've kept this company going in spite of Lillian's threats. I can't go through that again."

After reading the detective's information, Robert slammed it down on the desk. "This Logan guy won't stop at one payment. He'll bleed you dry."

"I know. I know. Look at these figures," Edward said, tapping his finger on the paper. "He's gambled more than he earned."

"How did you come by these figures?"

"My detectives followed him at the racetrack. They picked up his losing stubs." Edwards raised his eyebrows and his voice grew serious. "What if I admit it's my child?"

The legal ramifications of a paternity suit flooded Robert's brain. "Let's find out what Sarah has to say before we jump to any conclusions."

Edward raised his hands, halting the conversation. "No! Sarah doesn't know he's sterile."

"Whew! That puts a sticky twist on this whole matter. Lillian doesn't know either, right?"

"I don't think so," Edward mumbled.

"When are you meeting this man?"

"Tomorrow. He's coming back for the money."

"Send him to my office in the morning. I'll talk to him. Do you want me to confide with any other attorneys?"

"No!" Edward snapped. "Just you."

"I'll get a crew of investigators on this guy. Don't worry yourself sick about this." Robert's eyes were still fixed on the report. He softened his voice. "We've been through worse than this, haven't we?"

"It's a girl," he murmured softly. "If that's my baby, I'm going to support her."

"Whoa!" Robert interrupted. "Let's not jump to conclusions. We can't do anything until we get a blood test. I know a nurse who can get me the information. She owes me a favor."

The following morning Robert entered the office and handed Edward the hospital's report. "The baby's blood type is AB negative, the same as yours. Definitely not Paul's."

"Then it's true," Edward mumbled, his voice barely audible. "I remember the night." He paused, reflecting on his memories. "The baby is mine."

"Just because she has the same blood type, doesn't mean she's yours. There are a lot of other men walking this earth."

"No. Sarah's not like that. I'm satisfied the baby is mine. What do we do now?"

"Don't acknowledge the paternity, yet. Let's sit on this for a while."

"Why? What are we waiting for?"

"For that bastard to make the next move."

"What will happen if I declare the baby? Can I offer her financial assistance?"

"Don't declare anything. This Logan guy is after more than just child support."

"He probably needs cash. What if Lillian finds out and files for divorce?"

"If your wife finds out, that's a horse of a different color. First, let's concentrate on how to protect you, and the business. The legal father is Paul. He's married to Sarah and is living with her. As of now, you have no legal rights."

"What do you mean?" Edward sputtered, thrusting his chin forward.

"You have no control over raising the child."

Edward's hands tightened into a fist, and his words turned sour. "That gambler has control of my daughter's life? He isn't a fit husband. How can he be a good father? He's an adulterer. Any court would find him immoral."

"And you're different?" Robert replied with an accusatory grin.

Edward acknowledged the comment with a submissive nod. "If the child is mine, we can't let this get in the newspapers. It'll embarrass Sarah for sure."

"Sarah hell! What about your wife? For Christ's sake, this could lead to divorce. An illegitimate child can jeopardize the corporation. Society has little tolerance for adultery. Your wife can sue for a larger share of the stock."

Edward tightened his grip the medical report, looked up at Robert and lowered voice submissively. "Talk to that man tomorrow. See what he wants."

The next morning, having researched the legalities of a paternity claim, Robert was well-prepared. He intentionally kept Paul waiting more than an hour before calling him into his office. A long wait usually cools the heels of a client. It was a way of intimidating his opponent, and it usually worked.

Paul sauntered into the office, stopped and scanned the office. "Where's your boss?"

Robert, standing tall, stared defiantly and addressed Paul in a deep, authoritative voice. "There'll be a delay, pending an investigation of your allegations."

Paul stepped back, startled by the unexpected refusal. "Allegations, hell! I'll expose him. I'll call the newspaper. He's the baby's father."

Robert lowered his voice and glared at Paul. "You don't know that. Sit down. Listen to what I have to say." Robert took several threatening steps forward. "You owe some hefty gambling debts, don't you?" he chided with a snide grin.

"How do you know what I owe?"

"Suppose I inform the police. Gamblers have painful methods of collecting, don't they?" Though Robert had no proof, he continued to provoke accusingly. "My detectives tell me your life's been threatened."

Paul stumbled backward, then made his way to the door. He glanced back over his shoulder, and shouted in an angry voice. "I'll pay those damn markers off. He's gonna pay for what he did."

Several month later, Edward picked up the current detective's report. After scanning the report, he again summoned Robert into his office. "It's been months and still no word from Paul." Edward held the report out to his friend. "Look at this! Paul quit his job at the factory. Sarah must be devastated."

Robert snatched the report and thumbed through the pages. "The detectives picked up a few betting stubs they saw Paul tossing at the track. They're date stamped, so now we know how many horses he bets on in one day. But, even with these, we still can't prove they're his."

"Why not? His finger prints are on them."

"He'll claim he was holding them for someone else. Or, he'll deny being at the track."

"Paul hasn't worked in months. Where is he getting his money?"

Robert flipped through the pages. "He re-mortgaged the house. There's not much equity left."

"He must be running low on cash by now."

"That might be the key to stopping this man. Find out where he's getting this money. Let's put a twenty-four-hour surveillance on him."

Edward nodded in agreement. "This waiting is making me nervous. Do you think he'll expose me to the newspapers?"

"No. I think he's running scared. There might have been an attempt on his life. If he paid off his markers, he would have been back by now," Robert turned toward his friend and murmured in a soft voice. "I wonder? Is there a way to see his mail?"

Edward's head shot up. "No. Don't mess with the U.S. government. That's dangerous."

"You're right," Robert replied with a nod and a slight smile.

"Maybe he's winning inside bets."

"They're hard to track."

"It's only a matter of time. I'll have to pay him, eventually."

"Maybe not. Let's keep an eye on him." Robert scanned the pages. "Just sit tight. Something else is going on. I can't put my finger on it, yet."

The loud ring of the telephone interrupted the conversation.

Edward answered in a gruff voice. "I'm not taking calls. Is this important?"

"It's Sarah Logan," Betty replied. "Do you want to speak with her?"

A curious frown crossed Edward's face. "Yes. Put her on."

"Hello Edward," Sarah said, her voice sounded strained and fragile. "It seems I'm always asking you for help. Is it possible to get my job back?"

"Yes, of course," Edward replied, momentarily caught off guard. "You can start any time." Then, he thought of the baby-his baby. "I mean, ah. Who will take care of the baby?"

"My mother will watch Heidi."

A proud smile spread across his face. "Heidi. That's a pretty name. How old is she?"

"A year and a half. She's beautiful."

Edward's heart swelled with paternal pride. Though he longed to see the child, he dared not ask. "Are you all right? You don't need to work. I'll help you." He glanced up and saw Robert shaking his head, but it was too late. The offer had poured out before he had time to consider the legal ramifications.

"I have to find a job. I'm filing for divorce. My husband isn't working, and I'm at my wits end."

"What! Divorce?" Edward gasped.

Robert's head snapped to attention, and he stepped closer to the desk.

"I need someone to talk to," Sarah whimpered. "Things have gone from bad to worse. He's never home, and his gambling is out of control."

"I didn't realize it was that bad. Does he resent the baby?" Edward hesitated. Then his voice rose to a high pitch. "Is the baby okay?"

Robert leaned over the desk, tilted his head to the phone and whispered in Edward's ear. "What's wrong?"

Edward shook his head and waved his friend aside.

"Heidi is fine. I need to work. Paul doesn't hide his gambling from me anymore."

"He's probably addicted," Edward answered, placing his hand over the investigator's report.

Sarah's voice trembled as she spoke. "Am I doing the right thing?"

"Yes. You can't continue living like this. Let me help you. I'll pay your attorney fees."

Robert slapped his hand on his forehead. "Oh no," he whispered.

Edward gripped the phone tighter, turned his face away, ignoring Robert's gestures.

"I'm not asking for financial help. You've done so much already. I need emotional support."

Edward again waved Robert aside and lowered his voice. "I want to help."

"I'll sell the house to pay the attorney. I'll move in with my mother."

"That's not necessary," Edward replied. "Come to my suite Saturday. I'll find a way to help you. I'm at the Book Cadillac Hotel." Edward waited for a response. He heard a soft sigh, and the phone went dead. He glanced up at Robert. "Sarah's filing for divorce. I'm going to help her financially."

"Whoa!" Robert backed away from the desk. "You can't help her. The attorneys will have a field-day with that. If this ends up in court, your money will make her look bad. Does she understand the judge seldom grants a divorce?"

"She's too naïve. She doesn't understand how shocking this is."

"You're damn right. It's rare to get a divorce nowadays."

Edward raised his eyebrows and nodded, acknowledging the problem.

"The court intentionally makes a divorce difficult, if not impossible. They claim a stable family is for the sake of the children."

"Yes. I understand that. But, under the circumstance, Paul isn't providing for Sarah or his family."

"I know, but it's the law." Robert unbuttoned his jacket and sat down. "That man's got you over a barrel. He's using Sarah as leverage to control to you."

"If I don't play his game, he'll expose me as the father," Edward muttered under his breath.

"You can bet on that."

"On the other hand, if I refuse to help, Sarah will think I've forsaken her."

"You still care, don't you?"

Edward nodded. "I always will."

"If you want to help Sarah, we'll find a way. This won't be easy."

Edward leaned back and heaved a sigh of relief. "I'm glad for Sarah's sake she's ending this marriage. The next step is to find out how I can take care of her, and my baby."

"Whew! Let me think about that. They were married more than a year. Is that right?"

"Eighteen months and six days."

Robert raised his eyebrows at the unexpected response. Changing his tone of voice, he spoke firmly, but with authority. "Right now, we deny your paternity."

"If that's my daughter, I want to give her a safe home and financial security." Edward knew the risk he would be taking, but his conscience made the decision. "I've got to help her, no matter what the consequence."

CHAPTER 26

Henry Robbins, a short, stocky man with a pasty complexion and thin, receding gray hair, greeted Sarah with a limp handshake. He led her down a narrow hall to a small, cluttered office. After lighting a brown-tipped cigarette, he elbowed a pile of papers aside and placed a yellow, legal pad on the desk.

"All right my dear. I understand you want a divorce. How long have you been married?"

"We were married in May 1945, over two years ago."

Robbins took a deep drag of his cigarette and laid it across an ashtray. "Do you have any children?"

"Yes, a girl. She's seventeen months."

"Hum," Robbins murmured with raised eyebrows. He had taken little notice of the smoke drifting from his cigarette until Sarah wheezed and gasped for air. After a nod of recognition he shuffled across the room and hoisted a window open. "Tell me why you want a divorce," he said as he returned to his desk.

A waft of cold air drifted in, and with it the sound of distant traffic.

Sarah perched on the edge of her chair. She had always been a private person and found it difficult to talk about intimate matters. "My husband is a gambler," she said, her voice trembling with uncertainty. "He drinks to excess and is verbally abusive."

"Did you know he gambled before you married him?"

"No. He started gambling and drinking after the birth of our baby."

"Hum. And when was that? Oh, yeah. I have that information, don't I? That's when your husband started gambling." Robbins smirked and smoothed the sides of his pencil thin mustache with the tips of his fingers. He leaned forward, giving the appearance of genuine concern. "He was okay before that, huh?"

"No. Not really. He always drank. I didn't realize how much until after we were married."

"Was he abusive?" Robbins asked, positioning his pen, ready to jot down the answer.

"Well, when he drinks, he gets mean." Sarah felt a flush of heat spread across her face. "He's seeing other women. Sometimes his clothes smell like cheap perfume."

"Where does your husband work?"

"He used to worked at a factory. I don't know if he quit, or got fired."

Robbins scribble more notes across the page, and with an icy stare waited for her to continue.

"I don't think he's working now, but he always has money." Sarah rummaged through her purse, pulled out her checkbook and held it toward the attorney. "I can prove he took money from our bank account."

Robbins flipped through the pages, noting the available cash. "Um, huh. Stop worrying. I'll get you out of this marriage." Robbins shoved the bankbook across the desk. "I'll need a retainer fee before I file the motion. Here's the contract," he said, sliding a sheet of paper across the desk.

"Do I have to pay this right now?"

Robbins raised his eyebrows. "Is that a problem?"

"No. I'll get the money."

"Divorce is very difficult now days. Are you ready for the stigma attached to a divorce? Don't worry. I'll take care of everything." He stood up and snuffed his cigarette out with a firm twist, signaling the end of the meeting.

Sarah left his office feeling a great burden had been lifted. After all, didn't he say he would take care of everything?

Several days later, as planned, Edward waited at his suite for Sarah's arrival. He hadn't seen her since her marriage and when he opened the door, her frail appearance startled him. Even though she lost the sparkle in her eyes, she was more beautiful than he remembered. He wanted to take her in his arms, to comfort her. But, sensing her despair, he stepped back, allowing her to enter.

"I feel terrible asking you for attorney fees." Sarah cast her eyes down and hurried past him. "You're always there when I need you."

"Don't worry about the money," Edward replied with a wave of his hand.

Sarah glanced across the elegant living room, and headed toward a long, plush couch.

Edward waited until she was seated, then sat beside her. "Are you all right? How can I help?"

Sarah fumbled through her purse and handed him the contract. "This is how much it will cost. I'll pay you back as soon as I sell my house."

"That's not necessary," Edward interrupted, pushing her hand aside. He opened his wallet and laid a pile of bills on the cushion, more than the required amount.

Sarah's face reddened, and a faint smile of relief slipped across her lips.

Seeing the flush on Sarah's face, he grasped her hand lightly. "Forget about paying this back." *It's my parental duty*, he thought.

His conscience would have it no other way. "You refused to accept the country house I built for you." He paused, hesitant to bring up old memories. "I'm sorry. Let's not talk about the past." Edward leaned across the couch, his eyes twinkled with curiosity. "How is Heidi?"

"Fine, just fine."

"Do you have a picture of her?"

Sarah opened her purse and laid several photographs on the cushion.

Edward examined the pictures and a feeling of pride swelled within. He studied the child's pale blue eyes, wispy blond hair and dimpled chin. *She has my chin,* he thought. "She's beautiful," he murmured. Though he wanted to ask for a photograph, he reluctantly laid them on the cushion. "I'm glad you're divorcing Paul. Please, let me buy you a house."

Sarah raised her hand up as a protest. "No. The court will ask where I live. How will I explain that?"

"You're right. It would give the wrong impression."

Sarah picked up the money and photographs, then tucked them in her purse. "I appreciative your help," Sarah said as she rose to leave.

Edward stood up and wrapped his arms around Sarah, pressing her to him. "I'll take care of you," he whispered in her ear. It was apparent that living with Paul had taken an emotional toll. She had been the victim of false promises, and her innocence touched his heart. He felt her body melting into his, her warm tears dampened his shoulder. Though he wanted to reveal their love child, and explain his parental responsibility, he remained silent. He held her close until he felt her pulling away. Reluctantly, he loosened his grip.

Later that evening, Edward returned to the west wing. The living room was quiet, except for the muffled sound of voices coming from the servant's quarters in the attic. Before turning on the lamp, he went to the window, shoved aside the drape, and scanned the yard.

The moonlight cast eerie shadows across the snow-covered ground. The main house was dark, except for a single light that shone through a kitchen window.

He searched the back of the yard where the swing once hung under the old oak tree. Now, only two long cords of hemp rope dangled from the branches. He turned away, shaking the dreary images from his mind.

Will Sarah's divorce lead to further investigation? Will I be exposed as the baby's father? As the questions raced across his mind, an icy breeze brushed across his face, and he thought of his mother. *Mama told me to play the piano when I felt troubled.* He turned on the lamp and headed for the piano.

His fingers danced across the keys as he reminisced on pleasant memories. He tried to keep the music cheerful, but his emotions took over and the tone of music grew heavy. His fingers moved by instinct, slowing down the tempo. Music usually relaxed him, but tonight his problems came crashing down around him. *Will Lillian file for divorce? Will Sarah be charged with alienation of affection? Lillian hadn't filed before. Will she do it this time?* His fingers pressed the keys harder, pushing the melancholy away.

His body trembled thinking of the consequences, for he knew how vindictive his wife could be. *Will she take control of the company? Will she interfere with management?* The melody turned sour, then finished in an intense crescendo. He slammed the keyboard closed and turned off the lamp. *I have a beautiful little girl, and I can't cradle her in my arms.*

An eerie chill swept through his body, causing the hair on his arms to stand up. He glanced across the room, expecting to see someone or something, but the room remained empty. "It's all my fault," he murmured under his breath.

The following day Sarah delivered the retainer fee to the lawyer's office. "I found these betting stubs," she said, laying a stack of tickets on his desk. "They're worth hundreds of dollars. That's more than he earns in a month, when he is working."

Robbins copied the ticket numbers, then with the back of his hand, shoved them aside. "Where does he get this kind of money?"

"He leaves the house every day, but I don't know if he's working. I've never seen his paycheck."

"And?" Robbins asked as he jotted the information on a legal pad.

"I pay the household bills."

"Yes? And?"

"I caught him stealing money out of my wallet."

"All right, continue," Robbins groaned. It was obvious this client didn't control the family finances, and he didn't intend to spend too much time on this case. "What else?" he grumbled, eager to finish the interview.

"He's verbally and physically abusive. I'm sure he's running around with other women."

"What other women?"

Sarah fingered the straps of her purse, twisting them around her fingers. "I found lipstick on his shirts. Sometimes he doesn't come home for days." She turned away, too embarrassed to face the attorney.

"Do you have money for the filing? Will you have to sell the house?" he asked, intentionally changing the subject.

"What?" Sarah sputtered, unprepared for the insensitive request.

"I'll need a copy of your bank accounts and any property you own."

"My only asset is the equity in our home." Sarah folded her arms across her chest and scowled. "What does our savings account, have to do with my divorce?"

"Perhaps you should sell your house," he said, even though he knew the judge would frown on such a request.

"What?" Sarah blustered, taken aback by the attorney's hostile questioning.

"Don't worry. In most cases the judge allows the woman to stay in the marital home, especially where a small child is involved."

"Can I sell it without Paul's approval? After all, we have both our names on the deed. He didn't put any money toward the down payment, but he still owns half the equity."

"You can try selling, if you want to," Robbins said, tapping his pen impatiently. "I need a retainer before I file the papers."

"Isn't the husband supposed to pay a part of the legal fees?"

"Well, usually he's obligated to pay. But, whether he will, is a different story." Robbins continued tapping his pencil, waiting for an answer.

"I've got the money," Sarah replied as she handed him several large bills, the exact amount indicated on the contract.

The following week, Paul Logan was served with a 'Complaint for Divorce.' He burst into Lenny Mousa's office waving the pleading in the air. "Son of a bitch," he yelled, slamming a document on the desk. "My wife filed for divorce."

The papers landed on top of an ashtray, sending cigar butts and ashes flying in the air.

Lenny Mousa, a swarthy, leather skinned man, covered his nose and let out a shallow cough. He pushed himself away from the desk until the cloud of ash settled. Being accustomed to emotional outbursts by his clients, he accepted Paul's anger as typical. "What? I didn't know you were married," Mousa replied as he elbowed the ashes off his desk.

"I didn't think she had the guts. Damn it! This ruins all my plans."

Mousa blew the cinders away with a hearty puff, picked up the pleadings and read aloud. "Your wife is accusing you of adultery, verbal abuse, physical abuse, excessive use of alcohol, extreme mental cruelty, spousal neglect, gambling, and willful negligence to provide common necessities to the family, thereby destroying the object of matrimony. Phew! What the hell have you been doing?"

"She's a damn liar!" Paul grumbled.

Mousa glanced at the top of the page, noting the opposing attorney's name. "I know this guy," he said with a boastful smirk. It is an unsaid agreement between certain attorneys to stretch a case, thus increasing legal fees, and, he was sure this attorney would cooperate.

Paul leaned over and braced his hands on the desk. "I don't want this divorce!"

An envious grin swept across Mousa's face. "Hell. I didn't know you had a wife. I never saw her at the racetrack."

"Yeah, I'm married. I never brought the old lady with me."

"You brought some good-lookers," he quipped with a lustful grin that bared his yellow-stained teeth. "What the hell have you been doing? Screwing around?" Mousa ran his hand through his curly black hair, raising his bushy eyebrows with envy.

Paul shrugged off the remark as inconsequential. "You gotta stop this divorce."

Mousa crunched down on a soggy cigar and grinned. "I'll file an 'Answer to Plaintiff's Complaint.' Let's see what she had to say."

Paul's recent drinking binge left him bleary-eyed and shaky. He nodded his reply, weaved unsteadily and clutched the desk.

"Sit down, before you fall down," Mousa growled as he flipped through the pages. "You wanna stay married, huh?"

"Yeah."

"Okay. We'll deny the charges." Mousa studied Paul's anxiety and wondered if his concern was genuine. "I'll file this right away. Can you get money to cover my fee?"

"Sure. You know me. I'm gonna hit the long-shot" Paul chided, making light of the situation with a cocky grin. He withdrew a wad of money from his pocket and flipped several hundred-dollar bills on the desk.

The following week, Robbins summoned Sarah to his office. "I received your husband's 'Counter Complaint.' He's denying all allegations." Robbins nodded toward a chair. "Please sit down while I read this. Your husband alleges everything in your motion is untrue, misleading, and unfounded in law and fact. He's challenging you to support those accusations with proof."

"Every thing I said is true," Sarah whined.

"Did you receive your copy in the mail?"

Sarah looked up in surprise. "No! What copy?"

"Your husband's attorney is obligated to mail you a copy. Here. Look at this," he said, pushing a document across his desk.

"What is this?" Sarah pulled the document toward her and scanned the pages. "It says I'm vindictive and unsympathetic toward Paul's needs." Unprepared for the accusations filed against her, Sarah felt light-headed, and drew a long breath. "That's not true!"

Robbins leaned back and folded his arms across his chest. "Continue reading."

"It claims I failed to take care of my daughter and Paul properly. That's not true either. None of this is true?"

"That's what he claims."

"He's accusing me of." Sarah stopped and quoted from the motion. "Working outside the home to evade custodial responsibility to husband and daughter."

"Are you working?"

"Yes. To pay the bills. I've never neglected my child, or Paul."

"He also accused you, and again, let me quote. 'Grossly fabricating allegations of alcohol and gambling to intentionally cause harm and injury to Paul's good name.'"

"What good name?"

"What's your defense?" Robbins slid a legal pad toward him, gripped a pencil and waited for her reply.

Although Sarah wanted to burst out in tears, she held her composure. "How can I defend lies?"

"You must prove these allegations are false." Robbins, recalling the small amount in her bankbook, surmised there wouldn't be much money to be made on her case. "Misses Logan. He's challenging you with 'Cause for Fault.' What's good for the goose, is good for the gander."

"What about the racetrack tickets I gave you? Isn't that proof he gambled?"

Robbins leaned back in his chair with a satisfied smile on his face. "We can't prove those are his. He could have picked them up off the street. They could belong to a friend."

"I found them in his pockets. Most were in his dresser drawer." Sarah felt vulnerable, disillusioned by her attorney's insensitive attitude.

"That isn't proof he bought them," Robbins answered with a snide grin.

Sarah slumped back in her chair, disappointed and disgusted.

"We need to prove his gambling is out of control and is causing you emotional and financial harm."

"How do I prove it? Aren't you supposed to do something?"

"Sure, but it takes money to investigate. Have you ever hired a detective?"

"No. What for?"

Robbins shoved several papers aside as he searched for a contract. "Ah, here it is," he said, dragging a document toward him.

"What is that?"

"If you want me to defend you, you'll have to hire an investigator."

"I told you, he's abusive."

"You haven't proven that!" Robbins said, holding his hand up as if it were a red flag. "Show me some bruises. Did you ever file a complaint with the police?"

Sarah frowned and shook her head.

"Misses Logan. We need evidence." Robbins voice turned cold and emotionless. "If you want this divorce, we must hire a detective."

Sarah squirmed, and a nauseating sensation filled her stomach. "How much will that cost?"

"We'll start with three hundred dollars. It depends on what the investigator finds. We'll keep him on the books in case we need more evidence."

Sarah set six, fifty-dollar bills on the desk.

Robbins raised his eyebrows. "You have the money?" he said, dragging the bills toward him.

"What else do I need?"

"I'll phone you next week," Robbins replied as he guided her toward the door. As soon as Sarah left, he dialed the opposing attorney's phone. Robbins started with a casual conversation. "Hi Lenny. How's your golf?"

Mousa, recognizing the voice, replied with a long-winded explanation. "Perfect. Went to Florida and played golf last month."

Robbins listened patiently even though he suspected Mousa was stalling. "Good! Anything new going on?"

The phone echoed a deadened silence.

Mousa's voice broke the silence. "I see we're going to court."

"Yeah. It looks like it." Robbins changed the tone of his voice. "I'm curious. My client claims she married to a penniless gambler, yet didn't hesitate when I asked to hire a detective."

"Oh, yeah?"

"That lady didn't flinch. She paid the detective without batting an eye." Robbins paused, waiting for Mousa to slip up and divulge personal information.

Once again, the phone grew silent.

"Oh yeah," Mousa mumbled.

"What's the deal? Who's this Logan guy?"

"He's a friend of mine," Mousa quipped, still tight-lipped.

"Quite a pleading you filed. Your client doesn't want this divorce, does he?"

"You don't know who your client is, do you?" Mousa boasted, barely able to contain his good fortune.

"Sarah Logan? Seems like a dull, timid woman."

"Ha! That's what you think," Mousa snickered as he rolled a wet cigar between his teeth. "I did a little research of my own. That lady was once Edward Hansen's kept woman."

"You mean the Edward Hansen?" Robbins' eyes widened, and he pressed the phone closer to his ear. "Are you sure he was running around with that mousy looking woman?"

"Yeah. Her husband, Paul, worked at the Hansen Corporation. That's when I put the puzzle together."

"She mentioned her husband worked at several places."

"There might be more to this than meets the eye."

"Let's see where this goes," Robbins replied, then ended the conversation quickly. The Hansen name piqued his curiosity, and he regretted having treated Sarah with such hostility. He postponed the next court hearing until March. This would give him time to investigate if Edward Hansen was somehow involved. Later that day, though it was unethical, he telephoned Edward.

"Hello. I'm Henry Robbins, attorney at law. I'm representing Sarah Logan in her divorce. Thought you might want to know."

Edward hesitated, taken off guard by the unfamiliar voice. "How the hell did you get my number? Why are you calling me?"

"I'm just trying to help Sarah Logan."

"Get her out of that marriage quickly, and quietly."

"Okay. You want this kept quiet, huh?" Robbins asked, encouraging Edward to carry on a casual conversation.

The phone grew silent.

When Robbins realized he couldn't draw more information, he changed the tone of his voice. "Call me any time. I'm in the phone book. Henry Robbins, that my name. Robbins, attorney at law."

The following morning, Mousa phoned Edward's office. He hoped to speak to Edward before his attorneys warned him not to comment on Sarah's divorce.

"Hello. Lenny Mousa here. I'm Paul Logan's attorney. My client doesn't want a divorce," he said, intending to provoke an argument.

"Why are you calling me?" Edward blustered, irritated by the second unsolicited telephone call.

"I understand you want this divorce to go through quietly," Mousa said in a deep voice, emphasizing the word *quiet*. He knew Robbins would have contacted Sarah's male acquaintances. And, if it involved Edward Hansen, then his money is involved as well.

"How did you know that?"

Mousa snapped his finger and grinned. He had hit the secret word. "Ain't gonna happen. My client won't keep quiet," he chided, again goading Edward into divulging valuable information.

Edward slammed the phone down. After he calmed down, he phoned his personal attorney.

Robert, hearing the frustration in Edward's voice, hurried to his office. When he entered the room, he saw a perplexed look on Edward's face. "What happened?"

"Two attorneys phoned me about Sarah's divorce. What's going on?"

"They what?" Robert bellowed. "That's unethical. They're way out of line." Robert flopped in a chair and lowered his voice. "Did they mention the baby?"

"No. The call took me off guard. I told them to settle the matter quietly."

Robert slapped his hand against his forehead. "Oh no! You shouldn't have said that! That's exactly what they want to hear."

"What do you mean?"

"They're not interested in helping you. They want to know if you're financially supporting Sarah. What else did they say?"

"Not too much. Only that they want to help me."

"Ha! I'll bet they sounded sincere."

"Oh yeah. They were real friendly. I didn't tell them anything."

"Oh, yes you did," Robert interrupted, pointing his finger accusingly.

"I don't understand the law like you do. I only made an innocent comment."

"You told them to keep it quiet. Now they suspect you're helping Sarah. Those attorneys won't stop until they find out *why* you want this kept quiet. How the hell did they get your private home phone?"

"Maybe Paul got it from Sarah?"

"Probably," Robert mumbled under his breath.

"That call took me off guard. Damn it! It's illegal for them to phone me, isn't it?"

"Not illegal, but it's unethical. They didn't ask you for money, did they?"

"No."

"It's not a crime unless they're caught taking money under false pretenses. Even then, they could make it appear legitimate, as a service. You can't prosecute an attorney for trying to help."

"Do you think they'll call again?"

"No. They know you spoke with your legal staff by now. The damage is done. If anyone asks about Sarah's divorce, refer them to me."

CHAPTER 27

In July Sarah's attorney requested a fourth meeting. Robbins set a document in front of Sarah. "Here's the detective's report and his bill."

After reading the short, two-page account of her husband's actions, Sarah slammed the report down on the desk. "Your detective spent two weeks, and this is all they came up with? We already knew Paul was gambling. Didn't they find out if he was still running around?"

"Sorry. They only found he was gambling. That's not a crime."

"You still have the racetrack tickets. That proves how much money he gambled."

"Oh, those tickets? Didn't I give them back to you?"

"No. I left them with you. You put them right here," Sarah snapped, tapping her finger on the spot he had placed the tickets.

"They're not here. You're sure you didn't lose them?"

"No. I didn't! They must be in this office." Sarah swiped her hand across the desk, spreading aside a stack of papers. *Could he be that incompetent?*

"I didn't keep those tickets." Robbins replied with a confused look on his faced. "What were they? Racetrack stubs? The court demand more than gambling as grounds for divorce."

"What about harassment? He always starts an argument. Living with him is miserable."

"Don't argue with him."

"He hasn't paid the household bills."

"You'll have to pay the bills until I file for support. Anything else happen?"

"I've had three flat tires in the past month."

"Hum. Continue," Robbins grumbled as he jotted information on his legal pad.

"Someone is following me. One day I parked my car while shopping. When I returned, the rear-view mirror had been tilted."

"Tilted?" Robbins groaned.

"Yes. That means someone was in my car."

"Maybe you bumped the mirror."

"I don't think so. It's happened several times. That's not all. Someone moved the hands of the clock forward six minutes."

Robbins frowned quizzically. "Only six minutes?" he replied with a snicker.

"Yes. Six minutes. You know. Like the sign of the devil. Six, six, six. I always lock my car, but it still happens."

"You're overreacting. The judge will think you're crazy if I name the devil in your complaint." Robbins scratched out the notes with exaggerated swipes of the pencil. "I don't mean to belittle your evidence, but we can't use that. It's meaningless."

"But it's true. Paul's making me a nervous wreck. I don't feel safe in my car anymore. Can't you make him stop?"

"I can't accuse him unless you saw him messing with your car. Your husband's attorney is a coward. When he's losing a case, he terrorizes his opponents. I'll find out who sabotaged your tires. Let's get back to the facts we can prove."

"All right," Sarah grumbled. "He's spending all the money."

"He has a right to spend his own money. You can't divorce him for that."

Sarah, feeling defeated, slumped down in her chair. "He's never home in the evening. I think he's still gambling."

"If your husband doesn't earn money, how can you accuse him of spending it? It's a hard sell to prove he's still gambling."

"What if I take the baby and run away?"

Robbin's voice rose to a high pitch. "You plan to move somewhere?"

"I have a place in mind," Sarah said, remembering Edward's offer.

"Who with? You have another house in mind?"

Seeing she had piqued her attorney's curiosity, Sarah decided not to explain. "I'll stay with my mother."

"You can't remove his daughter from the marital home. Your husband will file a complaint. The court will take action against you."

"I have no rights?" Sarah whimpered.

"You must prove he broke the marital vows. And so far, we don't have evidence he dated other women."

"What about the law, Cause for Fault? What does that mean?"

"That is when the court decides who is entitled to the greater share of the marital assets. If we prove your husband is at fault, the court would consider those charges against him. In that case, you would get the larger settlement."

"But this is his fault."

"Now, Fault Divorce is another issue. It means the plaintiff, that's you, must prove your husband is at fault. Then the judge will grant a divorce. Lots of people are confused by those two legal issues."

"Do you mean, if I can't *prove* he's a rotten man, I can't get a divorce?"

"That's right. It's your burden of proof."

"I'm stuck in this loveless marriage?"

"This is 1947. Our courts demand Fault Divorce. Maybe the law will change in the future. Then it will be easier for women to get out of a bad marriage. Until then, you, and women like you, will be prisoners in your own homes."

"I can't live with him anymore."

"Sorry. My hands are tied. Until you bring strong evidence of abuse or adultery, you must stay with your husband."

Several days later, Mousa sheltered himself behind his desk before he spoke. "I agreed to let your wife's attorney delay the proceedings."

"Why the hell did you do that?" Paul grumbled.

"We need time for discovery. It'll cost, if you want this to go away."

"Ha! You brag about your connections. Do something."

Mousa folded his arms across his chest and crunched a cigar between his teeth. "Yeah. I do, but there's a possibility Edward Hansen might intervene."

Paul's head jolted upright. "What the hell are you talking about?"

Mousa continued, implying he knew more than he actually did. "Edward Hansen can afford to buy the plaintiff's freedom."

"How did you find out about him?" Paul leaned over the desk and glared at his attorney. "I don't want that son-of-a-bitch's name mentioned."

"Hey! What can I do? Money talks!" Mousa chided, keeping a safe distance behind the desk.

Paul stepped back, setting himself aside of the situation. "Keep that bastard's name out of this," he grumbled as he hurried toward the door.

"I'll do what I can," Mousa called out as he watched Paul slam the door behind him. After lighting another cigar, he thumbed carefully through the pleadings. "I wonder why he doesn't want Hansen's name mentioned? There must be more to this than meets the eye."

Paul, determined to stop the divorce, came up with a scheme. He attended the racetrack daily where he had previously seen the judge who was presiding over his case. Day after day, he scoured the crowd. At the end of the second week his hunch paid off.

Judge Burris, a squatly, gray haired man, was standing in line at the betting window.

Paul pulled out his camera, adjusted the telephoto lens and began snapping pictures. Later that evening, keeping his car at a safe distance, he tailed the judge and his lady-friend down the dark, winding streets.

The judge pulled his car into the parking lot of a secluded motel off the highway.

Paul coasted into a dark corner, waiting to see which bungalow the couple would occupy. After several minutes, he peeked in the window and started taking pictures.

Several days later, after his friend had developed the film, he telephoned Judge Burris. "Your Honor. This is Paul Logan. I met you at the racetrack a couple of years ago."

"What? Do I know you?" the judge answered in a friendly voice.

"Probably not. But I know you. My divorce is coming up in your court. Logan verses Logan," Paul replied, keeping his voice firm and convincing.

"How did you get my private phone number?"

"This is important," Paul countered in a strong, assertive voice.

"Logan versus Logan? Yeah. I read that motion. You're in deep shit my friend," the judge quipped with a chuckle.

"I wanna tell you something. I gotta a few pictures of you and your lady friend at the racetrack. And, at the motel if ya know what I mean."

Cupping his hand around the mouthpiece, the judge lowered his voice to a whisper. "What the hell do you want?"

"I need your help. I'll keep those pictures out of the newspaper if you deny the divorce. Ya wouldn't want your wife to see them, would ya?"

"You son-of-a-bitch," the judge mumbled under his breath.

Hearing the uncertainty in the judge's voice, Paul felt he had the situation under control. "Let's keep this between you and me. You can't afford a scandal. Not in an election year."

"All right," the judge muttered, holding his hand near the mouthpiece. "Be careful, Mister Logan. I'm watching you. If you so much as blink the wrong way, I'll have you arrested."

The day of the trial, Sarah followed her attorney to the front of the courtroom where Paul and his attorney were seated. The large size of the courtroom overwhelmed her, and she felt scared and emotionally fragile.

A chatter of whispers was heard throughout the room, and the benches were filling up fast.

Robert Michaels slipped in the side-door and made his way to the back of the room. He sat down and scanned the visitors. A curious frown crossed his face when he spotted Lillian's attorneys, Shilling and Goldstein, looking back at him with the same perplexing frown.

The courtroom hummed with chattering voices until the bailiff, a gruff looking man in a gray uniform, faced the people and shouted, "The Honorable Judge Burris. All rise."

The judge entered the courtroom and, as was his daily routine, he looked over his silver-rimmed spectacles and scanned the room for familiar faces. He immediately recognized Robert seated at the back of the room. He sat down and dragged the docket-sheet across the desk, checking to see why a corporation attorney was in court. His eyes shifted to Shilling and Goldstein seated in a corner with their heads bent and their faces shielded by documents. Though Judge Burris's face gave no hint of concern, he was curious why they were trying to be inconspicuous.

"Please be seated," a husky voice echoed. The courtroom grew quiet.

Judge Burris ran his fingers down the page. Being familiar with most of the attorneys, he mentally matched each to their client. None seemed to involve the Hansen Corporation. Setting the docket-sheet aside, he sent a damning glance to Paul Logan which went unnoticed by most spectators, then nodded to the bailiff.

The bailiff shouted. "Logan versus Logan."

Robbins and Mousa jumped up and made their way to the front of the courtroom.

Robbins approached first. "Good morning your Honor. I'm Henry Robbins. Counsel for Plaintiff, Sarah Logan. She is asking for a divorce as stated in this motion." The words spewed from his lips with an air of confidence as he presented his case. When he finished, he glanced at Mousa with a cocky grin and strutted back to the plaintiff's table.

Mousa swaggered across the room. He stopped midway and faced the spectators. With a smirking grin he nodded, then turned his attention to the judge.

"Good morning your Honor. Lenny Mousa. Attorney for Defendant, Paul Logan." Mousa's smile disappeared as he began his presentation. "Your Honor! There's no proof the defendant committed the accusations as alleged in this motion. The plaintiff's motion is misleading. It's been filed in bad faith to cause emotional harm to my client." Mousa spouted on and on, confident of his personal relationship with the judge. "My client is innocent of all allegations," he said, playing out the scene as if he was on stage.

The judge glanced over his spectacles, again scanning the courtroom. He noticed the attorneys, Shilling and Goldstein, feverishly taking notes. It was apparent there was a connection between the Hansen Corporation, Shilling and Goldstein, and Paul Logan. He was in a quandary; Hansen's political influence had fund raising potential for his election, but Paul's incriminating photographs could be damaging. Needing time to sort out his advantage, he bowed his head pretending to review the documents. "Counselor. Continue," he mumbled, keeping his voice unemotional and firm.

"Your Honor!" Robbins interrupted. "Counsel failed to present evidence to dismiss Plaintiff's allegations." When Robbins felt he was losing ground, he blurted out before considering the implications. "We're requesting more time for discovery."

Judge Burris raised his eyebrows and glanced around the room. Here was his chance to hold Paul at bay until he found out more. He held his hand up, notifying the attorneys to stop talking. "Time for discovery? Okay. I'm setting the next hearing for February. That's *next* year, counselors," he replied with a satisfying grin, tossing the file aside with obvious indifference. "Bailiff. Let's take a break."

Paul glanced up, and when he saw the judge glaring at him, he mouthed the words under his breath. "You son-of-a-bitch."

The judge smirked, stood up and looked over his eyeglasses. Again, he scanned the audience, making a point to stare directly at the back of the courtroom.

"All rise," the bailiff shouted.

Paul stood until the judge left the room, then followed Mousa into the corridor. "Why didn't he hear my case today?"

Mousa put his hand to the side of his mouth and whispered. "We need evidence against your wife before we try this case."

"Against Sarah?" Paul whispered. "What do you mean?"

"Let me handle this. I'll stop her from divorcing you. Trust me. I know what I'm doing," Mousa replied with a cocky grin, turned and sauntered down the noisy corridor.

"Why the long delay?" Sarah asked as she followed her attorney into the hall.

"We need time to prepare for his case."

"But February is too long to wait"

"The court has a full docket. Their cases are backed up," Robbins mumbled, then turned on his heels and headed toward the exit, leaving Sarah standing alone in the corridor.

Shilling and Goldstein hurried out of the courtroom. When they saw Sarah standing alone, they kept their heads down and merged in the crowded corridor.

Goldstein placed his hand across his mouth. "I wonder why Misses Hansen insists that we monitor this case?"

Shilling shrugged his shoulder. "Maybe she thinks her husband is still running with that teacher."

Goldstein let out a low chuckle. "I wonder about that too."

"Did you notice Robert Michaels in court today?" Shilling whispered as he edged his way through the crowded hall. "He was hiding at the back. He saw us."

"I'm sure the judge noticed all of us. He's probably wondering what the hell is going on."

Shilling nodded. "The last time Misses Hansen was in my office, she was raving mad. She demanded I prepare her divorce. It took a lot of persuading to convince her to stay married."

"Maybe she wants to know about Sarah and keep her eye on her husband. What are *you* going to tell misses Hansen today?" Goldstein asked as he followed his friend down the corridor.

"Why me? You're going to tell her something too, aren't you?"

"I'll prepare an account of today's hearing. I'll tell her the case is going in Paul Logan's favor."

"Convince her that Sarah may *not* get her divorce. That's what she wants to hear." Shilling made his way past a crowd of people and mumbled under his breath. "Misses Hansen scares the piss out of me."

In the meantime, Robert made his way to the clerk's office and approached a clerk. "I want two copies of the Logan versus Logan file."

The woman nodded and began searching through a stack of pleading. "That file isn't back yet."

"What? It should have left the courtroom by now."

"I'll try to locate it." The clerk searched through several file cabinets, after talking on the phone for several minutes, she leaned over the counter. "That file is in the judge's chamber. Judge Burris wants to review that case. It might be quite a while before he releases it."

"I'll wait," Robert replied, then made his way to a long, wooden bench against the wall.

Several hours later, the clerk set two green folders on the counter. "Your copies are here. Sign the register," she said, pushing the sign-in sheet across the counter.

Robert signed the register, and returned to the Hansen Corporation. He had a grim look on his face as entered Edward's office. He set his briefcase on the floor and withdrew two folders.

"What took you so long? I expected you back hours ago."

After clearing his throat, Robert placed the copies on the desk. "The judge held the file in his chamber. That's not a good sign. That means he's interested in this case."

"He held it over two hours?"

"The judge noticed the attorneys were stretching this case. He wants to know why."

Edward glanced up and frowned. "Stretching it? What the hell for?"

"Be prepared Mister Hansen. Those attorneys could approach you again." Robert unbuttoned his jacket and sat down. "Even though it's common knowledge you severed your relationship with Sarah, I suspect they got a whiff of money."

Edward picked up the pleadings and set his jaw stubbornly. "I don't give a damn about the money. How can we help Sarah?"

"I took notes." Robert pulled a legal pad from his briefcase. "We've got to be careful. Don't talk to Sarah. Not a word to her attorney, either."

Edward nodded in agreement, then scanned the file. "It says Paul hasn't held a job in months. Sarah paid all the household bills."

"The bills are trivial. Those attorneys were arguing superficial issues. It looks like they'll financially bleed Sarah…, until."

"Until what?" Edward interrupted.

"Until she's out of money. They're forcing your hand. They're waiting for you to intercede. Or, if I'm right, they may force her to drop the legal proceeding."

"Drop it? I won't let her do that! I'll hire a high profile attorney."

"You can't. That'll tip your hand." Robert flipped the page, scanning the notes on his legal pad. "I can't put my finger on it, but something else is going on. I noticed the judge glaring at Paul Logan. It looks like he has a personal vendetta against him. The judge set this case aside much too quickly."

Edward interrupted. "He can't do that. Can he?"

"It's perfectly legal. It's his courtroom. He's using his judicial power to serve his own agenda."

"What? They can't do that!"

Robert ran his finger down the page and scanned his notes. "If the judge doesn't like Paul Logan, he could have made a fool of him today. But, he didn't. He could have dismissed the allegations for lack of evidence, but he didn't. Instead, he gave the attorneys extra time for discovery. It looks like the judge and Mousa are playing games. This could be a long, drawn out battle."

"I've got to help Sarah. This has been so stressful for her."

"Look! No matter what you do, you are still married."

"You don't understand. I never knew real love until I met Sarah."

"You can't intercede. What if your wife finds out you're backing Sarah financially? She could cause a lot of trouble."

Edward slumped back in his chair, his shoulders drooped wearily. "I have to help. Sarah's the mother of my child."

CHAPTER 28

———•◆•———

February arrived and Sarah made her way to the front of the courtroom. She acknowledged her attorney with a weak smile and slid into the wooden bench beside him. "It looks like we're early. Does that mean our case will be heard first?"

"Not necessarily. I checked the docket sheet. The judge will be hearing three cases today."

The bailiff, a husky, stern looking man, entered the courtroom through a side door. He waited until he had the spectator's attention, then shouted, "All rise. The Honorable Judge Burris."

The judge entered from the same side door and glanced across the courtroom, mentally placing each attorney with his litigant. He sat down, nodded to the bailiff and the trials began.

After two, long boring trials, most of the spectators had left the courtroom. It was past four o'clock when the bailiff shouted. "Logan verses Logan."

Robbins shook the drowsy feeling from his head and approached the judge's bench. He began his presentation, speaking articulately, as if he enjoyed hearing his own voice. He rambled on, intentionally rushing through critical evidence.

The judge, seeing Paul squirming in his seat, interrupted the hearing. "Counselor! Present your evidence in more detail. You're rushing through too quickly." He glanced at Paul and nodded with a smirk of satisfaction.

From that moment on the trial proceeded at a snail's pace.

Robbins pleaded Sarah's right to be divorced, yet failed to present the gambling tickets as evidence. After a long, drawn out presentation, which accomplished very little, he strolled back to his seat with a satisfied grin on his face.

Now, it was Mousa's turn. Lenny Mousa presented his client as a bereaved husband who still loved his wife. Pleading the defendant had been wrongly accused of gambling and was innocent of any wrongful acts. With a pitiable voice Mousa claimed his client could not find work, therefore, had no money for gambling.

The hours passed. The attorneys droned on and on, reciting the law as if rehearsing for a stage play. Each citing trivial matters and frivolous issues. At the end of the long day, the attorneys had made little progress, and the judge again failed to rule on any issues.

Months passed and the court hearings went according to the attorneys' intention to stretch the proceedings. The attorneys put on a sham display of half-truths. They explained why *their* client is best suited to care for Heidi, and who should be responsible for the child's support. Each concealed valid evidence, opening the door to more court appearances.

After several more frivolous court hearings, Sarah was ready to give up. She telephoned Edward.

"The case is dragging on. The bills are piling up. Maybe it would be easier to drop the divorce and stay with Paul."

"Don't give up," Edward pleaded. "Talk to your attorney. Ask him when this will be finalized."

"I've phoned him many times. He's never in his office. His secretary claims he's at a meeting or on vacation. It's impossible to reach him."

"Please be patient. I know you can't move into the house I purchased for you, but I had it furnished, anyway. The key will be delivered to your office."

Sarah heaved a sigh of relief. "How can I ever thank you? If this continues much longer, I might need a place to get away."

Without informing his personal attorney, Edward sent a courier to Sarah's office with the key, then summoned Robert to his office. "Why is Sarah's divorce taking so long?"

"They're stalling," Robert replied. "Either they want to milk the client, or . . . ."

"Or what!" Edward growled, finding it difficult to control his frustration. "Why are they doing this to her?"

Robert dragged a chair to the desk and sat down. He could tell by Edward's frustration it was going to be a long morning. "They're stalling, stretching the trial with frivolous issues."

"Why? What's the purpose?"

"Each court appearance means more money in their pockets."

"Why are they doing this? Sarah doesn't have much money."

"They waiting to see if you'll intercede on her behalf."

"Well. I won't let them find out. They can go to hell!"

"Has Sarah discussed the delays with her attorney?"

"She claims she made a dozen calls, but he's always out of the office. Why is he avoiding her?"

"His intent is to try her patience; to make her emotionally fragile."

Edward's head jerked up and a frown spread across his face. "What the hell does that mean?"

"He's wearing Sarah down, so he can manipulate her easily."

"I thought he's supposed to protect her?"

"Yeah, he is. It's just another way to victimize a client without violating the law."

"That son-of-bitch. How long can he drag this out?"

"Until he finds who is financing Sarah's divorce."

"Does he suspect I'm helping her?"

"Of course. Your wife probably suspects too. Why else would Shilling and Goldstein attend every court hearing? They're probably reporting to your wife."

"I don't give a damn what Lillian thinks."

A curious frown creased Robert's forehead. "Have you talked to your wife lately?"

"No. Why do you ask?"

Robert shifted in his chair, studying Edward's face. "Have you been inside the main-house recently?"

"Not in years. I'm sorry if this is affecting Lillian, but I have a responsibility to Sarah. I saw how tired she looked."

"What?" Robert jumped up, gripping the desk with both hands. "When did you see Sarah? Don't you know detectives are following her?"

"Relax. I saw Sarah days before she filed."

Robert flopped back in his chair and heaved a sigh of relief. "Those attorneys aren't positive who's funding Sarah. Be careful. Don't show your hand."

Edward gazed aimlessly across his desk. "This isn't just about Sarah. It's about my daughter too."

"I know it's upsetting, but you can't let them know you're helping her financially."

"What about Shilling and Goldstein? Should we ask them why they were in court?"

"No! We can't do that."

"Why not?"

"Don't worry about those two. They won't hurt you. They're acting as Lillian's attorneys, but they'll protect you as much as they can."

Edward set his jaw firmly. "I have a right to know why my wife is interested."

"Let Shilling and Goldstein deal with her. By the way. How is your wife?"

Edward glanced up curiously. "I don't know?"

"I was talking to Goldstein the other day. He made a comment about her living room being dark and depressing."

"When was he there?"

"Probably had an appointment with her."

"With all the money Lillian spent on decorating, that house should look like a showplace."

"This is probably affecting your wife's health."

"She's a big girl. She can take care of herself."

Robert's voice turned sullen. "Is she on medication?"

"How should I know?"

"Have you seen your wife's latest medical bills?"

A curious frown wrinkled Edward's brow. "Why are you asking?"

"Your accountant is concerned about her spending."

"Just let her be. This whole mess is my fault, anyway."

The September hearing finally arrived.

Robert again found a seat in the back of the courtroom. He assumed Sarah's case would be last, and the judge would again clear the spectators from the courtroom. So, to make sure the proceedings went in compliance with the law, he hired twenty men and women to sit as court-watchers.

It was well after four o'clock when the bailiff called the Logan case.

The attorneys collected their files and approached the bench.

Judge Burris studied the unfamiliar faces sprinkled through the courtroom. Though his facial expression showed no interest, it unnerved him to see observers with paper and pen in hand. He wasn't sure who hired them, or if they were court-watchers or investigators. Yet, he was determined to use his judicial power to his advantage.

Robbins spoke first. "Your Honor. As stated in this motion, Defendant has not financially cared for his family. Plaintiff is required to pay all the household bills."

The judge, intent upon collecting more information, instructed the attorneys to present their evidence in extensive detail. He listened for several minutes then opened the Logan-versus-Logan file folder. His head jolted back and his eyes widened. A startled expression crossed his face.

Paper-clipped to the top of the file were two photographs. One of horses running at a racetrack and one of the motel he visited.

Judge Burris slammed his hand over the picture and glanced across the room, studying the faces of the spectators. He could feel the heat rising beneath his robe and warm perspiration covering his forehead. When he regained his composure, he scanned he courtroom, hoping no one noticed the startled look on his face.

Most spectators seemed unaware. However, several experienced court-watchers took notice of the judge's startled expression. They glanced at each other, wondering what had upset him.

Snatching the pictures, the judge palmed them under his hand. He wasn't sure where to hid them. His robe didn't have a pocket and slipping them in his pants pocket would be too obvious. He pressed his hand hard on the pictures and scanned his desk for a place to conceal them. The only solution was to slide them in his sock. Slowly, he edged his hand across his desk, and shoved a pencil off, onto the floor.

The bailiff, hearing the pencil hit the floor, headed toward the bench.

"No, I've got it," the judge said, raising his eyebrows toward the bailiff.

The bailiff understood, nodded slightly and placed himself in front of the bench, blocking the spectator's view.

The judge grinned sheepishly, then turned toward the audience. "Just dropped a pencil," he said aloud. Slipping the photos in his right hand, he crunched them together, folding them from view. He reached down, and with his left hand, snatched the pencil off the floor. As he rose slowly, he moved his right hand toward his pant leg.

The bailiff, sensing a problem, glanced over his shoulder. Seeing the judges' dilemma, he sidestepped, positioning himself directly in front of the desk.

When the judge was sure the bailiff had blocked his view, he shoved the photos in his sock. A short-winded huff, and a groan slipped from his lips as he rose from the awkward position. Resuming his stoic expression, he leered over his glasses and spoke sternly. "Continue counselor. The bills are paid, are they not?"

"Misses Logan is not out on the street, your Honor," Mousa shouted out of turn. "The Defendant has provided her with a home, has he not?"

"Proceed," the judge mumbled as he leafed through each page of the file-folder in case there were more photographs.

Robbins continued. "The Defendant hasn't bought groceries or paid the gas bill."

"I object! Argumentative. It's September. This is Michigan. There were no heating bills in August." Mousa turned and faced the spectators, hoisted his pants up over his belly, and released a humorous chuckle.

"Your Honor!" Robbins protested.

The judge uttered a dry cough, acknowledging the protest. He knew the court-watchers were well versed in law, and that the attorneys were intentionally stretching court time. He ignored Robbins' protest and encouraged the trivial arguing to continue. "Yes. What about the heating bill?" the judge asked, keeping his voice cold and unemotional.

Robbins edged closer to the judge's bench. "Your Honor! The heating bill is not the issue. My client claims Defendant's gambling is out of control."

"Objection. Unsupported," Mousa bellowed, waving a sheet of paper in the air. "Counsel presented no evidence to prove the defendant gambled."

"Counselor! Clarify your point on the gambling," the judge demanded, prompting Mousa to continue.

"My client doesn't have money to spend foolishly, much less on gambling. The Defendant is out of work! He's been looking for a job, but the poor man has a bad back. His wife is a vindictive, selfish woman. She doesn't want to part with the money she earns."

Sarah blushed with embarrassment, and a rush of heat reddened her face.

The judge turned his attention toward Mousa. "Thank you, Counselor." Even though he wanted to retaliate against Paul, he held his composure. He still needed the incriminating film. "Anything else about this alleged gambling?" he again prompted with raised eyebrows.

Robbins, seeing he was losing ground, appealed to the judge's sympathy. "Your honor! Plaintiff claims the defendant is a gambler."

Judge Burris leaned forward and glared at Robbins. "Counselor. Do you have evidence to support this accusation? Is there a witness to prove Defendant has gambled to excess?"

Robbins' voice turned submissive. "We can't prove it yet your honor, but . . . ."

"This court demands proof!"

Robbins backed away from the judge's bench. "Your Honor. I'll get the proof."

Judge Burris stiffened upright and reprimanded with pointed finger. "Counselor! If you continue presenting unsubstantiated accusations before this court, I'll have this case..., ah, I mean, ah . . . ." The judge hesitated, his mind racing through his legal options. After clearing his throat, he spoke firmly, imposing his judicial authority. "This matter of gambling, hereafter shall *not* be an issue before this court. That is a direct order!"

Robbins stared at the judge in disbelief, then took a deep breath. "Plaintiff claims Defendant threatened her. He abused her on several occasions."

"I object. Uncorroborated," Mousa blustered, stepping closer to the judges bench. "She has no marks on her body. She can't prove he ever hit her."

Robbins, seeing he was losing ground, stepped back and scowled. "My client claims her husband threatened her many times."

"Objection," Mousa shouted. "Where are the police reports? Where is the evidence to substantiate those charges?"

Judge Burris raised his hand, motioning for the proceedings to stop. After taking a moment to mull over the situation, he spoke in a stern, commanding voice. "This court finds no evidence that Misses Logan has ever been threatened. If your client persists in making unfounded allegations, I'll have someone put in jail. Do you hear me, Counselor?"

Robbins head drooped, and again backed away from the bench. "Yes, your Honor."

Mousa turned toward the judge and raised his eyebrows. "Misses Logan is a vindictive woman. If she thinks she's going to use this court, so she can run around . . . ." He stopped in mid-sentence, again raising his eyebrows, signaling the importance of the issue, then turned toward Sarah. "Is there another man?"

Robbins scowled at Mousa, and took several steps forward. "Your Honor! There is no other man."

The judge glanced up at the flurry of motion at the back of the courtroom. Even though he suspected the other man could be Edward Hansen, his stoic expression displayed no interest.

Mousa raised his eyebrows and grinned mischievously. "I'm asking time to file a motion of Discovery. We'll prove this woman was dating another man."

The judge nodded, giving no indication of interested.

Sarah gasped, and she shook her head. "No. No," she whispered in an attempt to get her attorney's attention. Seeing he had paid no attention, she slammed her pencil hard on the table with a loud cracking sound, raised her hand, shook her head, and mouthed the words, "There is no other man."

Robbins glanced at Sarah, frowned curiously, and stepped forward. "Your Honor. The Plaintiff does not wish to proceed with the divorce."

A flurry of movement at the back of the courtroom drew the judge's attention. A subtle smile crossed his face. Without hesitating, he held his hand up, halting the proceedings.

The courtroom grew dead silent.

Sarah felt the blood draining from her brain. She looked around the room, wondering how her attorney misunderstood her objection.

The judge, noticing the shocked expression on Shilling and Goldman's face, picked up the file-folder and made a pretense of examining the papers. He needed time to calculate the situation. If Hansen is the paramour, then he must protect him. Still, he had to find a way to retrieve the photographs. Waving the attorneys away from the bench, he cleared his throat and began. "After reviewing the issues . . .," his voice droned in a monotone voice. "And, fault being charged, but not proven . . . . And, giving full consideration to all evidence . . . . And, by indication of the Plaintiff 's attorney Misses Logan does not wish to proceed." He raised his voice as he issued the order. "Therefore, it is the order of this court, this divorce case is dismissed."

The bailiff noticed the judge's private signal to dismiss the room quickly. Taking the cue, he stood up and shouted, "All rise!"

Sarah, stunned by the court's ruling, followed her attorney into the hall. "I can't believe what just happened."

"You indicated you didn't want to continue," Robbins grumbled.

"No! I didn't. I tried to tell you I'm not interested in anyone else."

"You were shaking your head like you wanted to drop the case," he grumbled, then turned brusquely and started down the hall.

Sarah grabbed his arm and yanked him back. "What am I going to do now?"

Robbins wrenched his arm free. "Sorry. I did my best."

"No. You didn't. You did nothing but take my money." Finding it difficult to catch her breath, she gasped for air.

"Misses Logan, what's the matter with you? Can't you breathe? Are you hyperventilating?"

Sarah's eyes grew wild. The corridor seemed to darken. People faded into blurred images. Feeling faint, she grabbed Robbin's sleeve. "I think I'm going to pass out."

"God lady! Don't do that. Let's go over there." He tightened his grip on her arm and lead her to a row of wooden benches against the wall.

Sarah stumbled blindly across the hall. Spastic gasping sounds poured from her lips. Tears streamed down her face.

"Stop crying!"

"I can't," Sarah sobbed as she flopped down on the bench.

Robbins leaned close and whispered. "Sorry. The judge's order is final." He grabbed his briefcase, turned, and walked away.

Sarah watched him walking away. The long corridor blurred, and his image faded in a haze. Even the sound of his footsteps echoing down the hall seemed surreal. After regaining her composure, she made her way toward the elevator with tears streaming down her face. "I can't live with Paul anymore. I just can't."

CHAPTER 29

The office staff left for the day and the building took on a somber silence. It was well past six o'clock when Edward heard footsteps echoing down the hall, and in that brief moment, a wave of fear swept over him. *Was it over? Have I been exposed?*

The office door flew open.

Edward could tell by the expression on Robert's face, it had not gone well. He stood up and braced his hands on the desk to steady himself. "What happened?" he asked, his voice quivering with uncertainty.

Robert entered the room shaking his head. "No divorce."

Edward eased himself down into his chair. The words *no divorce* still ringing in his ears. "How could this have happened?"

Having been in court since early morning, Robert's body slouched with disappointment. "That damn judge made the attorneys present every scrap of evidence." Robert loosened his tie and plopped his briefcase on the desk. "Sarah's attorney failed to prove Paul was at fault. Then, it looked like Mousa was going to implicate you."

Edward's head bolted upright. "Me! Was my name mentioned?"

Robert raised his hand in the air, halting the conversation. "No. Your name wasn't mentioned. Mousa implied another man. That's when the judge dismissed the case. He must have known about your affair with Sarah."

"I don't understand. Why did he dismiss it?"

"To prevent your name from being mentioned." Robert slipped off his jacket and spread it over the back of the chair."The judge was being careful. He knew if your name came up, there would be an inquiry. That would bring a flock of attorneys rushing to defend you or Sarah."

"Defend me?"

"Yeah. Mousa was up to something. I don't know what the hell he was doing." Robert withdrew a legal pad from his briefcase. "Here's a copy of my notes."

"Let me see." Edward grabbed the legal pad and ran his finger down the page, searching for his name. "Are you sure the judge knew about Sarah and me?"

"Why else would he have dismissed it?"

"You think he was protecting me?"

"The judge was protecting someone. He didn't start Sarah's case until he cleared the courtroom. That was his way of protecting you. He suspects something, or he would have handled it differently."

"Your notes say the judge denied the divorce because Sarah stopped the proceeding. Why? How did she stop the proceedings?

"I saw Sarah raise her hand. That's when her lawyer came up to the bench and talked to the judge."

"What's going on here?"

"The judge followed the law. He complied with her request. I don't think he should have, but he did." A grim look crossed Robert's face. "I was sitting too far back. I couldn't hear what Sarah told her attorney."

"What can she do now?"

"She can file an appeal, but that won't set well with Judge Burris. He gets pissed off when his legal opinions are challenged." Robert hesitated, and softened his voice. "Perhaps Sarah should get a new attorney."

"Do you think her lawyer deliberately screwed up?"

"He saw the writing on the wall. Robbins knew he wasn't going to win, no matter what. I think he just quit."

"What should Sarah do now?"

"File an appeal. Her attorney failed to defend her. But it's expensive. Sarah doesn't have that kind of money."

An image of Sarah's frightened face flashed before Edward's eyes. "If that's what it takes, then find someone to file the appeal."

"You can't get involved," Robert pleaded, shaking his head in protest. "You're playing right into their hands. That's exactly what they're anticipating."

"They? What do you mean, they?" Edward asked, his eyes fixed sternly on Robert.

Robert stood up, turned his face away from his friend, and began pacing the floor. "It's what the attorney's call the 'revolving door.' It works like this. The first attorney files a frivolous motion, or intentionally screws up the proceedings. So technically, the judge has to follow the law. He could deny the motion, or rule with an unfavorable opinion."

"Why would he do that?"

"Don't you see?" Robert turned and faced his friend. "The judge knows her case can be appealed. It's...."

"What's this all about?" Edward shouted. "I don't understand how this can happen."

"It works like this. Some attorneys keep revolving court cases." Robert raised his hand, circling his finger in the air. "The first attorney makes his money then, through selected incompetence, fails to win his case. Then, a second attorney files to correct the first attorney's mistakes. And, in doing so, the second attorney makes his share of the money. It's perpetuating legal action. You know. A revolving door. Bleeding a client."

"This is unethical!" Edward blustered.

"Well. Yes and no."

A curious frown covered Edward's face. "What do you mean? The attorneys are taking advantage of the legal system."

"That's common knowledge. They're intentionally perpetuating their services through unethical procedures. They're building an enterprise. Securing a job for themselves." Robert waved his hand toward the window. "Look around you. It's happening in other professions."

Edward clenched his fist and slammed it hard on the desk. "Well, isn't that's convenient! That's a conflict of interest. They're deliberately misusing the law."

"Yep," Robert replied, jutting his chin out in a stubborn gesture. "That's what you call a self-serving enterprise."

"I'll hire a high profile attorney. I can afford to pay whatever it takes."

"Oh no!" Robert shouted. "You can't get involved in her problems. Sarah has to do this on her own?"

"You don't understand." Edward swiveled his chair toward the window. He didn't want to bare his soul. To expose his intense love for Sarah.

"Yes I do understand. You're still in love with her. As your friend and legal adviser I have to ask. Is it Sarah, or your child that you love?"

Edward turned toward his friend and lowered his voice. "Sarah is always on my mind. I can't change that, even if I tried."

"Remember," Robert said, pointing his finger sternly. "You have a wife, and Sarah has a husband. You've got to back off."

"I can't," Edward cast his eyes down and murmured under his breath. "She's my promise of tomorrow. I'm paying for her appeal."

Robert picked up his documents and slid them in his briefcase. "What do you want me to do?" he said, shaking his head in disgust.

HIGH SOCIETY MURDER IN DETROIT

"Nothing yet. I'll have the cash delivered to Sarah by courier."

"My legal advice is to stay out of it." Robert leaned over the desk and looked Edward square in the eye. "The newspapers could get wind of this."

"It's my fault Lillian is such a bitch. I never had the nerve to stand up to her. After Bridget died, Lillian seemed cold. I can't explain it, she just wasn't right after that."

"Let's hope your wife doesn't find out about the money."

Later that day, Edward couriered the cash, and included a note requesting Sarah meet him at his hotel the following Saturday.

Several days later, Sarah arrived at Edward's suite. When she saw him waiting at the door, she couldn't hold back the tears. "I can't live with Paul anymore," she sobbed.

Edward wrapped his arms around her, feeling her pain as if it were his own.

"This whole trial was unfair. My attorney did everything wrong."

"I'm going to help you," he said as he guided her into the living room. "I thought you might bring your daughter."

"She's with my mother for the weekend."

"Oh. The whole weekend?" Edward asked, encouraged by the news. "Don't worry. We'll hire an attorney to file an appeal."

"What good will that do?" Tears rolled down Sarah's eyes, and she began to sob. "I didn't get a fair shot in court. Will a higher court make any difference?" Sarah pushed Edward away and lowered her voice. "I wish I could take Heidi and run away."

"No! That'll make matters worse." Edward took Sarah's hand and guided her toward the couch. "We'll figure this out together."

"I'm exhausted. I didn't know where to turn." Sarah collapsed on the couch. "My mother can't help. She knows nothing about the law. Neither does my brother. He's deaf. This would be too stressful for him."

Edward understood how it felt to be insecure, and his heart went out to her. He stood for a few minutes looking at her, not sure how to comfort her. "Would you like a drink?" Edward said, breaking the awkward silence. "It might help you relax."

Sarah looked up, and with a weak smile nodded her reply.

Edward headed for the wet bar across the room. When he returned, he set a silver tray with two martini glasses, and a tall crystal carafe on the coffee table. "Maybe this will take the edge off," he said as he handed her a glass.

Sarah took a large gulp, then looked up at Edward who had been standing at the edge of the couch. "Do you think there's still a chance?"

Taking her question as an invitation, Edward picked up his drink and sat down beside her. "Yes. I'm sure the court will decide in your favor."

Having been stressed for months, Sarah felt a sense of relief. His words were comforting and reassuring. "Paul left for Las Vegas. He said he was going away for the weekend. I peeked in the bedroom when he was packing. There was a wad of bills on the bed. When he saw me, he stuffed the money in his pocket, grabbed his suitcase and ran out the door."

"Where does he get that kind of money? Does he win at the racetrack?"

"I don't know," Sarah replied with a frustrated shrug. "I don't think he's won lately. When he comes home late at night, he's usually in a bad mood."

"Well, maybe he's ah…" Edward stammered, hesitant to pursue the matter any further.

Sarah interrupted. "No. It's not because I'm not sleeping with him. He doesn't care one way or another about that." Sarah finished her drink, leaned back against a soft pillow and closed her eyes. With the reassuring feeling of being protected, Sarah fell asleep.

Edward gazed at her resting her head on the azure pillow. He sat quiet, content just to hear the calm rhythm of her breathing, grateful just to be near her.

The setting sun spread a shade of mauve across the evening sky, darkening the room. A waft of cool air sifted through the lace curtains, and the room took on a peaceful silence.

In the languor of sleep, Sarah's hand relaxed, loosening her grip on the glass.

Edward leaned closer, and being careful not to disturb her, removed the glass from her hand. The odor of her warm body drew him back. He gazed longingly at her face framed by the velvet pillow. A waft of cologne drifted from the cleavage of her breasts, drawing him closer. He kissed her neck, and with his lips on hers, he whispered, "Will you stay the night with me?"

Sarah opened her eyes and returned his answer with a sensual smile. She stretched seductively, and lifted her long, auburn hair off the back of her neck. A warm, calming flush crossed her face as the alcohol lessened her inhibitions. Feeling amorously relaxed, she drew him closer. "Yes," she whispered. "I love you, Edward. I always will."

Edward turned off the lamp and moved closer until he felt her body beneath him. "When your divorce is final, will you marry me?"

"You're still married."

"I'll take care of that," Edward replied as he caressed her body.

Feeling his warm breath on her face, Sarah reached up and drew his head closer to hers, then touched his lips with her fingers. Conscious of his desire, she slid down on the couch and responded to his sensual touch.

CHAPTER 30

The following week Sarah met with her new attorney. Goldie Schick, a heavy-set woman in her late fifty's, thumbed through the file. "You have quite a few investigative reports here."

"I gave you all the legal papers I had last week. They prove my husband's gambling is out of control. That's why I want to file an appeal."

"I went to the court and pulled your case. Most of these reports weren't in your file. Where did you get them?"

"Ah . . ., look at these." Sarah withdrew a stack of racing stubs from her purse and slammed them flat on the desk. "These are new. I found them in my husband's dresser."

"Eh, huh," Schick replied, eying the tickets out of the corner of her eye. "How did you come by so many detective reports?"

"Ah," Sarah mumbled. "I hired a different detective agency." Though she felt uneasy lying, she dared not explain how Edward's material ended up in her file.

"Must have cost plenty. Most of these are quite extensive." Schick scanned the pages, stopping several times and shaking her head in disgust at the judicial misconduct. "Why didn't your attorney present these?"

"I don't know. He suppressed a lot of evidence. These reports prove Paul was gambling. That's the main reason I want a divorce. How can I raise a child with a gambler in the house?"

Schick riffled through the papers, raised her eyebrows and her voice rose cordially "Oh, I see you have a daughter. How lovely."

"Her name is Heidi," Sarah replied, setting a photograph on the desk. "Here is a picture of her."

Schick took a quick, unconcerned glance. "Pretty girl," she said, shoving the photograph back, across the desk.

Sarah placed the photo in her purse. This was her first clue Miss Schick wasn't too interested. Certainly, she was wasn't interested in her daughter's photo.

"I see you withdrew your complaint against your husband."

"No! It was a mistake. I only waved my hand."

"Clearly, there was a misunderstanding." Schick placed the betting stubs in a folder and slid them to the side. "These new tickets may not be of any use. The judge ruled out your husband's gambling months ago."

"My attorney didn't object to that ruling. I don't know if he was lazy, or just incompetent. My trial has been dragging on for a long time."

Schick lowered her spectacles and leered at Sarah suspiciously. "Your husband gambled all your money? How will you pay for an appeal?"

Sarah gripped her purse. "I have the cash."

"Okay," Schick said with renewed confidence. "Let's go over the evidence. We attorneys are bound by a code of ethics. Anything you say will remain confidential."

The next several hours Sarah pointed out the suppressed evidence and unethical court procedure. At the end of a long meeting, Schick agreed to file.

Though Sarah felt uncertain of Schick's sincerity, she paid the retainer fee and left the office.

Edward had been on pins and needles waiting to hear if Sarah had filed. It was late afternoon when he heard a faint rapping at his office door.

Robert peeked through the half open door. "Busy?"

"No. Did Sarah file the papers yet?"

"I don't know," Robert replied with a shrug as he entered the office.

"What about Paul? We haven't heard from him in months. Do you think he's given up on the blackmail?"

"I don't think so." Robert set his briefcase on the edge of the desk, gripping it firmly with both hands. "Paul's silence bothers me."

"Look at these." Edward slid several photographs across his desk. "The detectives followed Paul to Las Vegas. This shows him gambling large amounts of money. They claim he was losing. He could be out of cash by now."

Robert's face turned sullen and his voice somber. "That's what I want to talk to you about." He opened his briefcase, hesitated with a frown, then withdrew a blue folder and slid it across the desk.

"What is this?"

"It's from the detective agency. It came this morning."

After reading the first page, Edward gasped. A nauseating taste rose from the pit of his stomach, and a flush of sweat covered his forehead. "Is this true? Why is Paul seeing my wife?"

"I'm not sure yet." Robert set his briefcase on the floor, then pulled out an envelope. "I have something else." He spread several photographs across the desk. "These were taken in the dark, but you can still make out what's happening."

Edward held the photograph close to his face. "That's my wife's car. What does this mean?"

Robert braced his hands on the edge of the desk. "That's a picture of Paul leaning in Lillian's car window. They appear to be talking."

"Lillian was talking to Paul?"

"Look at this one," Robert said, shoving a photograph forward. "This shows Paul holding something in his hand. It was nighttime. Too dark to see clearly."

"What the hell is Lillian doing?"

"It looks like she's giving Paul an envelope. The detectives claim she never got out of her car. After Lillian drove away, they followed Paul to a beer garden." Robert laid several more pictures on the desk. "This shows Paul paying the bar-tab. He's holding a wad of bills."

"My God! Is that where he's getting his money? From my wife?"

"Right now, we're not sure what your wife is doing. Let's consider the facts. Paul hasn't worked in a while, yet these pictures show a wad of cash." Robert stopped talking when he saw the fear in Edward's eyes.

"My wife is giving him money?"

"Could be," Robert replied with a slight nod. "But, I don't think Paul is done hassling you, either. He has the ace card, and he knows it." Robert reached in his briefcase and withdrew a legal document and slid it across the desk. "Paul re-mortgaged his house again. There's not much equity left."

Edward scanned the document. "This doesn't look like Sarah's signature."

"I agree. It looks like someone traced her name. It's written exactly like the first re-mortgage."

Edward shook his head in disgust. "I wonder if Sarah knows how much equity is left."

"There are a lot of things she doesn't know. That man is a sneaky bastard. He suspects you're still involved. He's waiting to catch you with Sarah."

"No one knows I'm helping her," Edward grumbled, protesting in his defense.

"It's a good thing you haven't seen her lately."

Edward dared not look up, for surely his friend would see the guilt in his eyes. "Sarah has no one else to turn to," he mumbled, keeping his eyes fixed on the photographs.

"Don't tell Sarah about this re-mortgage. If Paul's attorney finds out you're talking to her, he'll assume you're still her paramour. He can accuse you of adultery. Sarah could lose custody of her daughter."

"What? He can take my child?"

"The court doesn't know she's your child. Legally, Heidi is Paul's daughter. He knows a paternity trial will open up a can of worms. He's betting you'll pay to keep it quiet."

"I'll never let that man take my daughter. Is this about collecting child support?"

"No. He's sure he'll get child support from you one way or another. Paul knows how to work the system. All he has to do is prevent you from seeing your own child, and he can get whatever he asks for."

"What! How can he do that?"

"Legally, he can take her on vacation. Most likely Sin City. He knows dragging Heidi to Las Vegas will get your attention."

"The courts won't let him do that, will they?"

"You have no legal right to object. He's just taking his daughter on a vacation. Sarah might be too frightened to object."

"I can't protect my own child?"

"Extortion isn't new to this gambler. If he's getting money from Lillian, we'll have to look further." Robert lowered his voice and spoke sternly. "Have your accountant examine Lillian's expenditures. Get a history of unusual activity. Get the dates she withdrew large amounts of cash."

"Okay, but I feel ashamed spying on my wife."

The shrill ring of the telephone interrupted their conversation.

Edward grabbed the phone and bellowed. "I'm not receiving calls this morning."

"I'm sorry to bother you. It's Sarah Logan," Betty replied. "She wants to speak with you. Shall I put her through?"

"Yes, of course." Edward glanced at his friend with a concerned look in his eyes. "I have to take this call," he said, dismissing Robert with a wave of his hand.

Robert nodded and stepped away from the desk.

"Sarah? Is something wrong? Is Heidi all right?"

Robert started to leave, but hearing the anxiety in Edward's voice, he set the door ajar. "Can I help?"

"No. I have to take this call." Edward pressed the phone closer his mouth. "You sound terrified. What's the matter?"

"I must talk to you today." Sarah lowered her voice and whispered. "I'm pregnant."

"What?" Edward gasped, cupping his hand around the mouthpiece.

Robert, seeing his friend's face turn ashen, headed toward the desk. "What's wrong?"

Edward waved Robert away and gripped the phone tighter. "Are you sure?"

"Yes. Paul is not the father."

"Stay right where you are. I'm coming to your office." Edward turned toward Robert who was now hovering over his desk. "This meeting is over," Edward blurted, and setting the phone down gently. "I'll tell you about it later."

Robert, seeing his friend badly shaken, responded softly. "I'm here if you need me." He turned and scurried out of the office.

Edward, stunned by the announcement, paced the floor. He couldn't hide the truth any longer. It was time to tell Sarah everything. "What do I need?" he muttered, thinking out loud. He opened the wall safe, frantically shoving folders aside. His heart beat wildly as he removed several manila envelopes and shoved them in his briefcase. He gazed around the room, pausing at times to gather his thoughts. Seeing the investigator's reports and the current court notes on his desk, he hurried across the office. With a clean swipe of his arm, he shoved the documents into his briefcase.

A warm sweat covered Edward's brow as he sped across town. He barged into Sarah's private office, and seeing the fear on her face, he closed the door behind him. *What do I tell her first?*

"I can't believe it. I'm pregnant," Sarah cried, tears streaming down her cheeks. She rushed to Edward, wrapped her arms around him and buried her face in his chest.

"It's all right," he whispered in her ear. He felt her body trembling and her warm tears dampen his shirt.

"You don't understand. This is your baby," Sarah said, muffling her voice in the warmth of his body. "I haven't slept with Paul since I filed for divorce."

"I know." Edward tightened his grip, assuring her of his love.

"You know?" Sarah pressed her hands against his chest, pushing him away gently. "What are you saying?" She looked up curiously, waiting for an answer.

"Heidi is our child too. Please," he begged, raising his hand to halt her fears. "Hear me out."

Sarah's eyes widened and a shocked expression stiffened her face. "Heidi is your child? I don't understand." Sarah clutched

Edward's shoulder, then wavered unsteadily. "I think I'm going to faint."

"Please, sit down." He wrapped his arm around Sarah's waist and lead her to a chair. "Let me explain."

Sarah collapsed on the chair and stared deep in Edward's eyes. "Heidi does look like you," she said studying his round face, pale blue eyes and wispy blond hair. "How long have you known?"

"It's a long story. I don't know where to start." Edward picked up his briefcase and dumped the contents across her desk. "Your husband is sterile. It wasn't about the divorce. He wanted control of Heidi, so he could get money from me."

"My husband is sterile? How do you know that?"

"I had investigators look into his background."

"Why?" Sarah asked, her voice crisp and curt. "Do you investigate everyone in your employ?"

"No! You don't understand. Paul was trying to blackmail me. He threatened to expose our daughter to the newspaper. Do you know what that would mean?"

"Blackmail? He wouldn't do that!"

"Yes. It's true. Not only is he a gambler, he's a swindler too. He threatened to expose our affair to the press."

"How long have you known about Heidi? Why didn't you tell me?"

"I was waiting until your divorce was final."

After Sarah regaining her composure, she pointed to the pile of papers strewn across her desk. "What are these?"

"Evidence. Let me explain." Edward spread the documents out on the desk. One by one, he revealed Paul's unscrupulous scheme. "I didn't care what the newspapers wrote about me. I didn't want them to exploit you. To expose this as a sex scandal. I couldn't put you through that."

"Is this why you stopped coming to the country house?"

Edward nodded his reply.

"You broke my heart. It shattered my faith in men. But, if I had known this, I might have . . . ." Sarah hesitated, then a suspicious frown crossed her brow. "You left before I met Paul, before I was married."

"I know! It was to protect you. To keep the newspapers from scandalizing our affair. I had to consider what my wife might do. You know how unpredictable Lillian can be."

"Is that why you went to Traverse City? Why you started drinking?"

"I fell apart when I lost you." Edward wrapped his arms around Sarah and whispered in her ear. "I didn't realize what I was doing."

"When your wife finds out, she'll still turn on you." Sarah stepped back and stared hard at Edward. "Remember how she treated Bridget. How she bullied the household staff."

"Yes. I remember that strange look in her eyes when she went on a rampage. Now that you know the truth, can we get married as soon as our divorces are final?"

"When? I'm pregnant. How long can I wait?"

Edward, knowing an appeal would take months, understood the fear he saw in Sarah's eyes. "I'm prepared to give Lillian whatever she wants."

"What if the court finds out I'm pregnant? Paul can accuse me of adultery. He can take my children."

"No! I won't let him do that," Edward shouted. "Whatever happens, we'll face it together."

"What if your wife refuses to divorce you?"

"I expect her to be unreasonable. I'm willing to give her more than the half she's entitled too. The financial matters I can handle. The paternity will be the problem. It'll take time to sort this out."

"I don't have time. People will notice I'm pregnant. Paul will too."

"Do your best to hide it."

"Paul doesn't know yet. I saw your attorney sitting at the back of the courtroom. Did he say my case looked promising?"

Edward wrapped his arms around Sarah, pressing her close to his body. "I'm here for you. We'll face this together."

Early the next morning Edward summoned Robert to his office. "I didn't sleep a wink last night. How did the appeal hearing go?"

"As I expected. The justices' held a tight lip. You never know what they're thinking. They looked uneasy when they saw me taking notes. Goldstein and Shilling were taking notes too."

"It appears Lillian s interested in Sarah's case, but how did the hearing go?"

"Miss Schick presented some evidence that had been suppressed. I'm sure the justices understood what Mousa had done."

Edward's eyes sparkled with enthusiasm. "Then it looks good for Sarah?"

"Nothing is certain. I listened closely. Everything I heard suggested Sarah can refile."

Edward leaned back and heaved a sigh of relief. "How long before she receives an answer?"

"I asked the clerk. She claims the cases are backed up. It could be months before they mail the Per curiam."

"Months? We can't wait that long." Edward glanced up at his friend, and thinking of Sarah's condition, his voice turned cold. "I want you to prepare a divorce settlement for Lillian."

"What?" Robert stammered, stumbling back in surprise.

Edward raised his hand, palm forward. "Don't try to talk me out of this. I've considered the consequences. I'm ready to relinquish some control of the corporation."

Robert gasped, and when he caught his breath, his voice rose to a high pitch. "Do you know what you're doing? The corporation will be split in two. Your wife isn't a rational woman. What the hell made you decide this?"

"I can't wait any longer. I asked Sarah to marry me."

Gripping the back of the chair to steady himself, Robert lowered his voice. "You're really going through with this?"

"Yes. Get your best attorneys together. Prepare a settlement. Hash out the details. I've thought long and hard about Sarah and my children. I should have done this years ago."

"Your *children*?" Robert stammered.

"Sarah's pregnant."

"What are you saying? Pregnant!" The legal complications flooded Robert's mind, and he flopped down in a chair. "Whew! Give me a minute to think."

"There's nothing to think about."

"Your wife is going to raise holy hell. This new baby? Ah, are you sure?"

"Yes. I don't tell you every time I visit Sarah."

"Apparently not! I warned you about seeing her? You knew it wasn't safe."

"I know," Edward mumbled.

"We don't know what your wife will do when she learns you've fathered two illegitimate children?" Robert's head dropped, and he slapped his hand on his forehead. "What if this is flashed across the newspapers?

"My life with Sarah was a real awakening. It forced me to start fighting for my own happiness."

"Okay. I see you're determined. Do you realize the paternity issue will make negotiations difficult?"

Edward nodded.

"I'll set up a meeting with the attorneys. We'll start right away."

"Keep this in strict confidence, especially from Goldstein and Schilling."

A select group of attorneys worked at a furious pace to offer Lillian a fair settlement, yet prevent her from interfering in the corporation.

Several days later Robert laid the proposed settlement on Edward's desk. "Here's the first draft. What do you think?"

Edward studied the proposal, stopping several times, shaking his head in disgust. "I don't like the devious tactics we're using against Lillian. This is an unfair settlement."

"We took into consideration the money your wife spent. The stock she sold without your consent or knowledge."

"This makes me look vindictive. It'll only piss her off. We can't penalize her for selling her own stock."

"You've got to be assertive. She's going to demand more, no matter what she's offered."

"I can't do this to her. She did nothing wrong. This is all my fault. Revise the proposal. Come to a more equitable agreement."

"If your wife gets vindictive, we'll have to use the missing money as leverage."

"No! If Lillian used that money for, God knows what for, that's a Pandora's box I don't want to open."

Robert lowered his voice in frustration. "We have to minimize your losses."

"Wait!" Edward said, holding his finger in the air as an afterthought. "Is there any way you mention Lillian's strange behavior during the last few years?"

"No! The courts will hear that loud and clear. Don't you know it's almost impossible to divorce a mentally ill person? You charge her as incompetent and you'll never get out of this marriage."

"What are my chances?"

"It isn't a matter of chance. The slander could destroy your reputation. Have a devastating effect financially."

"All right! I didn't realize it would hurt the company."

"My job as your attorney is to protect you. Second, to protect the business."

"Okay. Take this proposal back." Edward reluctantly shoved the document across the desk. "Rewrite the settlement. I'll read the second draft after you've made the changes."

A serious expression crossed Robert's face. "Edward, I'm saying this as a personal friend. Your wife doesn't think like most people. She can't conceive of anyone being different than she is. You've been estranged from her for a long time. She's probably mad as hell. If you don't fight for your rights, she'll take you to the cleaners."

"She's always been unreasonable. It's my own fault. I never had the nerve to buck her."

"Then start now. Your corporation is at stake."

"I wish I could be aggressive like you. But it's not in my nature." Edward's shoulders slumped forward, and he slid deeper in his chair. "My mother did a job on me when I was a child. She suppressed every bit of courage I had." As the last of his words left his lips, Edward's head jerked aside, ducking as if he had been attacked.

"What's the matter?"

Panic shown in Edward's eyes. "Did you feel that breeze?" he whispered as he rolled his chair away from his desk. "What the hell was that?"

Robert glanced across the office. "You mean the cold draft?"

"Look! The hair on my arms is standing up. I don't want to sound like a weirdo, but that icy air seems to appear when I mention my mother."

"Your mother?"

"It's just something the housekeeper said," Edward said with a curious frown.

"What are you talking about? Your mother's been dead for years." Robert backed away from the desk, then scanned the office suspiciously. "Icy air? Are you saying your mother's spirit is here?"

Again, Edward jerked aside. "That damn cold air just hit me in the face again."

A curious expression crossed Robert's forehead. His face turned ashen. "She's here? The old lady is here? Shit! You mean she can hear us?"

"I don't know, but I feel something is in this room. Maybe my mother heard me complaining about what she did to me." A slight grin crossed his face. "Ha! I wonder if that's part of Karma. You get back what you give out." Edward took a deep breath, and after regaining his composer, replied sternly. "Modify the proposal."

"Are you sure?"

"I'm prepared to face Lillian in court. Offer her a reasonable settlement."

CHAPTER 31

———◆•◆•◆———

Edward was about to retire for the evening when he heard a timid knocking on the back door. He hurried to the kitchen, opened the door and set it ajar. "What are you doing here?"

Hilda stood on the back porch shivering. "I saw your lights on. I hope I didn't disturb you," she said, as she tightened the wool shawl around her shoulders.

"No. No. I wasn't ready for bed yet. What brings you out on such a chilly night? Come in."

Hilda stepped in the kitchen, lifted the shawl from her shoulders, and gave it a firm shake. "It looks like the snow is going to get deep," she said as she followed Edward into the elegant living room.

"Why did you come across the back? The yard is pitch-black. You should have come to the front door."

"I used a flashlight to cross the backyard."

"Why didn't you turn on the floodlights?"

"Oh no! I don't want the missus to know I'm here."

"Is everything all right?" Edward asked as he guided her to a plush, velvet chair. "Please, sit down."

Hilda eased her bulky body down and heaved a mournful sigh. "I know you and the missus aren't getting along, but when you don't visit, she acts real strange."

"What's Lillian done now?"

"The missus has too much time on her hands. I think it's killing her when you don't visit."

"I have no reason to visit the main-house," Edward, impatient with his wife's complaints, flopped down on the couch. "I haven't talked to Lillian in years."

"Why are you staying away? Is it because Sarah is getting a divorce?"

"No," he replied with a quick shake of his head. "This is strictly between Lillian and me."

"You say it's not about Sarah, but I see it in your eyes. You're nervous about something. What's going on?"

"Nothing," Edward muttered, shaking his head in denial.

"I didn't want to bother you, but the missus is acting real strange. I don't know what to do."

"What do you mean, strange?"

"She rarely goes out anymore. Doesn't visit her friends like she used to."

"I can't do anything about that."

"I'm worried. She spends too much time in the attic."

"The attic?"

"Yes sir."

"That's not my problem. Why don't you call Doctor Johnson?"

"A doctor can't help. I think she blames Sarah for, ah." Hilda stopped in mid-sentence, hesitated a moment before she again spoke. "I think it's her hatred toward Sarah. It's killing her."

"I can't help that. My relationship with Sarah is my business."

"If Sarah really cared for you, she wouldn't have married somebody else."

"Hilda. You've been my friend for a long time. You've seen how Lillian changed over the years. She destroyed our marriage long ago."

"Please. You gotta stop blaming your wife."

Edward cleared his throat, leaned forward on his haunches and whispered, "I think Lillian knows something about Bridget's death." He didn't mean to be quite so blunt, but his daughter's death still weighed heavy on his mind, and the words slipped out before he could stop them.

Tears rolled down Hilda's cheeks. "Your wife is ill. I mean, real sick. She needs help."

"What do you want me to do? I've given her everything she needs, and whatever she wants."

"She doesn't need material things. She needs a doctor."

"I've asked her to see another doctor many times. What else can I do?"

"Your wife still loves you. Sometimes, in the middle of the night, I hear her crying. Then she carries on. Oh, the foul words that come out of that woman's mouth. She says you'll never marry Sarah."

"She's crazy!" Edward blurted out, feeling this justified his defense.

"The missus has a sickness in her head. I'm not saying she's daft." Hilda paused, then spoke in a serious tone of voice. "That's why I'm here. The missus is doing peculiar things, like staying in the attic for hours at a time."

"What's she doing up there?"

"I don't know. It sounds like she's talking to someone," Hilda said, shaking her head ever so slowly.

"Talking to herself?"

"Mr Hansen. I think she's grieving. She sits all alone in the attic. That's not normal. One day I sneaked up the attic and peeked. She was talking to the mirror."

A frown crossed Edward's forehead. "What? The movers set it way back in the attic. How did she find it?"

"I don't know. It sounds like she's talking to someone. Don't you think that's peculiar?"

"She sees a face in the mirror?"

"I don't know what she sees. She got me worried."

"Maybe she feels guilty because she didn't hear the mirror fall?"

"Ah. Don't say that." Hilda shifted nervously, and her voice turned defensive. "The missus was in the parlor the day Bridget died. The radio was on real loud. That's why she didn't hear the mirror fall."

"I don't know *when* Lillian was in the parlor. Was it before, or after Bridget died?"

Hilda reached for her shawl, cast her eyes down, and lowered her voice. "I got no right to talk against the missus. What should I do?"

"I'll talk to Doctor Johnson in the morning. Maybe Lillian is having a reaction from her medication."

Hilda braced her hands against the arms of the chair and pushed herself up. "You come to the house. You see what I mean."

"What if I remove the mirror from the attic? Would that help?"

"Oh my. She's gonna make such a fuss. I ain't gonna tell her." Hilda made her way to the kitchen, paused, and turned toward Edward. "I remember when the missus was delirious with a high fever. She was babbling some strange things about Bridget's death."

"What did she say?"

Hilda glanced up, surprised she had spoken her inner thoughts. "Never mind." She wrapped the shawl around her shoulders and left, determined to take Lillian's comments to the grave.

Several days later, Edward and two men made their way up the snow-covered sidewalk to the main-house. He knew it wasn't going to be easy, and he was prepared for the worse scenario. He paused on the front porch, and after drawing in a deep breath, eased the door open. "Follow me," he whispered, waving the men into the foyer.

The foyer was depressingly dark, eerily silent, and a stuffy odor permeated the atmosphere.

Edward flipped the light switch.

Two small light bulbs scarcely illuminated the dusty chandelier. The dangling crystals cast an eerie gloom, barely lighting the musty foyer.

"For Christ's sake it's dark in here," Edward grumbled as he reached for the window shade. He gave it a quick yank, sending it flying up with a loud snapping noise.

The cracking sound brought Lillian to the upstairs balcony. She leaned over the banister and stared at her husband who was standing in the foyer. "What do you want?" she asked, in a frail voice.

Edward intentionally ignored her question. *There's no point in starting an argument.* He tapped his homburg against his knee, knocking snowflakes off the brim. "Let's go. It's up here," he said as he led the men up the staircase.

Lillian met her husband at the top of the stairs with her arms folded across her chest. "What do you want?"

Edward drew back, startled by Lillian's shallow complexion and haggard appearance. After regaining his composure, he pushed Lillian aside and made his way to the hall.

"Where are they going?" she demanded, stepping in front of the men, blocking their way.

His wife's sickly appearance had taken him off guard, but he was determined to end this matter, today. "Let them through," he demanded, extending his arm out, shoving her aside.

"Why are they going in the attic?"

"We're taking the mirror."

"No! You're not," Lillian screamed, then shoved Edward, flattening him against the wall. She dashed down the hall, stretched her arms across the doorway, blocking the entrance to the attic.

The men stopped, and the husky man called out. "What should we do boss?"

"You're not going up there," Lillian bellowed, flattening her back against the attic door.

Edward stood frozen, startled by his wife's frenzied reaction. A nauseating taste rose from his belly as he realized the depth of his wife's fury. "Let them pass," Edward shouted. Though it was against his nature to be aggressive, he grabbed Lillian's wrist, yanking her away from the attic doorway.

Lillian thrust her body forward and elbowed him in the stomach.

Edward grabbed his belly. Even though she looked frail, she had landed a solid punch. Startled by his wife's strength, he grabbed her around the waist, jutted his chin toward the attic and shouted. "Hurry! Find that damn mirror."

The men scurried past Lillian and dashed up the stairs.

"Get that gold-framed mirror. It's up there somewhere."

"You son-of-a-bitch!" Lillian screamed, pushing Edward's hand aside.

Startled by his wife's violent reaction, he responded without hesitation. Though he had never laid his hand on any woman, especially not his wife, he gripped her tighter and held on.

"What are you doing?" Lillian screamed, twisting and squirming to wrestle herself loose. When she couldn't free herself, she reached back and clawed Edward's face.

"Ye-ow!" Edward released his grip on his wife and covered his face.

Lillian spread her arms across the doorway. "They're not taking my mirror. Get those men out of my attic!"

The men, having located the mirror, started down the steps. When they saw Lillian blocking the way, they set the mirror on the top step and shouted, "What should we do boss?"

"Bring that damn thing down here," Edward snarled, waving the men forward. Again, he grabbed Lillian around the waist. With renewed strength, he hoisted her away from the doorway.

The movers carried the mirror past Lillian's outstretched hands.

"Get that thing out of here," Edward shouted, holding Lillian firmly. He waited until he heard the front door close, then released his wife.

"You son-of-a-bitch! That's my mirror. Make them bring it back."

"For God's sake stop making such a fuss," he snarled as he hurried down the stairs.

Hilda and four maids, having heard the commotion, ran to the foyer. "What should I do?" Hilda called out.

Edward stopped at the front door and scanned the foyer. "Get the maids to clean this place up. It's a mess."

"The missus won't let us," Hilda wailed, twisted her hands through her apron. "She screams at us when we run the vacuum."

Lillian leaned over the railing, glaring down with hatred burning in her eyes.

"This is for your own good," Edward shouted up to his wife, then slammed the door behind him.

Lillian dashed to her bedroom. She pulled aside the curtain just in time to read the sign on the truck. Exhausted and frustrated, she turned to the new mirror bolted against the wall. Her reflection portrayed a deteriorating body. The gray at her temples cut a line of truth across her dyed, black hair. Her eyes, hollow and empty, reflected her fear. Stress had wrinkled her face and guilt had siphoned her sanity.

CHAPTER 32

"It's been five months," Edward said as he paced the office floor. "Why is Sarah's appeal taking so long?"

"The clerk claims there's a long waiting list," Robert replied, rolling his eyes to the ceiling in jest.

"That's absurd. Don't they know she's living with an abusive husband? What can we do to hurry this along?"

"Nothing. Not now, anyway." Robert's steel-blue eyes stared hard at his friend, and he raised his voice as a warning. "Don't show your hand. And, for God's sake, don't visit Sarah."

Edward cast his eyes down as the message fell on deaf ears. "I'm concerned about Lillian. Her housekeeper claims she's spending too much time in the attic."

"What's she doing up there?"

"I'm told she was sitting in front of that damn mirror. That's not normal behavior."

"What are you going to do?"

"I had it removed from the attic."

"Your wife was okay with that?"

"Hell no! I've never seen her in such a frenzy. She attack me like a crazy woman. I don't know where I got the nerve, but I grabbed her and held her until the movers carried that damn mirror out of the house."

"You stopped your wife?" Robert tossed his head back with a gratifying smirk. "Wow!"

"Yeah," he chuckled, and smiled with satisfaction.

"Why is she so attached to that mirror?"

"Never asked. I didn't realize how neurotic Lillian had become. I'm starting to question her sanity."

A serious expression crossed Robert's face. "That's what I want to talk to you about. Your wife's mental health."

"What do you mean?"

"Your wife knows about Sarah. I'm concerned about how she'll retaliate."

"I'll cross that bridge when I come to it," Edward grumbled, nervously fumbling a pencil through his fingers.

Robert unbuttoned his jacket and sat down. When he spoke, his voice turned deliberate and sobering. "If Sarah is remanded back to a lower court, your name is sure to be mentioned. You may have to testify. What are you going to tell the judge? You committed adultery because of your wife's strange behavior?"

Edward glanced up, wrinkled his brow and replied meekly. "Lillian's always been temperamental."

"Do you realize she can sue you for alienation of affection?"

"Ha! That's a laugh," Edward fired back. "What affection?"

"Never the less, your wife's instability is a threat to you and the corporation."

"There's nothing I can do."

"You're procrastinating again. It amazes me how calm you are."

"I'm not calm. I'm furious," Edward barked, swiping his hand across the desk, sending papers flying across the floor. "I can't vent my anger the way you do. I wish I could, but I can't."

The smile disappeared from Robert's face. "Sorry."

"When I was a child, my mother smothered every bit of self-confidence out of me."

"I guess I spoke out of turn," Robert said as he gathered the papers off the floor.

"Why Lillian wants to keep the mirror that killed our daughter, is beyond me."

Robert picked the last document off the floor and laid it on the desk, then leaned closer. "If your wife is acting peculiar, maybe you should take charge." Robert paused, thinking about the advice he had just given. "On second thought, if you admit Lillian has a mental problem, you could lose your chance to divorce her."

"What do you mean, if she had a problem? You should have seen how frantic she was. She was out of control."

"That's exactly what I mean. Has your wife seen a doctor lately?"

"How should I know? As long as we were married, she never listened to me." Edward stacked the papers in a neat pile, looked up at his friend and replied humbly. "It's my fault. When we were first married, Lillian took over where my mother left off, and I let her. I didn't realize how different life could be until I met Sarah. Now, I see my marriage was a sham. A shallow lie."

"The court doesn't care how your wife treated you. You allowed it for years. The lawyers will argue your tolerance makes the issue moot. The bigger problem is, will your wife claim your illegitimate children as the cause of her illness?"

Unable to defend his actions, Edward shook his head sadly as a rush of heat surged beneath his collar.

"Paul is after money," Robert replied in an attempt to change the subject.

Edward leaned forward and a glimpse of hope brightened his eyes. "If Paul wants to extort money from me, then he won't accuse me of being the father."

"That bastard is street smart. He'll take advantage of the paternity issue. You've got to stay away from Sarah."

"I don't know if I can," Edward murmured under his breath. Although he had great respect for Robert, his heart had made the decision. He was determined to meet Sarah secretly.

A rapping on the office door interrupted his conversation.

"Yes? Come in."

Betty poked her head in the door. "You have a personal call from Sarah on line one. Do you want to take it?"

Seeing the serious expression on his secretary's face, he glanced up at Robert. "We'll discuss this tomorrow."

Robert nodded, took the hint and followed Betty out of the office.

Edward cleared his voice and tightened his grip on the phone. "Hello."

"I'm frightened," Sarah whispered. "Paul's been acting paranoid all morning, like he's afraid of something."

"You shouldn't have called me," Edward whispered, swiveling his chair nervously from side to side. "Your phone might be tapped."

"I know, but I'm afraid for Heidi and myself."

Hearing the anxiety in Sarah's plea, he softened the tone of his voice. "I'm sorry. I didn't mean to be so curt. Is Paul gone now?"

"Yes. We had a big argument this morning. He was jittery. I think someone is after him. He peeked out the front door, then ran to his car, and drove away."

"Just hang on a while longer. Your appeal should be coming through soon."

"Paul threatened to tell the newspapers I'm having your baby. I told him I would stop the divorce if, ah."

"No! Don't stop the divorce. Let him say what he wants."

"I'm in my fifth month. I can't hide it from the employees much longer."

"It's only a matter of time before everything is out in the open. I know Paul is terrorizing you, but can you hang on a little longer?"

"It's hard. He's so hateful, especially when he loses at the track."

"I wish I could do more, but my hands are tied. As least, I can take care of you financially. I've issued a leave of absence for you. With full pay," he added.

A slight sigh slipped from her lips, relieved that he genuinely cared. "You didn't have to do that. I can still work."

"Not if you're starting to show. I want you to rest. Please, do this for me. For our baby."

"How will I explain the money? Paul will know I'm not working."

"Tell him it's company policy. We pay for maternity leave. He'll believe that." Edward hung up the telephone and began pacing the floor. *How can I protect Sarah from that bastard? It's too late to cover up the paternity. My only hope is to keep Paul quiet.* Although it was against his better judgment, and would have been against his attorney's advice if he had confided in them, he arranged to meet Paul at a local diner.

It was past nine o'clock that evening when Edward pulled into the parking lot of the diner. Though he despised dealing with Paul, he hoped an offer of money would make him go away. He swiped his hand across the rain-veiled glass and peeked through the window.

Paul was sitting, hunched over the counter, drinking a cup of coffee. Cigarette smoke drifted from an ashtray, and a greasy donut lay half-eaten on a plate.

A strong gust of wind kicked up, forcing Edward to scurry inside. He waved his hand toward Paul, and made his way to the back of the diner.

Paul raised his eyebrows, nodded with raised chin, grabbed his cup and followed Edward. "I'm here. Now what?" Paul snarled as he slid into the booth.

After ordering two coffees, Edward waited until the waitress left before he spoke. "I want you out of Sarah's life. I want you to move out!"

Paul folded his arm across his chest and glared across the table. "You want *me* out!"

"I think this will change your mind." Edward pulled an envelope out of his pocket and shoved it across the table. "This is the only money you're getting."

A surprised expression raised Paul's eyebrows, and a sneer spread across his face. "Yeah, thanks." He grabbed the envelope and ran his thumb across a stack of hundred-dollar bills. "Anything else you wanna say?"

"Leave her alone!" Edward growled, managing to hide the quiver in his voice.

"Don't threaten me! I'm not going anywhere. Neither is Sarah."

"She doesn't want to live with you anymore."

"Well, she can't move out. I'll ask for custody of my daughter if she tries to leave."

Edward clenched his fist. "You know damn well that's not your daughter. I'm warning you. Leave Sarah alone."

"What are you gonna do?" Paul taunted as he shoved the envelope in his pocket.

Edward scanned the diner, making sure no one was watching. Leaning over the table, he snarled under his breath. "You're not getting anymore. This is it!"

Paul leaned back, grinned, and took a deep drag on his cigarette. "Hell. I can get more suing for alienation of affection. You wrecked my marriage."

"You're using Sarah for money."

A gust of smoke curled from Paul's nostrils. He nodded his head repeatedly, but would not answer. Assuming that Edward wasn't going to offer more, Paul leaned back casually, and flicked his cigarette, letting the ashes drop in the ashtray. "She's my wife. I can do whatever I want."

"You're not going to get away with this."

"What are you going to do? The court knows you're an adulterer and a womanizer. I'll tell them about your trips to Traverse city. I've got newspaper articles showing the trashy broads you hung around with." Paul patted the envelope in his pocket and rose to leave. "Let's see who has the ace card. You, or me?"

On May 17, 1951, Sarah delivered a baby boy. Even though Edward had been warned to stay away, he couldn't resist. He waited in the parking lot until he saw Paul leave the hospital . His heart was beating as he hurried through the hospital door. The muffled sound of crying babies drew him down the wide corridor. The crying grew louder as he reached the glass windows.

Row after row of white cribs filled the room.

Edward searched the name tags at the foot of each crib.

There it was. The name 'John Edward Logan.' A beautiful baby boy.

He had been standing at the window several minutes when he sensed someone staring at him. Glancing out of the corner of his eye, he saw two nurses watching him. Fearing he would be recognized, he turned his back and headed down the hall toward the exit. He had hoped to visit Sarah that day, but now it was too risky. He decided to wait until she left the hospital, then secretly visit her.

CHAPTER 33

In November 1952, Sarah received an answer from the Court of Appeals. She ripped open the envelope and withdrew a single sheet of paper. The Per curiam read as follows;

Logan-v-Logan. The Court of Appeal concurs
with the lower court's decision.
Based on a lack of evidence, Defendant, Paul
Logan, is not charged with fault.
Divorce is denied.

Sarah was stunned. This is not what she heard in court. The more she read, the more confusing the order became. The sentences were scrambled, and the words didn't make sense. Sarah gasped as she read the last line.

THEREFORE; it is the Opinion of the Court of Appeals,
Logan-v-Logan divorce is denied.
To be remanded back to the lower court for re-hearing.

Sarah flopped down in a chair. "Back to court again. I can't live with Paul another day. There must be something I can do." After she stopped crying, she hurried to the drugstore and phoned Edward.

"I received the answer to the appeal today."

"What happened?"

"They denied my divorce." Sarah's voice quiver as she continued. "I've never read a Per curiam before, but this doesn't look right. It contradicts what I heard in court. Someone changed the words."

"Denied? Why?"

"The whole document is full of contradictions."

"I don't think you should have phoned me."

"It's okay. I'm at the drugstore. This call won't be traced."

"That phone may not be tapped, but mine might."

"I never thought of that. I'm sorry. The court's decision is based solely on Mousa's statements. Listen to what it says." Sarah's voice cracked as she paraphrased the document. "Paul is an honest man. He's trying to find a job to support his family."

Edward softened his voice. "There must be something we can do. I'll send a courier to pick up the Per curiam. My attorneys will take a look at it." After hanging up the telephone, he summoned Robert to his office. "What the hell's going on. Sarah's divorce was denied."

"I expected this," Robert replied calmly. "This is nothing new. It's difficult for a woman to get a divorce, especially when children are involved."

"Why do the courts do this?"

"First, this is 1952 and 'Fault Divorce' is the law. Second, that law gives power to the judge's discretion. And third, the court knows a woman, or any litigant, will pay to keep their children. Sure, the court claims it keeps families together, but that's a lot of bullshit. The court knows most women will fight to keep custody of their children. Especially, to get away from an abusive husband. That's why it's easy to stretch a case."

"Stretch a case? What the hell are you talking about?"

"I told you about the 'revolving door.' I've seen attorneys force a litigant to file one appeal after another." Robert stared hard at his friend to make a point. "Justice isn't always served."

"Will Sarah ever be free?"

"I don't know," Robert said with a shrug of disgust.

"Why did her case take so long?"

"Nearly two years is reprehensible," Robert grumbled, nodding in agreement. "Someone deliberately misplaced it."

"What?" Edward sputtered. "Someone hid it?"

"Probably shoved it in a dead-file. It stayed there until someone was ready to retrieve it."

"Then this was just a sham. Sarah waited all that time for nothing. The justices' intended to deny her divorce all along."

"I didn't say *they* knew. I'll know more when I read the Per curiam."

"Why did someone hide the documents? Are all attorneys corrupt?"

"No! The entire legal system isn't corrupt, but this kind of misconduct is increasing. If the attorneys had tried this case fairly, it could have been finished in a couple months"

"The Appeal wouldn't have been necessary?"

"The attorneys are spinning the revolving door. They're increasing their fees."

Edward rose and began pacing the floor. "Where the hell are the watchdogs? Who makes the court comply with the law?"

"Watch dogs? Ha!" Robert replied with a snide snicker. "That's another story."

"What do you mean?"

"Very few attorneys will file a complaint against another attorney."

"This is why attorneys have a lousy reputation," Edward grumbled as he flopped down in his chair.

"They earned their reputation. When I was in private practice years ago, I saw this misconduct increasing." Robert's head bowed and his eyes searched the floor. "I have a guilty conscience about my own divorce. I wanted to quit practicing law after I won my divorce through unethical tactics." Robert glanced at Edward and shoved his hands deep in his pockets. "It bothered me for a long time. That's why I changed to corporate law."

"You mean corporate law is more honest?"

"Not always," Robert chuckled. "But your corporation has scruples. We deal with people honestly. Get me the Per curiam. I'll can tell you more after I've read it."

The following day, Robert received a copy of the Appeal Court's decision. He scanned the page, shaking his head in dismay. "Oh my God! What a mess." Robert's eyes never left the page as he made his way to a chair in the corner of the office. After reading the first paragraph, he lowered his eyebrows in a frown. "These paragraphs are deliberately garbled. This doesn't make sense!"

"Is Sarah's attorney stupid?"

"That's not it. Someone scrambled the sentences." Robert's finger followed the words across the paper. "Someone tampered with the justices' opinion."

"What! Does that match what you heard in court?" Edward asked.

"Not even close."

"Can Sarah ask the court to make corrections?"

"That won't do much good." Robert continued reading, then stopped abruptly. "Aha! We may have something here. This is not what Justice Jackson said." Robert made his way across the room, reading aloud as he walked. "The justice didn't use the term, 'lack of evidence'." Robert slid the document across the desk. "Jackson questioned if some evidence had been *overlooked*. That's when he remanded it back to court for a re-hearing."

"So? What does that mean?" Edward blustered.

"A divorce *can't be denied*, then *remanded* back to the lower court for a re-hearing," Robert replied, emphasizing the main points.

"Explain that."

"When an appeal is denied, it's a final order. It's done. You can't have it both ways. Either Sarah's divorce is denied, or it's remanded back for a retrial."

"Then this document is a sham."

"I heard Justice Jackson say '*not all the evidence was considered*. That's why it was remanded back for a rehearing."

Edward leaned across the desk, his forehead wrinkled with curiosity. "I don't understand."

"Someone changed the words." Robert coughed, cleared his throat, and explained the law. "When a Per curiam is written, the justices' *must* issue a clear and concise opinion. This is a piece of garbage. It has too many conflicting arguments. Hell, it misquotes Michigan law and court rules!"

"Do you mean someone altered the transcript? They can't get away with this."

Robert placed the document firmly on the desk. "Someone is forcing your hand. They suspect you're paying Sarah's court fees. They want to find out for sure."

"Can Sarah have a new trial?"

"Don't you understand? If Sarah goes to court, you could be exposed as the baby's father. My God man! This could lead to an investigation into Bridget's death."

"What about her death?" Edward bolted out of his chair and glared at Robert.

"The way your daughter died. Even now, you struggle with how that mirror could have fallen."

Edward's eyes widened, and he gripped the edge of the desk. "Why would the court inquire about Bridget's death?"

"The attorney's want to open the paternity issue. They'll file one motion after another, so they can examine more evidence."

"File more motions?"

"They want this case to stay active. Sarah will be forced to declare you as the father of her children. That means you'll have to go to court."

"Why? It's not my divorce."

"The attorneys will implicate you. They'll ask if you have any other children. What are you going to say?"

Edward felt faint, as if the world was crashing down around him. A rush of heat rose beneath his collar. He jutted his neck out and loosened his tie. "Do you think they will summon me to court? I can't lie on the stand."

"Your face will turn red. They can spot a liar instantly. They'll track your past like a bloodhound."

"Why would they do that?" Edward asked, plopping down in his chair. "This is Sarah's divorce."

"You are a part of it. They will ask why you committed adultery. Are you going to say your wife's craziness caused you to run around?" Robert waved the document in the air and continued. "That will open the door to other issues. Your wife's health. Are you sure Bridget's death was an accident?"

Edward's eyes widened. "What? I don't know what happened that day."

"I repeat! Do you think your daughter's death was an accident?"

"It never occurred to me. I wasn't thinking straight the day Bridget died."

"Well. I had my suspicions. Several other attorneys agreed with me."

"They suspected it wasn't an accident?"

"You were in bad shape that day, so I couldn't confide in you. Now you see why it's dangerous for Sarah to refile. It will open more inquiries." Robert paced the floor, waving the court's order in the air. "If you suggest your wife is mentally disturbed, she'll defend herself. She'll come after you like a bull in a china shop. Her attorneys will tear you to shreds."

"Oh, I'm sure they will. Lillian likes to be in charge."

"Be careful! If the court proves your wife is mentally incompetent, you can't divorce her. That means you'll never be able to marry Sarah. Either way, your corporation is at stake."

Edward laid his head on his desk and closed his eyes. "Damned if I do, and damned if I don't. My wife has my life on hold, and I can't do a thing about it."

Robert sat down, and spoke in a calm, reassuring voice. "Don't get discouraged. You have a brilliant staff of attorneys. They'll protect you and the corporation."

Edward raised his head and frowned. "Will it help to know who messed with the per Curiam?"

"Can't you see where this is heading?"

"What do you mean?"

"Someone was paid under the table to screw this up." Robert tapped his finger hard on the document. "And, they didn't do a good job of it, either."

"But look! It has three justices' signatures," Edward argued, pointing to the bottom of the page.

"Na. Those are just rubber stamps."

"The justices had to see it. They wrote it."

"Maybe," Robert replied, raising his eyebrows. "They may have written a Per curiam, but I don't think they wrote *this* one. In fact, they may not have seen this at all."

"Can Sarah file a complaint?"

"Ha! That's a lost cause. The Judicial Grievance Committee may refuse to look at this. They'll say the judge already issued a final order."

"I want a private investigator to look into this."

Robert nodded his head. "We'll find out who is behind this. Transcript tampering is serious."

"It could be Paul. He has crooked friends."

"It could be an attorney. It could be anyone. Hell, it could be your wife!"

"What!" Edward demand.

"I'll take care of this. I know a man who can investigate without stirring up attention."

CHAPTER 34

"Is the private investigator coming this morning?"

"He should be here anytime." Robert raised his arm and glanced at his watch. "Bogart's usually punctual."

"Can he find out who tampered with Sarah's Per curiam?"

Robert nodded. "He can be very friendly with court clerks. An artful impersonator when necessary."

"Can he be trusted?"

"I've known him over ten years and never had a problem." Edward's head shot up at the sound of loud rapping on the door.

The office door flew open.

A short, muscular man entered. He scanned the office walls, nodded toward Robert, and made his way across the office. "Your secretary said you were expecting me. What can I do for you, gentlemen?"

Robert reached out and grasped the man's hand firmly. "Hi Bogie. Good to see you again. I want you to meet my boss, Edward Hansen."

"Nice to meet ya." Bogart reached out and greeted Edward with a firm handshake. Again, he scanned the elaborate office. "Ya got a fantastic place here. Sorry, guys. Don't mean to be nosy, but noticing things is an occupational habit."

"We have a situation that needs investigating," Robert said, pointing toward several documents on the desk.

"How can I help?" Bogart replied, stepping closer to the desk.

"It's confidential," Edward warned.

"Um, hum," Bogart responded with a slight nod. "What ya need?"

"This brief is written by an attorney, Linda Schick." Robert handed Bogart the document. "It's not great, but she did address the appealable issues. Do you know this attorney?"

"I know of her, but never dealt with her."

Edward studied the detective, then slid the Per curian across the desk. "After you've read the brief, take a look at the court's opinion. It's a mess."

Robert tapped his finger hard on the paper. "We don't think the justices' wrote this. Someone tampered with this."

"Um, hum." Bogart picked up both documents. Again, he scanned the office, paying particular attention to the photographs and honorary degrees hanging on the wall. "Very impressive," he murmured with an approving smile. He made his way toward a comfortable chair in the corner. "Gimme a few minutes," he mumbled, then flopped down in the leather armchair. After reading the documents thoroughly, he joined the two men. "I see what you mean. Words are intentionally scrambled. I'm sure the justices' didn't write this."

"It looks amateurish, like a clerk edited it," Robert replied.

Bogart's eyes lit up, and he responded with an impish grin. "You want me to investigate a clerk?"

"Might be a female clerk," Robert replied with a mischievous snicker.

"That's my specialty," Bogart jested with a quick snap of his fingers. "Make me a copy of the file. I need a few days to study the motions. Then I'll go to the Court of Appeals."

Several days later, Bogart was ready to investigate. He shaved extra close, splashed on an expensive after-shave lotion, and slid two-inch lifts in his shoes. To complete his facade, he clothed his gruff exterior with an expensive black, silk suit. As a cover, he rented a pricey, black Lincoln to reinforce his deception.

Bogart pulled into the court parking lot and parked directly in front of a large window. He wanted to be sure his highly polished automobile would be seen by the office staff. He strutted into the building carrying an expensive leather briefcase and scanned the office staff.

Several girls raised their head, eager to make eye contact with the attractive stranger.

Bogart breathed a silent sigh of relief when he saw a short, heavy-set girl seated in the corner. *Aha. I've spotted my mark. She isn't wearing a wedding ring.* Bogart headed toward a matronly, gray-haired woman at the front counter. "I'd like to research old case files," he said, handing the clerk a sheet of paper. "These cases date back ten years."

The clerk offered a friendly smile and accepted the paper.

Bogart leaned over the counter, pointed to a young, naïve looking girl and whispered, "Who is that lovely lady in the flowered dress?"

The clerk raised her eyebrows, turned, and searched the office. "You mean Antoinette?"

"Do you think she could help me? Oh, by the way, is she single?"

"Yes. She's single," the clerk responded with a friendly smile. "I'll ask her to help you." The woman ran her finger down the paper. "These are old appellant cases. You'll have to go downstairs to pull these files." The woman cupped her hand near her mouth and chuckled. "We call it the dungeon."

"Do you think she'll mind?" Bogart winked and smiled flirtatiously. He had expected the files to be in a storage room, but alone in the basement was even better.

The clerk hurried across the office and whispered in the girl's ear.

The girl's head shot up and her eyes twinkled. A broad grin spread across her face.

Bogart nodded, acknowledging the girl's approval. All he needed was a few minutes to work his charm.

The young girl jumped up and beckoned Bogart with a wave of her hand. She led him down narrow stairs to a dimly lit basement. Through rows of khaki-green metal shelves stacked with cardboard file boxes.

Bogart worked his charm as he moved through the aisles. At times, following too closely, and colliding with the clerk. "Oh. I'm sorry. I didn't mean to bump into you," Bogart murmured, while slipping his hands around her waist, and leaning close to apologize.

The clerk couldn't keep from smiling as she led him down the dimly lit aisles. "These files date back to 1930." She placed a small ladder in front of the shelf and stepped up. "What you want is in that box."

Bogart sensually breathed her name. "Antoinette. Be careful. I wouldn't want a gorgeous girl like you to fall." He looked up at the girl and raised his hands outward. "I might have to catch you in my arms."

Antoinette responded with rapid fluttering eyelids, and reached for the file box.

Bogart slipped his hands around her waist and gazed into her eyes. "Can I help?"

Antoinette, aroused by his sensual, low voice, gazed down at him. "Maybe you could reach that box. You're so much taller."

Bogart nodded and tightened his grip on her waist. Although she was pleasantly plump, he made it seem effortless as he lifted her off the step. "It's too bad we found these files so quickly. I wish we had more time to talk," he whispered, then set the cardboard file box on the floor.

Antoinette bent over, holding her hand over the top of her blouse. She glanced up coyly, then released her hand, exposing the soft curves of her breasts. She took her time searching the files. After a while, she removed several folders, stood up, and stretched her hand out. "Are these the cases you want?"

"Um, hum," Bogart murmured, leaning close, making sure he touched her hand as he retrieved the files.

Antoinette again bent over, wiggled her behind a few times, then placed the lid on the file box.

"Let me put those boxes back," Bogart murmured in a seductively deep voice. After placing the boxes on the proper shelf, he looked deep into the girl's eyes. "Do you like to dance? I know a restaurant that has a good band."

"I love to dance," Antoinette replied, her voice rising with enthusiasm.

Now, all he needed was to make the final commitment. "Are you free this evening? We could go out to dinner?"

"I'm free," she responded with a sultry smile.

"Good. I'll pick you up after work. If that's okay?"

Later that evening Bogart placed a recorder in the trunk of his car. Reel-to-reel tape recorders were new on the market and quite large, so it had to be concealed in the trunk of his car. He ran an electrical wire from the trunk, threaded it under the front seat, and into the glove compartment. After attaching the wire to a small microphone, he cleverly disguised it by wrapping plastic flowers around the base. He set the microphone on top of the dashboard, hiding it in plain view. Bogart splashed on more after-shave lotion and headed for Antoinette's office.

After an expensive dinner, which included a third bottle of wine, Bogart worked his charm. It wasn't difficult once he got the clerk alone in his car.

Antoinette was a talker, rambling on and on about the office staff.

Bogart knew how to ask the right questions. By the end of the evening, he had most of the answers. "Maybe we could do this again," he cooed.

"That would be nice," Antoinette murmured.

"Oh, I just remembered. I'll be out of town on a legal matter. I'll phone you when I return." Bogart wasn't about to lose this valuable connection. He might need more information in the future.

The next few days, Bogart continued his investigation until he ran out of new leads. The following week he met with Edward and his attorney. "Good morning gentlemen," he said as he entered the office carrying a black satchel. After unbuckling the cover, he lifted a large, black metal box out, and placed it on the desk.

"What the hell is this?" Edward asked.

Bogart grinned. "A tape recorder. You're gonna like this."

Robert stepped closer to inspect the machine. "I've used a small recorder a few times, but they are not reliable for court. Too much static. Do these big machines sound any clearer?"

"The small ones don't pick up from a distance, so I rigged this one myself. I've got the girl on tape," Bogart replied with an impish grin. He reached in his briefcase and set two folders on the desk. "My secretary transcribed the tape. It's all in the report."

Edward picked up the report, and slid the second copy toward Robert. "Didn't the clerk see this big machine?"

"No. It was hidden in the trunk of my car. I ran a wire from the trunk, to the glove compartment. That's where I put the switch to the microphone."

"Where was the mike?" Robert asked.

"It was disguised. I wrapped plastic flowers around it and stuck it on the dashboard."

"Right out in view. Very clever," Edward chuckled.

Robert eyed the recorder, grinned, and leaned back in his chair. "This ought to be interesting."

"Did you find out who wrote the Per curiam?" Edward asked.

"Oh yeah!" Bogart's eyes sparkled as he flipped the switch.

Robert leaned close to the desk, straining to hear. "All I hear is static. What's happening?"

"Be patient. After I switched on the recorder, it took a minute to close the glove compartment."

"How did you turn it on without the clerk seeing the switch?" Robert asked.

Bogart grinned. "I reached in front of her, you know, real close. She saw me putting my gloves in the glove compartment, that's all."

The recorder picked up music from the radio, barely masking the whirling sound of the recorder.

Antoinette's voice could be heard, along with the sound of scratchy static. "That was a fantastic restaurant. Do you go there often?"

"Um, hum. They have the best music for dancing. You're a terrific dancer."

The muffled sound of shuffling continued for several minutes, then inaudible mumbling in the background.

Bogart's voice is heard. "Do you know who was assigned to the Logan file?"

A feminine voice followed. "I know who edited that Per curiam."

Static, then muffled giggling.

Antoinette's voice continued. "A clerk earned a nice bonus for doing that."

Bogart's voice came through in a sensual murmur. "We attorneys pay well."

More shuffling sounds are heard closer to the microphone.

"Um-mm, that tickles my ear," Antoinette purred, her voice muffled as if she had leaned into Bogart's chest.

"Which clerk edited Logan's opinion?" Bogart whispered.

Antoinette's voice now appeared farther from the microphone. "My friend Rita. She added some legal jargon and scrambled the words. An attorney helped her with the editing."

"Oh?" Bogart murmured in a breathy voice.

"Rita was paid well, if you know what I mean."

Again, a shuffling sound is heard in the background.

Antoinette's voice came through giggling, followed by a shrill squeal. "Oh, are you getting fresh?"

"No. You're just so pretty. Hey. That attorney? Was it Lenny Mousa? A short, dark haired man with a paunchy stomach?"

Antoinette's voice faded as if she had moved away from the microphone. "No. It wasn't Mousa. All the clerks know him. We call him the slime bag."

More shuffling noises.

"Um-mm. That tickles my neck."

"Do you know who helped Rita?" Bogart asked, his voice distant and muffled.

"He must be new a new attorney. I never saw him before. I hear his name is Shell, or something like that. He's a tall man with black hair and a receding hairline."

Edward glanced up and raised his eyebrows. "Could that be Lillian's attorney? Shilling?"

Robert tilted his ear closer toward the recorder.

Along with static, came heavy breathing, then more shuffling sounds.

Bogart's voice is heard in a soft whisper. "Have you seen this man before?"

Robert leaned closer, bending his ear toward the recorder.

Bogart's voice continued. "Do you know his name?"

"No. I didn't recognize him," Antoinette replied.

The tape registered the sound of someone moving close to the mike.

Bogart's voice is heard whispering in the background. Then a feminine giggle, and an inaudible protest.

Robert slapped his hand on his thighs and burst out laughing. "Very good!"

"It's all in a day's work," Bogart replied with a twinkle in his eyes. "Next time, I'll edit out my charming ways."

"Charm?" Robert grinned, smacking his lips on the tips of his fingers. "Um, Bogie."

Bogart, still grinning, stepped toward the desk. "Wait. There's more."

Antoinette's voice now sounded close to the microphone. "This isn't the first time Rita fixed an appeal. She's too quick to mess with legal documents."

"Good money?" Bogart's voice murmured.

A rustling sound was heard, then Antoinette's voice. "The justices don't oversee everything. Sometimes they don't examine the final edit. We just rubber stamp it and mail it out."

Edward reeled back in his chair, shocked and disgusted. "That's enough. Notify the court. This has to stop."

"Wait," Robert pleaded, holding up his hand. "Let's hear the rest before we make any decisions."

Bogart stepped closer to the desk, and laid his finger over his mouth. "Shh. You gotta hear this last part."

The sound of soft music is heard in the background, then Bogart's voice whispering. "How many girls do this?"

Antoinette answered in a matter-of-fact, tone of voice. "Word gets around. The attorneys know who'll fix an appeal."

"Does this happen often?"

"No. Not really. Rita's going to get caught if she's not careful."

"That's it," Bogart said, then turned off the recorder. "Better not use this information in court. I taped it without the clerks' permission, and I'm sure that's illegal."

Robert stood up and stretched his arms out. "I'm not good at sitting still. What else do you have?"

"That's all I got that evening." Bogart placed the recorder back in his satchel. "Oh yeah," Bogart said, pausing in thought. "I questioned the clerk, Rita. She's street-smart and clammed up real fast. It's all in the report."

"Enough," Edward growled. "The court should be told what's going on."

"Whoa. Not so fast," Robert interrupted. "How do we explain why we're butting our nose in Sarah's business?"

Bogart nodded his head in agreement."He's right. You can't expose how I got the information. What I did is illegal."

"Sarah has to comply with the court's order," Robert warned. "It's been remanded back to the lower court. Let her go back."

A scowl covered Edward's face. "But, the order has been tampered with. The justices' should know what their staff is doing."

"That's not as easy as you think."

"Why?" Edward asked.

"Because of the clerks."

"The clerks? They can't stop the justices from examining an appeal. Those girls aren't attorneys. I bet they're not even paralegals."

"It's too late," Bogart replied. "Once a fix is in, the clerks can do plenty. Rita probably warned the Chief Clerk by now."

Robert nodded. "He's right. If a case has been fixed, the Chief Clerk can prevent anyone from reviewing it."

"How the hell can she do that?" Edward grumbled.

"The Chief Clerk has jurisdiction to reject an appeal," Robert replied. "It's all quite legal. A brief must meet specific requirements. If one little thing is misspelled, or one word out of pace, she can toss it out."

"I'll hire a high-profile attorney for Sarah," Edward growled. "He'll make sure it's heard."

Robert cast his eyes down, scanning the floor as he paced the office. "Don't bother. Once an order is fixed, it's almost impossible to tell a judge it's been fixed. The clerks will intercept it."

"They what?" Edward bellowed. "How?"

"When they see Sarah's name on the envelope, they'll mail it back unopened. Or, if they open the mail, they'll say pages are missing, so it can't be accepted. They'll give any lame excuse, no matter how stupid."

"What happens if it's hand delivered and gets past the clerks?" Edward asked.

Bogart interrupted. "The Chief Clerk gets to see all mail before a trial date is set. She'll reject it on a technicality."

"The Chief Clerk is in on this?" Edward asked.

Robert stopped pacing and a grim look crossed his face. "She could be. If not, she still has to protect her clerks from being charged with any wrong doing. Her job is at stake. No matter how skillful the appeal is written, it's still red tagged."

"Get a copy of the transcript? That'll prove what happened in court," Edward growled.

"Ha!" Robert huffed in disgust. "That won't work either. The case is fixed. Those transcripts can be altered in a moment's notice. Words can be changed."

Edward slammed his fist on the desk. "Tampering with court evidence is a crime! It's illegal."

"Yeah, but who's going to charge an attorney with transcript tampering?" Robert held his hands up in the air as one would when being arrested. "Hell, they'd all be in jail."

Edward slouched down in his chair and swiveled back and forth. "What's Sarah's next move?"

"Back to the lower court. Through the revolving door."

"Can we hire a shrewder attorney?"

Robert shook his head. "Paul's attorney is counting on that. As long as you're willing to pay, Mousa will refile, and re-file, and re-file. He can do this until you're out of money or patience. You're wasting your time."

"Sarah has to sit through another trial?" Edward whined.

Bogart stepped forward and interrupted. "I get the impression the Per curiam was hidden for a while. Do you know who misfiled it?"

Robert returned to his chair and flopped down. "No. I suspect a clerk put it in a dead file. It stayed out of sight until someone was told to mail it."

Edward lowered his voice. "Do you think a judge is involved? What about Jackson? Maybe Judge Burris. Could a judge be interested in Sarah's case?"

Robert began pacing back and forth, deep in though. "Let's not jump to conclusions. Let's not point our finger at a judge. So far, it looks like only one attorney stands to profit."

Bogart nodded his head in agreement. "Ya. Mousa."

"Mousa doesn't fit the clerk's description. Could it be Lillian's attorney, Shilling?" Edward asked.

Bogart shook his head. "I don't know who paid for the fix. I couldn't find any connection to Shilling, except he is your wife's attorney."

Edward ran his finger across the paper, reading each line carefully. "Not a single argument against Paul. It's got to be Paul."

Bogart picked up his notes and stacked them in a pile. "The only connection between Paul and Judge Burris is they both go to race track."

"That doesn't mean a thing. Anyone can go to the track," Robert replied.

Bogart stretched his arms out and shrugged his shoulders. "It's hard for me to stay in one spot for long. So far, I haven't found the man who fits the clerk's description. Should I continue investigating? Am I still on the books?"

A scowl of determination crossed Edward's face. "Money's not an object. You're on the payroll. Find out about Rita. I want her in jail."

Bogart nodded with a smile. Again, his eyes wandered, mentally taking notes while scanning the elaborate office.

Robert jutted his chin out and loosened his tie. "I don't think the justices are involved."

Bogart moved closer to the desk. "Maybe it's not the higher court, but my nose tells me to investigate Judge Burris. Can't put my finger on it, but there's something we're missing."

"What if I donate to Burris's political campaign? Would that help?"

Robert held his hand up, halting the discussion. "No! Let's not get involved. This will take time."

"Sarah doesn't have time. Heidi is starting school soon." Edward's voice turned somber. "My daughter needs a stable environment."

"It can't be helped," Robert grumbled. "It's a done deal. Back to the lower court."

Bogart headed toward a massive window. "Beautiful, seeing the Detroit River from the seventh floor." He leaned over the marble window sill and looked down at the traffic below. Even with his back turned, his stoic voice demanded attention. "I wouldn't get involved with the higher courts if I were you."

Edward crossed the room and stood beside Bogart. "We have the altered document."

"Ah, huh. Sometimes we misinterpret what we see."

"How did I get into this mess? I have children I'm not allowed to see. I can't visit Sarah. Worst of all, I'm married to a woman I fear."

Robert's voice turned firm. "You have to stay married. Your wife owns too much stock."

Edward stared out the window and grumbled in a determined voice. "I don't care what will happen in court. Prepare my divorce papers."

Robert's voice rose to a high pitch. "What about the corporation? Your stock-holders will take a hit. Do you realize what you could lose?"

"My family comes first," Edward grumbled.

"Are your ready to face your wife in court?" Robert asked.

"Don't discourage me when I finally have the nerve to fight back."

"This will take more than nerve. Your wife isn't well. You may have to hire a psychiatrist." Robert shook his head in disgust. "Ugh. I dread dealing with your wife. We have no idea what she'll do when this whole mess is exposed."

"I understand, but I'll have to face her sooner or later. It's only a matter of time before everything is out in the open, anyway. I've got to help Sarah. Start preparing my divorce papers."

CHAPTER 35

It had been a long day at the office, and the reality of facing his wife in court left Edward feeling tense and uptight. He arrived home, and after a light dinner, he dismissed the household staff for the evening, intending to retire early. He switched off the lamp and started for the stairs, but a streak of moonlight shone through the living room window, drawing him back.

Once again, he found himself standing at the window, looking across the pitch-black yard.

Darkness had set in and a blanket of snow covered the frozen ground. A bitter wind blew a veil of snow across the yard, shrouding the main house in an eerie mist. A single light shone through an upstairs window, offering a hint of Lillian's presence.

Am I ready to lose her completely? We've been living apart for years, and I've grown used to the familiarity, whatever it was. Still, it's frightening to step into the unknown.

Edward recalled the day he removed mirror from the main house, and the startling decline in his wife's appearance. *Could her eccentric attachment to the mirror have caused her health to fail? Should I accuse her of mental incompetence? Better not. She has resourceful attorneys who will challenge me, if only to safeguard their own position. If she is declared incompetent, then I would keep control of the corporation.* Edward heaved a mournful sigh. *I'll never be able to marry Sarah.*

The light in the upstairs window of the main house went dark.

The sudden darkness left Edward feeling empty. Sensing a presence, he stepped away from the window and scanned the dark living room. *Is someone here?*

A rush of icy air brushed against his face.

His body quivered and his hand responded instinctively, brushing the cold from his cheek. *What would mother do?* As the thought passed his mind, a peaceful feeling swept over him, and he felt comforted by it.

Again, a waft of cool air touched his cheek, and with it came a familiar fragrance.

He sniffed the air, recognizing the scent of his mother's perfume, and he felt uneasy. Though he didn't believe in spirits, he stood searching through the darkness. *It feels like someone is watching me.* Again, whether it was a habit, or loneliness, he pushed the curtain aside and took one more look out the window.

The main house was totally dark.

Edward let the curtain fall back in place, shrugged his shoulders, and plodded up the stairs. That night, unable to sleep, his thoughts intensified beyond logic. He pictured his staff under Lillian's control, and his employees resigning. *What will Lillian do when she learns I want out of this marriage?* Fear of his wife's retaliation attack his mind for hours until he finally fell asleep.

The sun was beginning to lighten the sky when Edward woke to the faint sound of the servants bustling about in the kitchen. Though he dreaded the day he would have to face his wife in court, he was determined to finalize the divorce settlement. When he arrived at the office, he saw Robert waiting outside his office door.

"I know I'm late. I had a tough time sleeping."

"I'm sure you did." Robert said, as he entered the office. He tossed the amended settlement on the desk. "I hope you know what you're doing." He pulled a yellow legal pad from his briefcase, pushed a chair up to Edward's desk, and sat down.

Edward sat at his desk and dragged the papers toward him. "I'm in no mood to argue. Did you cover all the terms we discussed?"

"Everything. Down to the last penny." Robert ran his fingers down his legal pad. "We still don't know what your wife did with the money from your joint account."

Edward kept his eyes fixed on the documents, for they would expose his uncertainty. "That was Lillian's money, as well as mine. We're not discussing that."

"All right. It's your decision. The missing money isn't mentioned in the 'Complaint for Divorce,' but your attorneys considered it when preparing the settlement." Robert softened his voice and a curious frown furrowed his brow. "You're sure you want to file this now?"

Edward glanced up inquisitively. "Yes. I'm sure. Why?"

"It's Christmas for God's sake. You want to file this during the holidays?"

"I'm sorry it's come to this. Don't discourage me. It took a lot of guts to get to this point."

"Your wife won't take this lying down," Robert grumbled, and paced the floor. "She could charge you with adultery. This could jeopardize your executive position."

"I know. I know," Edward mumbled under his breath. He glanced up at his friend, and in an optimistic voice, he said. "Lillian never mentioned my..., ah, she never accused me of adultery before. Maybe she won't give me a hard time. What do you think?"

Robert leaned over the desk and looked hard at his friend. "This isn't going to be easy. Your staff examined a lot of legal defenses pertaining to extramarital affairs."

Edward cast his eyes down and muttered under his breath. "I know you did." He flipped through the proposal, reviewing each page carefully. "I didn't realize how much this involves. I'm taking quite a hit, aren't I?"

"If your wife retaliates, it could jeopardize your position in the corporation."

Edward placed his hand firmly on the documents as if holding them down. "My future with Sarah is worth the risk. Nothing will change my mind."

The following day Edward and his legal staff reviewed the amended settlement. The meeting became boisterous at times as the staff argued what tactics to use in Edward's defense.

"We revised the alimony, the property settlement, and household maintenance. You are giving your wife full ownership of the main house."

Edward nodded in agreement. "Did you add a clause that would prevent her from interfering in management decisions?"

"Yes, but I expect it will be challenged," Robert replied.

After a short lunch break, the men worked well past seven o'clock, and with Edward's approval, the settlement was finalized.

After the staff left the office, Robert stacked the documents neatly in a pile on the desk. "I hope these terms are acceptable to your wife. Filing this is against my better judgment."

"Let's get this done." Edward turned with a jerk, startled by the sharp ring of the telephone. Already disgusted and angry, he slammed his hand on the intercom and bellowed. "I am not taking calls."

Betty's voice sounded urgent. "You have an emergency call from Sarah Logan. Shall I put her through?"

"Yes. Of course," Edward replied. *My children? Are they all right?* A curious frown crossed his forehead when he heard Sarah's voice.

"Paul is dead," Sarah whispered.

Edward stared in disbelief, the words still echoing in his mind. For a brief second a bittersweet feeling of relief spread over him. He turned to Robert and whispered, "Paul is dead."

"What happened?" Robert bolted out of his chair, and stood behind Edward, bending his ear close to the phone.

Edward held the phone out so Robert could listen.

Sarah continued, weeping as she spoke. "The police were here. They found Paul's body in the front seat of his car, slumped over the steering wheel." Sarah took a deep breath and with a deep sob, she continued. "With a bullet hole in his forehead."

"Paul. Shot in the forehead," Edward repeated, relaying the information.

Robert edged closer, calculating the legal implications. "Sounds like a professional hit."

Sarah's voice quivered between sobs. "They asked all kind of questions. They wanted to know if Paul had any enemies. I told them he had gambling debts. Then a man, I think he was an attorney, mentioned a warrant."

"What?" Edward raised his eyes curiously toward Robert. "They came with a Search Warrant."

"My God. They think Sarah is a suspect," Robert whispered.

Edward felt his chest tightening, and a rush of heat rose beneath his collar. He glanced at Robert and fear shown in his eyes. "A suspect?"

"The police asked where I was between eleven thirty and two o'clock this afternoon."

Edward gasped and held his hand on his chest. "They asked you what?"

"I told them I was at home with my children."

"What did they say to that?"

"The officer said it's just routine questioning. A man in a suit, searched our legal papers and Paul's personal items. I gave the police everything, even our bankbook. They asked for the names of Paul's friends. I told them Paul never brought friends home."

Edward pressed the phone to his ear. "Yes. Go on. What happened next?"

Sarah lowered her voice. "They asked if we had life insurance."

Edward's throat tightened, making it difficult to speak. "Did you?" he sputtered, then turned to Robert and whispered. "They asked about an insurance policy."

Robert slapped his hand on his forehead. "Whew! That's not a good sign."

"I didn't know if Paul had insurance, but they searched the house anyway. They emptied every drawer."

The phone went silent.

Edward listened, and the silence frightened him like a foreboding warning.

Sarah took a deep breath before she again spoke. "The officer asked if you and I were lovers."

The words fell hard on Edward's conscience. How could he deny the truth? "What did you say?"

"I told them, no. I mean yes, but a long time ago." Sarah's voice turned apologetic. "I was so scared. I had to tell them. I said our affair ended years ago."

Edward gripped the phone tighter and replied forgivingly. "It's okay. I understand."

"It doesn't matter. We have nothing to hide." Sarah paused, and a sigh slipped from her lips. "Oh. We do, don't we?"

"Yes. Our children must remain a secret until they find the person who killed Paul."

Sarah's voice quivered as she continued. "The officer wanted to test my hands for gunpowder. I agreed. They drove me to the police station. It proved I didn't shoot a gun."

"That's good. I'm glad you did that. Now calm down. I'll be right there." Edward eased the phone down slowly and clutched his chest. His mind running in all directions. "I've got to go!" He shoved Robert aside and headed for the door. "I've got to see Sarah."

"Whoa!" Robert yelled and grabbed Edward's arm. "You can't be seen with Sarah. The police will wonder why you are there. Stay out of this."

Edward stopped when he saw a suspicious look on Robert's face. He raised his eyebrows and shook his head. "Oh no! Not me! I hated Paul, but I could never do that." His voice turned unforgiving. "You know me better than that." Edward jerked his arm away and headed toward the door.

"Sure. I know you. But the police don't," Robert called out. "You could be a suspect."

Edward gripped the doorknob and set the door ajar. As the accusation sunk in, he turned toward his friend. "A suspect?"

"Yes. You're the lover. After the loan sharks, you're next on their list."

Edward stared aimlessly at the floor, nervously twisting his car keys through his fingers. The seriousness of the situation was beginning to take hold. He returned to his chair and tossed his keys on the desk. "This changes everything, doesn't it?"

"You can't divorce Lillian until this is cleared up. It wouldn't look good. A murder. Then a divorce."

A sudden banging shook the office door.

Robert moved quickly, snatched the documents off the desk, and shoved them in his briefcase.

The door flew open. Two policemen barged in. Officer Meyers, a husky man in full uniform, marched across the office. "Are you Edward Hansen?" he demanded coldly.

Edward, taken off guard by the officer's hostile mannerism, stood defensively behind his desk. "Yes. What can I do for you?"

"Do you know Sarah Logan?" Meyers growled, jutting his jaw out and griping his holstered gun in a combative manner.

"You don't have to answer!" Robert shouted as he approached the officer. "I am Mister Hansen's attorney. What can we do for you?"

"It's okay. I can handle this." Edward waved Robert aside. "Yes. Sarah was an employee of mine. She worked in an office across town years ago."

"Did you know that Sarah Logan's husband was murdered?"

Robert interrupted quickly. "No! We didn't know. How did it happen?"

Meyers turned toward Edward and quipped sarcastically. "Sarah Logan was one of your lovers, wasn't she?" He slipped a notebook out of his pocket and, to avoid eye contact, stared down at the paper. "Isn't that true?"

Edward gripped the edge of the desk and clenched his fist. "What?"

Robert, in an attempt to prevent further questions, stood in front of Edward's desk. "My client has nothing to say."

"It's okay. I'll handle this." Edward replied "My affair with Sarah ended years ago. Please handled this discreetly. I'm married."

"Of course. We understand," the officer answered, feigning a weak smile. He flipped the page of his notebook. "Where were you between eleven this morning and two this afternoon?"

Robert, concerned that Edward had already said too much, stepped forward. "This questioning stops right now."

"It's a simple question. He'll have to answer it sooner or later. Where were you?"

"I was with my attorney. We never left this office. My chauffeur drove me here at eight this morning. My office staff and my secretary will confirm that I was in my office all day."

Robert threw his arm out blocking the officer from approaching the desk. "Do you have a signed warrant?"

"No. This is just routine questioning."

"It's okay. I can handle this." Edward again motioned Robert aside.

Officer Meyers stared suspiciously at Edward. "With-his-attorney," he repeated aloud as he printed across the page. He pressed the pencil hard, scratching dark lines under each word. "Do you always work this late?"

Edward reacted quickly. "No. Not usually. We had an important, ah, what the hell does it matter how late we work?"

Meyers scanned the walls, studying the elaborate office.

On the wall behind the desk hung prestigious awards from the United States Army and certificates of honor from the Department of Defense. Another wall displayed photographs of Edward with the governor, celebrities, and noted public officials.

"No photographs of a wife," Meyers muttered loud enough to be heard as he penned the words. "That's all for now. Don't go anywhere." Meyers motioned to the other officer. "Let's go," he called across the room, then marched toward the door.

After the officers left, Edward collapsed in his chair. "They didn't waste time getting here."

Robert, contemplating the legal complications, gripped his briefcase closer. "You've said too much already. They know you're estranged from Lillian. Hell, everyone knows that. They also know you were Sarah's lover. Let's face it. You and Sarah are prime suspects."

Edward leaned back, stunned by the accusations and fear shone in his eyes.

"Please! Let me handle any further questioning."

"Did you hear that? Sarah was one of my lovers! That officer made it sound so sleazy."

"They're hassling you so you'll say something incriminating."

"I could never commit murder," Edward mumbled under his breath.

"The newspapers will get wind of this. You have money, motive, and connections. So naturally, you're first on the list."

"How deep will they probe into my relationship with Sarah?"

"They're looking for a shooter, or a conspiracy to hire an assassin."

Edward's voice rose to a high pitch of desperation and his hands flew up in the air. "It could have been anyone. Loan sharks. Gamblers."

"What about your wife?"

Edward's head jerked, and he raised his eyebrow. "What?"

Robert changed the tone of his voice. "Let's look at the possibilities. Who else could it be?"

"It could be gangsters. Paul was involved in gambling and shady deals."

Robert glanced down at his briefcase. "We can't let anyone know about this impending divorce. That alone will make you look guilty."

Edward slammed his fists hard on the desk. "Damn it! Get me a private investigator. I want Sarah and my name cleared of this murder."

Robert, seeing the fear in his friend's eyes, nodded in agreement. "Okay, but remember, you're not in charge of this investigation.

The police know more than they're saying. Let them get the person who shot Paul."

"Phone Bogart," Edward insisted.

"All right." Robert nodded and patted his briefcase. "I'll keep this under my hat for the time being."

The following morning Bogart met with his friend, Detective Collier at the police station. He knocked at the office door and poked his head in. "Got anything on the Logan case?"

Detective Collier hurried Bogart inside his office, and peeked out through the half-open door. "Did anyone see you come in?"

"No. I don't think so." Bogart set his brief case on the floor and sat down. "I understand the police came with a Search warrant for Paul Logan's house."

"No. Not really. If it's any consolation, the officers didn't go there waving a warrant. They asked permission to search the house."

"What did they expect to find?"

Collier headed toward his desk. "Look. About that warrant. I knew it wasn't right, but I had to sign it. I couldn't tell the commissioner to go to hell."

"Who called for the search?"

"Judge's Burris. He sent Jason, his staff attorney to overseeing it."

"What? He can't do that. He's without jurisdiction to oversee a search."

"I know. They knew better too, so they never actually presented the warrant."

"Yeah. I know how they get around unethical searches. I understand the police visited Edward Hansen's office too."

"It was Officer Meyers. He's a hothead. Real cocky because he's a close friend of the judge."

"My sources tell me Meyers was insulting and disrespectful."

"That sounds like him. The police wanted more information, but Hansen's attorney squelched the questioning." Collier unlocked his desk drawn and pulled out a manila envelope. "I didn't forget that I owe you big time. What I have is strictly confidential." Collier pushed an envelope across his desk.

Bogart nodded with a sly grin. "Strictly between you and me."

The sound of a drunken man shouting echoed through the outer office.

Detective Colliers rushed to the door and peeked out. "I gotta go. Ya better leave while there's a lot of commotion out there."

Bogart slipped the envelope in his satchel. "Thanks." A quick nod, and he hurried past the officers wrestling with a belligerent drunk.

Several days later, Bogart laid the reports on the Edward's desk. "Be careful who sees this. It's confidential." Bogart slipped two folders out of his briefcase. "It looks like a professional hit," he said, raising his hand to his forehead as if holding a gun. "Wham! Right between the eyes. This Logan guy racked up some hefty gambling debts."

Robert picked up a folder, then pushed the second copy across the desk. "Did they find the gun?"

"No gun was found. The driver's side window was down. So, whoever fired the gun was at close range. Blood splattered everywhere. No obvious signs of a struggle."

"If the window was down, Paul must have been talking to the shooter," Robert interjected.

Edward read the report aloud. "Two women claim to have heard a single gunshot at approximately one-thirty in the afternoon. They saw a person, average height, wearing a dark coat fleeing the scene. They were too far away to see the face. The person's coat collar was up, or was wearing a hood.

"There's more confirmation on the shooter." Bogart flipped the page. "A male neighbor, Harry Johnson, claims it was about one-forty in the afternoon. He saw a person in a black coat running down the street and enter a black Chrysler. He claims the person ran like a female."

"It could be a woman," Robert replied. "Paul had lady friends."

Edward's voice turned optimistic. "This shifts the blame to Paul's girlfriends. Doesn't it?"

"Not sure yet," Bogart answered. "I've located several women who knew Paul Logan. They admitted to having dated him. I gave their names to the police department." Bogart grinned and rolled his eyes humorously. "Ya know. As a private citizen."

"It could be any of his lady friends," Edward responded, flipping to the next page.

"Not likely," Bogart interrupted. "Paul Logan's ladies don't drive expensive cars."

"Sarah has a Lincoln, not a Chrysler. She was home with the children," Edward retaliated.

"That black Chrysler could belong to anyone," Robert replied. "It's not unusual to see an expensive black car in Detroit."

Bogart pulled a chair up to the desk and sat down. "The police confiscated the title of Paul Logan's car. They found you purchased that Lincoln for Sarah. It's the same car Paul Logan was killed in."

"Paul was in Sarah's car?" Edward stammered, tracing the words across the page with his finger.

"Yeah," Bogart replied. "Paul Logan drove his wife's Lincoln the morning he was killed. Misses Logan didn't have a car that morning."

"I have several cars. One's a black Chrysler," Edward muttered under his breath. "Does that make me a suspect?"

"Let's not jump to conclusions," Robert interrupted. "Your legal staff can testify you were here all morning."

Bogart continued. "The wife claimed Paul Logan was acting paranoid earlier that morning. That sounds like he suspected someone was after him."

"The shooter could have been someone Paul knew," Robert replied.

Bogart turned toward Edward and lowered his voice. "They know you're estranged from your wife. You have money, motive, and power. They're investigating a possible conspiracy, or a hired gun." Bogart pulled another document from his briefcase. "This is a copy of the warrant for Paul's house."

Robert yanked the document from Bogart's hand. "A warrant?"

"Yep," Bogart replied with raised eyebrows. "Signed by Judge Burris. His personal attorney monitored the search."

Robert's head shot up, and he scowled curiously. "What the hells going on! He's without jurisdiction to oversee a search."

Bogart raised his hand, stopping the conversation. "No. No. They only mentioned a warrant. They never served it. The wife agreed to the search."

"Damn son-of-bitches," Robert growled. "They coerced her into a search, so they wouldn't have to execute the warrant."

Edward interrupted. "Sarah must have been upset. Maybe she didn't understand what they were asking."

"Actually, the judge can sign a search warrant. Having his office employee oversee the search might not be illegal, but it's certainly unethical," Bogart replied.

Edward scanned the document. "This shows Detective Colliers is the person who requested the search."

"Ya, but the warrant wasn't actually implemented."

Robert studied the document closely. "Why would the judge be interested in Paul Logan? What did he expect to find at Sarah's house?"

"The file is red tagged," Bogart replied, arching his back and stretching his shoulders. "I'll find the connection between Paul and the judge."

"Watch your step. Investigating a judge is risky business," Robert warned. "Keep investigating Paul's gambling connections. There's more to this than meets the eye."

CHAPTER 36

"It's been weeks. Still nothing about Paul's murder," Edward said as he scanned the morning newspaper. "What's going on?"

"It could involve someone important," Robert replied with a concerned shrug. "The press is careful what they print."

"I'm a nervous wreck. It's only a matter of time before my relationship with Sarah is all over the newspapers."

"Try not to worry. The Detroit News named you Citizen of the Year. They'll keep this under cover until they have all the facts."

"Anything new on the investigation?" Edward crumpled the newspaper and tossed it in the trash basket.

"Bogart dropped off his latest report." Robert opened his briefcase and withdrew a manila envelope. "He claims the police are withholding information from the media."

"Why is the press suppressing Paul's death too?"

Robert slammed the report hard on the desk and raised his eyebrows. "Again I'll say. It could involve someone very powerful."

"Could it be Judge Burris? He has a personal connection to the Governor."

Robert brushed off the issue with a slight nod.

"I spoke with Sarah. The police came back and questioned her again."

Robert's head jerked up and his eyes widened. "What! You're not seeing her, are you?"

"No. No," Edward replied, waving his hand in the air. "We only spoke over the phone. Why are they harassing her? She had nothing to do with her husband's death."

"Everyone is a suspect." Robert unbuttoned his jacket, sat down and his voice turned solemn. "I received a call from your office manager, Mister Kelsey. The police came to his office with a Search warrant. They confiscated information on Sarah's salary."

"Her salary? What the hell for?"

"They questioned your employees about checks cut in Sarah's name. Mister Kelsey admitted he has been sending Sarah checks, even though she isn't working."

Edward shoved his chair back, stood up and placed his hands firmly on the desk. "That's none of their damn business! I don't have to explain how I run my company."

"Don't you understand? That implicates you. It suggests you're involved with Sarah. You're a prime suspect."

Edward voice rose to a high pitch, revealing his frustration. "They should have asked *me* about the checks. I would have told them." Edward stopped in mid sentence, and lowered his voice. "I couldn't have told them anything, could I? Especially not the truth."

"Sarah's a kept woman," Robert responded coldly.

"I feel so powerless." Edward head dropped and his shoulders slouched forward. "I don't know how to help her."

"This isn't your battle. It's Sarah's divorce."

"It *is* my battle. Those are my children."

"You're right. Sorry. I didn't mean to be insensitive. I've been up half the night researching the law. We need to defend Sarah's income without damaging your reputation."

"Can't we say she's on maternity leave."

"Hell no! That would open Pandora's box. I hope she didn't tell the police you're the father of her children."

The reality of exposing his paternity hit hard. Edward felt like someone punched him in the stomach, and he collapsed back in his chair. "My God. Do you think Sarah mentioned our kids?"

"The police have a way of getting information, especially from an emotionally fragile person. And believe me, after dealing with the courts, Sarah is emotionally fragile."

"I'll phone her." Edward paused, glanced at his friend and asked. "I should, shouldn't I?"

"You might as well," Robert said, as he rose to leave.

Edward jutted his chin toward his friend. "Wait, a minute," he called out as he dialed Sarah's phone number. "Stay here in case Sarah has any questions."

"Sure." Robert retraced his steps back and sat down. "I'll answer them if I can."

When Sarah heard Edward's voice, she began to cry. "I'm sorry. I told the police you were the father of my children. They asked so many questions, and I got scared."

"Don't cry. I'll take care of everything."

"I didn't know how to explain my paychecks. They made me feel like a slut."

Edward covered the mouthpiece with his hand and whispered. "Damn it. The police know about my kids. What should we do?"

"Nothing. Just sit tight. Let's see what they do with the information."

Edward nodded, then turned his attention to Sarah and softened his voice. "Don't worry. It was bound to come out sooner or later. I'll call you tomorrow."

Robert scanned the latest detective report. "No one identified the person running from Paul's car."

Edward picked up his copy of the report and read the first line of each paragraph aloud. "The investigation is at a standstill. The attorneys clammed up. No new leads. Edward closed the report. "I wonder if the police questioned Lillian?"

"I'll talk to the police commissioner tomorrow. Don't expect too much. There's still a red flag on this case." Robert crossed the room, gripped the doorknob and set the door ajar. "If the police told your wife about your children, you're in deep shit my friend."

Edward followed his friend across the office and shoved his hands deep in his pockets. "I don't think Lillian knows. If she did, she'd be making one hell of a scene."

Robert stood in the doorway and called across the room. "For Christ's sake, don't put your hands in your pockets when you talk to the police."

Edward, puzzled by the odd request, looked down at his pants. "My pockets! Why?"

"The police read body language. Hiding your hands suggest you're concealing something."

"You've known me for a long time," Edward said, as he fumbled the keys in his pocket. "It's not my nature to be deceptive."

"Don't fumble with your keys, either. That tells the police you're nervous about what you're hiding. Be aware of your body language."

Edward yanked his hands out of his pockets and clenched his jaw. "You're talking as if I'm guilty."

"Your face is turning red. The police will spot that too. Keep a poker face when you talk to them. They're reading every move you make." Robert stopped and softened his voice. "Sorry. I don't mean to be so blunt."

"It's okay. These are things I need to know. I appreciate your honesty." Edward thought about how inexperienced he was when they first met. "Ever since we roomed together in college, you were like the older brother I never had."

"Yeah, I could see you were overprotected," Robert chided with a wide grin.

"Glad you were there to advise me."

The days were growing colder, and the evening lonelier. Edward was concerned because the police investigation was still undercover, and the Detroit News remained silent about Paul's death. Even Bogart's information from Detective Colliers had dried up. He stood at the window looking across the yard.

The main house was dark except for a single light that shone through a downstairs window.

It's probably Hilda in the maid's kitchen.

A faint light turned on in an upstairs window. A shadowy figure moved past the dimly lit window of Lillian's bedroom.

Edward stepped closer and pressed his face against the glass. The loneliness of the moment pierced his soul. *Is she as lonely, as I am.* He tried to remember why he had fallen in love with her, but those memories had faded long ago. Now, he could only think of his wife as a stranger.

The light in the upstairs window went dark.

Edward returned to his favorite chair in the living room and switched off the lamp. *I'm not sorry Paul is dead. Sarah is finally rid of him.* A twinge of guilt prodded his conscience because he had no regret for Paul's death. *At least Sarah won't have to go through another court trial.* He closed his eyes and thought about the future. *Will I ever be with Sarah and my children?* As the thought crossed his mind, an icy breeze brushed against his cheek. Edward opened his eyes, stuck his neck out and sniffed the air.

That's the same scent as my mother's perfume.

The fragrance brought a comforting feeling, like being wrapped in a blanket of security. But the peaceful moment didn't last. His thoughts drew him back to his tragic marriage, and the familiar scent vanished.

His Libra mind began weighing his personal fears. He recalled Lillian's temper exploding at the slightest provocation. And, the times she locked herself in the bedroom. *Did she hide in her room just to torment me? And, what about Lillian's mysterious meeting with Paul? And the stock she sold without the company's knowledge? Is there reason to suspect my wife?* "If only my mother was alive," he murmured as he again closed his eyes.

Once again, an icy breeze brushed against his face.

Edward's eyes popped open, the hair on the back of his neck stood up, and his heart beat wildly. He bolted out of his chair and dashed to the center of the room. Even though he felt comforted by the cold breeze, he scanned the room suspiciously.

The dark room remained quiet. A shaft of pale moonlight shone through the lace curtains, casting eerie shadows against the wall.

Feeling uneasy, Edward switched on a lamp. "Lillian drives a black Chrysler. I've never known her to own a gun. At least, I don't think she has a gun," he mumbled under his breath.

Over the next several weeks, Edward buried himself in his work, hoping to take his mind off the police investigation.

Robert entered the office and placed a stack of documents on the desk. "The soldiers are returning home, and a baby boom will be underway. Your legal staff proposed several sites to build factories. What do you want to do?"

"I know there'll be a demand for housing, but I can't consider building right now. When this police investigation is over, I still intend to file for divorce. Lillian would be a thorn in my side if I start any new projects."

"Am I to reject these sites without an explanation?"

Edward waved his friend aside. "Stall the committee for a while."

"How do I explain your refusal to build?"

"Damn it. Lillian has my life on hold. What the hell can I do?"

"Hey. Remember me. I'm your friend. I'm having a tough time stalling them. Are you sure your wife will interfere if you build?"

"You're damn right she will, just to spite me." Edward raised his voice defensively. "I've hired more employees. I've increased production. Isn't that enough?"

"Several members of the legal staff say you're procrastinating again."

"Just support me," Edward barked. "No new construction."

"You're missing a great opportunity. We could corner the housing market."

"Making money is not my first priority. If I break ground on a factory, Lillian owns enough stock that she can stop construction. That woman can be vindictive when she wants too."

Robert was about to leave when he heard a soft rapping on the office door. He opened the door and stood face to face with Edward's secretary.

Betty Chalmers smiled sensual, gripped the door ajar, and intentionally blocked him from leaving.

The strong scent of perfume filled Robert's nostrils. He stepped back and glanced at Edward with a bewildered look on his face.

Edward, seeing the frustrated look on his friend's face, tossed his head back and chuckled.

Miss Chalmers remained broadside in the doorway, making it difficult for Robert to pass.

Robert stepped forward, determined to leave the office.

Betty closed her eyes, jutted her chin out and puckered her lips.

Robert sent a damning glance at Edward, who was grinning from ear to ear. He forced a weak smile, sucked in his stomach and squeezed past the secretary.

Betty stepped closer, making sure Robert would brush against her breast as he made his way through the door. A soft murmur oozed from her lips as Robert's body touched her. Betty, still grinning, strolled sensually across the office. "I don't mean to bother you, but your wife's housekeeper has been phoning all morning. I told her you were in a meeting, but she insists upon speaking with you today."

"What does she want?"

"She wouldn't tell me. Do you want to speak with her?"

Edward frowned. "Don't I have enough trouble? Yes. I'll take the call." Edward waited until his secretary left the room, then softened his voice. "Hello, Hilda. Is there a problem?"

"I think your wife is sick."

"What's the matter now?" Edward grumbled, irritated by what he assumed was Lillian's way of getting attention.

"The police came to see the missus a few weeks ago. Ever since then, she's been acting real strange."

"The police?" Edward shrieked. "Why didn't someone tell me? What did they want?"

"They asked where the missus was on the day that guy was shot. I told them she went shopping. Then they asked if she drove a Chrysler. I told them, sometimes she drives that car, and sometimes she drives the Ford. They asked a lot of questions. Ya know, like what kinda man you are."

"What did they want?"

"The police sent me away. But I listened at the parlor door."

Edward gripped the telephone tighter, his mind racing with uncertainty. *Did the police disclose the financial arrangement I had with Sarah? Does Lillian know about the impending divorce?* A warm sweat formed across his forehead. "What else did they ask? Did they question my wife just because she drives a black Chrysler?"

"I told the officer I don't pay much attention to what she drives. When they left, I peeked in the parlor. The missus looked real scared, like she was sick or something. Then, she started bad mouthing you. Saying you're ruining her reputation."

"What else happened?"

"The missus complained of a headache. Her eyes looked funny, like they're blurry. You know, like she can't see. She went up the stairs real slow, like she didn't feel good. I heard her lock the bedroom door. She didn't come out for two days. Ever since then, she's been looking sickly."

"Is she drinking?" Edward waited for an answer, but when Hilda didn't reply, he assumed Lillian's incoherence was alcohol related. *If she's been drinking, she'll make one hell of a scene. Today wouldn't be the best time to visit.* "Phone the doctor. I'll talk to him after he's seen her."

"No, sir. She forbid me to call Doctor Johnson. What should I do?"

"I'll call the doctor. Maybe I can stop by in a few days." Edward assumed Lillian wanted attention, just as she had done most of their married life. Even though he resented catering to his wife's whims, he felt it was his duty. Plus, he was curious to learn more about the police visit.

"Okay," Hilda replied. "I won't tell her you're coming. She'll be carrying on something fierce when she finds out you called Doctor Johnson."

CHAPTER 37

Lillian woke feeling uncontrollably angry, cursing the weather for her throbbing headache. After locking the bedroom door, she staggered across the bedroom and entered the large walk-in closet. Shoving several dresses aside, she pulled out a small metal box, and dumped the contents on the bed.

Photographs, scrunched-up papers, and packs of hundred-dollar bills lay scattered across the unmade bed. A plastic bag, half-filled with medicine bottles, lay beside the box.

Lillian picked up a piece of paper, squinted as she tried to read it, but the writing appeared blurred. *What's wrong with me?* A dull throbbing hammered within her head. Feeling faint, she cupped her hands on her temples and collapsed on the bed. After resting for a while, she returned to the closet. Edging her way to the back, she yanked a white sheet off a gold-framed mirror. Though it was heavy, she dragged it across the room, scraping the edge of the frame against the oak floor, and set it against the wall.

Why is the glass so dingy? With a broad sweep of her hand, she brushed the dust off the glass.

A beam of morning sun shone through the windows, brightening the bedroom. Shafts of sunlight reflected on the dingy glass, giving an illusion of a gray mist moving within.

Is something moving inside the mirror? Lillian blinked to focus her eyes. Again, she brushed her hand across the glass.

The gray mist looked like smoke, twisting and turning behind the glass. A flash of sun streamed through the lace curtains, setting the gold frame aglow. The sculptured curves of the frame appeared to move, giving the effect of grotesque figures dancing around the mirror's edge.

Lillian, mesmerized by the movement, sat on the floor and watched the phantom mist changing shape. She squinted. *Are my eyes deceiving me?*

The gray vapors melted together, forming a ghost-like image. From the shadows, a ghostly face emerged, moving closer, and closer, as if it had a purpose. After a while, the mist faded away, leaving the imprint of two coal-black eyes staring accusingly through the glass.

Startled by the black orbs, Lillian arched her back against the bed and pushed herself away from the mirror. In her attempt to get away, her foot struck the edge of the frame.

The mirror wobbled, yet remained steadfast against the wall. The black orbs vanished, and through the gray mist a face with an open mouth materialized. Phantom lips, though barely visible, pleaded from within the mirror.

"Why, ma? Why?"

The message stabbed at her conscience like a sharp sword. She clasped her hands on her temples. A piercing pain raced through her head.

When the pain subsided, she wiped the tears from her eyes. Traumatized by the apparition, she could not turn away. She resumed her position squatting on the floor in front of the mirror.

The curious face had now faded into the mist, and from the swirling vapors, scenes of her past appeared.

Lillian visualized her temper tantrums, and acts of violence against her daughter. She recalled the days she hid in her room and now realized the damaged it caused her marriage. The hostile actions of her past became clearer, each scene more lucid, more intense.

Lillian watched the day Bridget was born, and the anger she felt when she saw the baby's misshapen face. "I didn't want you," Lillian whimpered. "I didn't want an ugly child. Why didn't you die when I fell down the stairs?"

The memory of her daughter's misshapen face intensified, assaulting her body with guilt.

Within the mirror, the image of a wood board emerged from the mist, and hovered in midair.

Lillian closed her eyes, and shook her head, to push the image away. When she opened her eyes, she saw the board begin to grow larger, and larger, levitating behind the glass.

Lillian relived her actions on that fatal day. She watched the board crashing down, striking Bridget across the back. She turned away from the mirror and buried her face in the bed sheet. The image of Bridget struggling to rise from the floor, played across her mind. When she again looked at the mirror, the board was slowly rising.

It loomed in midair, threatening its next move. Again, it came crashing down, striking the second blow across Bridget's neck.

Lillian grabbed the bed linens, pulling them down to cover her body.

"Why, ma? Why?" A disembodied voice wailed from within the mirror.

A sharp pain raced across her temples like hot rubber bands splitting inside her head. Feeling disoriented, she collapsed on the floor. As she lay quietly, she felt the warm sensation of blood surging through her brain. A tranquil calmness swept over her, and she felt strangely detached from her surroundings.

The room darkened and became eerily quiet.

Lillian felt a part of herself separating her from her physical body, floating up toward the ceiling. Movement seemed to slow down. Her surroundings appeared surreal, void of meaning, and empty.

"Oh, my God! What have I done?"

With the repentant plea of remorse, a tranquil emotion swept over Lillian. She felt her soul rising in slow motion, drifting silently toward a brilliant light. With her mind at peace, Lillian embraced the celestial atmosphere, floating as if in a trance, without recognition of time or space. After a while, she wondered. *Should I look for Bridget?*

As the thought crossed her mind, the memory of her guilt manifested into sinister black figures. They swooped down and dragged her from the tranquil light.

She struggled to wrench herself free, but it was no use. She felt a part of herself slamming back into her physical body. An excruciating pain raced across her forehead. Lillian opened her eyes, face to face with the mirror.

The vague image of her daughter, with arms outstretched, appeared within the glass.

"Oh, God! Please help me." Lillian's repentant cry removed her from the horrifying scene, and again she felt herself floating toward the ceiling. She looked down.

A women's body lay lifeless, clad only in a silk nightgown.

Lillian felt no connection to the lifeless body below. She felt herself drifting in serene peacefulness toward a brilliant light. The feeling of unconditional love embraced her, and she knew she was returning to her real home.

But the guilty thought of her daughter's death was too strong. The sin, for which she thought there was no forgiveness, forced her back to reality.

Once again, darkness swept over the room. Ghostly black figures appeared from all directions, dragging Lillian's soul toward her physical body.

In her attempt to return to the light, Lillian thrust her body forward, into her own reflection in the mirror.

The mirror crashed down, slamming hard against Lillian's head.

Again, she felt her soul slipping out of her physical body. The sensation of having no control frightened her. She called for help, but no voice came from her lips. She reached for the bed, but her hands had no substance and her fingers slid through the bed linen. She tried to lift the mirror off her body, but her hands passed through the frame. Even though her body was pinned beneath the mirror, she could see all around the room. She was looking from within the mirror, and there was no way out.

The brilliant God light had vanished. The menacing black blobs of fear had left as well. The room grew eerily still.

In her attempt to escape, she touched the glass. The glass had no substance, yet it was impenetrable. Panic-stricken with fear, she realized that her soul, the essence of her being, was encapsulated inside the mirror.

It was nearly noon when Hilda and Ester made the third trip up the stairs. The breakfast tray was still outside the door and the food remained untouched.

Hilda rapped lightly. "Misses Hansen, are you awake?" She pressed her ear against the door and listened. "Please open this door."

No sound came from the bedroom.

"Ester! Run downstairs and call Mister Hansen. Tell him the missus locked herself in her bedroom again. She won't let us in."

Ester, sensing no urgency, ambled down the stairs. She had seen Lillian hide in her room many times before, and thought today was no different. Ester phoned Edward at his office and drawled her complaint. "Miss Lillian done locked herself in her bedroom again. She ain't eating her breakfast. What should we do?"

"What now?" Edward grumbled. "When will she stop this nonsense? Have the gardener jimmy the lock."

"Hilda wants you to open the door," Ester whined.

"If Lillian doesn't open that damn door, have the police knock it down. I've had enough of that woman's craziness. She just wants attention."

Ester hung up the telephone and trudged up the stairs. "He ain't coming. He say, have the gardener jimmy the lock."

"Hush," Hilda whispered, again pressing her ear against the door.

"The mister sounded mad. He say, have the police knock it down."

"Shush. Can't you see I'm listening?" A curious look crossed Hilda's face. "I can't hear a thing."

Ester hoisted the breakfast tray onto her hip. "Maybe she's gonna stay in her room," Ester quipped as she headed for the stairs.

"Something is wrong. I feel it in my bones," Hilda mumbled as she followed Ester down the stairs. She stopped halfway, turned, and shouted, "Misses Hansen, if you don't open that door in one hour, I'm gonna call the police. Do you hear me?"

"She's in one of her bad moods," Ester whispered.

The women returned to the kitchen. Hilda, still concerned, found herself looking at the clock every few minutes. She waited until one o'clock and again sent Ester upstairs.

Several minutes later Ester sauntered into the kitchen. "The misses ain't gonna answer. Her door is still locked."

"That's it. I'm calling the police." Hilda, mindful of Lillian's violent temper, hesitated to take matters in her own hands, but today, she had an uncomfortable feeling.

Within minutes, a police car raced to the house with lights flashing and sirens blaring.

Hilda, waiting in the foyer, directed the officers up the stairs with a pointed finger.

Officer Schmidt pounded on the bedroom door. "Misses Hansen. This is the police! We must talk to you." He pressed his ear against the door and listened. "Open this door, or we'll break it down."

The older, gray-haired officer, edged his way past Schmidt. He sniffed the keyhole, then looked up and whispered. "We have a problem."

Schmidt, recognizing the implication, shoved the officer aside, unhooked a ring of keys from his belt and began inserting one key at a time. After several attempts, a key clicked, and he eased the door open.

Lillian's body, still dressed in a nightgown, lay slumped at the foot of the bed. A large gold framed mirror lay on top of her body.

Officer Schmidt opened the door open wider.

The odor of foul-smelling air wafted from the room.

Schmidt gagged and heaved a coarse cough. With a wave of his hand, he directed two policemen into the room.

In unison, the men lifted the mirror off the body and set it against the wall.

The older officer lifted Lillian's wrist. "She's gone," he said, then laid his fingers against Lillian's eyes, closing them gently. "She's cold. Probably dead a couple hours."

Hilda let out a mournful wail. "Goot en himmel. My poor baby. It's all my fault. I should have known something was wrong." Hilda buried her face in her hands and wept.

Officer Schmidt, realizing he was in the midst of a breaking story, shouted across the room. "Do you have another phone? I don't want to touch this one."

"In the kitchen," Hilda whimpered.

Schmidt dashed down the stairs. His hand trembled as he dialed the phone. "Commissioner. We've got a dead body at the Hansen estate. It could be Misses Hansen."

"Are you sure?"

"Yeah. I'm sure. Ya gonna tell Judge Burris what's happening?"

"Are you positive it's the Hansen residence?" the commissioner growled.

"Ya. I'm sure. You ought to see the size of this house. It's huge!"

"Don't touch a thing. I'll send homicide down there."

"This isn't a homicide," Schmidt bellowed back. "It looks like a stroke. The woman's face is distorted. The muscles on her mouth are pulled down on one side. That's a stroke if I ever saw one."

"Was there blood at the scene? Does it look like foul play?"

"No. The housekeeper said the woman has been sick."

"Damn it. I asked if there was blood at the scene!"

"Yeah. On her face. The damn mirror fell on her face."

"Was the mirror cracked? Did it cut her?" The commissioner spoke rapidly, anxious to get every detail immediately.

"Yeah. The mirror is cracked. It's a small crack. I think the mirror could have caused the blood."

The commissioner interrupted. "I didn't ask you to think. You're supposed to take orders."

Schmidt hesitated, a thought of recognition crossed his face. "Didn't their daughter die the same way? Bludgeoned by a mirror?"

"I remember that. This sounds suspicious. Don't touch the body until homicide gets there with a Search Warrant."

"A warrant?"

"Yeah! Don't let anyone in that room. Didn't we question Misses Hansen about Paul Logan's death? This could be important. I'll call the judge."

That same afternoon, the bailiff entered the courtroom and approached the judge's bench. Leaning close, he whispered in his ear.

Judge Burris' head snapped up and an astonished look crossed his face. He glanced across the courtroom with furrowed brow, hoping no one had noticed his startled reaction. Regaining his stoical demeanor, he stood up and addressed the crowded courtroom in an authoritative voice. "I have an important phone call. There will be an hour delay." He stepped off the platform and hurried to his chamber.

Jason Martin, the judge's personal attorney, was waiting in the chamber. When he saw the judge entering, he waved the bailiff out of the room.

The judge lowered his voice to a whisper. "What happened? The bailiff said it was important."

"The commissioner just phoned. There's been a death at the Hansen estate. There could be a connection to Paul Logan's unsolved murder. He said you'd understand."

"Shh. Damn it. Turn off the in-office microphone before you say one more word."

Jason nodded, then hurried to the outer office and turned off the hidden tape recorder.

"Issue a Search Warrant right away," Judge Burris shouted across the room.

Jason returned to the judge's chamber. "What? Why?"

"I want to search that house."

"It's not a homicide. Schmidt thinks the woman had a stroke."

"Screw Officer Schmidt. Issue the warrant." The judge glanced at his wristwatch. "Hurry. Every minute counts."

"We don't have cause for a search. It looks like an accident."

"Son-of-a-bitch," the judge growled, slamming his fist on the desk. "Get over there now, before anyone hears about this. I'll think of something to validate the search." The judge lowered his voice. "If we don't find those photos, you could be out of a job come election time."

"Do you think Misses Hansen knew Paul Logan? Why would she know about the photograph?"

"I'm not accusing anyone. If we find the racetrack pictures, then we're okay." The judge turned and shouted to his secretary in the outer office. "Get me a Search Warrant for the Hansen premise. Now!"

Several minutes later, the bailiff entered the chamber waving a piece of paper in the air. "What charges are we siting for this search?"

"Just say, ah, . . . circumstances support a homicide, ah, . . . undetermined death," the judge muttered as he scribbled his name on the document.

"I don't think that's probable cause."

"Damn it. Just do it," the judge bellowed. "Phone the commissioner. Tell him to send homicide over there. You get over there too. Do a thorough search."

Edward, having been notified of Lillian's death, hurried to the main house. He edged his way through a crowd of policemen milling about the foyer and dashed up the stairs. As he leaned in the bedroom doorway, the repugnant odor of death invaded his nostrils. He covered his mouth with his hand and heaved a dry cough.

Lillian's body lay on the floor covered by a silk sheet. Several police hovered over the body, talking in low whispers. A large, gold-framed mirror leaned against the wall.

Edward braced his body against the door-frame to steady himself. "What happened?" Before he could get an answer, he felt someone pushing him aside.

"Excuse me. Coming through." Jason and two policemen barged in the room waving a document in the air. "Start your search there," he shouted to the officers.

Edward followed the attorney in the bedroom. "Hey! Who are you?"

"Jason Martin, Judge Burris' personal attorney. I have a Search Warrant."

"What's going on?" Edward snatched the warrant out of Jason's hand and examined the paper. "Homicide? Undetermined death? What the hell are you looking for?"

Jason ignored the questions and hurried across the room where stacks of money and papers lay scattered across an unmade bed. He waited until the police photographer finished, then rummaged through the items. Several small photographs had slipped out of an envelope.

Jason glanced suspiciously across the room. When he was sure no one was looking, he slipped the photographs up his sleeve. Satisfied there was nothing more of interest, he headed toward a large, tall dresser.

"Why is homicide here? For Christ's sake! My wife was ill." Edward followed Jason across the bedroom. "The housekeeper said my wife locked herself in her room. The door was locked from the inside, wasn't it?"

Again, Jason ignored Edward's question. Seeing an officer rummaging through a dresser drawer, he shouted. "Hey! I'll do that." He darted across the room and, starting at the top, opened each drawer and examined the contents. After shaking each piece of lingerie gently, he dropped them back in the drawer.

Edward glanced down at Lillian's feet protruding from beneath the silk sheet. He felt his knees growing weak, and to keep from falling, he leaned against the wall.

A group of men in white jackets continued to examine Lillian's body. Faint whispers came from behind a closet door.

Jason stopped searching the dresser, cocked his head, and listened. Realizing the voices were coming from the closet, he slammed the drawer shut and hurried across the room.

"What the hell are you looking for?" Edward asked as he followed Jason across the room.

Jason entered the closet and slammed the door closed.

Edward, angry and bewildered, eased the door open and poked his head in. "What's going on in here?"

"Please, step back Mister Hansen." Jason shoved Edward away from the door. "Let us do our job."

Edward heaved a sigh of relief when he saw Robert enter the bedroom. "Why are they searching my house?"

Robert hurried into the bedroom when he saw Lillian's body laying on the floor. "How did this happen?"

"I don't know anything yet. Hilda phoned me this afternoon. She was frantic. Lillian locked herself in the bedroom.

"How did you find out?"

"The police phoned me at the office." Edward held his hand out. "They have a Search Warrant."

Robert grabbed the warrant out of Edward's hand. After scanning the paper, he leaned close and whispered. "Just as I suspected. It's signed by Judge Burris." Robert stomped across the room waving the warrant in the air. "Who's in charge? What's the reason for this search?"

Jason Martin, opened the closet door slightly and stood broad-shouldered across the doorway. "We have to find, . . . ah, I mean. This is a Search Warrant. That's all that matters."

"Who the hell are you? Why are you here?" Robert bellowed as he hurried toward the closet.

Jason placed his hands across the doorway. "Sorry. You can't come in here."

Robert knew he couldn't legally stop the search, but felt compelled to try. "What the hell are you looking for? This woman was ill. This is not a homicide."

Jason stepped back, into the closet and slammed the door. Several minutes later, he emerged holding a small revolver dangling from the end of a pencil. "Recognize this?"

A puzzled expression crossed Edward's face. He glanced at Robert for assurance, then back at Jason. "No. Never saw it before."

"I have everything I need," Jason announced with a satisfied grin. After dropping the gun in a plastic bag, he handed it to the homicide detective. "Mark this as an exhibit. Jason turned his back and with sleight of hand, slipped several white envelopes in his pocket then headed toward the door.

Later that afternoon, Lillian's body was removed, and the house was quiet once again. Though Edward tried to comfort Hilda and the household staff, the words didn't come easy. He couldn't find words that came from his heart. His wife had become a stranger, and he struggled with bittersweet emotions.

CHAPTER 38

———— ❖ ————

"I'm glad you came," Edward said, guiding his friend through the spacious foyer, into the dimly lit living room. "I didn't want to be alone this evening."

"Your wife's death was quite a shock. This has been unnerving for me, too. I can only imagine what you're going through."

"Why were the police searching her bedroom? It looked like the mirror fell and killed her."

"They don't think it was heavy enough to cause her death. They ordered an autopsy. That will tell us the real cause."

"I feel guilty not taking her complaints seriously. But, she's always complained about one thing or another. Hilda tried to tell me, but I was bogged down with my own problems."

"I know. You came to work stressed out every day. I figured it was your wife's fault."

"I didn't pay any attention. Sorry I sloughed it off today."

Robert snorted and let out a slight chuckle. "I've been told we men just don't get it. We need more than just clues. It wasn't just you. We all saw Lillian as a bully. Every one of us. I could use a drink," Robert said as he headed across the room. "How about you?"

Edward ambled to the wet bar and filled two glasses to the brim. "It's hard to believe Lillian's dead. This has been one hell of a year, hasn't it? One thing after another. Everything came crashing down all at once."

"Did you know your wife had a gun?" Robert asked, staring hard at his friend as he extended his hand and took the glass.

"No! We didn't have guns in the house. At least, I didn't."

Robert laid a friendly hand on Edward's shoulder. "You're sure you never touched it?"

"Never saw it before. She must have hidden it in the closet."

"Let's face it. Lillian's gun and two deaths in a couple months is cause for suspicion."

A surge of nausea filled Edward's stomach. "My God! They don't think I killed my wife, do they?"

"Most husbands are considered prime suspects." Robert crossed the room and turned on a brighter lamp. "They know the same mirror was involved in Bridget's death."

"I regret giving Lillian that damn mirror," Edward whimpered, then flopped down on the couch, slouching deep in the cushions. "As far back as I remember Lillian locked the bedroom door when she was upset."

"I thought you got rid of the mirror months ago."

"I did. Somehow, she got it back." Edward glanced up at his friend, and his eyes misted with tears. "That damn thing killed her."

"We don't know that for sure. Let's wait for the autopsy report."

"She complained most of our married life. I got used to her bitching." Edward lowered his head and stared absentmindedly across the floor. "After a while, I didn't take her seriously."

"No one took her seriously. I'm sorry to speak ill about the dead, but talking might help release your frustration."

"That's okay. It's good to get my true feelings out."

"What are you doing about Lillian's staff?" Robert asked, lightening the conversation.

"I can't fire Hilda. She's been with us for years. She needs the income."

"What about the other maids? And the gardener?"

Edward hesitated, undecided about the future. "They can stay on until I make other arrangements."

Robert raised his empty glass and gestured with a smile.

"Pour me another too," Edward said, extending his glass to his friend.

Robert ambled to the wet bar and refilled the glasses. "I hear your wife let the house fall apart after you moved out. It might need a good cleaning, anyway."

"It's been a mess for a long time. I don't know why Lillian wouldn't let the maids clean." Edward heard his friend's voice rambling on, and on, but found it difficult to focus his attention.

It was well past midnight when Robert stretched his arms and released a low-pitched yawn. "I think I'll go home. Try to get some sleep tonight. I don't expect to see you tomorrow. You have funeral arrangements to make." Robert paused by the door, ready to leave. "I'll be in the office all day if you need me."

Edward nodded. "Cancel my appointments. My head is still in a fog."

Several weeks later, the commissioner summoned Edward and his attorney to the police station. "We're satisfied Misses Hansen died of a brain hemorrhage. Here's the autopsy report. Please sit down," he said, drawing two chairs up to his desk.

Edward stiffened up when he heard the word *hemorrhage*. Though it took him by surprise, he snatched the report, slammed his hand on it, pressing it down on the commissioner's desk. "I told you she was ill," he snarled, remembering the unjustified search. "Your men overreacted. You had no right to search my house."

Robert raised his hand, halting further comment. "Let's hear what the commissioner has to say," he said, with a slight raise of his eyebrows. He unbuttoned his coat and sat down, ready to hear details of the investigation.

The commissioner, thankful for the interruption, continued. "You haven't heard me out. We found the gun in your wife's closet. It's the same weapon that killed Paul Logan. It was splattered with Logan's blood. Lillian Hansen's fingerprints are on the handle."

Edward, feeling light-headed, leaned against a file cabinet, but declined to answer.

"This is the ballistic report." the commissioner continued, sliding the second document across the desk. "Why don't you sit down. You look a little pale."

The commissioner's words fell on deaf ears. Edward examined the document for several minutes, then placed it in Robert's outstretched hand.

"These are your wife's bank withdrawals," he said, shoving several papers forward. "They match Paul Logan's deposits. Not exactly each dollar, but certainly each date. Please sit down. You don't look well."

Edward flopped in a chair and dragged the withdrawal slips toward him. "This looks like Lillian's signature. This is her account number," he replied, pushing the papers toward Robert.

Clearing his throat with a hoarse grunt, the commissioner continued. "Sarah Logan's name isn't on her husband's bank account. She wasn't in on the . . ., ah, I mean . . ., there was no conspiracy."

"Conspiracy? Not Sarah."

"No! No! She's not involved," the commissioner replied, holding his hand up to halt further speculation. "We're satisfied she didn't know about her husband's savings account."

Robert tapped his finger several times on the withdrawal slips. "This appears to be your wife's signature," he said, then slipped them in his briefcase.

Seeing the bewildered look on Edward's face, the commissioner was eager to finish his explanation. "The evidence indicates Paul Logan was blackmailing Lillian Hansen."

Edward slumped back in his chair. Even though he suspected Lillian had given money to Paul, he was astonished by the amount of details the police had collected. "Blackmail? Why? This doesn't make sense."

Robert set his hand on Edward's shoulder and gave a gentle squeeze. "Let's hear the facts before we make any comments. What did Paul have against Misses Hansen?"

"My men confiscated these notes written to Paul Logan. They were in your wife's closet." He slid a folder across the desk. "These are copies of the letters your wife wrote. It says she begged Paul to keep her husband's infidelity a secret. Look at the date this was written. She knew about your children for quite some time."

Edward was about to speak when he felt Robert's hand tighten on his shoulder.

"Please continue," Robert urged.

"Paul Logan threatened to tell the newspapers that you fathered both of Sarah's children."

A warm blush reddened Edward's face, and he felt heat rising beneath his collar.

The commissioner placed a green folder on the desk. His voice rose, confident of his investigator's research. "Judging by the notes we found, Paul Logan was bleeding your wife's bank account."

"You're not going to release these to the press, are you? This would slander Sarah's good name." Edward gripped the folder until he felt Robert pulling it from his clenched fists.

"No. No," the commissioner responded. "I talked to a judge about this. He suggested we keep this matter closed to the public. You, personally, were not involved in Paul Logan's death."

Edward heaved a sigh of relief and his voice softened. "Thank you."

"Your wife knew Paul Logan was about to file a lawsuit against you." Again, he shoved several legal documents across the desk. "It's a paternity suit."

Edward, too unnerved to answer, glanced up at Robert for approval.

"Please continue," Robert replied, scooping up the documents.

"The department is returning everything confiscated from your home," he said, heaving a sigh of relief. "You can take the evidence and the mirror today."

"What? Oh, no," Edward replied with a wave of his hand. "My chauffeur will collect the evidence later. As for the mirror, throw it away."

"I'll send it to the Salvation Army if that's okay with you?"

"Anywhere. Get rid of it"

The commissioner stood up, braced his hands on the desk and leaned forward. "This case is officially closed. There won't be a press release on this matter. Paul Logan's killer is not named, just identified as deceased."

Edward offered a weak smile, still too shaken to respond.

"There will be no further investigation. With the size of your wife's brain tumor, it could have caused uncontrollable rage. Maybe she snapped."

Edward's head shot up. "What? Who said Lillian had a tumor?"

"We subpoenaed Doctor Kokeny's records. He confirmed it. Our investigation shows he treated Misses Hansen for years. Because of your wife's condition, she probably didn't know what she was doing." The commissioner rose and edged his way toward the door, eager for the men to leave. "It's all in the autopsy report."

Robert set his hand on Edward's shoulder. "Thank you," he said, nudging him toward the office door.

The following day, Edward called upon Robert to accompany him to the doctor's office.

Doctor Kokeny, an elderly, gray haired man, reached out with a firm handshake. "I'm so sorry for your loss." After studying Edward's face, he leaned forward with a friendly smile. "So, I finally get to meet you."

Edward sat down and returned the greeting with a submissive smile. "My wife never mentioned you."

"I've been her physician for years."

"For years? I had no idea she was seeing another doctor, much less had a tumor. How long has she had the tumor?"

"Since she was a teenager. It got worse as she aged."

"This is quite a shock. Lillian never talked about a tumor."

"I'm sure she didn't. Would you have married her if you knew she had a life-threatening tumor?"

Edward responded with a blank stare.

"Would you?" the doctor repeated.

A flash of recognition lit Edward's eyes, and he shook his head slowly. "Probably not."

"That's why she didn't tell you. She insisted I keep it a secret."

"I never received medical bills from you."

"Lillian always paid with cash." The doctor leaned back and studied Edward's face. "Didn't you notice your wife's uncontrollable rage?"

"I thought it was her personality," Edward replied, the pitch of his voice rising defensively.

"Didn't she mention her toothaches?"

Edward nodded his head several times. "Yes. I remember her complaining about her teeth. I didn't pay much attention. She complained so much."

The doctor let out a soft chuckle. "They say we men seldom listen when our wives speak."

Edward responded with a nonchalant shrug.

"It wasn't her teeth that ached, it was her head. I'm sure the pain became intense just before the seizure."

"What?" Edward blurted out, gripping the arms of the chair. "I didn't know she had seizures too."

Robert, who had been standing behind Edward's chair, laid his hand on his shoulder. "Are you okay?"

"Yeah," Edward replied, glancing up at his friend.

"I treated your wife's seizures for many years. After each bout, she refused to stay in the hospital. I had no choice but to send her home with medicine and ordered bed-rest."

"That may explain why your wife hid in her bedroom," Robert said, patting Edward on the shoulder.

Edward, giving little thought to the doctor's words, retaliated in his own defense. "Lillian knew it upset me, but she locked the bedroom door, anyway."

"She wasn't doing it to upset you."

"Lillian never told me she was seriously ill."

"She didn't want you to know. I warned her the headaches would get worse if she got pregnant."

"You what?" Edward snapped, taken off guard by another condition that threatened his wife's health.

"I warned Lillian the birth could kill her."

"Oh my God! Our doctor never told us," Edward muttered, his voice fading apologetically.

"Your family doctor didn't know about her tumor, or the severity of her illness."

"No wonder Lillian was upset about having the baby," Edward mumbled, his head bobbed up and down, remembering his wife's uncontrollable temper during the pregnancy.

"She took every precaution, but somehow she miscalculated."

"Lillian didn't want to get pregnant?" Edward hesitated, and a heavy frown creased his brow. "That explains why it took ten years." Edward glanced up at Robert. "I wonder why Hilda never mentioned the tumor?"

The doctor lowered his voice. "Your wife took a risk. The birth could have killed her."

Edward began to fit the pieces together. "As I recall, Lillian's temper did get worse after Bridget's birth."

"With the tumor growing, and her uncontrollable mood swings, your wife wasn't a good candidate for motherhood."

"I just assumed she was bitter about having a baby."

"The word *bitter* doesn't suit us well here. Your wife was frightened."

Edward's voice turned hostile in an attempt to change the subject. "She had a bad temper, she tormented Bridget. I tried reasoning with Lillian, but she wouldn't listen."

"You don't understand. It wasn't that she *wouldn't* listen. She *couldn't* do anything about her temper."

"Oh, his wife had a quite a temper," Robert replied, nodding in agreement.

Doctor Kokeny clenched his jaw in frustration. "Again, you didn't hear me. Lillian's tumor grew after the birth. Didn't you notice her behavior getting worse?"

"Yes. It got so bad I wanted to divorce her."

The doctor leaned across his desk and frowned. "I'm curious. Why didn't you?"

"I was afraid of retaliation."

"Your wife was too ill. She wouldn't have stopped you."

"Why didn't she divorce me? I gave her justification."

"We talked about that too," the doctor replied. "Your wife confided in me. True, your public affairs humiliated her, but that wasn't the real reason she didn't file for a divorce. She didn't have the energy to fight."

"She threatened me with divorce once. Did she tell you that?"

"Yes, she told me. It was only a threat. She hoped it would bring you to your sense."

"I stopped going to Traverse City." Edward softened his voice. "I gave up the woman I loved. Lillian was so vindictive, I was afraid she would smear Sarah's name across the newspapers."

"Your wife knew about Sarah for years. This probably aggravated her paranoia."

"Paranoia? She knew for years?"

"Your wife's illness played a big part in the break-up of your marriage. I'm not putting the blame on anyone," the doctor said, offering a sympathetic smile.

"She had no motherly instinct when it came to raising our daughter," Edward snapped back. "That's what pushed me away. You can't blame me for falling in love with someone else."

"I'm sure Lillian was hard to live with."

"She made my life a living hell."

"How? What did she actually do to you?"

Edward's head jerked up, startled by the blunt question. "She, ah, she was mean to our daughter."

"She knew her tumor was growing. That's why she was taking it out on Bridget."

"Lillian was suspicious. Impossible to live with. After I moved out, she started acting strange. She refused to let the maids clean the house."

"I suspect the noise of the vacuum bothered her. A tumor can do funny things, even to our ears."

Again, Edward tried to defend his actions. "I've lived in a shadow of fear most of my married life."

"That was your own fear. Think about it. What did she do? Did she strike you? Did she fight with you?"

"No," Edward replied with a frown. "She locked herself in her bedroom."

"And?"

"She slammed the bedroom door. She knew it infuriated me."

"And?"

"What? She did it on purpose."

"Mister Hansen. You're misreading what was really happening. You missed the clue again."

Edward straightened up in his chair and leaned forward. "I don't understand."

"You've misread her symptoms. She was hiding her illness."

"She screamed at Bridget for no reason at all," Edward blustered in his defense.

"Did she lash out at you when she seemed normal? Ah, I mean, when she was rational."

Edward wrinkled his brow, pondering the question.

"Your public affairs humiliated her. She suffered even more when she lost your love."

Edward dropped his head and he lowered his voice. "I went off the deep end after Bridget died. I wanted to run away. Escaping to Traverse City was my way of coping. That's not an excuse for my affairs, it's just something I did."

The doctor nodded his head several times, "I followed the newspapers, and surmised what was happening. I'm glad you found your way back."

"After our daughter's death, I needed someone to talk to. Lillian locked the bedroom door and refused to talk to me. I thought she was just being hateful."

"No, she wasn't being hateful. Lillian lived in fear every day of her life. She didn't know who would take care of her when her tumor got worse. Listen to what I said. Not *if* her tumor got worse. *When* it got worse."

"I was the *one* living in fear," Edward mumbled defensively.

"What's the remark President Roosevelt said? There's nothing to fear, but fear itself."

"Are you saying I feared my wife for no reason at all?"

"None what-so-ever. You misread the signs. What you thought was temperamental, was part of her sickness. When she screamed at you, she couldn't control her rage. The truth is, Lillian lived in fear from the moment she became pregnant. That's why she hid her seizures from you. Your wife's pride may seem excessive, but it's a part of her personalty. You knew that when you married her."

Edward nodded ever so slightly as he recognized the depth of his wife's illness. "I often wondered if the fall down the stairs was intentional."

Doctor Kokeny interrupted. "I'd like to think it was accidental."

"I feel strange asking this, but is it possible Lillian had something to do with Bridget's death?"

The doctor lowered his head and looked down, nervously fingered the medical report. "I read your daughter's autopsy years ago. In my mind, there was something missing."

"You wondered how my baby died?" Edward replied, the pitch of his voice rising with curiosity.

"Your wife was ill," the doctor responded quickly.

"She was ashamed of our deaf daughter. That's why she was mean to Bridget."

"No. Let me explain again. Your wife didn't always have control of her actions."

"Lillian was too proud. She didn't want to be known as the rejected wife," Edward babbled, in an attempt to save his humiliation.

"I suppose that's true."

"But then, Lillian could have killed Paul to protect our marriage." Edward stopped rambling when he felt Robert's hand gently squeezing his shoulder.

Robert stuffed the medical reports in his briefcase. "Let's go. We'll talk about this later."

The following week, Edward entered Sarah's house carrying a dozen red roses, a Shirley Temple doll, and a teddy bear. He dropped the gifts on a chair, and though it should have been a solemn moment, he didn't mean to smile so broadly, but it just slipped out. He wrapped his arms around Sarah, and in that single moment, he knew his life had finally come together.

Sarah melted in his arms. "I'm so sorry about your wife."

"I completely misread Lillian. Judged her by her actions, by what I saw. I thought her headaches were a way of getting attention."

"Our affair had a lot to do with her anger. I'm at fault too. I don't blame her for hating me, but I didn't know she was sick."

"Would it have made a difference? Even if Lillian wasn't so hateful toward Bridget, I still would have fallen in love with you." He took Sarah's hand and drew her closer. "That's not what drove me away from her. From the first day I met you, I realized something was missing in my marriage."

"Even I could see something was wrong, but...," Sarah paused, hesitating to explain further.

"Shortly after you moved in, it became clear. You cared about my daughter and treated her with such tenderness."

"I felt the same way about you. Especially when I saw how gentle you were with Bridget."

"It's taken years and heartaches to get up the courage to stand up to Lillian. Even before she died I was ready to give up everything to marry you."

Sarah released her grip on Edward and pushed him back. "I talked with the police the other day. They explained why Lillian killed Paul."

"I thought I knew my wife." Edward glanced around the room and whispered. "Are the children asleep?"

Sarah returned his answer with a sultry nod, squeezing his hand reassuringly. She sat down on the couch and patted the cushion as an invitation. "What will you do now?"

Edward sat own and moved close. "I've decided to sell the house and furniture, except for a few things my mother left me."

"What about the housekeeper?"

"Hilda has been a loyal servant. I've considered her age and arthritic condition. I'm retiring her with a generous pension."

"And Ester? What happens to her?"

"Would you consider having her as our housekeeper?"

A wide smile spread across Sarah's lips. "Our housekeeper? Are we getting married?"

"Of course. Shall I get on my knees?"

Sarah smiled and wrapped her arms around Edward. "I'm so glad you considered Ester."

"Ester's a good person. She started working for us when she was barely a teenager. Coming from a large family, she had to help financially. She only finished grade school. I'm sure you can overlook her lack of education. She's not book-smart, but I think she can learn."

"The past few years, Ester and I became great friends. While I was teaching Bridget to read and write, I also taught Ester. We knew your wife wouldn't approve, so we kept it a secret."

Edward leaned close and took Sarah's hand. "I guess we all kept secrets from Lillian, didn't we?"

"I feel guilty too. Our affair caused her a great deal of pain. But, when your wife acted so hateful, I didn't care how she felt." Sarah's voice turned serious. "There's something I must tell you about the mirror."

"What about it?"

"A few days ago, I stopped by my friend, Jane's house. She bought Lillian's mirror from a Salvation Army store."

"Your friend bought it?"

"It was scratched, and the gold was worn off, but I knew it was Lillian's mirror. This has haunted me, but I'm going to say it, no matter how strange it may sound."

Seeing the serious expression on Sarah's face, he clutched her hand tighter, offering his full attention.

"I saw something strange inside the mirror. It looked like a woman's face. When I touched the glass, it sent chills up my spine."

"What do you mean, a face?"

"It wasn't real clear, but it looked like Lillian."

"You mean like a ghost?" Edward asked, creasing his forehead into a frown. "That's impossible."

"I know what I saw. I spoke with priests and reverends, but they couldn't give me an answer. So yesterday, I went to a psychic. This woman communicates with the dead. She claims a soul can be trapped in a mirror, especially if the soul dwells on its own guilt."

"Trapped? How?" Edward asked, perching on the edge of the couch.

"Lillian's soul could be trapped in the mirror. Earthbound by her own thoughts."

"What do you mean, earthbound?"

"Held in-between this life and the next dimension. What if it was Lillian's face I saw?"

"Maybe you only thought you saw a face"

"No," Sarah replied, her voice firm and adamant. "Those dark eyes are burned in my memory. I can't forget them. The psychic said that after a person dies, the soul reviews its past life. It examines its own actions, deeds, and guilt."

"Do you believe that?" Edward muttered.

"Maybe the guilt of killing Paul is holding her earthbound. What if Lillian can't leave this earthly dimension until she's forgiven herself? Or, even worse, what if she believes God won't forgive her?"

"I think you saw something in the mirror, but I don't know if it was a ghost. What can we do about it anyway?"

"I guess we're supposed to understand and forgive."

"Forgive her?"

"If the tumor caused your wife's mental illness, how can she be guilty? And, guilty of what? The psychic said perhaps Lillian *believes* she's guilty. Or, she could be guilty of something else. Whatever it is, Lillian needs to forgive herself." Sarah leaned close and looked deep in Edward's eyes. "My friend still has the mirror. Do you want to see it?"

"No! No!" Edward blustered, waving his hand defensively. "I understand how the tumor made Lillian irritable, but she was driving me crazy too."

"Even if you had stayed married, the tumor might have driven her to madness anyway." Sarah gripped Edward's hand squeezing it gently. "God knows what else she might have done."

"If she was ill, should *she be punished* for killing Paul? Or, should *I be punished* for misinterpreting her illness?"

"I'm to blame too. I judged her by what I saw. What I wanted to believe."

"You're saying, Lillian might have to make restitution, like a penance or atonement? We can't take all the blame. She's to blame too. We saw what she wanted us to see, not what she was hiding."

"What if her guilty thoughts are holding her captive in the mirror?" Sarah remembered the pathetic face in the mirror and the pleading dark eyes. "Maybe Lillian is punishing herself?"

The end.

BIOGRAPHY

MARIE HARRIETTE KAY is a writer, author, artist, psychic, natural medium, and a teacher of parapsychology. She was married and raised three children. Marie was born the seventh of eight children in Detroit, Michigan. Coincidentally, it is said the seventh child is often psychic. Marie was trained by June Black, a psychic medium who came to United States from London England. She became Mrs. Black's assistant, and for seven years studied meditation, psychometry, healing, spirit communication, past life regression, mediumship, and much more. She has mentored, instructed, and lectured on many phases of parapsychology.

Marie studied creative writing at a local community college. On her first try at writing, she won top prize for her story, 'A DAY IN COURT.' She has written an instruction manual for novice and/or teachers demonstrating easy methods to develop one's innate sixth-sense and spiritual awareness. **AWAKEN YOUR PSYCHIC ABILITIES**, by Marie Harriette Kay, Published by Balboa Press.

HIGH SOCIETY MURDER IN DETROIT, Peacock-tail Mirror, an historical murder mystery and love triangle with paranormal encounters. The story demonstrates the human frailty of misinterpreting information, and the destructive psychological effect of self guilt. It challenges the reader to decide who is to blame for each tragedy as it occurred.

Marie was a member of the Shelby Township Writers Group. She completed a course from the Gotach Center for Health, for Healing Touch Therapy. She has lectured on "Psychic Phenomena" and "How to Meditate" at numerous events and organizations over the years including; Women's political Clubs, Lawyer's Wives Group, Utica Library, and the Sterling Heights Public Library, Foxfire Series. She was a member of the Utica Cultural Arts Council and had received awards and letters of recognition for her paintings and charity work in the field of Art. She received a letter of appreciation from Sterling Heights Cultural Commission for "Artist of the Month," and for artistic and charitable contributions.

Painting of Milkmaid painted by Marie Harriette Kay

Oil painting of 'Swiss Side of the Alps'
painted by Marie Harriette Kay

Lightning Source UK Ltd.
Milton Keynes UK
UKHW012151050320
359866UK00006B/104